THE LONDON TRILOGY: BOOK III

autumn
EXODUS

THE LONDON TRILOGY: BOOK III

autumn
EXODUS

DAVID MOODY

Author's note:
Although many of the locations featured in this
novel are real, I have taken fictional liberties with them.
This is a work of fiction, not a travel guide.
Please also note - 'The Highway' is the full name
of a street in London and should be capitalised as such.

First published in 2022 by Infected Books

A CIP catalogue record for this book
is available from the British Library

ISBN 978-1-7397535-3-5

Cover design by Craig Paton
www.craigpaton.com

www.davidmoody.net

www.lastoftheliving.net

www.infectedbooks.co.uk

DAY EIGHTY-SIX

The third and final Great Fire of London burned unchallenged for a week before the rains came. Unlike the first great fire, the seventeenth-century blaze everyone knew from history lessons at school, and the second that came as the result of a spectacularly brutal and lengthy bombing of the city during World War II, this was unequivocally the final great fire because, this time, there was no one left to rebuild the capital, and nothing left to rebuild it with.

The downpour started in the early hours the day before yesterday and showed no signs of abating. The roiling clouds were heavy and black with oily smoke, as was everything else, making it hard to find the point where the sky ended and the scorched remains of this once unyielding city and its undead population began.

The Tower of London had stood here for centuries, and it showed no signs of falling today. Though now surrounded by tons of compacted and charred rot, its grey stone walls remained, for the most part, intact. In comparison, many of the more modern structures around it had twisted and buckled and collapsed in the intense heat of the recent inferno. Those that were still upright were immense in their towering dilapidation, strikingly pared back to colossal skeletons of metal and concrete. Barely a single pane of glass remained unbroken, anywhere. Ceilings had become floors, collapsed downwards and now lay heaped on top of each other like the pages of discarded books. Many buildings had been reduced to basic shapes, their interiors as bland as their exteriors, no fine details remaining. From fast-food joints to exclusive penthouse suites, from newspaper stands to proud museums, embassies, and monuments and mansions, the fire had spared nothing. All life extinguished, everything had become monochrome and dull, barely a glimpse of colour left anywhere.

The wind whistled as it whipped through the empty spaces that people used to inhabit. There were other sounds too; water trickling from ruptured pipes and buckled gutters, birds calling out as they swooped to peck meat from corpses, rodents scurrying through the debris, foraging for any sort of scrap that had escaped the burn.

And even the base infrastructure, the roads, lanes and alleyways were no longer recognisable. Asphalt had buckled and cracked in the heat, and most throughways were blocked with fallen rubble. It was clear that there would be no easy avenue of escape from this hellscape for either the living or the dead.

Tens of thousands of corpses had congregated around the Tower in the days before the fire and had been trapped, wedged in position as a never-ending flood of followers had made an instinctive pilgrimage towards the flames, overburdening the space. As a result of the pressure and the heat, the compressed hordes had gradually reduced to a single compacted, carbonised, waist-high mass of diseased flesh. From a distance it looked like a lava field. Wisps of smoke rose from vent holes in the crisped flesh, and occasional bursts of flame spurted as pockets of noxious gases bubbled up and were ignited by smoulders and sparks, brief flashes of light that disappeared almost as quickly as they'd appeared. The scab-like surface remained reassuringly featureless for the most part, but occasional tiny details would bring the horror back into focus: a withered hand clutching at the air, the cremated remnants of a child's foot dangling from the end of a blackened tibia, half a face, its lipless mouth frozen mid-scream, its tongue a brittle twig of ash, shocked dead as flames burst across it.

David, Chapman, Joanne, and Sam waited on the river for the situation to change, and the coming of the rains had been the trigger. Vicky had volunteered to attempt to reach the people trapped in the Tower once it was safe enough for her to go ashore. She'd had to edge slowly through the ocean of grim remains, dragging her feet most of the time because picking up her boots and taking steps was out of the question. What was the name of that game she used to play when she was a kid? *Jack Straws*, she seemed to remember. You dumped a pile of plastic sticks and other objects on the table, then used little hooks to fish out individual items without disturbing others. This morning, her feet had been the hooks, repeatedly getting caught among broken limbs, spinal cords, rib cages and pelvises that were buried out of sight. She'd been terrified of getting stuck, but she'd lost so much weight recently that for the most part she'd been able to walk on top of the sunken bits and not sink deeper into the waterlogged torsos. Once she made it to the outer wall of the Tower, Ruth used a rope to haul her up and over the battlements and she climbed down onto the other side where a path through the charred remains had already been cleared.

When she entered White Tower where the others were hiding out, they gave her a hero's welcome, but she didn't have time for any of that nonsense. The message she'd come to deliver was simple: 'Pack everything. We've got a boat. We're getting out of London today.'

'They're coming,' Joanne said when she saw someone signalling from the roof of the Tower, and she sank the blade of her shovel through the burnt crust that covered everything, deep into the semi-solid sludge of human remains beneath the surface. Next to her, Sam quickened his pace, the pair of them frantically trying to dig a path from the pier to the Byward Tower entrance.

After days of relative inactivity, the sudden frenzy was a rude awakening. Sam was already feeling the pace of the gruelling, physical work. He looked back to see how much they'd cleared so far. 'Shit, you seen this?'

Joanne glanced back and saw that the remains of the dead were oozing back across the section of pathway they'd already dug out.

At first, she thought it was just the weight of the sloppy morass spilling in from either side but, when she looked closer, she could see signs of activity deep within the mire, stirring up the sludge. Incredibly, things that had been buried for days were still trying to remove themselves. A shuffle, a twitch here, a spasm there – if she stared hard enough, she could see teeming movement everywhere. Worms and maggots squirmed around and between things which used to be human. The open jaw of a lop-sided face was constantly grinding. She hadn't realised she was staring at the thing's one remaining eye until it blinked. Near the heel of her boot, the clawed fingers of a wizened hand flexed, and she stamped hard on the crab-like thing so it couldn't grip the cobbles and pull whatever remained of the rest of its body along.

At this rate there was a very real possibility the path might close behind them, leaving them stranded midway along the hundred metres or so they needed to clear, but there was no other way of doing this. They had to be ready for when the boat came, and she didn't think that would be long. She could already hear its grumbling engine in the distance.

When the others had sealed themselves in, they'd left a van blocking the Byward Tower entrance. Sam could hear movement on the other side of the vehicle now, people scrambling to try and shift it. Sanjay climbed through its burnt-out interior then slid down through the hole where its windscreen had been, landing feet-first in the muck. He used the shovel he'd been carrying to steady himself from going over. 'Good to see you, Sanj!' Sam shouted, and Sanjay looked across in disbelief.

'Sam? Bloody hell, I thought you were dead.'

'Sorry to disappoint, mate.'

'But how...?'

'I'll tell you later. For now, get digging. The boat's on its way.'

Sanjay started scooping out muck from around the van's front wheels. He'd harboured a naïve hope that they might have been able to simply release the handbrake and roll it forward, but the fire had put pay to that. The tyres had been burnt away to nothing and the wheels were locked, rusted into position. At the back of the van, Gary Welch led the efforts to shift it, invigorated by the prospect of finally escaping the impenetrable stone walls they'd been imprisoned within for a week that had felt like a decade. He sank his hands into the foetid junk that was wedged along the side of the vehicle, grabbed whatever bones he could get a grip of, then dragged what was left of the next corpse out of the way. Other people began following his lead. Beside him, Orla managed to haul up almost an entire skeleton intact, and when she heaved it over her shoulder into the air, much of its remaining flesh fell away from its bones, churned innards spilling out through the gaps between exposed ribs. Gary was splashed with gore, but he was long past the point of caring. They all were. The deterioration of the dead was such that they no longer looked like people, the way sausage no longer resembles a sow, and it was all but impossible to tell where one body ended and the next began. He and Orla both managed to grab hold of different parts of the same two corpses that had become intertwined, and between them they hurled the conjoined cadavers away from the back of the van.

Now Gary could see daylight.

'We're almost there. Get ready to push,' he ordered. 'One, two, *three.*'

A group of folks helped shunt the vehicle forward. Its wheels scraped along each time they shoved it, making constant but unsteady progress across cobbles that had been lubricated by the greasy ex-human sludge that coated everything.

Almost there. Almost free. Word was passed back along the line for the evacuation to begin.

Conditions inside the Tower had been harsh. According to Georgie's meticulously kept paper records, a total of two hundred and thirty-three people remained in here, leaving more than a hundred of their original number unaccounted for. Some cowards had escaped in the clipper with Piotr and Dominic and were long gone, but the majority of the lost souls had likely perished in the fire. To those who'd been left behind, it didn't matter: regardless of their fate, everyone else was as good as dead.

Until Vicky had appeared this morning, the prospect of getting away from the Tower had seemed remote, let alone escaping London. Hunkered down in the dark for much of the time, cramped and uncomfortable and with the world in flames around them, claustrophobia and grim uncertainty had been rife. But now they'd been given a glimmer of a chance of escape, and in the dark recesses of White Tower, frantic activity had replaced the gloomy inertia of the last week. Supplies were being boxed up, ready to be shipped out. People were getting ready to move. In one corner, Audrey Adebayo and a handful of others were deep in prayer. It pissed Vicky off more than it should have. 'They could try helping,' she said to Ruth. Ruth shrugged.

'Different strokes for different folks.'

'Yeah, but how is wishful thinking supposed to be useful? Honestly, if it hadn't been for you and Selena and a couple of others stuck in here, I might not have bothered coming back.'

'Don't say that.'

'You don't know what I went through to get here. I'm sick of risking my neck for nothing. We're top-heavy with lazy bastards. It's always the same few doing the work.'

And before Ruth could respond, Vicky had gone. She waded into the middle of the chaos to try and get things moving.

Marianne was floundering. 'I've got this Marianne,' Vicky said. 'You move out with the others.'

The fear in her face was clear. 'I'm sorry. I thought I was helping, but I'm just getting in the way.'

'Doesn't matter. Just go.'

'I just thought I should—'

'Go!' Vicky said again, and this time Marianne did, though she was forced to move to the side when Lisa Kaur came barging through from outside.

'Leave the rest of the stuff,' she shouted, her voice loud enough to silence everyone left inside the Tower. 'Just get yourselves out

6

of here fast. Carry what you can, forget everything else.'

Vicky grabbed her arm. 'What's wrong? Boat here?'

'Not yet.'

'What then?'

'The dead are coming.'

The dead are coming.

2

David stood at the back of the bridge and nervously watched Chapman navigating the Thames. To say Chapman was a novice at this would have been an understatement, but at least he'd managed to get the engine started and get the boat moving, thanks in no small part to the crash course he'd had from Allison when they'd taken the clipper from Surrey Quays. He'd hoped they'd have been able to find a similar suitable vessel, but the only other clipper they'd found had been nowhere near large enough. They'd eventually commandeered a party boat – the *London Sunset* – as inappropriate as it was impractical. There was little in the way of seating inside, just an open expanse stretching side to side on the lower deck, with an opulent wooden dancefloor upstairs that opened out onto a viewing deck. There were two bars (they both wished were still serving alcohol), but there'd be time for that later. *The London Sunset's* engine running, and it looked like there was enough fuel in her tank: the only thing that mattered now was getting well away from this hellhole.

'Jesus Christ,' David said, distracting Chapman.

'What's the problem?'

'Nothing. Don't worry about it. You just stay focused on what you're doing.'

Too late. David regretted having spoken out loud, but it had been an involuntary reaction. Chapman looked up and saw what he'd seen. 'Fuck me.'

The dead were, as always, reacting to the noise. As they sailed upriver, a wave of undead activity followed them on either edge. On the relatively untouched south bank of the Thames, there was absolute fury among the remaining crowds. They seethed and surged, piling down towards the icy water with unquestionable intent, splashing into the murk as they reacted to the sound of the boat's engine.

'It's November, for fuck's sake,' Chapman said. 'Fucking things have been dead for three months. It's about time they gave up, I reckon.'

David shook his head. 'Judging by what I'm seeing, I really don't think they will.'

He turned to look at the other side of the river, and even over on the north bank, where the devastation was unprecedented, the scurrying creatures continued to crawl, half burnt, mashed by pressure, some barely mobile, over the ruins. On the fringes of the worst of the fire damage, relatively intact cadavers continued their unsteady march towards the Tower of London. Their progress was hampered by the fact there were no longer clear streets for them to move along, the ground now covered with a layer of rubble, ash, and roasted meat, but it didn't stop them. David and the others had known the dead would react this way, of course, but the silent tenacity of their enemy was chilling. If there was a way though, they'd find it. If there was a weak point anywhere, the dead would inevitably exploit it.

But what David could now see happening closer to the Tower of London was worrying him most of all. They had perhaps another five minutes on the water, and he could see that the group had made good progress evacuating the Tower. All around them, though, there were other signs of movement. Some of the dead had escaped the worst of the heat and the flames, and in the space where Sam and Joanne were working between the walls of the Tower and the pier, a few cadavers had now begun to rise up in deliberate response to the increased activity around them. He watched as a lone figure lying in a shallow pool of gore slowly hauled itself back upright, breaking the thin crust that had formed from the residue of others on top of it. It stood and swayed, clearly contemplating its next move, dripping with muck like it had crawled out of a tar pit. And though it was just a single corpse with barely any physical strength, the impact of its determined

9

resurrection was considerable. The shift in its position created sudden pockets of space around it that allowed other similarly preserved monsters to begin to rise. At the same time, when the foul-looking thing took an unsteady step forward, it caused panic in a crowd of evacuees who were trying to get down the steadily shrinking path that had been cleared to get them to the pier.

'He's coming in a bit fast, don't you think?' Sam said. Chapman had sailed past the jetty and turned the party boat around under the arches of London Bridge, and though he looked to be on a good course for the pier, his speed seemed excessive.

Joanne didn't even look up from her digging. As fast as she was clearing the path, the dead were re-filling it again. 'As long as he slows down enough for us to get on, who cares?'

Sam threw his shovel down and pushed his way to the front of the crowd now gathering on the pier. 'Stay back until he's docked,' he told them. He was relieved when he heard Chapman finally cut the engines, but the boat still seemed to be coming in at a hell of a speed. He could see David up on deck now, coiling the mooring line, ready to throw it ashore and secure the ship.

A metre and a half away from the jetty.

Still too fast.

'Throw it to me,' Sam yelled, and David hurled the hawser across the gap. It landed near his feet and immediately began whipping away, but Ruth was there too, and she managed to catch it. Between the pair of them they got a good grip on the line. Other people who could see what was happening tried to help, some adding their hands to the rope, others wrapping their arms around Ruth and Sam's waists to stop them being dragged into the river.

Chapman put the engine in reverse, cursing himself for not doing it sooner, but they were already in danger of overshooting the jetty. Ruth had managed to wrap the rope several times around the mooring, but the boat was still moving downriver. On deck, David raced to the stern and threw another rope ashore.

Lisa almost caught it, but it slipped through her fingers. Without another anchor, the bow of the *London Sunset* clipped the end of the jetty then came to an unsteady stop, completely out of position, but finally stationary. 'Fuck it,' David shouted down. 'That'll have to do. Get everyone onboard *now*. The dead are coming!'

It was a blessing that the folks on dry land didn't have the same view as he had from up on the deck, because there would have been absolute bedlam if they'd realised the number of corpses that were now dragging themselves back up onto their feet and advancing towards the group. Those that were mobile might only have been a fraction of the vast total, but their numbers were irrelevant; right now, even a handful looked like a horde. They tripped through the slop, stumbling across the churned remains of their brethren. A handful or a hundred, it didn't matter. They were closing in.

Standing on the edge of the pathway they'd cleared, with one foot in the rot and the other on dry ground, Gary swung his machete wildly at the nearest of the ghastly upright creatures, splitting the paper-thin skin of its distended abdomen. Through their swaying shapes he saw that the bow of the boat was head-on to the riverbank, making it difficult for people to get onboard via the jetty as planned. They'd need an alternative route. 'Get some ladders down here,' he screamed at anyone who'd listen.

Sanjay had seen some ancient-looking wooden ladders in the White Tower, part of a display, and he was sure he'd also seen a couple of sets of aluminium stepladders knocking around the place since they'd been locked down last week. He ran back to find them, fighting against the tide of people still coming the other way. The plunge back into darkness once he'd reached the building was disorientating and he tripped and fell forward, the ground around his feet covered with filth. He fumbled through the ancient stone passageways, feeling his way along the rough walls.

Then he stopped.

There was something else in here with him.

He grabbed the knife he always carried, ready to slice through the corpse he felt sure was about to attack. 'Don't,' it said.

He stepped back, almost losing his footing completely when he came up against another pile of abandoned junk. 'Who's that?'

They didn't answer, but as Sanjay's eyes became accustomed to the low light, he saw that there was a group of people still huddled in the dark. Despite them all being incarcerated in the White Tower together for days and, before that, holed-up in the Monument base for weeks, he didn't immediately recognise any of them, couldn't put names to the faces. They were part of a quiet, reclusive few who had preferred to remain isolated. They'd stayed apart, hidden in the shadows, trying not to get involved.

'You need to get out of here,' Sanjay said. 'We're leaving.'

'We're not going,' one of them said. It was a woman, and when the limited light caught her, he saw that she was pregnant. He'd seen her around; she'd already been a couple of months along when he'd first arrived at the Tower.

'Look, we don't have time to piss around here. Chapman's got us a boat. We're leaving now.'

Someone else switched on a torch. Christ, there had to be twenty people in here. 'We're not going anywhere.'

This was someone Sanjay recognised. It was Nick Hubbard. He'd been one of Piotr's lot, often helping Mihai, the group's quartermaster. Had they left him behind, or had he had a fit of conscience when his bunch had taken the clipper and abandoned the rest of the group?

'Come on, Nick. Don't be stupid.'

'There's no point running. You go if you want, Sanjay, but it's gonna be just as bad wherever you go.'

'You don't know that.'

'No, and neither do you. We've got some food, we've got this place, we've got each other. We don't need nothing else.'

And although a thousand thoughts were running through Sanjay's head, a thousand things he thought he should say, he instead said nothing.

Not my fucking problem.

He grabbed the long wooden ladders he'd been looking for and ran back to the others, terrified he'd missed the boat.

Outside, the channel that had been dug through the undead mire was narrowing again. It was as if the barely distinguishable body parts were reaching across the gap, desperate to reconnect with each other. 'Get that frigging ladder over here now!' Gary screamed at Sanjay as he weaved through the chaos. Things had deteriorated in the few minutes he'd been away. Now, more people were spaced along the jetty, holding onto various ropes that had been thrown down from the deck of the ship, doing everything they could to keep it from drifting. 'Sanjay!' Gary screamed at him again. 'Now!'

Ruth was gesturing for him to get the ladders down to the end of the pier so they could use them to bridge the gap between the floating structure and the side of the boat. She snatched them from him, and he was immediately shunted back, pushed out of the way by a swarm of folks desperate to leave. Ruth held the bottom of the ladder and swung the other end over to David who wedged it into the railings on the deck. He'd barely got it secure before people were using it to scurry up to safety, the wooden ladder bowing and groaning under their weight. Sanjay lost his balance and gripped the side of the pier to steady himself, before realising it wasn't him off kilter, it was the pier. The entire structure felt like it was about to collapse into the river.

Back on the footpath, Orla and Gary were frantically defending the space that Sam and Joanne had managed to clear. Even more of the dead were approaching now. Gary hacked at another foul ghoul then flung wet chunks of its sliced-up frame out of the way and into the river. In the sliver of clear space now ahead, he watched in horror as another rancid cadaver began rising. It didn't have the strength to stand fully upright, so instead just dragged itself along on the stumps of its knees. The sudden pocket of space it created gave two more carcasses enough room for manoeuvre, and they too started to shift their sloppy bulks.

Someone close by let out a piercing scream.

Sam spun around and wrestled with a horrifically decayed skeletal thing that had grabbed hold of the woman standing behind him. The corpse was dealt with quickly, but the terror was infectious, spreading like a bushfire through the group of people still jostling for position in the escape line on the footpath. He could see folks scrambling up the ladder from the jetty, but they weren't moving quick enough, and a bottleneck had formed. With a couple hundred people still to shift, they needed to speed things up.

Weakened by the impact of the boat and under increasing strain, the end of the pier creaked then began to tip. It dropped by half a metre, a sudden downward lurch that caused another wave of panic to tear through the crowd. The guy who'd been halfway across the ladder was thrown sideways and landed in the heavily polluted waters below. A couple of people looked for him, but he was already gone, swept away by the current and lost among the once-human flotsam and jetsam that now covered much of the surface of the Thames. People surged forward to take his place on the ladder. That the pier would soon collapse and break free of its moorings felt inevitable.

Chapman found a safety ladder on the boat and unfurled it down the bow, as close to the bank as he could. There was a narrow strip of shingle between the wall along the footpath and the water. People began climbing over the railings, dropping down hard then immediately picking themselves up again and stretching for the bottom rungs of the safety ladder. Packed up supplies and belongings were also hurled over the wall, boxes and crates hitting the gravel riverbank with wet thuds. 'Leave all that,' Joanne said, and while some people listened, others desperately clung onto their last possessions, deadweight from a lost world.

A second safety ladder appeared and was unfurled. Sam tried to marshal the crowds still on the footpath, doing what he could to divide them equally between the different routes to safety that had now been established. He shouted instructions, but no one was listening. Could they even hear him? The noise out here this morning was becoming uncomfortably loud – constant screams and shouts combined with the roar of the current and the sound of the boat's idling engine. The cacophony was causing more of the dead to emerge from their bizarre hibernation. He'd assumed that the endless urban undead had been burned and welded into position, congealed by the heat, but many had been preserved under the burnt crust of countless others. In places, entire sections of the featureless mass undulated as more of them reacted to the chaotic noise. He thought he'd seen all the horrific sights the world could throw at him, but Christ, some of these monsters were more repulsive than anything his nightmares could conjure. Their rotting flesh had been hardened by the heat; grotesque sneers permanently baked onto what was left of their faces. Others were incomplete, limbs missing, features eaten away by fire and decay, and yet they continued their unsteady advance towards the living.

There was a groan of straining metal followed by a loud, splintering crack as the pier continued to collapse. The section that had been damaged by the collision with the boat threatened to break free from the narrow end of the structure that remained anchored to the shore.

Sam hacked down another trio of loathsome, dripping corpses so that he had a clear view back to the entrance to the Tower. A final few folks were stepping gingerly through pools of flesh where the path that he and Joanne had dug had finally sealed itself up again.

We must be nearly there now.

He looked down over the wall and realised there were still around a hundred people waiting down by the river, fighting for space in the narrow strip between the wall and the water. There was a smaller crowd on the unsteady jetty and a decent number had already made it up onto the deck of the boat. He didn't want to leave anyone behind, but he instinctively scanned the crowds because there were people here that he cared about, people he'd already sacrificed his own safety to save by blocking London Bridge with a bus, then again trying to get back here via the Thames Tunnel. He saw Ruth on the jetty, helping Selena, Omar, and a couple of other kids to get across the ladder, and there was Dr Liz Hunter with Orla helping others climb the safety ladders. On the boat, he could see David and Chapman helping people up and over, and down on the jetty, Gary and Sanjay were ushering the last few stragglers along. Joanne caught his eye and he gestured for her to find a way onto the boat now too. Was that everyone accounted for?

Where's Vicky?

She was still on the footpath, looking back in the direction of the Tower, watching the dead. She recoiled when he put a hand on her shoulder. 'Come on, Vic. We need to get going.'

She nodded, but still didn't move.

'Look at it.'

She gestured at a corpse standing a few metres away from her. Sheets of sloughed flesh had peeled away from its torso and were fluttering in the wind like loose gauze. The creature appeared to be mired in the goop, stuck, unable to move. It was staring back at her, a bizarre standoff.

'Now's not the time,' Sam said, and he tried to move her along, but she shrugged him off.

'I think it's looking at me,' she said.

'Plenty of time for corpse watching from the boat,' he said, and he led her to the railings at the edge of the footpath and lifted her down. She was light, like a ragdoll, barely any meat left on her bones.

Sam felt skeletal fingers scraping down his back. The ghoul that Vicky had been studying had broken free from its moorings. It had barely any strength, yet it came at him with such ferocity that it almost knocked him over the top of the railings. He swung his fist and his hand sank into what was left of its face. He caught it as it crumbled to the ground then hurled it into a crowd of several others that were trying to fight their way towards him. He realised he was the only one left on the footpath now.

Fucking typical.

Sam climbed over the railings and lowered himself down. His hands were still slippery with gore, and he fell the last metre. A vicious dagger of pain shot up along his injured leg that took his breath away. Joanne called out to him for help and when he looked up, he saw that Marianne was frozen halfway up the closest ladder, unable to keep climbing. She was in a bad way - tired, unfit, unwell, afraid – and the few people waiting behind her to escape showed no compassion whatsoever. Sam pushed through them, dragged someone off the bottom rung, then climbed as high as he could and unceremoniously shoved Marianne's backside upwards, helping her get high enough so that Joanne and David could reach down and pull her up the rest of the way. He followed her up, much to the disgust of those still waiting. He was past caring. People had to learn to help themselves.

He collapsed on the deck, his leg in agony. When he looked back, he saw a corpse fall over the top of the railings and land like a sack of rotten fruit. Those people still waiting to get up the ladder recoiled from the monster in the mud. It had snapped its spine in the fall, but it continued to attack regardless. 'Deal with it!' Sam screamed. It hooked a wizened claw around a man's ankle, and he panicked, struggling to shake it off.

'Thank you, Sam,' Marianne said. 'It's good to see you again.'

He wasn't interested in small talk. He pointed down at the people he'd left behind. 'They've got to learn to fight.'

'We're not all like you, Sam. Some of these people are terrified. *I'm* terrified. It doesn't come naturally. We can't all fight the way you do.'

'With the greatest respect, Marianne, right now we don't have the luxury of choice.'

Orla pushed her way through the crowd to get to the troublesome corpse. She stamped on the monster's upturned face, instantly ending its dogged resistance. Another one landed at her feet and she punted it into the river. It flapped and splashed furiously as the grey waters of the Thames carried it away.

'See,' Sam said to Marianne. 'She gets it.'

David pushed past them both and leant over the bow of the boat, keen to give Chapman the signal to get them away from this hellish place. It looked like most people had made it onboard now, but it was increasingly difficult to be certain. Up on the path along the front of the Tower, the area the group had cleared had been completely reclaimed by the dead. The congealed mass of rotting creatures had seeped into the empty spaces, and those that had been able to get up and move had crowded forward as far as the railings, blocking his view. Though the differences were stark close-up, from here it was hard to separate the living from the walking dead. They all stumbled forward desperately.

Elsewhere, other corpses remained anchored in the waist-high rot. They stood like scarecrows with their dripping arms outstretched, grasping furiously at thin air. They posed little immediate threat, but to David they were the ghastliest of all, pure nightmare fuel. And way beyond them, just visible on the outermost edges of the area that had been destroyed by fire, he could see yet more of them. They never stopped coming, never got tired. *Jesus Christ*, he thought, *will we ever see the end of those fucking things?*

The evacuation of the final few people from the pier was taking too long. Ruth, Gary, and Sanjay were trying to hurry things along, but the jetty felt increasingly precarious, and traversing the ladder was no easy task with both the pier and the boat moving unsteadily. 'Gary, go!' Ruth said, and she shoved him in the small of his back towards the ladder. He started making excuses, trying to get her to go before him, but she was having none of it. 'Just fucking move!'

He crawled along with more speed than any of them expected. Sanjay urged Ruth to follow him, 'You next.'

She put one hand on the next rung, then stopped. 'Everyone's out of the Tower, aren't they? We haven't left anyone behind?'

Sanjay hesitated just for the briefest of moments, thinking about Nick Hubbard and the others. *Their decision, not yours. Leave now or you're stuck here forever.* 'We're good,' he said, hoping he sounded more convincing than he felt. 'Go, Ruth. I'll sort the ropes.'

Ruth climbed across the ladder, bracing herself when the end of the pier lurched again, almost tipping her off.

Sanjay raced across to the mooring to untie the last rope. It had been badly tied and came away easily, and he was about to drop it into the water when the jetty dropped again.

Ruth scrambled up onto the deck of the boat and turned around, but all she could do was watch as the ladder fell and was swept away. 'Hold onto that bloody rope, Sanj,' she screamed. The end of the pier collapsing now, coming apart under his feet. The *London Sunset* drifted out into the river.

The distance between Sanjay and safety was increasing and he knew it. In a split-second of frozen terror, he imagined various versions of his own demise: being left here alone, drowning in the stagnant Thames, being torn apart by the endless hordes of the living dead that occupied London... He could see multiple nightmare scenarios, but only one possible way out.

As the end of the pier broke away, Sanjay wrapped the rope around himself, gripped it tight, then ran to the end of the woodwork and jumped.

It was impossible to know what hurt more, the pain of smashing into the hull, or the intense shock of dropping into the foul, ice-cold water. They hauled him up onto the deck as Sanjay clung onto the rope like his life depended on it, because he knew that it did.

3

'So, what's the plan?' Orla asked. 'I'm assuming there is one?' She looked around at the others on the bridge, hoping for inspiration but getting nothing back. Chapman stood at the controls, staring out at the expanse of grey water ahead of them. 'There was a plan,' he said, 'but to be honest, it didn't go much further than getting you lot out of the Tower.'

'People are gonna start asking.'

'Fuck 'em,' he said, and he meant it.

Orla turned to David. 'Look, even if it's vague, we need to tell them something. People need something to hold on to. They know we're not just going to keep sailing down the Thames indefinitely. Once the buzz of getting away from the Tower has worn off, they'll start asking questions.'

'Why are you looking at me?' he asked.

'Because people look up to you, Dave. And they listen to you. They trust you.'

'But what if I don't want that responsibility?'

'We're not asking you to take all the responsibility.'

'It feels that way.'

Sam interrupted. 'I'd do it, but they wouldn't like what I'd tell them. I'd be too honest.'

Joanne laughed. 'You're such a miserabilist, Sam. It's the frigging zombie apocalypse, for crying out loud. I don't reckon things can get much worse.'

'You'd be surprised.'

'You think about this stuff too much.'

'Somebody has to. I just choose not to share a lot of what I'm thinking. Go too far down the rabbit hole, and the few of us who are left will realise that trying to restart the human race is frigging futile.'

'That's a bit over the top, even for you,' David said.

'You think? I'm underplaying it if anything. I'll tell you lot, because I know you can take it, but I also happen to think Orla's right; we need to give people something to keep them afloat, a reason to keep going.'

'Go on then, how bad do you think this is really going to get?'

'For starters, there are about four hundred nuclear reactors dotted around the planet. That's four hundred potential meltdowns or explosions, right? Four hundred Chernobyls, but each one will be far, far worse because no one's left to put out the fires or take any kind of action to contain the radiation. I'd say it's pretty much a given that's going to bite us all on the arse before long one way or another.'

He paused, unsure if he should continue, but then did it anyway.

'Do you think London's the only city that's been razed? My guess is most towns and cities will have suffered some fire damage, some of them have likely been completely destroyed. Now that's bad enough, but think about the cumulative effect of all that destruction, all the ash and soot and other crap that's been thrown up into the air. I don't think we're talking about nuclear winters or anything on that kind of scale, but it's definitely going to take its toll. We could be looking at reduced levels of sunlight, reduced quality of sunlight, changes to the surface temperature of the planet... it might become harder for us to grow crops. And while we're on the subject of growing, one thing that probably will do well is weeds. They'll be unchecked and they'll start eating into things. Assuming there are buildings and other structures still standing, they won't be maintained. Foundations will be weakened, metal supports will start to rust... to me it feels pretty much inevitable that everything we've put up will come down, probably sooner rather than later.'

He stopped. Rant over. He'd said enough.

'You're a proper ray of sunshine, aren't you, mate?' David said.

'He does my head in when he talks like this,' Joanne said. 'It's never as bad as he says it is. It's not like we're starting from scratch again, is it?'

Sam shook his head. 'You're right, but how much of that knowledge is going to be accessible? I mean, everything we need to know will be in a book somewhere, but how do we find it? Entire libraries, archives, histories have been downloaded; how much information is stored solely on computers we'll never be able to access, or lost forever in the cloud? And if we do get hold of the information we need, what do we do with it? Say you get hold of the instructions for how to make a wind turbine, where do you get the parts? How do you source the materials to make spares? Everything's always been complicated, but at least we had the infrastructure before, and the engineers, the manpower. Now there's just us, and hell, not everyone could even climb the ladders to board the fucking boat.'

Chapman looked back over his shoulder. 'I don't know what's wrong with you people. We might be the last humans left alive. We've just rescued a couple of hundred people from almost certain death; can't you just be a little bit positive, for crying out loud?'

'Believe it or not, I am,' Sam said. 'I know I might not sound it, but I'm up for the challenge. If we can get far enough out of London and we manage to stay alive long enough to see the end of the dead, then we might still have a fighting chance. We're not going to be able to rebuild everything from the ashes like that prick Dominic Grove was always talking about doing, but people lived thousands of years without computers; I reckon we can do enough to build ourselves half-decent lives.'

David wiped a section of misted glass clear and peered out across the swollen Thames. Bloated bodies lapped with the waves. What looked like the upturned roof of a building floated past. 'Sam's right. I don't know about you lot, but I have to believe there's still a chance. I'm clinging onto the idea of getting back to Ireland and my kids. And before anyone starts on me, I know the odds of them being alive are pretty much zero, but I've got to try. That's all I've got left to aim for. If I lose that last little bit of hope, then there'll be no point in going on. So yeah, Orla, you're right, we need to give the others a reason to keep going. Give me a bit of time to make something up and I'll go and talk to them.'

When they'd been spread out in the chaos outside the Tower of London, the group had seemed sparse. Now that they were all crammed into the party boat, though, their numbers appeared more substantial. Georgie kept herself occupied ticking folks off her register. They'd lost another seventeen people today, she calculated. Two hundred and twenty-six left alive.

Marianne was traumatised. Her body ached, she was freezing cold, and she could barely move. Someone had found her a chair and she sat there unresponsive, her head in her hands. She didn't even acknowledge Selena when she brought her over a cup of coffee.

The bars on the party boat had been reasonably well-stocked, most likely in readiness for some social occasion that never took place. They'd also manage to salvage some food, carried over from the Tower in backpacks. Steve Armitage and Phillipa Rochester – the group's stalwart catering double-act – instinctively set to work, as much to keep themselves occupied as for the good of everyone else. They scraped together enough to give something to eat to everyone who wanted it; a few decent mouthfuls doing enough to calm nerves and stave away hunger pains.

Ruth stood at a window with Vicky, Selena, and Omar. Outside, she saw that the fire had spread far beyond the area they'd already seen. At first, she thought this was likely a continuation of the fire that had raged for days around the Tower, but they were too far away, and not everything between the Tower and here had been razed. No, this was likely the result of other uncontrolled blazes such as the one that had consumed the landmark buildings in and around Canary Wharf. *Hang on, perhaps this was Canary Wharf?*

The world looked nothing like it used to, but the twists and turns of the Thames they were following indicated that it probably was. All those impressive skyscraper office blocks, the financial hub through which trillions of pounds used to move every day, had been reduced to blackened stumps that were indistinguishable from anything else, all of it now valueless. The distinctive, circular husk of the nearby O2 Arena at Greenwich confirmed her suspicion, but for the most part, it was hard to discern anything from the vast mounds of rubble. Big Ben, the Sistine Chapel, the Empire State Building; even the most iconic landmarks all looked the same once they'd been reduced to piles of broken bricks and concrete.

Now, if her geography was correct, they were about to pass Surrey Quays. They'd left people behind there – friends of Joanne's – but there was no talk of mounting a rescue mission. Did they even need help? The area was still heaving with undead activity, but if those folks in their ivory tower had been as smart and well-protected as she'd been told, maybe they'd be better off staying put? Right now, it seemed a safer option than being on this boat with a couple of hundred others, sailing towards uncertainty.

On both sides of the river the dead were now more diffuse. Unlike the many thousands that had wedged themselves into every available space and surrounded them at the Monument, here they had space to be able to roam freely. Would this help the group when they left the boat and stepped ashore? It didn't matter. They'd have to deal with whatever they came up against. The only thing Ruth knew with any certainty was that they weren't going to be able to stay on the water indefinitely.

4

The Thames Flood Barrier had collected vast drifts of shite. Over the months, it looked like an entire flotilla of boats had become trapped, some upright, others capsized, and an unfathomable number of bloated bodies clogged the water between and around them, packing out the spaces. There were scavenging birds everywhere, swooping to peck at the plentiful supplies of flesh, feasting on the juicy scraps like a swarm of oversized locusts. The fouled waters on the other side of the barrier were slightly clearer. It felt like they'd crossed a significant threshold at last.

The wooden dancefloor on the top deck of the boat proved quite useful, the large open space lending itself to an impromptu townhall meeting. There was a small, raised stage at one end: a narrow performance space big enough for a DJ or a couple of musicians. David hesitated before stepping up. 'I don't know what to say.'

Orla urged him forward. 'Just tell them they're safe. Just tell them what you're thinking.'

Reluctantly, he took a deep breath and coughed to clear his throat. It was already quiet, but it immediately became quieter still. 'Can I just have a couple of minutes, please? Look, everyone, I'm no Dominic Grove—'

'Thank fuck for that,' Gary shouted from the back.

'—but I thought it would be a good idea to tell you what condition we're in and what's going on. Before you ask, I don't have a lot of information, and there's no real plan as such, but I think it's important we do this. We're going to need to work positively and collectively if we're going to get through this in one piece. Everyone must do their part. Understand?'

He paused for their response, half-expecting to be bottled off the stage. He got little back other than a couple of nodding heads and a few mumbles. There was no dissension. He kept going.

'The good news is we're well on our way out of London. Georgie reckons we lost quite a few people this morning, but other than that, we're in reasonably good shape as far as I can see.' He paused. Did he sound disingenuous? 'Christ, I'm not a public speaker. I really wish I could spin the bullshit like Dominic used to, like all our worthless politicians did for a century, but I can't. I'm just one of you, the same as everyone here, and all I can be is honest. I'm not sure if that's a good or a bad thing, but that's how it is. The reality of our situation is that we don't have a lot of fuel and we have even less food. We don't know where we're going, where we'll end up, or what we'll find when we get there. My guess is we'll try to stay on the river for a while longer, maybe make a stop for supplies if we can, then we'll look to find ourselves somewhere safe. Christ, I'm not even sure what safe looks like anymore. Logic says there will be fewer bodies, the further we get from the centre of the city, but hell, what's logic got to do with anything these days?'

'And that's it?' Audrey said, standing up to make herself heard. She was midway along the length of the room, holding onto a metal pillar as the boat rode the waves.

'What else do you want me to say, Audrey? We're all in the same boat here, figuratively and literally.'

A couple of people laughed at his comment. Audrey didn't. She remained stony-faced. 'We need to have a better plan. We can't just keep running.'

'Well, if you've got any suggestions, I'm all ears. We don't know what things are like anywhere. We know what places *used* to be like, but until we actually get somewhere and see for ourselves, we won't—'

Audrey shook her head violently. 'We need to have a little faith and trust that—'

'Look, I'm not going to start an argument with you about your beliefs at this stage, but we need a lot more than just hoping and praying. If anyone has any suggestions as to where we should go, then I'm all ears.'

Selena got to her feet. Everyone knew what she was going to say before she said it. 'Ledsey Cross.'

There were audible groans. David gestured for people to quieten down. He was beginning to bitterly regret speaking up. 'Look, Selena, I know Ledsey Cross is important to you, and we might well end up there eventually, but we need to face facts and start being realistic. We need to find somewhere safe, and we need to do it fast. We can't simply aim for somewhere that's several hundred miles away, not yet. There's too much at stake. It's taken us three months to get out of London, for crying out loud.'

'You're both right,' Vicky said, silencing everyone. 'We need to find somewhere immediately, but Ledsey Cross must be where we end up eventually.'

'I'm sick to the back teeth of hearing your Ledsey Cross bullshit,' Audrey said. 'You need to be realistic.'

'That's rich, coming from you.'

'I know the place has an appeal and you've got an association with it,' David said, 'but I have to admit, I'm still struggling to understand your obsession with it. It worries me that you just want to go there out of some misplaced loyalty to your friend.'

Vicky shook her head. 'Kath would want us to go, sure, and I made her a promise to try and get Selena there, but there's more to it than that. I haven't been completely honest with you. I've not told you the full story.'

'Go on,' David urged.

'I don't want anyone to think I've misled you or that I'm trying to manipulate the situation, but I can't ignore the facts. I didn't want to say too much before because I didn't know if we were ever going to get out of the capital.' She paused, struggling with her wretched cough again. Ruth passed her some water, and once the brief fit had passed, she continued. 'I strongly believe that everything and everyone we need in order to live long and comfortable lives will be there. I think we have to go.'

'You're going to need to give us more to go on than that,' Marianne said, sounding less than convinced. 'We've all seen the photos and the messages, but I'll be honest, right now I don't know if I could physically keep going long enough to make that kind of a trip.'

All eyes were on Vicky. 'I assume everyone knows what we're talking about here? Kath was still in contact with her friend Annalise *after* everyone died. She'd been living in Ledsey Cross for years. It's an intentionally remote place, the area's not easy to get through, it's well away from large population centres. It's up in the hills around the Yorkshire Dales. There's a single road that leads to it, passes through a village called Heddlewick.'

'Christ, could there be a more Yorkshire-sounding name?' Orla said.

'Kath said that once you get to Ledsey Cross, you're on your own. When we talk about a self-sufficient community, we're not just talking about houses with solar panels on the roof and wind turbines in the garden. Those things are there, sure, but Kath told me that the planning went far deeper than that. There are reservoirs and lakes in walking distance, so they have decent supplies of fresh drinking water and fish. They also had access to more farmland than we'll ever need. I mean, all that bullshit Dominic used to spout about growing crops on the parkland around Hatton House... he was living in cloud cuckoo land. Up there, though, they have established and maintained farms that were already supporting the community.' She paused. Had she given them enough? 'I guess what I'm saying is that Ledsey Cross wouldn't just be a good place for our immediate survival, it's a place where we'll be able to live longer-term. That's how the people up there were thinking, planning for the future. Even though they're a distance from the surrounding cities, the last time we spoke, they were talking about putting up fences at a distance to keep out whatever dead managed to find them. Imagine that.'

She stopped, sensing someone staring. Sam's eyes were burning into her, and she knew exactly what he was thinking: *how can she be talking about the long-term, when she might only have a few weeks left*? And he was right. She could feel her cancer eating away at a little more of her every day.

'So, we're going then?' Selena said. The way she phrased her comment made it sound half-question, half-order.

'Not yet,' David said, taking back control of the discussion. 'Maybe we'll end up there at some point, but right now we need to focus on our immediate priorities. I'm not ready to start planning for the future until I've survived today. We need to know where our next meal is coming from, and we need to find somewhere safe to rest for a while and build up our strength. I'm with Marianne here – I don't think any of us are in good enough shape to travel half the length of the country just yet.'

'There's another argument for taking our time,' Sam said. 'How do you think the folks at Ledsey Cross are going to feel if we turn up on their doorstep unannounced? A couple hundred new arrivals could undo all the work they've done. Personally, I think we need to hole-up for a while, maybe sit out the winter.'

'Now you're the one who's starting to sound like Dominic Grove,' Gary said, semi-serious.

David nodded. 'You know, for all his bullshit, Dominic did get a few things right. You can't argue with the logic of getting through winter before striking out. By next spring, there should hardly be anything left of the dead.'

The air had a constant, wretched stink these days, but this was different. It wasn't just the stench of death they could smell here; there was another layer to it. It wasn't as sickly sweet as decaying flesh, but it was no less repugnant. 'This is Coldharbour,' Selena announced.

Blank looks all round.

'It's a massive landfill site. It means we're getting close to Purfleet, my neck of the woods. I grew up with that stink. It was really bad on hot days when the wind was blowing a certain way.'

Joanne appeared, looking for David and Sam. 'Problem,' she told them, and they followed her back to the bridge. Chapman glanced over his shoulder when they appeared.

'I know I'm getting the hang of driving this thing,' he said, 'but I'm never going to be able to get us past that.'

A jumbo jet had crashed and was blocking almost the entire width of the river. It had sunk at an angle, with one wing dug down into the water and its nose twisted around, the tip resting on the south bank. Ahead of them, the fuselage of the plane appeared monolithic. It stretched across almost half of the width of the Thames, but over the last few months vast amounts of floating debris had been washed downriver and become caught up with the wreck, blocking all routes.

'Whoa, that's impressive,' David said. His comment was appropriate yet felt wildly inappropriate at the same time.

'I once heard that there used to be anywhere between eight and nine thousand planes in the sky at any given time,' Sam said. 'Imagine that. They all had to come down somewhere.'

'And all it took was just one of them to fuck up our plans,' Chapman grumbled, and he slowed the engine.

'There's a pier over there,' Joanne said, gesturing towards the north bank. 'The light will be fading soon. I reckon we should stop here for the night then see how the land lies first thing.'

David called Selena in. 'You know the area. Is there anywhere close where we might be able to stop for a while?'

'There's Lakeside, I suppose.'

'What's that?'

'Shopping centre. Massive, it is.'

Chapman shook his head and steered towards the jetty. 'Yeah, 'cause it went so well last time we visited a shopping centre,' he grumbled.

5

DAY EIGHTY-SEVEN

The shifts in perspective were predictable and infuriating. People had been desperate to get away from the Tower of London – until it had been time to move, and then some of them had needed to almost be dragged down to the boat. Now, less than twenty-four hours later, those same people were equally reluctant to leave the perceived security of their temporary home on the water. They'd had a choice, of course, but David had spelt it out to them all first thing: you leave with us, or you stay here and fend for yourselves.

Sanjay and Gary volunteered to check the jetty and make sure their way off the water was clear. The relative silence out here this morning was reassuring, emphasising the space around them. After their incarceration in the Tower, living on top of each other for months and not knowing if they were ever getting out, to now have the freedom to move around like this was truly liberating. It was cold and pissing down with rain, but that didn't matter one iota. 'It's a conspiracy, I swear it is,' Gary whispered. 'It's dry when we need it to be wet, wet when we need it to be dry. Audrey needs to have a word with her friends in high places. I reckon someone's got it in for us.'

They'd docked near a refinery. A series of metal gantries connected the jetty to the shore. Once they'd crossed the water, they found a ladder down to a well-trod path in the shadow of a lichen-encrusted wall. They followed the wall for another hundred metres or so, then used a torch to flash a silent signal back to the others.

Sam and Chapman led the group along the path. Some of these

people hadn't been out in the open for months. David had given them a pep talk before they'd set foot outside.

Stay close.

Stay quiet.

Don't panic.

Easier said than done. Chapman knew the area well and had left David in no doubt as to the potential dangers. 'Truth be told,' he'd said before they'd abandoned the boat, 'I'd have picked somewhere else to land if I'd had any choice. This was a busy spot. You'd got the M25 and the Dartford Crossing – a permanent bloody traffic jam. Then there's the refinery, Lakeside, a load of distribution centres... there's a hell of a lot of business crammed into a relatively small area here.'

But perhaps that would be to their advantage? Sam had suggested that they'd likely be able to find everything they needed here: food, clothes, medicines, equipment, all for the taking.

It was raining so hard that it hurt. Gary was at the very end of the line now with Vicky, bringing up the rear. 'Don't know which one of us is slowest,' he whispered, limping on his dodgy ankle. 'You not feeling up to it today?' Vicky shook her head, too breathless to answer. She was painfully gaunt, thin as a rake, and her face was as grey as the clouds. She constantly swigged from a bottle of water, doing what she could not to start coughing again. She'd had a brief conversation with Dr Liz before they'd left the boat just now. Liz had been shocked by her appearance, even though it had only been a little over a week. Liz wasn't a cancer doctor, but she hadn't needed a specialism to understand the extent of Vicky's illness. What she didn't say – the things she avoided – told Vicky far more than anything she'd actually spoken aloud.

The rest of the group stretched out in front of them, the distinctive shape of the Queen Elizabeth II bridge emerging from the gloom up ahead. As they neared, Gary saw that, even today, the Dartford Crossing was still congested. The crash barriers along the sides of the elevated road kept the dead corralled, but an articulated truck had bucked and smashed through a section, its cab now hanging over the edge like a passed out drunk. Every so often corpses dropped off, staggering up to the crest of the bridge, then straying too close and being caught by the whipping winds.

At the front, Sam was finding it harder to keep tabs on the rest of the group than he'd expected. When he was out on his own among the dead, his attention was undivided. Now, though, he was having to multi-task: keep everyone together, keep watching the dead, and find somewhere safe for them to aim for. He changed direction, moving away from the Thames and further inland, cutting across a patch of scrubland then leading them down onto a main road lined with deep vegetation on both sides. 'Good move,' Chapman said quietly. 'If memory serves, this'll take us straight into Lakeside.'

Sam caught glimpses of the rest of the world through the trees. There was an ugly industrial complex on one side: huge, box-shaped units, metal pipework mazes, and endless storage yards. On the other side of the road, a sharp contrast. Here, an odd-shaped housing estate had been built to fit the limited available space. There were corpses walking the streets of the estate that had likely been trapped there since day one. They had become grotesque parodies of the people they used to be. He could see dead school kids, parents, teachers, office workers, home workers, street cleaners, crossing wardens, police officers, couriers... all of them doomed to retrace the same steps again and again and again until they were no longer physically able.

They'd so far avoided any of the undead on this stretch of road, but there was no escaping them now. The heavy, drenching rain made it difficult to see any great distance ahead, and in the encroaching gloom it was hard to tell the difference between the living and the dead. Everyone moved with the same slow weariness. Often, though, the unsteady gait of a cadaver was a giveaway. Sam clocked the first of them by the way it was limping awkwardly. Its left foot was barely attached, and it dragged the exposed stump along the ground. It was moving in the same direction they were. He put on a quick burst of speed, caught up with it, then wrapped his arm around its neck and sank his knife into its exposed temple. He dumped the creature in an unruly heap in the gutter.

The dead were already having a disproportionate effect on the group. Sam gestured for them to stay quiet. 'For fuck's sake,' he whispered to Chapman, 'what's the matter with them? You'd think they hadn't seen a corpse before.'

'To be honest, most of this lot have managed to stay alive by keeping themselves away from the dead.'

'All that's changed now. They're all gonna have to step up.'

More corpses emerged from the gloom. One staggered out from between the trees and collided with Marianne. She grabbed the cadaver and bit her lip, stopping herself from yelling out at the last possible moment as its wet flesh oozed between her fingers. Gary wrestled it away from her and dealt with it with brutal effectiveness.

Still more coming. Far more of them now.

'We're getting close,' Chapman hissed. He could hear the unease in the ranks behind. 'What don't they understand? They need to stay quiet.'

'With the best will in the world, the noise two hundred and fifty people make just shuffling along, breathing, is going to be heard when everything else is so quiet, no matter how hard we try.'

Both men quickened their speed to head off the nearest cadavers. Immediately behind them, others unsheathed their weapons and began re-killing. It was second nature to many people now. David, Joanne, Ruth, Lisa, Sanjay, Steven, and Orla all fought with a weary determination: emotionally detached, doing it because it had to be done.

The bulk of the dead were approaching from the front, but still more crashed through the undergrowth to attack from the sides. 'Fuck's sake,' Gary cursed as another one of them burst through the trees immediately to his left, vicious branches ripping at its deteriorating flesh. He swung at the dead woman's neck with his machete, his first decisive strike instantly severing what was left of her spinal cord.

Liz found herself towards the back of the main bunch. She'd been focussed on moving forward, paying little attention to what was happening behind, but when she glanced back she realised that Vicky, Marianne, Gary and the others had been cut off. More corpses had emerged from an alleyway and were closing in on the stragglers like a gang, an accidental ambush. Liz grabbed Sanjay's arm. 'Shit. Look!'

Sanjay nodded and, without hesitation, he waded into the fight. Selena now had a clear view of what was happening. She'd been carrying a kitchen knife around for weeks, but she'd barely had the chance to use it. It pissed her off that Vicky continued trying to shield her from the death and destruction, treating her like one of the kids. But this was her moment. She sprinted the short distance back and plunged her blade into the neck of the nearest corpse. 'Easy,' she said under her breath.

'What the hell are you doing?' Vicky demanded.

'Keeping you lot safe,' she said, and she struck out at the next dead body before Vicky could argue.

6

They were fast approaching the main part of the shopping centre. The last few hundred metres had been non-stop slaughter, the stretch of road behind the group now awash with blood and guts and body parts, yet the number of oncoming corpses showed no signs of reducing. There was a carpark the size of several football pitches still to cross before they made it to the entrance doors. 'This isn't gonna work,' Chapman whispered to Sam in a momentary gap between kills. 'We can't just go waltzing in there without checking it out first. The mall might be just as busy as it is out here.'

'I know, but I don't see that we have any choice. Out here we're exposed.'

Joanne was close behind. She smashed the skull of a cadaver against a lamppost, then pushed through between the two men. 'I know this place. We go in that way, straight through by Primark. Carry on into the mall, then go right or left – whichever way's clearer – and get up the escalators. Logic says there'll be far fewer of them on the first floor.'

'Care to lead the way?' Chapman asked, bracing as yet another lurching cadaver clattered into him.

'My pleasure.'

She put on a burst of speed. Sam gestured for everyone else to do the same. He whispered to Steven, who was close behind, 'Time to get a fucking move on. Pass it on.'

There wasn't a direct route between Joanne's position and the entrance she was aiming for. Though it had been early in the morning when death swept across this part of the globe, the carparks nearest to the mall had already been busy; shopping at the mall was the last thing thousands did at death. By the looks of things, it had been peak arrival time, because for every car that had been left in a space, there seemed to be at least as many again that had crashed on the way in or were abandoned, waiting for spaces that would never clear. From here, the carpark looked like a maze without a guaranteed solution, absolute fucking chaos. She tried to find the shortest route, cutting between cars, taking sharp turns right and left in quick succession, slaloming through, constantly looking over her shoulder checking the rest of the group were still following. The unevenly spaced line of more than two hundred people seemed to stretch away into the distance forever.

A corpse, stuck behind the wheel of the car it had been trying to park when it died, slapped what was left of its palm against the window. The dull thud startled Joanne and threw her off her stride. She tried to block it out, but now she'd seen one undead body trapped inside a vehicle, they were everywhere. No matter where she looked, she saw gnarled, horrendously disfigured faces staring back at her.

They'd covered less than a quarter of the distance between the road and the entrance when another corpse that had been wedged between two crashed cars managed finally to squirm free. Incensed by so much sudden close activity after months of endless inertia, it lunged forward with such force that it ripped its belly open on a wing mirror and, its profile slightly narrower then, squeezed through the gap. It collided with Audrey, drenching her with what was left of its liquefied innards. She screamed at the top of her lungs in equal parts terror and disgust.

It was as if power had been restored to the inert undead masses. In response to Audrey's noise, huge swathes of them began to stagger towards the group, zeroing in. They came from all directions, the size of the swarm more than compensating for their lack of speed. Wherever Joanne looked now she could see more of them coming, so many that their individual shapes were indistinguishable, just a single wall of ghastly movement. 'Keep going,' Chapman said from close behind her.

'Like I was going to stop, you absolute fucking idiot,' she cursed, and she changed direction and stumbled on.

For a fraction of a second Sam considered breaking away from the others and trying to distract the undead, perhaps make enough noise to give the rest of the group time and space to get inside. Though he'd pulled similar stunts in the past, this was different. There were so many of them... too many of them... *where the fuck has all this rot come from?* He'd expected a certain level of undead activity in an area as built up as this, but what Audrey had just triggered was off the scale. Had there been other survivors here? It made sense – the rotting remains of the local population aside, the massive mall would have been an ideal place to plunder for supplies and even hole up for a while.

Joanne changed direction again.

Almost there.

She was close to the entrance now, but her way forward was blocked. A swarm of cadavers spilled out ahead of her, filling the space in front of one of the main entrances to the complex. She dropped her shoulder and charged through them, the rest of the group following in her wake.

It was only when she was inside that she realised the glass doors had been smashed. Diamond-like shards crunched under her boots as she disappeared under cover. She didn't stop to question – couldn't risk it – and instead just kept running, ploughing through even more bodies, trying to make sense of the interior of the mall. The lack of light wrong-footed her, because every memory she'd had of the inside of this cavernous place was filled with bright light, and space and a much more orderly clientele, and right now she had nothing but dim illumination from the door through which she'd just entered and the grubby glass skylights in the pitched roof many metres above. There was just enough brightness for her to be able to make out the silhouettes of thousands of wandering corpses. Just like Christmas, the inside of the mall was even busier than the carpark.

Committed.

No other option.
Keep going.

The dull light was as much a hindrance to the dead as it was to the living, and the constant heavy drumming of the persistent rain on the roof provided the group with a little cover. In the miserable tank-like conditions, the limited awareness of the undead made them sluggish and diminished their compulsion to attack. The deeper into the building Joanne went, the more torpid the occupants all around her became; some stood staring into shop windows, perhaps at their own reflection. As her eyes adjusted to the gloominess indoors, she gradually began to recognise her surroundings. She banked right, heading for where she thought the nearest escalator was, the rest of the group still following. The number of dead had slowed her down enough for everyone to be able to keep up.

Joanne ran past the husks of stores she recognised, pausing only once when she caught sight of a leather jacket she'd once coveted, then squirmed around benches and dried-up fountains and other street furniture remnants that now felt like obstacles deliberately strewn in her path to stop her getting to the escalator. That was as far as her plan currently went, and it was by no means a given that they'd all make it upstairs. Plenty of people in the following pack were running out of steam.

Now that they were indoors, the group's collective noise was amplified, echoing along the length of this vast, cathedral-like space. Up ahead now she could just make out the entrance to a sprawling toy shop where she'd bought presents for her brother's kids, and an overpriced sports shop opposite where she'd sometimes bought her running gear. The escalator was right between the two stores. She put her arms out in front of her now, the better to plough through the corpses, forcing a way through.

Fuck.

There was enough light trickling in through the glass ceiling for her to see that, from the bottom to the top, the steps up to the first floor were covered by the truly dead, flesh trampled and smeared, blocked. Backed-up with rot.

Joanne started digging, grabbing at scraps of clothing and yanking corpse after corpse out of the way to get closer to the escalator. She sensed the rest of the group bunching up behind her.

'Leave it,' Sam said. 'We're not getting through this way.'

She ignored him. Kept working. Worked faster. Had to get up.

'That's us fucked,' Chapman said, already pushing back the dead hordes alongside Sanjay and Ruth. They were grouped at the bottom of the escalator, lashing out at anything that came close enough to shove.

'Keep at it,' David shouted. 'If they get on top of us, we're screwed.'

Joanne was still trying to clear a route up the blocked escalator, but it was like shovelling snow from the bottom of an avalanche. The more she moved aside, the more rotting debris came tumbling down on top of her. *Fuck, are there as many of these damn things up on the first floor as there are down here?*

'Push them back!' Gary encouraged from his exposed position on the outermost edge of the group. The dead just kept on coming, no apparent end to their numbers. 'Why are there so many of the fuckers in here?'

'We'll work it out later,' Ruth said, swinging her rucksack around like it was a medieval mace, battering a swathe of spindly monsters out of the way. 'For now, just keep fighting.'

Sanjay was pushed back against the counter of a coffee stand. He began stripping anything he could from the displays and throwing it into the seething crowd in an effort to halt their advance. David saw what he was doing and helped him to hurl tables, chairs, and other bits of furniture into the crowd, whatever wasn't screwed down. Unfortunately, the need for silence and stealth had been abandoned in panic, and now David was acutely aware that the more they did to try and hold back the army of the dead, the more of them they'd be alerting to their presence. And now some silly bastard was hitting something against a metal railing way over to his right, deeper into the mall. It was like they were ringing a dinner bell, the clanging clearly audible over the rain. 'What the fuck are you doing?' he demanded. 'Sam, is that you?'

'I'm over here,' Sam said, gasping for breath as he lunged at corpse after corpse with his knife.

'Then who the hell is banging that fucking gong?'

Whoever they were, they had to be borderline suicidal. The incessant tolling noise continued, and David said a silent word of thanks as he felt the pressure of the crowd around him shift and then lighten slightly as the horde refocussed. By no means all of the dead were seduced, but a decent number had changed direction towards the source of the rhythmic sound.

Joanne was still hard at it, trying to find a way upstairs. She heaved another flaccid carcase out of the way, then realised it wasn't just flesh and bone blocking the escalator. She ran her hands over the angular outline of a gore-soaked shop display, and realisation dawned. 'Someone did this.'

'Did what?' Sam asked.

'Someone blocked the escalator. Trying to stop any more of the dead getting up there, I guess.'

'The same person who's making that bloody noise, I expect. It's coming from upstairs.'

'Whoever it is, they're not helping.'

'I'm sure they're just looking out for themselves. Looks like we've walked into someone's patch and wound up the crowds.'

'Oh, that's just fucking perfect,' she said, and she turned her attention from the impassable escalator to the ever-shifting crowds.

Ruth was dripping with sweat, struggling to keep fighting. Alongside her, Selena hacked tirelessly at those cadavers unfortunate enough to stagger into range. She raised her knife, ready to slice down into the ripe flesh of the monster now directly in front of her, only for the creature to catch her wrist. She froze, unable to compute. The corpse shone a light into her face.

The man was alive!

His face illuminated by the soft glow from his torch, he lifted his finger to his lips to tell her to stay quiet, then beckoned for her to follow him. She grabbed Vicky's hand and Vicky alerted Ruth who took hold of the back of her jacket, then reached for the next person behind and gestured for them to do the same. As the metal chiming continued somewhere overhead, and as more of the dead drifted away in search of its source, other members of the group began to realise what was happening. There was no argument. Whatever they were now walking towards couldn't be any worse than the prospect of staying put. Even the strongest fighters were flagging, impossibly outnumbered. The walls limited the escape routes for both the living and the undead, and the building was continuing to fill. They'd end up drowning in decay.

The message worked its way through the two hundred or so members of the group, and as the ugly, hammering noise continued elsewhere, the silent conga line of the living disappeared into the shadows of the mall.

7

The man led them back towards a branch of Marks and Spencer's they'd passed a short time earlier. He used a staff entrance at the side of the store for access, then took them up to the first floor. He was silent throughout, and no one else said a word. They walked in a snaking line through the shadowy store, too relieved to have escaped from the dead to be concerned about what might come next. At the back of the line with Joanne, Sam allowed his mind to wander. He imagined a whole community of survivors living up here in a similar way to how Brian, Eric, Joanne and the others had managed to eke out a decent existence in John Kennedy House on Surrey Quays. He made fleeting eye contact with Joanne, and she almost managed a smile. It was relief, more than anything, but he smiled in return. In just a few short minutes they'd gone from utterly hopeless to somewhat hopeful.

It won't last, Sam thought, keeping his optimism in check. *It never does.*

The department store felt like a haunted house. Wherever these people had chosen to base themselves in Lakeside, it wasn't here. It smelled musty, like it had been left undisturbed for centuries, not months. There was dust everywhere, cobwebs draped like curtains. Sam thought the mannequins terrifying; their vacant, frozen expressions somehow even more menacing than the disfigured faces of the dead. It was jarring just how abnormal the mundane had quickly become. Seeing clean faces and bodies dressed in coordinating, carefully chosen clothing was alien, a mockery. People dressed in scraps now, didn't shave, barely washed. He couldn't imagine ever giving a damn about his appearance again.

They left the store through a back door marked 'staff only' and were soon deep within the catacombs of the shopping centre; a maze of corridors, storage areas, access routes, and fire escapes that the public didn't usually see. Finally, they stopped in a cavernous loading bay. The man who'd led them to safety waited for them to all catch up. 'Thank you,' Vicky said.

'Don't mention it. You're from the Monument, right?'

'How did you know that?'

Another figure stepped out from the shadows at the back of the room. He seemed hesitant, reluctant to be seen. When Chapman recognised his face, he completely understood why he'd been keen to stay hidden. It was Mihai, Dominic Grove's beleaguered quartermaster. 'I wanted to explain—' he started to say, but Chapman wasn't having any of it. When Mihai came into range he swung for him, knocking him off his feet.

'You fucking Judas,' he said, and he spat at the crumpled heap of a man lying at his feet.

On hearing the noise, someone else had entered the loading bay. 'You're not going to punch me too, are you, Chappers?'

It was Allison Woodhouse, the clipper captain. Chapman's reaction this time was the complete opposite. He grabbed her and wrapped his arms around her.

'I can't believe you all made it,' she said.

'Not all of us did. We lost a few folks along the way.'

Allison pushed herself away from him. 'I didn't want to do it,' she said. 'I didn't know what was happening until it was too late. Piotr made me think we were all getting out. I didn't realise. I didn't have any choice.'

'I believe you.'

'Mihai was the same. Piotr lied to him too.'

David helped Mihai to his feet. 'It's true,' Mihai said, and he spat blood onto the ground. 'The fucker forced us to do it. He fed me a load of bullshit about getting the supplies onto the clipper to keep them safe from the fire. Next thing I know, we're on our way. He's a fucking psychopath.'

'Sounds about right,' David said.

Chapman wasn't convinced. 'I don't believe him.'

The man who'd led them to safety had been watching the reunions from a distance, but now stepped in. 'You're going to have to argue about it later, I'm afraid. We've got more pressing things to worry about. I'm Noah, by the way.'

'Pleased to meet you,' said Sam. 'Thanks for your help.'

'That's alright. By the way, if you're unsure about allegiances, it was Mihai who acted as bait so I could come and get you all just now.'

'You been living here long?'

'Me? Since all this started. I used to work here. Security. That's how I know all the back routes.'

'We appreciate it.'

'Don't mention it. Seriously. I'm not hanging around.'

Marianne pushed her way to the front, sweat-soaked and streaked with dirt and gore. 'What did you mean when you said there's more pressing things to worry about?'

'Did you not notice the bodies downstairs? Want to know why they're inside instead of outside? I was set up nicely here until your mate Piotr turned up. Fucker trashed the place.'

'Did you see the plane in the river?' Allison asked.

'Couldn't miss it,' Chapman said.

'There was no way past. I told Piotr I couldn't go any further downriver, so he made us get off the clipper and come this way.'

'Where did you dock? We didn't see it.'

'I let her drift. The last thing I wanted was for Sir Arsewipe to have a change of heart and decide we'd go back to the Tower.'

'So what happened?'

'It had been relatively peaceful until he showed up,' Noah said. 'The dead had been pretty spread out, lethargic, nothing to bother about. But the entire legion came flocking in from miles around as soon as the looting started. This lot came crashing through like a bloody steam train.'

'But that's just stupid. Why take such a risk?'

Allison was shaking her head. 'Because Piotr never has to deal with the consequences, does he. He was never planning on hanging around. You know what he's like... he takes what he likes from a situation then disappears, leaving nothing but chaos behind him. It's everyone else who takes the risk or has to deal with the consequences, never him.'

'He's gone now though?'

'Long gone, yes. He was planning to go east. Said they'd have a better chance somewhere quiet like Norfolk or Suffolk.'

'You're bloody lucky we're still here,' Noah said.

'You did say you weren't hanging around,' David said.

'We're just waiting for the right moment. A gap in the clouds, so to speak. Quite literally, actually. It's pissing down out there.'

'It's impossible to stay here now,' Mihai explained. 'We'll never get all the bodies out, and even if we did manage it, we won't be able to keep them out. It's too big a site for just a handful of us to defend. It's the same problem we were facing in London, only a bit smaller and with Boots and Body Shop.'

'It's nowhere near as bad as London though, is it?' Marianne said. 'There's only a fraction of the number of them here.'

'Thousands instead of millions, yes.'

'But there's more than a handful of us now. The odds are quite different.'

'But it's still too much of a risk,' David said. 'Too many ways to get ourselves trapped in a corner or surrounded. I for one don't fancy hanging around. No sense barricading ourselves in here with a few thousand corpses for company when there are so many similar places that might be empty.'

'It's not as straightforward as that, though, is it? Speaking for myself, I don't think I can keep running. We're not all as strong as you. I'm on my last legs here, and I know I'm not alone.'

She looked around. There were nods and mumbles of support.

'I'm sorry, but your friend here's right. Staying here's just not an option,' Noah said. 'Holing up in these dark backrooms? Staying quiet, hiding from the bloody dead masses? What sort of life is that? Nah. Your man Piotr fucked us over. This place is no good now.'

'Where were you planning on going?' Sam asked.

'I'm from Brentwood, just up the motorway. Going to see what's left of the place, then consider my options.'

'How will you get there?'

'Walk. Short bursts. It's too much of a risk to try anything else around here. My fear is they'll hear us if we're not careful leaving. If even a handful get the scent, the rest will follow.'

'Makes sense.'

'There's a service station less than a mile away,' Noah continued. 'It has a couple of food outlets and a Travelodge, and it's fairly isolated. We agreed we'd head there first, then move on. Take it step by step and see where we end up.'

'I might manage a mile,' Marianne interrupted. 'I know it won't be easy, but I think we can all manage one last push.'

'Sounds like this place will give us a little breathing space,' David said. 'If we're all in agreement, I think we should head out now and see what happens. The way I see it, other than heading back to the boat and maybe trying to get onto the south bank, right now we don't have a lot of viable options.'

8

Another coordinated burst of noise from Mihai up on the first floor of the shopping centre allowed the group a sliver of space to escape. Noah led them along cut-throughs and service roads that, without his insider knowledge, would otherwise have remained undiscovered. But the volume of bodies crammed into the mall was such that the undead were everywhere already, even in these remote, dark corners.

There was no doubt that Piotr's wrecking ball actions had left Lakeside uninhabitable. The population density of this part of Essex had been high, and there'd been a disproportionate concentration of workers and shoppers within a couple of miles of the mall when death had indiscriminately swept across the world. As the group had already discovered, the geographic complexities of such a built-up area had made it easy for corpses to accumulate, but difficult to drift away. Until something else caught their attention, tens of thousands of corpses were stuck, going nowhere. And the single factor most likely to trigger another unpredictable chain reaction within the massed ranks of the volatile undead was *them*.

It was a heavily industrialised, built-up area, but there was a surprising amount of open green space between Lakeside and the service station. David checked over his shoulder regularly as they marched across the grassy scrubland and wasn't at all surprised to see corpses following. 'It's because there's so many of us,' Noah explained. 'They're bound to see one of us, aren't they. I've only ever been up here on my own before now.'

They had a clear view of an elevated stretch of the A282 road directly ahead. There were stationary lines of traffic in both directions, but no obvious signs of movement. 'Looks quiet up

48

there,' David whispered.

Noah nodded. 'I've never seen many of them on the roads. Think about it – no one ever walked on the motorways and A roads, did they? All the bodies that were up there when it happened are likely still stuck in their cars.'

They scrambled through a copse of trees and emerged outside the service station. 'Now this looks promising,' Chapman said.

The building itself appeared surprisingly insignificant, given the acres of carparks and greenery which surrounded it. It was a sullen, angular grey construction with raised walkways leading up to its uninviting entrance. He walked up to the doors and peered inside through the grubby glass. Sanjay stepped up next to him and forced them open with relative ease.

Light seeped in through the windows around an open-plan seating area, but much of the rest of the building remained shrouded in darkness. The muffled quiet inside was immediately disturbed by the sounds of a handful of resident cadavers reacting to the break-in. Chapman dealt with them swiftly before the rest of the group arrived.

Those people who'd had most exposure to the dead world beyond the walls of the Monument base immediately knew what to do. Sanjay, Ruth, Selena, and even Omar went from room to room, space to space, removing corpses and collecting up anything of value. Others began securing the entrances, using tables, chairs, and shop displays to block the doorway through which they'd entered.

David headed deeper into the building. He rattled the door of the nearest cubicle in the large restroom area to bring out the dead. 'I get all the best jobs,' he grumbled to no one in particular, and he jumped with surprise when a cadaver lunged at him from around a corner. He gripped it by the back of the neck and smashed its face repeatedly into a stainless-steel urinal bowl until it stopped fighting. He found another one trapped in a locked stall, a third stuck in a cleaner's storeroom, and one more, butt naked in a shower, bouncing furiously off the walls. He slaughtered them all with nonchalance, barely a thought. He realised he'd long since stopped trying to work out their stories – who'd they'd been, how they'd come to be where they were on the day they'd died. He'd seen too much death to care anymore, and it worried him. The undead were empty shells, far removed from the people they used to be. He'd changed too; but what had he become?

He'd have probably killed Sanjay offhand if he hadn't stopped him. 'Jesus Christ, Sanj! What the hell are you doing creeping up on me like that?'

'I didn't creep up on you. You were properly in the zone. I've been trying to get your attention for the last couple of minutes.'

'I've been busy.'

'I can see that. It's a bloodbath in here, mate.'

'I've got a lot on my mind,' David said, and he slipped past Sanjay and went back to the others.

There'd been no opportunity to eat yet today. Until now, nervous uncertainty had meant that food had been the very last thing on most people's minds, but the adrenalin of their escape from the mall, coupled with the apparent safety and convenience of this new-found shelter, had rapidly altered the dynamic.

Marianne appeared more alive than at any time since they'd set sail from the centre of London. Most of the group had gravitated towards a seating area sandwiched between branches of Costa Coffee and Burger King, and she'd switched back to her old self again: energetically ordering folks about, coordinating the stockpiling of the supplies they'd found, and clearing a whole area so that people could rest and recover from their ordeal.

'Don't get comfortable,' Noah said.

'We need to rest.'

'Yeah, but don't get too settled. We're not stopping. Couple of hours max.'

'Who are you to tell me what we're doing? I hardly even know you.'

'Don't be difficult, Marianne,' David said. 'You were part of the conversation just now. You know we're not hanging around.'

'Yes, but that was before we saw this place. We could make it into a bloody fortress. It's safer than anywhere else we've been.'

'But still not safe enough.'

'We might not find anywhere else as good as this.'

'It's a frigging motorway service station,' Noah sighed. 'They're everywhere. If you're that much of a fan, let's go find you one that doesn't have thousands of corpses on the doorstep.'

'There's no need to be like that.'

'There is, actually.'

'Noah's right, Marianne,' David said. 'We can't stay.'

'We haven't even tried,' Audrey protested. 'Did you know there's a hotel here? There's a Travelodge at the back of us, room enough for everyone... this place is ideal. And anyway, how comes you get to make all the decisions?'

David shrugged. 'I don't. I'm not twisting anyone's arm. If you want to stay, stay.'

Marianne was indignant. 'I don't think our opinions should count for less just because we can't fight as efficiently as you can.'

David shook his head. 'What are you talking about? Your opinion has always been listened to, Marianne. Many of us wouldn't be here today if it wasn't for you and your opinions. You're a gobby, opinionated bugger, and we love you for it.'

'Don't try and butter me up, David. That's not what I'm saying, and you know it. We're out of London now, and we need to start thinking differently.'

'Out of London, yes, but not out of trouble.'

'I just think before we start running again, and before anyone else starts talking about Ledsey bloody Cross, we need to stop and think about our situation realistically.'

'Bit late for that,' Noah said, observing. 'It's the bloody zombie apocalypse. Realism went out the window months ago.'

She ignored him and continued. 'The problem is, David, and I mean no disrespect, but you're all still thinking about our situation in terms of your own skills and needs. The reality is we're not all the same, but there are other, equally valid perspectives to consider.'

'Let's hear them, then,' David said, looking around at everyone else. 'Come on, speak up. If you want to stay here, say so.'

'I'm with Marianne,' Audrey said. 'We've all got something we can contribute. If we all work together, I believe we could do well here. Those who can fight can hold the line, the rest of us will do whatever we need to make our lives more comfortable and secure. Cleaning, maintenance, preparing food, fortifying the building... there's all kinds of jobs will need doing.' She looked for a particular face in the crowd. 'Georgie, why don't you start going through everyone's details and identify the jobs they can do. We'll start drawing up a list of what needs doing and—'

'And before you know it, you'll be back in the exact same position you were all in at the Tower of London,' Sam said. 'You'll be cut off. Surrounded.'

Joanne noticed he was soaked and out of breath. 'Where've you been?'

'Up near the motorway.'

'And?'

'And we've got company.'

'Already?' Marianne gasped.

'Yes, already. Are you surprised? Have you not been paying attention?'

'How many?' David asked, concerned.

'Enough. Twenty or thirty getting close.'

'You can deal with that number, can't you?' Audrey said. 'Your lot must have killed thousands by now.'

'*Our lot*?' Ruth said, incensed. 'What the hell's that supposed to mean?'

Sam shook his head. 'You're missing the point. You're all missing the bloody point. They follow. It's what the dead do. One coming this way is as bad as a hundred.'

'Then all we need to do is stay quiet and wait for them to piss off again, same as always,' Marianne said.

'We're past that point now. It didn't work in London, and there's no reason to think it'll work today. We're far more exposed out here.'

Concerned mumbles rippled through the group. Sam waited for the low noise to die down, then continued.

'There's something else you need to know. There's a whole other herd.'

'Where?'

'There's another section of the centre just to the west of here. A huge supermarket then a whole load of other stores beyond. After that, massive housing estates.'

'And?'

'And they're closer than the bodies we came here to get away from. They're already drifting this way.'

'We can sit it out.'

'I don't think so. It's surprising how much you can see from up there. It all looks very different to how I expect it used to. The grass is overgrown, and there's litter everywhere. No one's been collecting leaves this year, so there are blocked drains and standing pools of water and—'

'And what bloody point are you making?' Audrey interrupted nervously.

'Because nature's taking everything back, it's far easier to see where we've been. It's harder for us to hide. From up on the road just now, I could see the damage Piotr and his cronies caused when they left. Looks like they looted everything on that side of the centre, then split, leaving a filthy trail. Tyre tracks on the road, bits of bodies everywhere.'

'So?'

'So, there are still corpses hanging around. There's a whole load of them just waiting, like they're holding on for them to come back.'

'Bullshit.'

'Go up there and look for yourself if you don't believe me. It's three days since Piotr was here, and they're still out there in large numbers. What I'm saying is, once they know we're here, we won't be able to get rid of them. And that other herd already knows.'

'We really can't risk stopping here,' David said.

Sanjay was at the window. 'Sam's right. I can see quite a few of them out there already. They look in better shape to the ones we were facing in London. They're stronger and faster... not as badly damaged. They haven't been crushed up against massive crowds, haven't been burnt to a crisp. Seriously, I think we need to go.'

Marianne sat down, defiant. 'I'm not leaving.'

'Sounds like we don't have much of a choice, Marianne,' David said. 'If what they're saying is right then we must—'

'I'm not leaving!' she yelled at him, her voice uncomfortably loud. Around her, people cringed at the volume. She paused to compose herself, then explained. 'I just can't face going back out there. I'm sorry; I can't do it. I know what you're saying is right, but I just don't think I can go any further.'

'We might be able to hold on for a couple of hours here if we're careful, just long enough so that everyone can get their breath back.'

Marianne shook her head. 'No, David, I'm sorry. It won't make any difference.'

Audrey put a reassuring hand on Marianne's shoulder. 'I'm with you, love. Seems to me that if we walk 'til the cows come home, we're never going to find anywhere better than this. If they followed us this far, they'll follow us to Kingdom Come. I say we stay and spend the time before the dead get here making the place as strong as possible.'

'Did you not hear me, Audrey?' Sanjay said. 'They're already here.'

'It's a pipe dream, Marianne,' David said. 'I heard what you said, I understand the lure of a place like this, but consider. The dead will converge, more coming every hour, and soon we'll be well and truly surrounded. Those nice fields we passed? It'll look like Glastonbury for the damned. There'll be no escape for us, ever. The hordes will park it here and won't be drawn away again. They'll eventually perish, but they'll likely outlast us. We have to go now. The situation gets worse with every minute we stay.'

He started getting his stuff together. Around him, more people followed his lead. Marianne remained in her seat. 'You're not listening to me, David. I'm not going anywhere. I can't start running again, not knowing if we'll ever stop.'

'Listen to me, Marianne, if you stay here you—'

Vicky grabbed his arm. 'Fuck it. You're wasting your breath. Let's go.'

He shook her off and tried again. 'If you stay here, you'll likely not survive. I can't put it any clearer than that.'

She looked up at him. 'I do understand. But it doesn't change anything. I know what my choices are; this is the safest I've felt all day, and I can't go back out there.'

In the space of just a couple of minutes a clear divide had opened in the group. Some people were frantically preparing to leave, but many others clearly intended on staying put. Some began piling furniture up against the windows and doors, herding other folks deeper into the building.

The interior of the service station was alive with movement now. David tried to talk to Marianne again, but Gary blocked him. 'Just go,' he said. 'I know you're right, but I'm staying too. I'm out of shape and I've still got a dodgy leg... I'd just slow you down.'

'Don't be stupid, Gary.'

'I'm not, I'm being sensible. Some of us can't keep going, and you just have to accept that. I'll get whoever's staying organised and we'll hold the fort. Take as many people as you can and get out of here. Set yourselves up somewhere down the road and send word back. We'll get there as soon as we can. We survived London. We'll survive this.'

David nodded but was struggling to find words. He looked over his shoulder and saw the leavers already making their way out of the back of the service station. He winced at the noise again when someone dropped a table against one of the windows, piling up furniture. Through a gap David saw that hordes of advancing cadavers were now visible. They really were a different sort than they'd fought in London; they'd have to hump it just to stay ahead of them.

Gary pushed him away.

'Go. Now. We'll sit out the storm then I'll get them to follow later.'

David nodded and looked around. There was a map on the wall nearby, a simplified diagram of the motorway network. 'We'll try and go north. Up towards Cambridge. If we think Piotr's gone east, then we'll definitely avoid going that way.'

'Okay. Leave signs along the way if you can.'

'Will do. Thanks, Gary.'

'Don't thank me, just go. We'll be with you as soon as we can.'

The first corpses slammed up against the entrance doors, pawing at the glass with greasy fists. Though they'd been conditioned to keep quiet, those people who were staying behind couldn't help but react. Some moved to pile more furniture up against the windows, others scurried away in the opposite direction, desperate to be swallowed up by the shadows.

Gary held his machete ready to fight. 'For the last time, go!'

David looked for Marianne. He caught a momentary glimpse of her sitting at a table, watching at the bodies clamouring to get inside. Between the dead flesh blocking the outside of the windows and the barricade being hurriedly constructed inside, the service station was rapidly filling with darkness and fear.

'Come *on*, David,' Sam shouted from near the rear exit. 'We need to move.'

David reluctantly followed him outside, the last of a line of people moving as quickly and quietly away from the service station as they could. Some were already up on the motorway. He knew they were well spaced out, but Christ, there only seemed to be a fraction of the number of people they'd arrived here with.

How many had stayed behind?

He ran to catch up with the others but stopped again when he made it up onto the motorway. From this height he had a clear view of the building he'd just escaped from and the rest of the vast shopping centre beyond.

Fuck.

There were tens thousands of bodies moving towards it, an unstoppable slick. Within the hour, all their exits would be blocked, and the place would be surrounded, encased by death. Eventually, inevitably, the dead would force their way inside. With nothing else to distract them, they'd just keep on coming.

He wanted to go back, but he knew there was no point. He'd drawn as clear a picture as he could, but Marianne and the others had been as determined to stay as he had been to leave. He couldn't have forced them.

It didn't compute. Irrespective of the speed of the dead, it had all happened so fast. A huge number of people, lost in a heartbeat.

9

Noah led the remains of the group along the silent M25. He estimated they had about six miles still to walk to get to Brentwood, and whilst he covered that distance each morning in half an hour, safe in his warm motor, they were resigned to a slog through rusting traffic and rotted muck. Close to London, this part of the motorway network had been heavily congested during the morning rush hour grind on the day the world ended. In places it was hard to find a way through the wreckage on foot. There were signs that Piotr and his cronies had managed to get vehicles through, but they'd had fewer people to worry about and had no doubt blitzed through without a care. Sam knew that, for now, this group needed to take it slow and steady. He hoped they'd find the amount of devastation reduced the further they got from the centre of the capital. If things stayed like this, he thought, they'd struggle to get far. At least one thing had gone in their favour. 'You were right about the number of bodies up here,' he said to Noah.

'I'm right about a lot of things. People should listen to me more often.'

'Who? We listened, didn't we?'

'Yeah, but look how many of your lot didn't. That frigging idiot Piotr didn't, neither.' Noah kept his voice to little more than a whisper, conditioned by weeks of living alongside the dead. 'I was doing alright until that dumb bastard turned up. I mean, it weren't the height of luxury or nothing, and I had more than my fair share of scrapes, but I was getting by.'

'Piotr has a habit of fucking things up for everyone.'

'I get that impression. I heard plenty from Allison and Mihai. They're not fans, believe me.'

Sam looked back at the rest of the group behind him. Every time he turned around, they seemed to be more spread out. He was worried they'd start leaving people behind at this rate. They were walking in almost complete silence, bunched up in twos and threes or alone, heads down, shuffling slowly...

Christ. Are we the zombies now?

He stopped and waited for the others to catch up.

Vicky was dropping further and further down the line, almost at the back now, unable to keep up despite their relatively slow speed. Selena and Ruth walked alongside her, but her regular walking partner was nowhere to be seen. 'Where's Gary?' she asked. 'He's the only one who can match my pathetic pace.'

Ruth took her arm. 'He stayed behind, love. He told me he was sick of slowing us down. He promised they'd follow later.'

Vicky shook her head. 'We both know that's not happening. He knew it too.'

Omar was behind them. 'Gary's gone?'

'Sorry, love. I thought you knew. I knew you two had a bit of a bond.'

'I knew him from before, that was all.'

Omar nonchalantly wiped his eyes with the back of his hand, trying to hide that he was crying, but serving only to draw attention to the fact.

'He told me you used to get on his nerves,' Vicky said. 'He told me he couldn't believe it when you first turned up with Sam.'

'Whatever.'

'He also said he thought you'd done well, though. He said you'd surprised him, considering you used to be an irritating little shite.'

'He said all that?'

'On the boat this morning, actually.'

Omar said nothing but sped up again, uncomfortable having his emotions on show.

Mid-afternoon. The winter daylight was already fading. Sam and David were waiting in a bubble of space formed between several different high-speed crashes. 'I can't keep going at this pace,' Vicky said, the last to catch up.

'Looks like we've got a way to go yet,' Sam said unhelpfully.

'We can do it in bursts,' David suggested. 'A mile or so at a time. Reckon you can cope with that?'

'Maybe,' Vicky said.

'We'll stop between walks. Find some food and shelter.'

'On the M25?' Ruth said, aghast. 'How's that going to work exactly?'

David gestured towards the inner lane where many of the crashed vehicles were clearly commercial. 'There's a Sainsbury's truck; might be something in there. We can use trucks like that for shelter, as long as we keep a look-out and don't hang around too long.'

Sam approached a tall-sided vehicle that straddled the hard shoulder, its nose buried in the embankment. The sides of the lorry were slatted. He peered in and wished she hadn't. Livestock, a misnomer. It was impossible to be sure what kind of animals the truck had been transporting, but they'd died cooped up. He imagined the horror of their frightened death throes; had they taken to eating each other? Joanne checked he was okay. 'Just when you think you've seen it all, there's something like this waiting for you around the next corner.'

'Makes you realise how much we've lost,' she said. 'There's absolutely nothing that's escaped this.'

A little further down the road, Chapman forced open the door of an empty trailer that was on lying its side. He herded everyone inside. Ruth, Orla, and Liz cleared out the contents of the supermarket delivery van they'd seen and shared the food around.

'We stop for an hour,' David announced, 'long enough to get our breath and our bearings. We need to keep moving. Keep looking forward, don't look back.'

A routine was quickly established: walk a mile or two in silence, pause and regroup, then repeat. Georgie kept herself busy each time they stopped, checking and double-checking who was here and who hadn't made it, noting names. They were about a mile and a half out of Brentwood now, ready for the final push.

They came upon an empty coach. After Sanjay tussled with the husk of its long dead driver who, even now, appeared loath to surrender his post, people climbed onboard and sank into relatively comfortable seats.

David stood at the door and looked along the length of the coach. It looked like a very large group - people were sitting on top of each other, and there were folks in the aisles and sitting on the steps - but it was an illusion. There was just about room for everyone who was left; the truth was, there wouldn't have been, just earlier that morning. They'd lost so many today.

Georgie did a headcount. 'I might as well give up with this. It's pointless now.'

'Don't,' David said. 'Please. Your records are important. It's the only way we have of keeping track of who we've got and what they're capable of.'

'And who and what we've lost. I just don't know if I've got it in me anymore, Dave. It hurts too much. When this all started,' she held up her worn notebook, 'people were continually arriving at the Monument. I kept myself crazy busy keeping everything up to date; felt like a real purpose, an important step to rebuilding. Now all I'm doing is crossing out the names of those who've gone. I'm sick of it.'

'How many of us are there?'

Georgie swallowed hard. 'Seventy-six.'

The numbers were sobering, confirmation of David's worst fears. It took a moment before he could respond. 'So we left around a hundred and fifty behind at Lakeside?'

'No, around a hundred and fifty people chose to stay behind,' Chapman said quickly, correcting David. 'There's a difference.'

'You think? Looks the same from where I'm standing. I should have done more to get them to leave.'

Chapman shook his head. 'No, absolutely not. I know it's shit, but they all did what they did for a reason. None of it was your fault.'

'I don't buy that.'

'And I don't care, mate. You take too much on yourself. If we hadn't left when we did, we'd have lost a lot more. We might have all died.'

Georgie agreed. 'And most of them wouldn't have made it this far even if you had forced them to leave. We'd never have got away.'

'She's right,' Chapman said. 'Stay positive.'

'*Stay positive?*' David repeated, incredulous.

'Yes. People take their lead from you, Dave.'

'I don't want the pressure.'

'Tough shit, you've got it.'

'You're like the group dad,' Georgie said.

'Is that supposed to be a compliment?'

'Why, yes, actually.'

Sam and Noah shuffled down the coach to where David and the others were talking. 'We need to decide where we're going when we get into Brentwood.'

'Any suggestions?' David asked.

'There's a decommissioned nuclear bunker,' Noah said.

Chapman scoffed. 'You think I'm sealing myself underground in the dark? No frigging way. Any alternatives?'

'There was a TA base not far from my place. How about that?'

'TA?' Georgie asked.

'Territorial Army. Reservists. It's well outside the centre of town, off the beaten track, strong fence around it. Maybe we should try there? Assuming they didn't leave the gates wide open, it's almost certainly going to be secure.'

Though no one wanted to lose the light, the end of this day couldn't come too soon. After many months of terrible days, today had been among the very worst that any of them could remember. At least the rain had stopped now, small mercies. The sky overhead was clear. It was a race to cover the final distance before the sun disappeared completely.

Noah drove this section of the motorway regularly. It was impossible to take a wrong turn, yet he felt hopelessly disorientated. It wasn't just that he was on foot, every other aspect of his surroundings conspired to confuse him. The once-bright lights that marked out the line of the road were all unlit, and the scrambled remains of doomsday traffic meant the lanes all merged without distinction, most painted markings obscured. As a result, every metre of tarmac felt the same as the next and the last. A while back they'd passed a sign that told them the next junction was a mile away, but the distance seemed to be taking forever to cover.

On an elevated section of the motorway, Noah stopped abruptly. 'What's wrong?' Sanjay asked, concerned.

'Look at this.'

'At what?'

'Exactly. There's nothing to see,' he replied. He swept his arm across from left to right, pointing out invisible landmarks. 'There's Upminster. Hornchurch, too. Hard to believe that over there is Romford. There's not a single bloody light left on anywhere. If you every want to get some perspective on what's happened to the world, come to a place you used to know and look around. There's nothing left out here. Nothing but us.'

'Do we have far to go?'

He pointed along the road. Sanjay squinted. 'See that bridge? From memory, I think that's got to be the Warley Road. That should take us straight there.'

'Should?'

'What's the matter? Don't you trust me?'

'No offence, but until this morning, I didn't even know you.'

'I'm not working with your mate Piotr, and I'm not dead. I think it's safe to assume we're on the same side,' he said, and he walked on, indignant.

'For the record, I think he's on the level,' Chapman said.

'I just don't know who to trust anymore, you know?'

'I do. But it's like the man says, as long as they're not Piotr and they have a pulse, I think we have to take our chances.'

Noah led the group up an embankment, over a fence, then onto the Warley Road. They were soon walking through a leafy, tree-lined area, a welcome contrast to the endless industrial brutality of Lakeside and the motorway they'd subsequently been following. Their surroundings felt worlds removed from the built-up urban chaos of central London. It was a long time since any of them had been anywhere like this.

'It's proper *Walking Dead* territory, this,' Joanne joked. Orla just looked at her.

'Never watched it.'

'They were always walking down roads like this. Didn't matter where they'd been or where they were going, they always seemed to end up on the same roads, weed strewn with forests on either side.'

'Yeah, and there was always zombies,' Omar said, and he immediately wished he hadn't, but it was okay. For once, there were no corpses around. They passed a nice-looking blue Audi that had carried on straight when the road had curved, ending up nose-first in a ditch. The driver must have been going at some speed because his neck had been snapped in the crash. His face was glued to the wheel by decay, yet his rheumy eyes swivelled to

64

watch as the group traipsed past. Other than him, they couldn't see a single dead body, ahead or behind.

'Can't see anything through the trees here,' Vicky said, panting with effort.

'This was always a quiet spot,' Noah said, 'way off the beaten track. Hopefully the dead will all be in the centre of town, not out here on the outskirts.'

'I'm not so sure,' Sam said. 'It might have been that way at the start, but they'll have been spreading out since then. You saw how dark Romford and all those places were just now. If Brentwood was the same, there'd have been no reason for the dead to hang around.'

'Christ, could you not give me a couple of minutes to enjoy the illusion of peace?'

They walked past grand, monolithic country houses, set well back from the road at the end of long, sweeping drives, drenched in shadows as if to highlight their gothic credentials. In one, the silhouette of a skittering figure could be seen moving back and forth, back and forth across a first-floor landing window. 'That is creepy as fuck,' Orla said under her breath.

'Should we try one of these pads?' Sanjay asked.

'If there were only a few of us, maybe,' David said. The tone of his voice left no room for negotiation. 'Too much of a risk with seventy. Let's stick to the plan. The fence around an army reservist base is going to be stronger than the fence around some old guy's garden.'

'Point taken. I'm just tired, that's all.'

'Not far now,' Noah said as they approached a large restaurant, the only visible building. He hesitated, drowning in the memories of the life he'd once had here.

Remember that time you came here with the lads and Mickey got so drunk he sat down at someone else's table and started eating some random guy's chips? Wonder if any of the lads made it through this?

'What now?' David asked, bringing him back to reality.

65

'There's a country lane round here,' Noah said. 'We can use it as a cut-through. Shave a few minutes off the walk.'

'I don't see any cut-through.'

The light hadn't so much faded tonight as it appeared to have been snuffed out. They'd been able to make out plenty of detail just a few minutes ago, but since they'd emerged from the trees, all Noah could see were shadows and the shadows of shadows.

He gestured into the dark. 'It's there. Probably just overgrown.'

'You sure about this?'

'Absolutely. If we keep going this way, we'll end up going through a residential area. Take that lane and we'll bypass it.'

Someone screamed.

Joanne was wearing a head-torch. She flicked it on and looked around.

Corpses!

Barely contained panic spread rapidly through the group as more of the dead lumbered towards them. They'd congregated in a bunch while Noah considered their change of direction, and their noise had attracted the unwanted attention of some of the undead from across the restaurant carpark; they had simply fallen in line behind the survivors. In the almost total darkness out here today, the living and the dead had become indistinguishable, all of them reduced to shadows.

Sam was first to react. He cracked the skull of a dead woman with a mallet he'd picked up on the motorway, caving it in like a chocolate easter egg, then lashing out several more times just to be certain. Alongside him, Joanne lunged for a stick-like ghoul that had wrapped its brittle-branch arms around Allison. She wrenched the cadaver away, wrestled it the ground, then stamped her boot on its upturned face.

Shit, but it was like herding cats now.

People were beginning to scatter, moving away from each other because the only way they could be certain they weren't next to a cadaver was to be standing next to no one at all.

'What the hell?' Chapman said, exasperated. 'Where did they

all come from?'

Joanne continued to look around for the dead. 'It's only a handful. For fuck's sake. Complete fucking overreaction.' Her anger was part-nerves, part-relief.

Sam took a torch from his rucksack and shone it around. Several more cadavers were closing in, drawn to the noise. Another minute, and there'd be more still. He shoved the torch into Noah's hand. 'Go. Get moving. Get to that bloody TA place and get inside. Keep this light on and keep it pointed up so that people can see it. Just don't stop again.'

'But I—'

'Just fucking do it!'

He pushed Noah towards the trees, then went back to the restaurant carpark. He climbed up onto the roof of the sole car remaining and jumped up, landing hard and denting the sun-bleached metalwork. Immediately the remaining corpses turned and began shuffling towards the noise. Once Sam was sure that the others were all following Noah, he climbed down off the car and pushed through the crowd.

He collided with a lone figure who was standing in the entrance to the country lane. What idiot had waited for him? He was about to berate them, cursing them for taking unnecessary risks, but he bit his lip when he realised it was one of the undead. The dead man swayed on unsteady feet, watching Sam watching him. '*What the hell are you?*' Sam asked under his breath. For half a second the corpse seemed poised to attack him, but it didn't. Distracted by something else in its periphery, it staggered away.

The behaviour of the dead man unnerved Sam. He hadn't fallen for the distraction, like the others. Had the corpse seen through his rouse? His position near the entrance to the lane left Sam wondering if the dead man had been caught in two minds: *do I react to that noise, or do I follow the crowd?*

But that was impossible, wasn't it?

They'd been right to trust Noah. His local knowledge was spot on, and for that they were grateful. Without him they'd have been wandering all night and would likely have walked right past this place. It was quiet, secluded and, until now, undisturbed. There was a good amount of space on almost all approaches, most notably the woods through which they'd walked to get here, with a water tower and covered reservoir on a patch of land behind. Tucked away on the outermost edge of a Brentwood suburb, the Reservist base looked ideal.

Steve Armitage was the only one with any relevant recent military experience. He got inside and scouted the place out, returning after a couple of minutes with a pair of cutters that he used to make a large enough hole in the wire-mesh fence for them to crawl through. The break-in felt deceptively simple. They had to remind themselves that, pre-apocalypse, it would have been impossible. These days even the most secure, well-protected locations were easy targets. Steve agreed to take responsibility for working out what they'd got and what was worth keeping. There was no discussion necessary. This place would do for tonight.

The site itself was little more than a yard and a handful of buildings: the barracks, secure stores, what appeared to have been a training and administration block, and a prefabricated hut that had been home to the local army cadets. One of the rooms in the barracks was a chapel, and someone had joked that Audrey could set up shop before remembering she wasn't there, that she'd been lost today along with so many others. Their exhaustion and the adrenalin rush of the trek here was enough to keep the loss and grief at bay, but barely. Most people could feel the darkness closing in. They knew they couldn't keep walking indefinitely, couldn't go another mile tonight, and this place seemed ideal. Except that the security, darkness and space would inevitably give them time to think.

Today's losses were painful and raw. They brought back memories of everyone they'd lost before. Sam remembered Charlie, who'd died helping them get out of the hotel on Fleet Street. David remembered Holly, who'd been so traumatised by the fighting around the Monument that she'd taken her own life rather than face going into battle again. Lisa thought about Richard, who'd gone off to help secure Thomas More Street on the night the final Great Fire of London had begun and who'd never returned. And both Vicky and Selena thought about Kath. They wished she was here, but they both knew she'd never have made it. Sanjay remembered the group of people he'd left behind in the Tower of London. He'd had no choice but to walk away, but that didn't make him feel any better. He'd just abandoned them, for crying out loud. Had he even tried? It felt like an age ago.

They were still hung up on past losses, hadn't had space to even start trying to deal with them. Today alone they'd lost more than one hundred and fifty of their friends – another mass of hurt that would eventually need to be unpacked. And no one yet dared to mention the countless family members, loved ones, colleagues, and other friends who'd been killed without explanation that first week of September. It felt like there was layer upon layer upon layer of loss, too deep for any of them to dig through.

They dined on ration packs in a musty mess-hall. With everyone occupied, David left the main building to look for Chapman and Steve. He saw that there were bodies in front of the gates. It was no surprise; wherever they went, the dead would find them. Their numbers were low for now, but David knew it wouldn't take much of a disturbance for a handful to become a crowd, then a mob, then a major problem.

They were waiting for him in the cadet headquarters on the

other side of the yard. It reminded David of the draughty old Scout hut he used to go to when he was a kid. In comparison to the other buildings on the site, it felt flimsy and prefabricated. 'Our reluctant leader,' Steve said when he entered the building.

David sighed. 'Fuck me, I keep telling everyone I'm not the leader.'

'And the rest of us keep telling you that you are. For now, at least. Anyway, want to know what we've got?'

'Go on.'

'For starters, three well-maintained trucks and a van. Not the most comfortable of rides, but they'll do. Plenty of room for all of us that's left and our gear. Next, quite a bit of useful kit. There's a reasonable stock of ration packs, some protective gear, lots of useful stuff we can use out in the field.'

'Sounds good. What about–?'

'Weapons?' Steve interrupted, pre-empting him. 'Yep, there's some stuff we can take, but I'd keep it between us. You know how it is, Dave, the dead are coming apart at the seams as it is, we don't need to start shooting at them.'

Chapman agreed. 'We need to steer away from guns and grenades. You'll get rid of a handful, but every single shot will let hundreds more corpses know where you are.'

Steve wasn't finished. 'I know my way around this kit, but I don't intend spending the next few weeks and months training civvies how to fight. I mean, can you imagine Omar getting his hands on a frigging automatic rifle? Terrifying! We're not that far gone.'

David managed half a smile. 'So, apart from the fact you don't trust Omar with a gun, what exactly are you telling me?'

'That we should be good here for a day or two, but no longer,' Chapman explained. 'As I'm sure you've noticed, we already have an audience building outside. We've got time to get some rest and get our heads together, talk about next steps, but that's about it. I reckon we're still far too close to London to risk hanging around for long.'

70

'People are going to want to stay,' David said.

'And we need to be ready to persuade them otherwise. Look around... things are nowhere near as bad as they were in the capital, and it should only get easier the further north we go. I'm not suggesting we go all the way up to la la land or wherever it is in Yorkshire that Vicky's determined to visit, just far enough. It'll be December in a couple of days. Winter's coming. Once we get a couple of months into the new year, everything will look different again.'

'Will it? I'm not so sure. You might have the appetite for it, but I'm not sure about everyone else. I'm not even sure I have. It's the wrong end of the wrong day to be having this conversation.'

'No, it's exactly the right day. We should let the others have a night off tonight, then start sowing the seeds tomorrow. And don't start with all that *I'm not a leader* bullshit again, because right now you're the closest thing we've got.'

'I'm no Dominic Grove,' he said quickly.

'Thank fuck for that,' Steve said. 'You're as far removed from that slimy little bastard as it's possible to get. Look, mate, I know what I'm talking about. You're good officer material. You lead from the front, and you're not opposed to getting your hands dirty. I heard people talking tonight like they'd found their forever home here, but I reckon that's just wishful thinking. We need to get them used to the idea that this is just another pitstop. In fact, we need to get them used to the fact that it's going to be pitstop after pitstop for the foreseeable future.'

12

DAY EIGHTY-EIGHT

They spent almost the entire following day trying to acclimatise, but it was easier said than done. Switching off and kicking back was a thing of the past, no matter how safe their surroundings had initially appeared. As the hours ticked by, the barracks began to feel less suitable, less secure, less permanent. As much of an improvement on their previous hideouts and boltholes as they clearly were, they still weren't good enough. Even here, surrounded by military kit and protected by walls and fences and open spaces, they still had to take risks just to fulfil their basic needs.

For starters, they needed food.

Sam and Mihai found a supermarket within walking distance. A group of ten volunteers left the base to collect enough to keep everyone fed and watered for a few days at least. Despite the fact they stayed quiet and moved slowly, and even though most of the people who went out to loot were used to tiptoeing around the dead and not taking chances, they still hit problems. There were too many wandering bodies in the area to be able to avoid all of them. The looters tried to balance safety and speed, and though they were largely successful, by the time the job was done, the crowd of cadavers hanging around the gates had more than doubled in size. The dead showed no signs of retreat. 'They're becoming more persistent,' Sam said. 'Their behaviours are changing. They're holding back more, reacting with less volatility. It's like they're thinking.'

His comments had initially been met with derision from certain quarters, but the evidence was mounting.

'I saw the same thing at the service station, and again on the

72

way here. And before you start ripping the piss out of me, I know exactly how ridiculous this sounds. Their physical condition is better than the ones in London, it makes sense that what's left of their brains are in better shape too. I swear I could see one making a rudimentary decision last night; I don't know... it sounds crazy, I know.'

'No, I think you're onto something,' Vicky said. 'I've seen it too. When I watch them now, I can feel them watching back. I think they're struggling to work out what's happening to them as much as we are.'

The food they'd scavenged had mostly been eaten by the end of the day. They'd have to go out again tomorrow and get more. The group's first night here had been relaxing and optimistic, but with a steadily growing crowd loitering outside the gates, and with Sam's words echoing around their heads, many people resigned themselves to sleepless second nights. David resisted the temptation to try and impose his views on the rest of the group, figuring instead that it would be better for them all to come naturally to the same conclusions. He paced around the barracks, no intention of trying to sleep. *Our time here is running out*, he thought. *Why are we delaying things? Why not just leave right now?*

He'd only been lying on his bed for a couple of minutes when Lisa collared him. 'You're needed,' she whispered, gesturing towards the cadet building, and his heart sank. He didn't bother asking questions because there was no point. It could only be bad news. *There's no such thing as good news anymore, if there ever was.*

Sanjay, Chapman, Sam, and Steven had three prisoners.

It wasn't too strong a word to use, because whoever these kids were – and he didn't recognise any of them – they weren't going anywhere. They were young and uniformly scrawny mid-teens, waifs, two lads and a girl, each of them draped in layers of ragged clothes that might have fitted once but which now looked several sizes too big.

73

'We caught these three trying to break in and help themselves,' Steve explained.

'It's not like it's your stuff,' one of the boys said. 'You broke in here too.'

The girl in the middle nudged him in the ribs. 'I told you, I'll do the talking,' she hissed. He crossed his arms and slumped back in his chair, suitably admonished. She looked up at David. 'We weren't after your stuff.'

He stood in front of the three of them, doing his best impression of a stern headteacher. 'If you're not on the take, do you want to tell us what it is you're doing here?'

'Trying to stay alive, same as you.'

'And how do you know anything about us?'

'We don't. All we know is that you're trouble. Are you something to do with that last lot that came through? We heard them on the motorway, frigging maniacs.'

David glanced at Chapman, then turned back to the girl. 'Believe me, we're nothing to do with them. And you'll stay away from them too if you've got any sense.'

'They didn't hang around. Were they friends of yours?'

'Hardly.'

'What do you mean, we're trouble?' Chapman demanded. She shrugged.

'We've only lasted so long here because we've been careful. We saw you lot walking along the Warley Road. We heard you a mile off. Ours is one of those big houses you went past.'

'And?'

'And if we heard you, *they'll* hear you too. It's not good. You'll fuck it up for all of us. You've already got a load of them hanging around outside.'

Much to Chapman's surprise and annoyance, David pulled up a chair and sat down in front of the kids. 'You're right. You've done well to have lasted so long here. We've had a bit of a shitty time, to be honest. I'm David. It's good to meet you.'

Taken aback, the girl shook his hand when he offered it. 'I'm

Mia. This is Callum and Ollie.'

'And you three have been doing okay here?'

'Better than everybody else,' Callum said. David laughed.

'Good answer. So, you've got a good set up at the house?'

Callum was about to answer, but Mia spoke first. 'Why should we tell you? You gonna come and take all our stuff next?'

'That's not going to happen, I promise. There's more than enough to go around these days. We're not going to be a threat to you unless you threaten us.'

'Carry on like this and you're gonna get us all killed,' Callum grunted. His voice was full of animosity. 'We heard you out shopping this morning, dumb fuckers. Every dead bastard a mile around heard you too.'

Chapman wasn't impressed. 'Who does he think he's talking to? Cocky little shit.'

David held up a hand to silence him. 'It's okay. I understand. We're on their turf, remember.' He turned back to Callum. 'We're just trying to find somewhere safe. We started off in central London, not through choice, and we've been trying to get out ever since.'

'There was a lot of smoke coming from that way,' Mia said.

'Yep. Long story short, there's not a lot of central London left anymore. There's not a lot of us left either, to be honest. Until a couple of days ago there were almost three hundred of us. We lost a lot of people along the way.'

'You got a plan, or are you making it up as you go along?'

'Bit of both. We're trying to get north. We think things will be better up there.'

'So who was that we heard on the motorway?'

'Trouble. People who sold us out and left us stranded. We're all better off without them.'

'To be honest, sounds like we had it easy in comparison,' Mia said. 'We just found the biggest house we could, away from everything else, and we're waiting it out. We're all from around here. We know the place. We went the long way whenever we

75

needed to go into town and fetch stuff – through the park then in and out on the train line. There was never many of the dead down there.'

'Sounds like you've done alright for yourselves.'

There was a pause, a definite hesitation before she continued. Her voice was different now, emotional, all the cockiness stripped away. 'We had another couple of people with us to start with.'

'What happened?'

'Crace had diabetes. This woman Simone had been with him from the start. She knew him from before it all happened. He ran out of insulin, and we couldn't find what he needed. We told Simone we'd been through all the hospitals and the chemists we knew, but she wanted to keep looking, even though she knew there was no point because she was only ever gonna keep him alive for a little bit longer. She went out on her own one day and never came back. Stupid, really. They didn't both have to die.'

The conversation faltered, everyone musing on what Mia had said. Then Ollie cleared his throat and spoke for the first time. 'You can't stay here.'

'Why not?' David asked.

'Too close to town. Too many deaders. It ain't gonna take a lot to bring them all over this way. You're lucky you never done it when you was in the supermarket, 'cause if that happens, we're all fucked.'

'We're not planning on hanging around.'

'I get it. You're just gonna stay here long enough to fuck everything up for us, then leave?'

'You could come with us. That's what you really came here for, isn't it?' David looked at each of their grubby faces, struggling to discern their reactions. He gestured at the bags they'd been carrying. 'We can drop all the pretence. You've come packed. There's no point hanging around here on your own.'

'Jesus, Dave, we don't even know them,' Chapman said.

'And we don't know you,' Ollie sneered. 'You could be paedos or anything.'

Mia glared at him again. 'If so many of your group have died, are we gonna be any safer with you?'

'Now that's the million-dollar question,' David explained. 'Things might work out for the best, but on the other hand, leaving here might be the biggest mistake any of us have made. We've got some ideas of where we're going, but nothing concrete. We're going to try and find ourselves somewhere away from the dead and wait until they've rotted away to nothing.'

'We were thinking the same,' she said, nonchalant.

'You were planning to stay in Brentwood, though?'

She shrugged. 'Couldn't really go anywhere.'

'Look, I'll level with you,' David said, 'it makes no difference to us either way. You're right, we've lost too many of our people; and a number of them chose not to come. I don't know... having you three onboard feels like a step in the right direction.'

'Are we sure about this?' Sanjay asked. 'Bit of a frigging risk if you ask me. They could be anybody.'

'So could we.'

'And what are they going to bring to the party? Just three more mouths to feed?'

'We can help you get out of Brentwood safe,' Callum said. 'We can get you back to the motorway, help you get around the crowds.'

'I'm sure we can manage,' Chapman said, sounding less than impressed. 'I don't need kids giving me directions.'

'You sure? You been into Brentwood recently?'

The layover at the barracks came to a natural end. By mid-morning the size of the crowd outside the gates was substantial and showed no signs of abating. The question was not if the group left, but when. There were no arguments when David made the announcement. 'We've dealt with bigger hordes, sure, but we all know things could go either way. They're unpredictable, and there might be another ten thousand waiting for us around the corner. Look at it this way, if we're not safe here in an army base, then we're not safe here at all.'

With vehicles and supplies, they could make actual progress.

The vote was unanimous.

The yard at the rear of the barracks was secluded enough that Steve, Chapman, and Ruth could work on getting the vehicles ready without antagonising the rotting crowd. Liz, Vicky, Orla, and David coordinated the rest of the group as they stripped the site.

Sam had been dispatched into town with Ollie and Callum, the three of them tasked with doing whatever they could to coax the dead away from the roads that would be used to get back to the motorway. Their respective routes had been meticulously planned, little margin for error. Everyone involved knew that the moment the engines burst into life, a slow-motion stampede would be triggered. Unless they could be persuaded otherwise, the entire remaining undead population of Brentwood would begin to herd in the direction of the barracks.

'I never realised there was so much green space here,' Sam said, keeping his voice low as they skulked between the trees. The forest stretched away in all directions. It was hard to believe they were so close to the centre of a London commuter town.

'Whole world's gonna look like this soon enough,' Ollie mumbled, 'how 'bout that? A fucking silver lining.'

At the northern tip of these woods, a path out of the trees led between a cemetery on one side and the backs of houses on the other. Sam pulled Ollie back. 'You're sure this is going to work?'

'It's all under control, mate. We've done this loads of times before. Go with the flow and don't slow us down. Just trust us.'

Cheeky fucker.

It was easier said than done, though. Callum and Ollie had little to gain but plenty to lose by screwing him over, but it stung his ego a bit to be putting his fate in the hands of two kids he'd only just met. Time past, he'd have put them in their place, but they'd so far survived and were in reasonably good *physical* shape. He thought they must have been doing something right.

Losing the cover of the trees made Sam feel unexpectedly vulnerable. In comparison, Ollie and Callum looked assured as they cut through an alleyway then strode along a well-to-do-looking street. Midway along was a black BMW convertible blocking the pavement. What was left of the driver remained strapped in her seat, dressed for the office. When they were just a couple of metres away, she heard them and began flapping her jaws wildly and flailing her spindly arms about, a hurricane of sudden movement. When Sam reacted, the others snickered.

'Morning, luv. You look nice today.' Callum said casually. This clearly wasn't the first time they'd met.

They crossed the road at the end of the street, not even pausing to check for corpses, and continued through the carpark of a large pub opposite. They carried on down the side of an empty outbuilding. Sam could see huge swarms of corpses nearby. He slowed down, and Callum shoved him in the back. 'They're alright. Just keep moving.'

They followed a narrow path between the side of the outbuilding and a wooden fence. Sam's heart was pounding. There were bodies on the other side of the fence. He could feel them colliding with it, no doubt reacting to their footsteps. They crossed an overgrown beer garden, then climbed through another broken fence into the back garden of a modest-looking semi-detached house. Out through the side gate, across another road, then straight through the front door and out into the back garden of the house opposite. Across another road, then they crawled under a buckled garage door before walking the length of a decent-sized garden with an oval swimming pool at the far end. The water was green, solid with algae. Sam almost didn't notice the bloated body bobbing on its back. It had swollen so badly that its tight trunks had cut into its belly and the tops of its legs. Another garden, then yet another house, then they stopped. Other than well-trod trails through the uncut grass, Sam knew he'd struggle to find his way back to base on his own.

'That's got to be far enough, right?' he asked.

'Yeah, this'll do us,' Ollie said.

Callum explained further. 'Train tracks are on the other side of this fence. We'll follow them into town, then get out through the station. It'll be busy but we know what we're doing. We've got a couple of buildings primed.'

Sam was confused. 'What, with explosives?'

'No, you dick. With *noise*.'

Fifteen minutes later and they were on a level halfway up a multi-storey carpark they'd blocked off at street level. It was pissing down with rain again. 'Want to wait until it eases off?' Callum asked.

'No,' Sam said. 'Do it now. It took long enough to get here, and I don't want to miss the pick-up.'

That didn't bear thinking about. They were about to whip the undead masses into a frenzy; no one wanted to be stranded at that rave.

'It'll be fine,' Ollie said. 'We've done this before.'

It was clear that they had. There was a car parked across two spaces – a souped-up Ford something-or-other, it had so many

80

modifications it was hard to tell – and Ollie grabbed a rucksack full of phones from the front seat. They'd been using the car's battery to keep a number of phones and a couple of power packs charged up. Next, they put Bluetooth speakers on the ledges of the outer walls, facing out into the street. Finally, they filled the world with German Death Metal.

Inside the carpark, the noise reverberated and echoed until Sam thought he'd lose his mind just before he went deaf, but pride kept him from covering his ears. The boys barely seemed to notice.

By the time they got back down, the rain-soaked streets were already swarming. The dead emerged from every corner and every direction, all zeroing in on the multi-storey.

'How long we got?' Callum asked.

'About half an hour,' Sam replied. 'How long will it take us to get to the rendezvous point?'

'About that.'

And before Sam could say anything else, Ollie spoke. 'Back to the station, down onto the tracks. Follow Callum and me and try to keep up. I know you've got a dodgy leg, I can see it when you walk. But if you fall behind, you'll be left behind.'

'Pirate code, is it? Got it,' Sam said.

Ollie charged straight into the advancing crowds, confident in the knowledge the hordes were temporarily distracted. Callum immediately followed and Sam did the same, realising that if he lost sight of the lads, he was screwed. There wouldn't be another chance if he missed his connection. The noise coming from the carpark could be heard from space. They'd lit a bomb under this place. It wouldn't be safe to come back to this part of town for weeks, if ever.

The barracks had been a hive of activity until about twenty minutes ago. Since then, the group had remained completely silent and stayed out of sight to give themselves maximum chance of getting away safely. But even maximum chance didn't feel like much of a chance at all. Sam, Ollie, and Callum had set out to keep the dead away from the roads, but what was happening at the barracks was always going to be more of a draw for those corpses that were drifting close to this place.

The fact there'd been more activity here in the last hour than the last three months hadn't helped. That they'd had to start the vehicles and leave them running for a while had added to the draw, but had they not started, the entire plan would be scrapped. They'd been successful; the vehicles were moved into position in the yard now, ready to go.

Chapman was behind the wheel of the first truck, Mia sitting alongside him to navigate. Ruth was to drive truck number two with David co-piloting. Sanjay would be driving the final truck with Noah there to help with directions, while Orla had agreed to drive the van. Vicky was with her, for no other reason than the seats were marginally more comfortable than any of the trucks. She'd lost so much weight it was starting to hurt to sit for prolonged periods.

The rest of the group and their belongings had been distributed evenly, taking seats on long benches in the open transport vehicles with only tarpaulin walls between them and the dead. They were as well prepared as they could be, considering that they were about to embark on yet another half-baked plan. They were focused on getting everyone out of Brentwood in one piece and hitting the road, and what happened after that was currently anyone's guess. Gripping the wheel of his truck tight, Chapman was beginning to think that getting that far would be enough of an achievement in itself.

The standing room only concert at the car park could be vaguely heard, but the temporary silence at the base now was eerie, almost unbearable. In an effort to prove his allegiance beyond doubt, Mihai had volunteered to be the one who'd make a last-ditch attempt at tempting the more persistent visitors away from the entrance to the barracks. Someone had suggested starting another fire, but an over-reliance on arson had been the catalyst for their downfall at the Monument, and it was decided that this operation needed something a little more straightforward. Old school.

Standing next to a skip on a building site, about half a kilometre away from everyone else, drenched by the cold rain and poised to make himself the centre of undead attention, Mihai was wondering what the hell he'd let himself in for. The urge to run for cover was strong, but he stood his ground knowing that a few minutes of danger now would prove that his loyalties lay with the group of people that he'd previously been tricked into screwing over. *Christ, if I never see Piotr or Dominic Grove again it will be too soon.*

There must have been a couple hundred shambling figures outside the barracks now, all of them with their backs to him, focussed on the breathing beings within. Their preoccupation with everyone else had made it easy to get out here, but getting back again was going to be more of a challenge. He'd soon find out, anyway, because he could see Chapman hanging out of the window of his cab, waving furiously.

Here goes everything...

Mihai began hammering a heavy wooden baton against the side of the skip, the empty metal bin ringing out like some huge, upturned bell. The clanging noise bounced off the walls of empty buildings and echoed along soulless streets, immediately having the desired effect. On cue, the corpses began to shuffle around, the entire congregation now lumbering towards him.

He'd been told to give it a couple of minutes, but he bottled it. He sprinted around the outer edge of the crowd and dove back through the hole they'd cut into the fence. '*What the hell are you doing*?!' Chapman screamed at him as he raced towards the trucks. 'That was nowhere near long enough.'

'Bit of a damp squib,' Mia said, 'but we're committed now. The lads will be waiting for us. Just drive and hope for the best.'

'To be honest, that was the plan all along.'

Chapman started the engine, revving hard to make sure it

caught. The other drivers all did the same, and in seconds the cumulative noise from four rattling engines had undone Mihai's paltry efforts and refocussed the attention of all the distracted dead. Chapman shoved the truck into gear and hit it, hurtling straight at the gate, crashing through, and swerving out into the fringes of the crowd.

'Left,' Mia ordered.

'You're sure about this?'

'LEFT!'

He did as he was told, swinging the truck wide and wiping out a few stragglers. For a moment he couldn't see. The decomposition of the dead was astonishing. Some of them burst on impact like overripe fruit, popping like balloons filled with offal. He flicked the wipers onto their fastest setting then wrenched the truck around the back of an overturned car he was about to collide with. His wheels skidded in the grue. 'Which way now?'

'Left again then straight on.'

'This doesn't feel right. You certain?'

'I live here, don't I? Do me a favour and just drive. This isn't the most direct route, but it's the safest.'

Trees to their left, a row of quaint-looking bungalows on their right... the apparent respectability of their immediate surroundings belied the fact that they were driving around the outskirts of an apocalyptic town centre. For a couple of seconds everything looked like it used to, but the illusion was shattered when the convoy roared towards a crossroads just as a surge of ghouls dragged themselves around the corner. Chapman braced and locked his arms, fighting against his instincts. He wanted to swerve, but the safest option was to drive straight through the lot of them and hope the force and power of his vehicle would do enough damage to wipe out the horde.

The truck barely slowed. The creatures all but disintegrated on impact, reduced to an impossible jigsaw of broken limbs and smashed up body parts.

'Too easy,' Chapman said, smug, but he was forced to eat his words when the bloody chaos cleared, and he realised the road ahead was blocked by tougher stuff. The cab of an agricultural tanker had veered off the road and into the frontage of a shop, leaving its load straddling almost the full width of the street. He braked hard, aquaplaning through puddles of standing rainwater, then carefully coaxed his truck up onto the pavement and around the tanker's rear end.

Mia was not impressed. 'It's not a time trial, you know. There's abandoned shit like this all over town.'

He bit his lip to stop himself snapping back, but he knew she had a point. He was letting his nerves show. He slowed down and watched his rear-view mirror until the other trucks and the van had safely squeezed through the gap.

'Hear that?' Callum asked. 'Trucks. As promised.'

'Thank god for that,' Sam said. 'Sounds like they're on the move at least. We need to speed up.'

'They said two hours,' Ollie protested.

'You want to risk missing them? We need to get a shift on.'

They pounded along the train tracks. There were four lines here, split into two pairs with a well-worn concrete strip between them. Nowhere was easy to run along. Their feet sank into or slid on the gravel on either side of the tracks, the rails themselves were too narrow to balance on, and the spacing of the sleepers stretched between them meant that running at a steady pace was impossible.

Sam found it disconcerting down here; not his purlieu. It was a separate slice of the world, disconnected from everything else. Whilst the simplicity of the straight lines and the protection of the embankments were useful, they took away their options and made an already uncomfortable situation feel even worse.

In the squally air, the washing of the engine noise banging into the Death Metal cacophony was disorientating. 'Are they still behind us?' Callum asked. 'If they're in front already then we're fucked.'

Sam was struggling to keep up. 'How far?'

'See that bridge up ahead?'

'Yep.'

'If they've followed Mia's route, they'll come that way.'

'And that's where we're supposed to meet them?'

'That's the plan. If you stop asking questions and speed up, we might even do it.'

Lippy little shite, Sam thought, but he put in a burst of extra speed now the finish line was in sight.

The convoy had made steady progress along Mascalls Lane, the same road they'd been following since navigating the wreck of the tanker. There'd been a constant stream of figures getting in the way along the more built-up sections, but now they'd reached the suburbs again, there were hardly any of them about.

Up ahead, the heavy rain had caused a flood, and the route of the road was lost in the water. Chapman's instincts were to accelerate through, but the risk outweighed the potential gain. He slowed down to a crawl, focusing on keeping moving and getting back onto dry land. It was deeper than it looked. Water on all sides.

There were things moving under the surface, thumping against the chassis. 'What's that?' Mia asked.

'Probably just bits of trees,' he said, and though there were boughs hanging over the road from both sides, they knew the truck wasn't driving over sticks or branches. Mia looked down and saw the face of an upturned corpse revealed momentarily in the wake from the front wheels.

The relief was palpable when they made it to the other side. Chapman drove far enough ahead to leave room for the others, then stopped and waited.

The second truck made it through with ease.

Sanjay nearly stalled the third truck when an almost completely fleshless arm reached up out of the middle of the murk and latched onto the running board, but he managed to keep the engine running and the wheels moving and when the skeletal fingers finally slipped, he drove straight over it.

Bringing up the rear, Orla looked terrified. The van was much lower than the trucks, the water more of an issue. There might only have been a couple of corpses in the water, but they'd become more active as each new vehicle had driven through. One, like a Darwinian link, had crawled onto its belly where the water lapped against the submerged gutter and was trying to straighten its arms and get upright. It managed to lift itself to waist height and scrape its bony fingers against the back of the van as it passed.

The vehicle noise was louder now. As reassuring as the sound was, Sam wished they weren't so close. He kept his eyes on the bridge they were racing towards, convinced he'd see the convoy cross before he and the lads could get anywhere near.

'Steps,' Callum shouted, and he raced up a long set of concrete steps set into the embankment immediately before the bridge. Sam would have gone straight past them. They were clearly intended for maintenance, barely used in normal times, and almost completely overgrown today, hard to make out through the weeds.

Sam reminded himself he was carrying an injury and that he was much older than both Callum and Ollie, but he felt in awful shape when he got to the top. His thighs were burning, and he could hardly breathe. He could hear the engines approaching but he was doubled-over, light-headed. He didn't know how long he could carry on like this. Life was constantly stop-start, stop-start now. He was at full speed or a dead stop, never anything in-between.

The boys were on the wrong side of a padlocked security gate. Built into a sturdy metal fence and topped with anti-vandal spikes, it was as adept at stopping them reaching the road as it had been from stopping live vagrants trespassing onto the tracks. The street on the other side was clogged with corpses.

The engine noise was getting louder, riling up the dead and ramping up his nerves. The corpses dragged themselves towards the oncoming traffic with renewed energy. 'Over here!' Sam yelled and waved his arms as the lead truck rumbled into view, but no one heard him. Chapman was behind the wheel, as focused on the dead as they were on him.

The snub nose of the truck thumped into the wedge of deteriorating flesh, the density of the swarm slowing it down but not stopping it.

'Give over, granddad,' Ollie said, shoving Sam out of the way and giving Callum a bunk up. Callum balanced precariously on the top of the gate – one foot on either side of the spikes – then tried to twist around but fell, landing on his back in the throng like a crowdsurfer at a gig. Their seething movements supported him momentarily, then he fell through to the ground. Winded, he rolled out of the way of the wheels of the second truck, its tyres grinding flesh and bone into the tarmac just centimetres away from his face, showering him with liquid muck.

The third truck was close. Callum scrambled to his feet and pushed his way towards the middle of the road. Sanjay stood on his brakes when he saw him, bringing the truck to a juddering halt just centimetres short.

Sam helped Ollie up, then Ollie stretched back down and helped Sam to the top and over. Ollie made the jump easily and followed Callum into the back of Sanjay's truck, but Sam was prevented from going the same way by another rush of corpses taking the place of those that had been smashed underwheel. Sam ran for the van at the back of the line and threw himself in through a door that was being held open for him. His feet were still hanging out the back when Orla accelerated, pushing through the crowd of flesh that had built up around them.

'This is it,' Mia said, dividing her attention between the crowded road ahead and the others following behind. 'Next left.'

Chapman wrenched the wheel hard left and slewed around the corner, almost mounting the pavement and colliding with a set of traffic lights. They raced past the front of an Aston Martin garage, rows of posh cars left outside, tarnished by the elements. 'Always fancied an Aston,' he said wistfully as he swerved around a six-car pile-up that had spilled across three-quarters of the width of the road.

'You need to get the hang of this truck first, mate,' Mia grumbled as she was thrown around in her seat. 'Just keep going straight. We'll hit the motorway soon.'

'How soon?'

'I don't know. Half a mile, something like that.'

'I'm loving these precise directions.'

'I'm loving nothing about this.'

Chapman glanced in the rear-view again, double-checking the others were still behind, then accelerated. He drove between two columns of stationary traffic, one facing either direction. The road was clearer here. The chaos was a little more ordered where the traffic had been queued: low-speed shunts rather than high-speed collisions.

They were nearing the motorway junction. He drifted to the left, ready to follow the curve of the roundabout he could see under the elevated M25, then he course-corrected and cursed himself. 'What the fuck am I doing? I'm still driving like there's gonna be other traffic on the road. No need to go the long way around.'

He raced the wrong way around the circular junction then drove up the slip road before powering up onto the M25. The wide road was silent and largely empty, much of the stationary traffic bunched towards the inside lanes of the opposite carriageway, the decaying ruins of the final, never to be completed, commute into the dead town of Brentwood.

14

Their speed was a fraction of what they would have expected, pre-apocalypse, but to be travelling at all was the only thing that mattered. Progress was steady. The motorway, whilst never completely clear, was passable for the most part. There were occasional delays and distractions where they came upon vehicles that had crashed, whole sections of road that resembled scrap heaps, but they found a way through. Sometimes it took a little patience and coaxing to unpick maze-like, tangled-up, multiple wrecks but, so far, they had always found a solution.

Though their destination hadn't yet been decided, before they'd left the barracks, they'd agreed upon a route away from London and the south-east. When they'd left the others at Lakeside, David had told Gary they were planning to head for Cambridge. From there, they'd keep going towards Peterborough. Vicky was happy so long as they kept travelling north. Though they didn't say it out loud, most people hoped they'd find somewhere suitable to stop long before they got anywhere near the Yorkshire Dales and Ledsey Cross.

Noah's hunch about the motorways being largely corpse-free had so far proved to be correct, and David hoped that would continue to be the case. Logic dictated that the major roads on this side of the country – the 'A' roads that ran through open countryside to connect cities, towns, and villages across great distances – should be similarly clear.

At the next junction, Chapman took them onto the M11. A section of the barrier along the central reservation had been destroyed by an enormous fire, and he crossed over onto the other carriageway to avoid the bulk of the debris. Although initially counter-intuitive, he realised it no longer mattered which way they drove so long as they kept moving. How many of the rules they used to live their lives by could be discarded now? This new-found freedom was strangely exhilarating: the open road, barely any corpses...

'Why the hell did we ever think sticking around in London was a smart move?' he asked, thinking out loud.

'Hindsight, innit? Frigging stupid move if you ask me,' Mia said.

'I didn't. It was rhetorical.'

'It was bad enough in Brentwood, but London? Sheesh, what were you all thinking?'

Something in his mirrors caught his eye.

'Shit.'

'What's wrong?'

'Sanjay's slowing down.'

The third truck was pulling up. Sanjay flashed his lights repeatedly until the two drivers ahead realised and slowed. They'd come to a halt on an elevated section of motorway just past Epping. Chapman froze, not daring to move. What was wrong? Was there a problem with the truck? Was someone sick?

Nope.

Omar jumped out of the back, ran over to hide behind a car that had come to rest on its side, and pissed up the wall. It was just a toilet break. An Omar-instigated pit stop.

Chapman remained in his seat for a while longer, the steering wheel gripped tight, ready to get away fast if – when – trouble came.

'Actually,' Mia said, 'I could do with going to the loo myself.' And she got out and went to find a private spot. Unsure at first, but then with a little more certainty, other folks started doing the same. Some just needed to stretch. Others wanted to see where they were and what was happening.

Soon, almost everyone was out on the road and the vehicle engines were temporarily silenced. Perversely, the fast lane on the wrong side of a once-busy motorway not far out of central

London was the safest, most peaceful spot they'd found in months.

There was only one corpse around that was mobile. Sam upended it over the side of the road and watched it drop. It fell into a bramble patch, cushioned by the vegetation, and immediately tried to get up. The more it struggled to right itself, the more it became hopelessly caught up. Long, thorn-covered strands tore at its skin. *The pointlessness of the living dead*, he thought to himself.

Distracted, he wandered over to where Vicky and Selena were admiring the view. It was cold, grey, wet, and unremarkable, and yet there was an undeniable beauty in what they could see. Space. Freedom. A place where they had room to breathe without the constant fear of triggering chain reactions within the legions of the undead that had, until now, plagued their every move.

Lisa, Joanne, and Liz had scavenged several trays of soft drinks from the back of a beached catering van that had been heading up the opposite carriageway. Joanne called Sam over.

'What's up?'

'I don't want to make a big thing of it but look.' She gestured at the ground by her feet. 'Someone's driven along here recently. Almost certainly your pal Piotr.'

Sam continued a little further north and inspected the road. There'd been much movement here since the apocalypse. Vehicles had been shunted out of the way. Most telling, though, were the remains of a random corpse. There were tyre tracks through its caved-in chest and what was left of its head.

'Good spot. Whoever it was is a few days ahead of us, though, so I don't think there's any point telling the others.'

'I agree. We just need to keep an eye out and stay well clear, just in case. I've not met any of those folks, and I'd like to keep it that way.'

15

When it rained these days, it felt like it would never stop. Constantly out in it, the grey was wearing on them. The atrocious weather had returned, as if whatever was responsible for controlling the elements was goading them. There were dark storm clouds overhead, alternating with random clear patches. For the last hour it had either been black as night or bright as summer, no in-between. It made driving along the debris-strewn motorway even harder; after every sudden downpour, the sun would appear temporarily, and the glare was unbearable. 'Wish it would make up its damned mind,' Ruth grumbled.

'This is how it is now,' David said, semi-serious. 'Nothing's straightforward anymore. My old dad would say it's character building.'

'Yeah, right.'

'Want me to drive for a bit?'

'No, I'm good.'

The sun disappeared again, plunging them back into darkness. She was at the front of the convoy now and the sudden drop in light levels disorientated her momentarily. She struggled to make out what she was now driving towards. It was as if an oil slick had spilled across the horizon.

Bollocks.

Bodies. Loads of them.

She slowed down and flicked on her hazard lights to warn the others behind. The heavens opened as they approached the largest gathering of dead flesh they'd seen since leaving Brentwood.

'Why are they all the way out here?'

'Makes no sense,' David said, scanning the horizon. 'We must be close to a town or something.'

'I thought you were following on the map?'

'I gave up. It's hard to work out where we are. We're still on the wrong side of the road. All I can see is the back of traffic signs.'

'We've hardly seen any bodies since we've been on the motorway, just stragglers.'

'Why they're here isn't important, we just need to get through them. The ones we saw in Brentwood virtually disintegrated when we hit them.'

'Yeah, but this crowd's filling the road. I can't see anything else. If I drive into something and we get stuck, then –'

'Don't. You don't have to explain. I get the picture.'

Ruth slowed the truck down and nudged through the crowd, sitting up in her seat to try and see over their bobbing heads, looking for hidden obstructions. The trucks were better suited to the atrocious conditions, and at the wheel of the van behind, the widening gap made Orla nervous. 'I don't like this at all,' she said. They were still a distance back from the edges of the crowd, but she could see how the dead were reacting to the deceleration of the convoy. The slower speed meant that they were able to swarm around the back of each vehicle, moving like a glutenous mass to swallow and separate each of them.

'Don't lose them,' Vicky said from the back. Next to her, Joanne and Selena craned their necks to try and see what fresh hell they were driving into.

Sam was sitting up front. 'I'm surprised we didn't hit problems like this sooner. What a pain in the ass.'

Orla tried to focus on the third truck's brake lights, which were now only intermittently visible, the vehicle all but completely obscured by the crowd. 'I can't see a frigging thing. I don't even know if–'

A woman ran out in front of the van and flagged them down. Orla slammed on the brakes, throwing Sam and her other passengers forward in their seats. The woman looked exhausted, her ragged clothes streaked with blood and grime. But there was no mistaking the crucial difference between her and every other figure out on the motorway: she was breathing.

'Help us!' she shouted, hammering on the bonnet of the van.

Some of the milling dead turned towards the commotion. The three lead trucks had disappeared into the crowd, and many of those on this side of the unruly assembly gravitated towards them in response to the woman's voice.

'Wait. There are two of them,' Sam said, pointing out a guy between the woman and the bulk of the crowd who was furiously swinging an axe, hacking down any corpses that lunged into range.

'We've got to help them,' Vicky said.

Sam gestured for the woman to go around to the back of the van. He saw that more bodies were dragging themselves out onto the motorway, coming through a gap in the trees that lined the side of the road. They weren't pouring through, but it was a steady, determined trickle.

'We're taking a serious risk here,' Orla said.

'Too late.'

The woman was inside the van, her companion close behind. 'Thank Christ you stopped,' she said, breathless. 'We heard your engines and just ran for it.'

'What happened?' Sam asked, one hand on the handle of his knife, just in case it was a set-up.

'We're at the airport.'

'What airport?'

'Stansted. It's on the other side of the embankment. We were doing okay until we had some pretty obnoxious visitors turn up a couple of days back. They caused carnage then buggered off again.'

Sam looked at Orla, both of them reaching the same obvious conclusion.

'We need to get moving and catch up with the others,' Orla said.

The man spoke up. 'You can't, mate. There are more of us.

We've got kids back there. There's a plane out on its own on the far side of the carparks. That's where we've been holing up. We can't go without them.'

The van was becoming surrounded by corpses, the beating on the sides had begun. 'Well we need to do something,' Sam said.

Orla agreed. 'Fuck it, we can't leave kids behind.'

'Thank you,' the woman said, relieved.

Next to her, Vicky sounded less convinced. 'This starts to look less than kosher, and I'll kill the fucking pair of you.'

'We're level, I swear,' the man said, wiping rainwater from his face.

Orla put the van into gear and drove into the crowd, nudging cadavers out of the way. Ahead of them now was nothing but darkness. 'The others won't wait for us.'

'They don't even know we've stopped. We'll catch up with them,' Sam said. 'We know the route they're taking. Even if they don't notice we're missing, they'll stop for the night soon enough, and they'll leave us a sign, same as we would for them.'

Orla couldn't tell if he believed that or if he was just saying it for her benefit. Either way, it didn't matter. For now, they were on their own.

The woman's name was April, the man was Rafe. Once they'd nudged through the bulk of the crowds, April guided Orla along the hard shoulder of the motorway to a point where the vegetation had been hacked away and a rough path cut through. 'We've been here from the start,' Rafe explained as the van rumbled over the uneven ground. 'Just a bunch of random travellers who all happened to be leaving for holiday the day the world fell apart.'

'Not the best place to be stuck,' Sam said.

'Yeah, I think I'd have preferred to be in Majorca.'

'Could have been worse. You could have been halfway there and lost your pilot.'

'Don't think I haven't thought about it. To be honest, things could have been much, much worse. This place was just about liveable until those fuckers came through last week.'

'Yeah, I'm not surprised.'

'Friends of yours?'

'Hardly.'

They stopped alongside a section of the airport boundary fence that had been brought down. The gap had been crudely blocked up with junk – enough of a challenge for the dead, but otherwise straightforward to pass through.

'This is it,' April said. 'I'll go get them.'

'I'll go with you,' Sam said. He hated the fact he'd become so cynical – his default position had shifted to distrust – but he needed to be sure April and Rafe didn't have any nasty surprises in store. They couldn't afford to take many more wrong steps.

'You sure about this?' Vicky asked.

'Yep. If I don't come back, just go.' It sounded overly dramatic, but they knew he had to go, and he knew they'd leave him if he didn't quickly return. 'No messing around, right?'

'Right,' Rafe said.

'Any bullshit and I'm off.'

'I get it, I get it.'

The air outside smelled different. The stench of death was prevalent here. There were more hordes nearby, of that much Sam was certain. They emerged on the edge of one of the vast long-stay carparks on the outskirts of the airport, huge numbers of holidaymakers' cars left waiting in concrete fields forever. It was foreign turf to Sam. He'd avoided international travel and the associated environmental costs, but now he felt strangely remorseful. He'd not seen much of the world, and now never would. *No more flying*, he told himself. *You're only gonna get as far as your feet will take you now.*

The sinking sun briefly broke through the gloom again, drenching the main airport hub in brilliant light. Corpses swarmed around the departure gates and terminals. 'That's us over there,' Rafe said, pointing at a jumbo jet abandoned out on its own on a blocked-off section of tarmac, away from the crowds. 'The plane had been ready to take off. There was plenty of food for us to start with, beds in business class. We used security routes to get in and out of the main buildings when we needed supplies.'

'Turned out there'd been other people sheltering here too,' April said as they ran. 'We didn't realise. When that lot drove through, they forced us all out of hiding and we ended up bunking in the same plane together. They really fucked everything up, you know. We're pretty much all out of food with no way of getting more. That's why we had to take a risk and leg it up onto the motorway when we heard you.'

'You were lucky. If it hadn't been for the crowd of dead bodies, we wouldn't have slowed down.'

'And if it hadn't been for the dead bodies, we wouldn't have needed you to.'

There was a set of boarding steps leading up to the plane's rear exit. Sam followed Rafe up. The door immediately swung inwards. 'Thank God for that,' Sam heard someone inside say. 'We thought you'd left us. Didn't think you two were ever coming back.' The voice was familiar, instantly recognisable. He pushed past Rafe, hoping he was mistaken, but fearing he wasn't.

'That's just fucking brilliant,' he said. 'What the hell are you doing here, Stan?'

Alec Stanley hesitated before answering. 'Sam? Is that you? I heard you were dead.'

'Sorry to disappoint.'

'You know each other?' April said, confused.

'Unfortunately, yes.'

And then another man appeared with two small girls following. He was coming down the aisle from the direction of business class, a torch aimed down at his feet to guide his way through the dark. 'This is Emily and Isabella,' April said, 'and—'

'Dominic Grove. Pleased to meet you.'

Dominic had only crossed paths with Sam fleetingly. 'We've

met,' Sam said.

'Have we?'

'Yes, Dom, you have,' Stan reminded him. 'Sam was with me and Dave Shires in that hotel on Fleet Street.'

Rafe was confused. He looked at Stan and Dominic. 'I don't understand. You told us you'd both been hiding in the airport since it all kicked off.'

Dominic squirmed. 'Did I say that? I don't think I did. What I actually said was—'

'Save it,' Sam said, cutting him off mid-flow. 'You can explain what happened when we get back to the others.'

'The others?'

'Yep. We've lost a lot of people, in no small part thanks to you, but there's still a decent number of us left. David, Ruth, Vicky... I'm sure they'll all be keen to hear why you abandoned them.'

'It wasn't like that. I didn't know that—'

Sam interrupted again. 'Was it not your fault, Dominic? Were you and Stan both poor, innocent victims? Did Piotr force you to go with him?'

'You don't know he's like. He's become a bloody dictator. I didn't realise what he was capable of.'

'Yeah, right. You expect me to believe that? Christ, I barely met the guy, and I could see it.'

'But I'm not the kind of person who—'

'Who what? Who gives a damn about anyone else? Doesn't matter what you say, both of you jumped in a boat knowing full well that you were condemning hundreds of people to death.'

'It wasn't like that. I was petrified, I don't mind admitting. I could see how bad things were starting to get around the Tower, so I simply suggested we move some of the supplies onto the water to keep them safe. I figured they'd be safer on the boat than anywhere else. I had no idea what Piotr was planning to do... I was talking to Mihai about how much we'd got, and the next thing I knew we were on the move. Once we'd launched there was no way I could get back and—'

'Save it. I'll ask Mihai for his version later.'

'Mihai's alive?'

'Very much so. Fortunately, not everyone is as spineless as you are. There are plenty of people who aren't going to let themselves be beaten by a thug like Piotr.'

Stan crumbled. 'I'll stay here. Leave me behind. I don't want to go.'

'No way, Stan. You're both coming with us. You're going to face the others and you're going to tell us everything you know about Piotr's plans.'

'You're not going to try and take this Piotr bloke on, are you?' Rafe asked, clearly concerned. 'He sounds like an absolute psycho.'

Sam shook his head. 'No, I don't want to take him on. I need more up to date info. Seems we've been misled regarding their destination, and I want to do everything I can to put maximum distance between him and the rest of us. Forget the dead, until Piot's out of the equation, none of us are safe.'

16

The trucks kept going. It was what they'd agreed. Ruth wanted nothing more than to stop and wait or even turn back, but the risks were too great. Orla knew the route they'd be taking. 'We're going to have to stop soon anyway,' David said, trying to reassure her. 'It'll be dark before long.'

'I understand the logic,' Ruth said. 'Doesn't make me feel any better, though.'

'You know full well that Vicky and Sam are in that van. You couldn't meet two more stubborn bastards. They know what they're doing. They've both been stranded on their own and have stayed alive. If I was asked to put a bet on anyone surviving, I'd stake everything I've got on those two.'

'Do you have anything left to gamble?'

'That's not the point,' he said, almost managing a smile.

The amount of frozen traffic was lighter here than the clogged-up carriageways they'd crawled along first thing after leaving London and the South. A pile-up near the end of the M11 had finally forced them back over onto the left-hand side of the road; two huge articulated lorries had come together and burst into flames, along with numerous other vehicles that had been caught-up in their wreckage like flies trapped in a mechanical web. If they'd come across such a sprawling, catastrophic accident earlier in the day, they might not have made it far from Brentwood. They were on the A14 now – just as wide a road, but quieter still. 'There's a service station not far from here,' Ruth said. 'It's a massive one. I used to use it regularly when I went to see my folks.'

'Because we've got such a good record with holdovers at motorway services...'

She ignored him. 'It's probably our best option for tonight.'

Ruth remembered the service station as having been like a small town, pre-apocalypse. Surrounded by fields, plenty of open spaces for weary travellers to stop and breathe, she'd hoped it would provide risk-free shelter for the night.

But it wasn't to be.

They made it as far as the slip road, then saw that the entire place had been wiped off the map in a brutal, yet remarkably well-contained, fire. The buildings had collapsed in on themselves in the heat, and the carparks were filled with burnt-out wrecks. There was a hole in the ground and piles of rubble where a fuel station had stood, just the melted remains of its welcome sign remaining.

In the absence of any alternatives, they kept going, following the road north. David and Ruth swapped places. The concentration required to keep the convoy moving forward was intense. It used to be that you could just point your car and go, safe in the knowledge that, for the most part, the road network would be accessible and clear, free flowing. Today, though, virtually every road was an obstacle course. Devastation was the new norm.

Ruth had her eyes closed and was sleeping; either that or she was avoiding talking to David. Until she was reunited with Vicky, what was there to say? Safe topics of conversation were in increasingly short supply, small talk impossible. Past lives were off-limits, and future plans were too vague to be discussed with any certainty and almost seemed like tempting fate. David couldn't even find anything positive in the fact they'd escaped the nightmare of London, or that he was still alive when so many billions of people were not; in fact he was so exhausted by it all he wasn't sure that was something to be grateful for. They'd done well to get this far but, ultimately, their survival had largely been down to luck, not skill. He was worried that luck was in danger of running out.

More corpses up ahead.

He slowed as they approached a dip in the road. At its lowest point, a snaking queue of figures traipsed across the carriageway like cows on their way to milking.

'What's wrong?' Ruth asked, immediately awake.

David gestured at the line of shambling shadows. They stretched beyond the tarmac and out into the fields. 'Look at that. What's got their attention?'

Ruth craned her neck. 'Is that a fire?'

David had assumed he'd been looking at more storm clouds but, now checked again, he saw that it was smoke billowing up into the winter sky. Ruth was right; there was another fire in the distance, a dull orange glow on the horizon.

'Think we should investigate?'

'Why on earth would we do that? Whatever's happening there, we should stay well away.' He accelerated down the hill and drove through the spread-out cadavers.

A short distance ahead, a bridge had collapsed.

The wandering masses had obscured David's view until it was almost too late. He swerved around the corner of a car lying on its roof like it had simply gone belly-up. 'Bloody hell, that was close,' Ruth said. 'Take it easy.'

'It's all good,' David said as they rumbled over the central reservation again, back onto the opposite lanes. He checked his mirrors: the other two trucks were still with him, barely any distance between them.

The road curved away to the right. David thought nothing of it initially, but as it swung further to the east, he began to become concerned. He felt the hairs on the back of his neck start to prickle. 'I think I might have fucked up here.'

'What? Why?'

'I've gone the wrong way. I don't think I'm on the right road anymore. Didn't even notice.'

'Just keep going and find somewhere to turn around. Shit happens.'

David thumped the wheel in frustration. 'Bloody idiot.'

'Don't be so hard on yourself, Dave. Let's keep things in perspective here. This morning we were still in Brentwood. We're past Cambridge now. We're well away from London, and well on our way to wherever. We're doing okay. Just take a breath, turn around, go back, and carry on.'

They went over a crossroads but didn't realise it was a junction. The roads on either side had been blocked by cars that looked like they'd been parked properly and abandoned. The lateness of the day and the heavy clouds combined to reduce visibility. Other than the trucks, there were no lights anywhere. Only the shapes of the shadows around them changed. They'd gone from a country lane with fields on either side to a residential street lined with houses without even noticing.

Chapman was furiously flashing the lights of the truck behind. 'I know, I know, I fucked up,' David said under his breath.

'Calm down, Dave,' Ruth said. 'It'll be okay. You're just tired. We need to find somewhere to park up for tonight and just—'

The truck ploughed headlong into a solid glut of rotting flesh. Where the hell had all these corpses come from? Seconds ago, the road had been deserted, but now it was teeming with movement, massive numbers of them flooding forward from either side. They were tumbling and stumbling along side-streets, swarming around wrecks, trickling through the gaps between buildings.

'We're committed now,' Ruth said. 'Keep going. Find a way through. We don't have any option.'

David accelerated. The noise of the engine echoed off the walls of buildings, amplifying the sound. 'Fuel station up ahead,' he said, spotting the distinctive outline of the tall price display sign and the lid-like covering over the forecourt. 'I'll turn around there then go back the way we came.'

His momentary relief was short-lived. Before they reached the fuel station, the road was blocked again. David slammed on the brakes. Chapman came to a juddering halt a metre behind, cursing, and Sanjay also stopped at the last moment, equally close.

And now the dead were everywhere: a slow-moving, ubiquitous swarm of death that moved like a collective sludge. It was a devastating, albeit small-scale replay of everything they'd fought so hard to escape in London. The inevitability of what was happening made it harder to accept. Even out here in the sticks, life hung in the balance. It made a certain sense; though there'd inevitably be some dispersion, when many people had died, they'd remained trapped where they were. Every housing estate, every business park, every school and other gathering place would be rife with the dead. The thinnest of margins separated security and chaos.

'And you lot thought I was some kind of leader?' David said, close to tears. 'You must have been out of your minds. The harder I try, the worse things get for everyone.'

17

Another cloudburst had delayed everything. Sam had tried valiantly to get Rafe, April, and the others off the plane and over to the van, but the torrential rain and drifting corpses had slowed everything down. It was pitch black when they made it back to the van. They didn't want to be out on the road much longer tonight.

'I'm pretty sure we haven't passed them,' Orla said. 'They'll have stuck to the plan. They'll be sat safe somewhere, waiting for us to catch up.'

'I think we should stop,' Selena said.

'Are you sure that's a good idea?' Dominic said from the seat furthest back. 'Don't you think it would be better if you—'

Vicky glared at him. 'You'll never be in charge again, you fucker. In fact, you don't even get to have an opinion.' The look she gave froze the words in Dominic's throat. She turned back to Sam and Orla. 'Remind me again why you didn't leave this piece of shit to fend for himself back at the airport?'

'Happy to stop the van and dump them both,' Orla said.

Stan sounded terrified that she'd do it. 'There's no need for that. Please.'

Sam pointed out a small building at the side of the road. It was a farmhouse with a couple of outbuildings, looking wildly out of place alongside what had, until recently, been a major six-lane road. They'd passed a couple of similar places – stubborn relics of history whose owners had steadfastly refused to be uprooted. In the case of a set-up like this, it made sense. The road had likely bisected this farmer's land, and the road planners of the day had done what they could to accommodate the landowner. There was a specially constructed slip road that appeared to lead nowhere

106

else. 'This'll do us for now,' Sam said.

Orla slowed down and took the turning. 'You sure?'

'It's isolated and we need to rest. If we keep going there's every chance we'll pass the others, if we haven't already. Seriously, park up.'

'Do it,' Vicky said. 'I really need to get up and move.'

The road continued round into a concrete yard. Orla stopped outside the homeliest looking building, then waited. Nothing happened for a while. After a minute had passed, a single cadaver lumbered slowly into view, wearing a housedress and filthy apron. It crossed the beam of the van's headlights. Sam got out and ended the thing's half-hearted resistance quickly.

When Orla switched off the engine, there was nothing but silence. Other than the wind and rain, it was absolute. No traffic noise, no electrical hum... nothing. He leant back into the van and grabbed his knife and a torch. 'This place should be okay for tonight. Stan and I will check the house.'

'M-me?' Stan immediately protested. 'Don't you think it would be better if—?'

'I'll drag you out if you don't move.'

Stan reluctantly followed him up to the front door of the farmhouse. It was unlocked, and led straight into a large, foul-smelling kitchen space. There was an enormous wooden table covered in all kinds of junk which was, in turn, covered with a thick layer of dust. Spiderwebs obscured a fruit bowl and candles. They looked like they'd been draped in lace.

Something was moving around in an adjacent room. 'All yours,' Sam said to Stan. Stan just stood there, shifting his weight from foot to foot. 'Just as I thought. Completely fucking useless. Have you ever yet killed even one of them?'

He marched into the room next-door, dragging Stan behind him. The corpse of another woman was stuck between the back of a sofa and a sideboard, moving continually but going nowhere. Sam caught her thrashing arm then pulled her closer and impaled her eye with the tip of his knife. She dropped to the ground, like she'd been switched off.

'It's just not my thing,' Stan said, jabbering uselessly. 'I-I don't know how you do it. I-I mean, I'm grateful you do, naturally, believe me, but I-I don't think I could—'

Sam shoved him back onto the sofa, sending great plumes of dust billowing up. He shone his torch into the other man's face. 'Tell me everything.'

'Ev-everything? What do you mean?'

'Why you really split from Piotr, everything you know about his plans... anything that might be useful.'

'I-I've already told you.'

'No, you told me what you thought I'd want to hear, the bare minimum. Let's be honest here for a second, *Stan*, you're of no value whatsoever. I'd finish you off in a heartbeat, and no one would even ask.'

'You-you wouldn't hurt me. You-you told me you were a pacifist.'

'Things change. Want to try me?'

'Why don't you talk to Dominic instead?'

'Because he's a much better liar than you are and I'm afraid I *will* kill him outright. Now talk. Why did the pair of you bail on Piotr?'

'It's like Dominic said, he's-he's out of control. We-we got scared.'

For the first time Sam sensed he might be telling the truth. 'Go on.'

'Piotr wanted to-to go further down the Thames than we did, but Allison wouldn't do it. When she did a runner with Mihai, he felt like he'd got a point to prove. He-he went right through the middle of Lakeside shopping centre... stirred the place up like you wouldn't believe.'

'Oh, I'd believe it alright. We lost more than a hundred people there. The dead were seething. We didn't stand a chance.'

'I'm-I'm sorry about that, Sam. I just did my usual, kept my head down, you know, but when we got to Stansted and the same thing started happening again, me and-and Dom realised we were in trouble. We saw the lights in that plane and just-just made a run for it. You've got to believe me, Sam, Piotr's lost it completely. He's king of the whole bloody world now.'

'There's not a lot left for him to be king of.'

'I-I know that, and you know that, but try telling him. If there's one person to lord it over, he runs his mouth. You remember Lynette, don't you? Lovely, she was. Dom told me he-he pushed her off a roof back by the Tower just because... because he didn't like what she was saying. We were all on eggshells around him; bloody maniac.'

'You're a fucking coward, Stan.'

'Guilty as-as charged. Look, shouldn't we be getting the others in now? The rest of the house sounds empty.'

'Not just yet.'

'What else do you want? I-I don't know anything. I told you I tried to keep my distance.'

'We heard that Piotr was planning to head east towards Norfolk. Is that still the case?'

'Eventually, yes.'

'Eventually? What's that supposed to mean?'

'Turns out Paul Duggan lived not far from here. Place called Corby. Don't know it myself.'

'And?'

'And, well, apparently there's some big RAF or Army base nearby. I think the plan was to head over that way, get themselves tooled up, then move on. It's like Piotr thinks he's on some kind of crusade; arming his followers to conquer what's left.'

As dawn broke, the three trucks remained stuck, wedged together midway along a nondescript suburban street. They were unable to go forward or back, every scrap of space between and around them packed tight with an ever-increasing amount of cold flesh. They'd had no choice but to wait for morning, despite knowing that by the time the sun came up, the crowds might have doubled.

During the night, Chapman had managed to get to David and Ruth, climbing from the back of one truck to the next, clambering over cab roofs and jumping the gaps. Squeezed into the front of the first truck together, the reality of their situation had hit home. The blockage stopping them from going any further forward had been deliberately placed. They'd walked into a trap.

Doing nothing wasn't an option.

Chapman, Ruth, and young Ollie, volunteered to carry out a recce.

From the roof of the cab of the lead truck, they jumped onto the roof of one of the cars that had been parked across the road. The noise of their heavy landings was enough to cause some of the dead crowd to react, but they were wedged together too tightly to pose any threat. Before climbing down, Chapman looked back. He saw that there were junctions on either side of the street, but only those on one side had been blocked. That, and the fact that the road on the other side of the blockade was almost completely clear of the undead, confirmed their suspicions. 'Definitely a set-up,' he said.

The silence of the morning was sobering. The December air was icy cold, and a layer of frost had settled on everything. The crystal sheen gave the decaying world a thin veil of beauty. Even the handful of corpses on this side of the barrier wore glistening masks of ice that partially obscured their decay. Their movements were more stilted than usual, ice crystals in their claggy blood. Chapman was reassured. If the temperature continued to drop far enough, the monsters would be reduced to grotesque, yet harmless mannequins.

The road crossed a railway bridge. The group took cover halfway across. Ruth scanned the scene through a pair of binoculars. 'Why set a trap out here?'

'Where even are we?' Ollie whispered.

'We're on the outskirts of Peterborough,' Chapman told him.

'Doesn't look like there's a lot round here.'

'Plenty of housing; I can see a few industrial units up ahead, but otherwise it's a bit of a wasteland.'

'Exactly,' Ruth said, handing the binoculars to Chapman. 'So why set a trap out here?'

'There's always a chance whoever was here has taken what they needed and fucked off,' Ollie suggested. 'I reckon that's what it'll be like now, going from place to place, nicking what we need from whatever's left, then moving on again.'

'You might be right,' Chapman said, 'but that doesn't explain what I'm seeing.'

There were fields beyond the buildings, the land opening-up. One of them was filled with bodies; fenced-in and penned-up. Further away, black smoke was rising from another area. He showed the others. 'That must be the fire we saw last night,' Ruth said. 'Didn't think much of it at the time. What do you reckon's going on?'

'I know this might sound crazy, but bear with me. It looks like the dead are being harvested.'

'Yep, sounds crazy,' Ollie agreed.

Chapman shook his head. 'Look at where we are... I think someone's keeping the dead at a distance, then burning them when their numbers get out of control. Jesus, this is wild. Really smart.'

'And dangerous,' Ruth warned. 'I'm sensing nothing but trouble; I'm proper freaked out. We need to get out of here. Vicky and Sam are still missing... we can't risk losing anyone else.'

Chapman wasn't convinced. He shook his head, 'There's something we're not seeing here.'

'I agree with her,' Ollie said. 'We don't need to see it. We just need to go.'

'Not yet. There has to be something about this location to make it worth defending.'

Chapman didn't wait for the others to react, he just started walking. They followed the same road a while longer until, feeling exposed, they climbed through a gap in the hedgerow that Ollie found and walked along the edge of an adjacent expanse of grassland. Ahead of them now were the beginnings of a sprawling housing development. Some homes had been completed, others were roof-less, scaffold-clad shells. On one edge of a large, gravel yard filled with building materials were four portacabin offices, stacked two by two. Chapman climbed the metal steps up and used the open door of one of the top cabins to haul himself onto its flat roof. Still carrying the binoculars, he crawled to the farthest edge and lay down.

This really was an unusual area. He could see the grey blur of Peterborough to the north now. The suburb where the trucks had become trapped was over to the west, and to the east he saw green spaces, small lakes, more houses, and then the fields of captive corpses further beyond.

And then he looked north again and picked out a couple of large white warehouses he'd simply looked past before. They were relatively nondescript, but when he studied them, he saw fleets of trucks sitting in loading bays along the longest side of one of them, and the sheer scale of the buildings came into focus. The vehicles looked like a kid's toys.

These days, most every surface was covered in a layer of dust and grime. Muck and mould clung to walls and floors. Nothing was clean anymore, and even the monolithic buildings up ahead looked grubby, windows and walls left uncleaned. Nevertheless, Chapman couldn't believe he'd overlooked the massive Amazon signs. He was looking at a vast distribution centre for the online marketplace. Now he understood. *Everything we could possibly need is likely stored in one of those buildings. Fuck Ledsey Cross... this place could be the holy grail of self-sufficiency.*

Ruth and Ollie were becoming impatient. Ollie threw a stone that clanged off the portacabin wall. Chapman ignored the noise. He could see movement around one of the warehouses now, a handful of people emerging from a side door. What kind of folks were they dealing with here? They hadn't been outwardly aggressive so far... the trap the convoy had become ensnared in, if they'd set it, was defensive more than anything. They hadn't attacked, they'd just done what they'd needed to try and keep people away. Perhaps they'd be willing to talk? But how might they react when upwards of eighty new arrivals turned up on their doorstep unannounced? Would they welcome them with open arms or—?

His train of thought was derailed.

Another figure had followed the group outside. Chapman immediately recognised his shape and demeanour.

Piotr.

19

They left the farmhouse early and got straight back on the road. Sam drove the van today, Vicky with him up front. Stan had baulked at the fact they'd left the keys in the ignition all night. 'Safest option,' Sam had explained. 'Means that whoever gets to the vehicles first can drive. Gives us the best chance of getting away quick if things get shitty.'

'Yes, but what if someone takes it?' Stan protested, aghast.

'Who? Vehicle theft is on the decline, I heard. Anyway, if it does happen, we just find another. Everything is replaceable these days except us.'

The pointless bickering annoyed Vicky. She'd almost decided to stay behind, not just because Stan and Dominic wound her up beyond belief, but also because, despite looking like a horror movie trope made real, the dust-ridden farmhouse had temporarily felt like the safest, most comfortable place on earth. They'd eaten reasonably well last night from the various tins and packets they'd found in the kitchen and had shared a bottle of wine Sam found on a shelf in the pantry. It had gone straight to their heads. Most importantly, once they'd drawn all the curtains and lit a few candles, the evening had remained blissfully corpse-free. She'd even played a little Monopoly with Sam, Joanne, and April; the game taking on a whole new resonance after their time spent in the centre of London. She'd slept on a proper, if allergy-inducing, bed, snug under a fresh duvet she'd found still in its plastic wrapper in a wardrobe. It had felt like something out of a dream, like she'd been catapulted back in time. At dinner they'd talked about how a small group of survivors like them might do well in an isolated place like this, away from the city sprawl and other centres of population.

When Vicky had opened her bedroom curtains first thing, she'd expected to see an army of the undead waiting for her outside. But the land around the house remained empty.

Back on the road, and back to the grind.

Barely metres from the front door of the farmhouse and they were surrounded by death and destruction again. Sam found his first taste of driving along the A14 exhausting, constantly having to weave around and between odd-shaped ruins. No wonder Orla had been so keen to swap. He wanted to drive faster but was afraid of missing signs that the others might have left for them along the road. 'What if you're wrong?' Rafe asked from the back. 'What if they went a different way? Or if we've already passed them?'

'Then for now we're on our own,' Vicky said, matter of fact.

Sam agreed. 'We have to keep going. I'm sure the others will have done the same. Second guessing would be a mistake. We stick to the route we agreed because if we end up going one way and they go another, the distance between us could get pretty bloody huge, pretty bloody quickly.'

'You're doing nothing to inspire confidence,' Dominic said. Sam stopped the van, got out, then stormed around to the back and dragged the wiry ex-politician out. He slammed him up against the side of a rusting 4x4.

'I don't want to hear another fucking peep out of you, Dominic, understand?'

'I don't know what you're getting so tetchy about.'

'Seriously? *All of this is your fault.*'

There was a lone corpse approaching, zeroing in on the noise. Dominic squirmed. 'I made a mistake sticking with Piotr. How long are you going to punish me?'

'I haven't decided.'

'It was his idea. You should blame him.'

'He's not here, so I'm blaming you.'

Little fucker just couldn't keep his mouth shut. 'Seriously, though, I get that you're not impressed with me, but what are you going to do? What's throwing your weight around like this going to achieve? That's the kind of thing I expect from Piotr.'

Sam pulled him forward then slammed him back again. Dominic winced with pain. The approaching corpse collided with them. Dominic recoiled but Sam held his ground. He straightened his arms, giving the ghoul plenty of space to get in Dominic's face. The more he reacted, the more interested in him the corpse became. When he'd had enough of Dominic's whining, Sam smashed the dead man's face into the 4x4.

'Thing is, Dominic, you need us a lot more than we need you. In fact, we don't need you at all. I'm keeping you close because it's convenient and because I've one less thing to worry about knowing where you are and what you're up to. But if you push me too far... if you keep making dumbass comments and stirring things up, you're gone. Understand?'

'I understand. There's no need to make such a song and dance about it.'

Vicky leant out of the window of the van. 'Sam, either get rid of him or get back in. We need to get going.'

He let Dominic go and pushed him back towards the van. He was about to follow but stopped and looked down at the road. There was another corpse on the ground nearby. One of the minority who had died and stayed dead when the infection (or whatever it was) had decimated the population. The woman's body was stuck to the tarmac with rot. There were several sets of tyre tracks where vehicles had driven over her deflated chest.

Someone else has been this way.

He hoped it was David and the others, but he knew it could equally have been Piotr.

20

Ruth and Ollie had gone back to warn the others. Chapman broke ranks, telling them he'd return in under an hour, then disappearing before either of them could argue. He knew Piotr better than most. To have set up camp here was out of character, too smart and too sensible, and the herding and harvesting of corpses was an initiative that was way out of Piotr's league. In comparison to the utter chaos Piotr had caused in London and at Lakeside, what Chapman had seen here was too organised and quiet. It made him feel uneasy. There had to be more to it. Right now, the convoy was prone and the people he was travelling with were vulnerable. He was sure they were missing something. They weren't yet seeing the full picture.

The warehouses had piqued his interest, and not just because of the potential treasure stockpiled inside. For them to have been built here they'd have needed excellent transport links and a plentiful supply of staff. He'd done a little research in the building site office. The neighbourhood where the trucks were stranded was called Yaxley, and this development covered a vast swathe of land between Yaxley and the outskirts of Peterborough. There was a fishing lake nearby, and ample farmland, all in close proximity to a city with a pre-apocalypse population of around two hundred thousand. No wonder traps had been set up to keep scavengers at bay. This was prime territory for survival – all the things they'd hoped to find in London, but with much more long-term potential and only a fraction of the undead to contend with. The distribution centres were the icing on the cake, and the more Chapman thought about it, the more certain he felt that this location had been carefully selected for survival. And the more he thought about that, the more certain he was that whoever had been living here, Piotr had come and torn their world apart.

It had started raining again and the clouds were black, but that was a good thing. The foul weather gave Chapman cover as he skirted wide of the warehouses to continue his reconnaissance. The biggest risk this morning, he realised, was being recognised. If Piotr, Harjinder, Paul Duggan or any of the thugs saw him, they'd realise people had survived the inferno and escaped from London. Knowing how their Neanderthal brains worked, they'd likely assume they'd come here for revenge.

He was out in the wilds now. There were corpses in the adjacent field, and it looked like they'd recently been held here too. The ground under his feet was churned up and waterlogged, reminding him of a festival site after everyone had gone home: scraps of discarded clothing and endless lines of muddy footprints. There was a rumble of thunder that caught him by surprise. His heart thumping, he looked across and saw he wasn't the only one who'd been startled by the ground-shaking noise. The dead next-door appeared to have momentarily lost all control. They were staggering aimlessly, colliding constantly, unfocussed eyes scanning the heavens. *They almost seem... are they afraid?* He told himself to get a grip and kept walking.

Through the criss-crossing corpses, something caught his eye. There were lights in the windows of a house in the distance. The quickest way to get there was straight across the corpse-filled field and, before the undead regained control, he vaulted over a metal gate and jogged between them. It was easy when they were distracted, less so when he was the distraction. He cursed with pain when he skidded in the mud and wrenched his knee, and they immediately lowered their gaze and surged towards him in uncomfortable numbers. He kept running until one caught his arm and another one of his legs, and he lost his balance and was on his back in the mud before he even realised what was happening. Another ominous thunder growl came to his rescue and the corpses scattered again, bewildered. The cadaver nearest to him began pawing at the air, as if trying to defend itself from

Zeus.

Chapman ran on, more of a skate than a sprint, then crashed into the hedgerow and fell out the other side into a long and overrun, jungle-like back garden.

The modest house he was now approaching looked busy. He could see a group of people crowded into a conservatory. Perhaps because of the dark of the storm, they didn't yet appear to have noticed him. The coating of mud and grime from his dash across the field was convenient camouflage.

It wasn't a new house, this. Probably built in the thirties or forties, he thought, certainly no later than the fifties, unremarkably ordinary. He inched slowly along the edge of the garden, trying to work out his plan of attack on the fly. He couldn't go back to the others yet. He needed to know more about these people and why they

The side door of the house flew open.

Chapman tried to run again, but the man who came at him was drier and faster and he was rugby tackled to the ground. Chapman panicked, thinking that in his bedraggled, mud-covered state, the man would assume he was one of the undead. On his knees, face down in the grass, he tried to raise his hands in submission. 'Don't! I'm alive.'

'Not for much longer if you're not careful,' his assailant said, and he grabbed Chapman by the scruff of his neck, picked him up, then span him around. 'Yeah, I thought it was you.'

Chapman wiped rainwater from his eyes and tried to focus. He recognised the voice. More to the point, he recognised the accent. Liverpudlian. He'd only met one Scouser since the end of the world. 'Tony? Is that you?'

'It's me lad, yeah.'

'What the hell are you doing here?'

'I was about to ask you the same thing. Come inside, yeah? Let's talk.'

Chapman followed him, then stopped. He was so taken aback at being confronted by a familiar face that, for a moment, he'd forgotten what David Shires had told him about this man. This was the man who'd deceived everyone and ensconced himself deep within the group at the Monument that he'd also tried hard to destroy. This bastard was Taylor, a cold-blooded killer. Chapman went for his knife, but Taylor was one step ahead of him. A quick, stinging jab to the face, and Chapman was out cold.

When Chapman came around, he was sitting on a kitchen chair, his hands tied behind his back. He'd only been out for a matter of minutes, but his head was full of wool. 'Fucker,' he said, looking up at Taylor. He noticed that there were two men in the doorway behind. He didn't recognise either of them.

'Ah, you're back with us then,' Taylor said. 'From that reaction, I take it you've spoken to David about me?'

'That's right.'

'And how much of what he told you did you actually listen to?'

'Enough to know you're a self-serving bastard who doesn't give a shit about anyone but themselves.'

'That's not remotely true.'

'Is it not? I heard all the crap you told him about how you were just helping everybody else, but that was just empty talk, wasn't it? The only person you're interested in looking after is yourself. If you'd meant any of it, if you'd truly given a shit, then you wouldn't have run out on the rest of us on that boat.'

'It wasn't like that.'

'Don't you think? From where I was standing – which was the top floor of a fucking burning building, by the way – that was *exactly* what it was like. You and all those other fuckers left us to die.'

'If I'm being completely honest, I thought you and Shires were already dead.'

'Yeah, well we both made it, no thanks to you.'

Taylor cut the cable-tie that he'd put around Chapman's wrists, then handed him a coffee. Chapman wiped a dribble of blood from his nose on the back of his sleeve.

'I've always done nothing but looked at a situation and then did what I could to help the people who've needed it most,' Taylor said. He sounded subdued now, unsure of himself.

'I find that very hard to believe. I think the people who needed help most were those you left stranded in the Tower of London while the city was burning. It's a miracle any of them made it out alive.'

'How many did make it?'

'We got nearly everyone away from the Tower; not all chose to come. We went downriver as far as we could—'

'Shit. Please tell me you didn't end up at Lakeside?'

'Don't act so surprised. You clearly know the river was blocked there, so what else where we going to do other than walk straight into that clusterfuck that Piotr left behind?'

'We had a plan...'

'Who, you and Piotr?'

'No, me and Allison. We were going to take the boat and sail back to the Tower.'

'You expect me to believe that?'

'That's up to you, mate. I get why you'd be doubtful, though. If I was in your shoes, I probably wouldn't believe me either.'

'Strange that Allison never mentioned anything.'

'Allie's still alive?'

'Yes, no thanks to Piotr. Mihai too. But we lost more than we gained at Lakeside. More than a hundred people died –'

Taylor seemed visibly shaken when he heard that. 'Good God.'

'Yep. Puts things in perspective, doesn't it. You can tell that to Piotr when you see him.'

'That's not going to be happening anytime soon. We didn't exactly part on good terms.'

Chapman laughed. 'Oh, my. This is priceless. So convenient. Do you plan and practice this nonsense, or does it just flow naturally?'

'I don't have a clue what you're on about.'

'You shoot people, then you claim you're only trying to help.

You blow up the barricades around the Monument, then you convince people you did it to keep them safe. You help steal the boat and leave us all to burn, then you announce you were going to steal the same boat back and come rescue everyone? You're just full of shit. You're a fucking snake. You switch sides at the drop of a hat. The only person you genuinely seem to give a damn about is yourself. So long as you're safe, that's all that matters.'

'Finished?'

'I was at Spitalfields, remember? I nearly died out there when you set a flood of dead bodies on us.'

'I was trying to protect Helen and keep things calm.'

'Yeah, that worked out just perfectly.'

The man who'd been loitering in the doorway stepped forward. 'I can vouch for Tony.'

'And who the hell are you?'

'Edward Hollins. I've lived and worked here all my life. There were thirty-eight of us here until that bastard Piotr turned up. He drove us out of our homes and took everything we had, everything we'd worked for.'

'Sorry to hear that.'

'Eight people joined him, and we lost another half dozen that him and his lot murdered. If it hadn't been for Tony here, we'd have lost a hell of a lot more.'

'There's no reasoning with Piotr anymore,' Taylor said. 'It was a tough ask trying to deal with him as it was.'

'Doesn't Dominic still have him on a leash?' Chapman asked.

'Dominic's gone. Missing. Presumed very, very dead.'

'That's no tragedy. What happened?'

'After leaving Lakeside, Piotr pulled the same stunt again at Stansted Airport. Dominic, Stan, Amit, and a few others bought it in the chaos.'

'Don't get me wrong, I'm no fan of Dominic Grove's, but he had a weird sort of sway over that lot; they'd listen to him. If he's gone, there really is no point trying to talk to Piotr.'

'There's no point at all,' Edward said. 'A couple of our lot, Sally and Alan, both tried. They're two of the six who died.'

'I'm sorry.'

'Beats me why he can't just fuck off somewhere else. The country's plenty big enough, surely. Why destroy what we'd worked to build?'

'Because that's how he rolls. He's a megalomaniac, complete with cronies to do his dirty deeds. The guy's an absolute fucking parasite, gets off on spreading fear. He surrounds himself with people who are frightened of him, and he gets them to take whatever he decides he wants. I should know. I was stupid enough to listen to him until he fucked me over too.'

Edward was fully in the room now. 'So, what do we do about it?'

'I'm not doing anything until my people are safe.'

'Where are they?' Taylor asked.

'Surrounded by dead bodies in the middle of Yaxley.'

'That's simple enough to put right,' Edward said, and Chapman laughed. Edward was less than impressed. 'I'm serious. Sounds like you got stuck halfway down Broadway.'

'Yeah, we walked straight into your trap.'

Edward scoffed. 'That wasn't a trap.'

'Felt that way to me.'

'You don't understand,' Taylor said. 'What Ed and the others have done here is nothing short of amazing. Dominic Grove might have had the ideas, but here in Yaxley, they've made them reality. That's why we've stayed close. We can't afford to give it all up.'

'I was a farmer,' Ed explained. 'I started off just trying to keep us all fed, then I realised I could use some of the same tools and techniques to keep the dead in check. You saw the fields, I take it?'

'You're farming corpses?'

'I wouldn't put it that way, but you're not a million miles off. Corralling and culling might be a better way of putting it. It's quite straightforward, actually. We're close to the city, you see, so we needed to find some way of controlling the numbers. We round them up and then, when there's too many, we get rid of them.'

Chapman shook his head. Were these people crazy or inspired?

Taylor sensed his uncertainty. 'Listen, pal, I've burned my bridges with Piotr.'

'He knows who you are?'

'Yeah. Allison already knew. Do you remember Mark Desai?'

'The kid who was one of the runners back in London?'

'That's him. He overheard Allison talking to Mihai about me, and he must have grassed me up to the boss. I sensed he knew something, so I'd been keeping my head low. Piotr was focused on taking control of the warehouses and pushing out this lot, so I jumped ship and helped them get away. Two birds with one stone, and all that.'

'It's true,' Ed said.

'So, until Piotr's out of the picture, I'm as fucked as the rest of you.'

'What are you going to do about it?' Chapman asked.

'Get as far away from here as we can. Which is a real bloody shame because this place is as good as it gets. Ed had everything running nicely, by all accounts, and the Amazon warehouses made things infinitely easier. Trouble is, even though there are more of us, most of them wouldn't last five minutes going up against Piotr's lot. They've gone proper *Mad Max*, follow me?'

Chapman looked at Ed. 'You said you could get my people out of that mess they're stuck in?'

'Yep. Might take a little while, but I can do that, no problem.'

'What are you thinking?' Taylor asked.

'I'm thinking I've got almost eighty people back there, all of them keen to see the back of Piotr. They're not all fighters, but they've made it this far, so they've got something about them. I'm thinking that with those kinds of numbers, and with everything you know about the area, Ed, we should force Piotr and his cronies out. From what I've seen of what's left of the country these last couple of days, this place is bloody Shangri-La.'

21

The warehouse was an absolute treasure trove. Since they'd been here, Harjinder had struggled to think of anything they might conceivably need that he hadn't yet been able to find on some shelf. Okay, so without power and computers, things were nowhere near as efficient as they otherwise might have been, but it was nothing they couldn't get around. He thought they could have done with that geeky kid Georgie here. Jeez, cataloguing the entire contents of two warehouses would have kept that nerd busy for weeks.

Right now, Harj wanted something to eat. That was the only thing that let this place down. They'd be comfortable here, of that much he was certain, but they'd need to go further afield to maintain a decent stock of food and drink. It would be worth a little more effort because this place was the fucking business.

It had taken him longer than expected to get to the point where he was comfortable with his position in the new world order, and if he was honest with himself, he still wasn't completely sold. He'd slept through Armageddon; it had come after three twelve-hour shifts in a row, and he'd been completely unaware. Literally from the moment he woke up and discovered what had happened, he'd been fantasising about what this post-apocalyptic world might hold. He'd daydreamed his way through the usual cliches... the freedom, the power, the sheer excitement of surviving each day, truly *living*. He could go wherever he wanted and do whatever he pleased, but as yet the reality hadn't quite matched the fantasy, particularly not when the dead began to rise. Still, he'd never lost sight of how it might one day be. It was never about rebuilding society or trying to reboot the old world, making humanity's mistakes all over again. All Harjinder had ever been worried about was making the most of whatever time he had left, set up in this monster-laden destruction, and even if he survived another few decades, there'd still be enough stuff lying around here to keep him occupied. They'd barely scratched the surface so far. A life of looting and pillaging lay ahead of him. He was looking forward to it after practicing for years in video games, but he wasn't there yet. It put him at odds with some of the others, most notably Paul Duggan. They wanted to party. He wanted to be certain they were in the clear, *then* party. There was a subtle difference; eat your vegetables first sort of thing.

Darren Adams walked past Harjinder with his arms loaded with books. 'I heard Piotr was looking for you,' he said, his face just visible over the top of his pile. Harjinder acknowledged him and changed direction.

One end of the larger of the two buildings was given over to a maze of rooms that had originally been offices and staffrooms. The desks and uncomfortable office chairs had been dumped in the carpark, replaced from the treasure stacked in the warehouse aisles. They'd no doubt move into more comfortable accommodation later, but for now this area was being used as a makeshift living space. There was a definite pecking order here, to which no one dared object. He'd quickly taken over one of the two training rooms for himself, leaving Paul to claim the other. On the opposite side of the same narrow corridor was a meeting room that was as big as all the training spaces combined. That was where Piotr hung out.

Harjinder knocked on the door. Kelly unlocked and opened it. Other than a long winter coat, she was wearing only underwear. Kelly and Laura were the only decent-looking women around, and Piotr had them both when he wanted them. The girls were another post-apocalyptic cliché made real; they flashed their tits on demand for the boss, the same way he flexed his muscles for him.

'He's over there,' Kelly said, sounding barely interested, vaguely gesturing somewhere towards the other end of the room.

They'd all taken their fair share of stuff from the warehouse since they'd been here, but Piotr had built up a stash that dwarfed everyone else's. The end of the room was packed to the rafters, more stuff than he could possibly need. The focal point was an unmade bed that was surrounded by empty bottles and food wrappers and an unexpected number of books. Piotr was sitting on a gaming chair, reading a novel, spinning idly. Harjinder coughed. Piotr stopped spinning but didn't look up.

'I heard you were looking for me, Piotr.'

'Just wanted to know what was going on.'

'Nothing, boss, why?'

'That's what I want to hear. I'd like it to stay that way.'

'Everybody seems happy. Pretty chill, to be honest.'

'Good.'

'Paul said something about going to look for food later. Other than that, I've not heard much from anyone.'

'Good,' he said again. 'Keep an eye on him, will you.'

'Who, Paul?'

'Who else do you think I mean? He's not as savvy as you. He's becoming a bit of a loose cannon.'

'Yes, boss.' Harjinder paused. 'Was that all, or was there something else?'

Piotr looked up at him. 'You tell me, Harj. Is there something else we need to talk about?'

Harjinder shrugged, awkward. 'Don't think so.'

'You seem tense.'

'Not at all.'

'Sure?'

'Absolutely.'

'I think you are. I've noticed it a couple of times now. You need to relax.'

'I am relaxed.'

'You don't seem it. You seem a bit tense. Do you want Laura to come and loosen you up later?'

Harjinder hesitated. Was he supposed to say no because she was with Piotr, or should he accept the offer? Would turning Piotr down make him look like less of a man? 'Yeah. That'd be good. I've got a couple of things to do first, then I—'

Piotr snapped his book shut, truncating Harjinder's words. 'See? I told you.'

'Told me what? Sorry, boss... I don't follow.'

'You don't switch off, Harj, and that's a good thing. People like Paul, they're already checked out. You and me, though, we need to keep our eyes open at all times. Understand?'

'Sure,' he said, and he genuinely did, though he had a sneaking suspicion Piotr might have delivered the exact same speech to Paul already and just swapped their names.

'Thing is, the troops are losing focus, and I get that. Yes, I know, we need food, and we have to watch out for the dead, but that's about all, innit. They already think we've won. Job well done and all that, time to relax. It's a good point; if we're smart, we won't have to leave this place for a long time. I just don't want people getting complacent. I want you to keep an eye on things for me, make sure nothing's getting missed.'

Harjinder felt uneasy. Unsure. Was he actually being tasked with something or challenged? 'I get it, Piotr. You can rely on me.'

'I know I can, but I sense your hesitation. It's going to take some getting used to the new way of things. It doesn't feel right yet because you're still living in the old world, playing by the old rules. Things are different now. Look at what happened at Lakeside. We're already unstoppable, just imagine what it'll be like once the dead are finished. It's all ours, mate. All of it.'

'**S**top the van,' Orla shouted. 'Fuck me, would you just look at that.'

Sam slammed on the brakes. It was still counter-intuitive to stop suddenly in the middle of a once-busy road like this, but before he could say anything, Orla had jumped out of the back and run across the carriageway. Joanne caught his eye in the mirror. 'I'll go with her,' she said.

Orla squeezed through the gap between two rusted wrecks, batting away the flapping hand of a corpse that stretched out through a broken window. The monster strained at its seatbelt restraint, its outstretched fingertips brushing against her. Unbothered, she climbed through a sparse hedge and over a waist-high wooden fence.

'Orla, hold on,' Joanne said, but her voice was lost in the noise of the rain. When she finally caught up, Orla was standing in the middle of a dirt track alongside a field that looked like it had been recently ploughed. Most everywhere else there were weeds taking over, but here the ground appeared to have been recently churned and was devoid of all vegetation.

It was the distinctive shapes that had caught Orla's eye from the van, the piles of skulls and bones. Far from being empty, the field in front of them was filled with burnt human remains. For the most part they lay level on the ground, but in places corpses had built up in clumps, burnt flesh, ash, and blackened bones wedged against each other where the living dead had been unable to escape. The relative elevation of these cremated heaps made them easier to distinguish. There was a very visible leg stuck straight up like a flagpole with the remains of a foot flapping at the top. Elsewhere, two corpses were locked together in an eternal

130

embrace, crisscrossed ribs intertwined like wickerwork, wrapped together... there had been hundreds of corpses here once, perhaps a thousand or more, all now reduced to a single, surreal, never-ending tangle. The stench of charred meat hung in the air.

'What the fuck is this?'

'I dunno,' Orla said. 'Some kind of freak accident, maybe?'

'Seriously?'

'Why not? We know how quickly the fires spread in London. It wouldn't have taken a lot. What if they were struck by lightning?'

'Do you have any idea how unlikely that is?'

'How unlikely would you say any of this was just last summer?'

'But why were they all in the same field?'

'Maybe they were having a game of cricket,' she smiled. 'Sorry. I'd say either there was something here that attracted them, or they were rounded up and torched.'

'What, some kind of ritualistic sacrifice? Can you even sacrifice something that's already dead?'

'Interesting question.'

'Why's that? Look, Orla, I don't really care what happened here, I just don't want it happening to me.'

Back at the van, they told the others what they'd seen. Sam questioned them as he drove away. 'How many bodies?'

'We didn't stop to count,' Joanne said, sarcastic.

'A dozen? Fifty? Give me an estimation.'

'A couple hundred at least.'

'And was it a recent fire?'

'Hard to tell with the rain. But, yeah. Few days, maybe?'

'That's good.'

'Is it?'

'Yes, for a while I was thinking it might have been something to do with David and the others.'

'But who'd do something like that?' April asked.

'You've not been properly introduced to Piotr, have you?' Vicky said. 'It's definitely his style.'

April watched Emily and Isabella's faces with concern. This

horror was hard enough for her to process, how the hell were kids as young as these two supposed to cope?

'It wouldn't have been Piotr,' Dominic said. 'Too classy for him. He'd have just set fire to them where he found then, wouldn't have taken the time to round them up.'

Sam thought he might be right but didn't give him the satisfaction of any acknowledgement.

Barely any further forward, Sam slowed the van again. They were on the summit of a hill now, facing down the slope on the other side. There was a crowd of bodies at the bottom. Their movements were unusual. Orla had noticed it too. 'This is weird. They don't know if they're coming or going, look at them.' She had a point; as many were walking out onto the road as those trying to go in the opposite direction.

'I think they're coming *and* going,' Sam said. 'There's more smoke way over in that direction, see? This might be a residual response. I think what we're seeing now are the remnants of their reaction to something that happened previously.'

'Like Piotr coming through, or David and the others?'

'Exactly. Imagine what it would have been like here last night... pitch black, pouring with rain. With all those bodies in the road, our lot could have ended up anywhere.'

'We're close to Peterborough,' Rafe said, checking a book of maps. 'Bloody hell, your friends might have driven blind into the middle of a city.'

'That's what I'm worried about.'

'So, what do we do?' Orla asked.

'I think we keep going.'

'What?'

'Just a little further. I'll get us through the crowd, then we'll stop somewhere on the other side.'

'This is a bad idea,' Stan said from the other end of the van.

'It might well be, but unlike you and Dominic, I give a shit about my friends. If there are no tracks on the other side of the bodies, then it looks like they've ended up in Peterborough, as

Rafe said. And if that's the case, then we're going in to look for them.'

23

Chapman returned to the convoy, accompanied by Ed and Marcus, another man from the Yaxley group. The two local men worked quickly and silently to ease the pressure of dead flesh from around the stranded trucks and release David, Ruth, and the rest of the remaining group. They shifted vehicles that had been left blocking specific side-streets, allowing the mass of corpses to flow away. Ed's dog Molly precipitated the flood. An incredibly smart and fast animal, she'd adapted to this new world as well as her owner. She'd been trained to round up sheep but proved equally adept at keeping corpses in line. She'd sprint away from them then stop and bark until they followed, wagging her tail like it was the greatest game. A maze-like system of further blockades deeper in the village kept the creatures moving along into a holding pen of sorts, a safe distance away from everyone else.

It was less of a risk to move the people rather than their vehicles. Ed and Marcus led them along whisper-silent streets to the south. They regrouped in the assembly hall of a small school on the far side of a playing field. Chapman sat with David and Ruth on one side of a table, and Ed and Marcus on the other, feeling like he was a politician about to try and broker a crucial peace deal. They were united in their disdain for Piotr and everything he represented, but Ed was staunchly protective of the community they'd built here.

'I think you'd got it part right,' Ed said after David had told him what they'd been through in London. 'You were too restricted there, though. Too many dead bodies. Your ratios were all wrong.'

'Forgive him,' Marcus said. 'He's always going on about ratios and stuff like that.'

'That's because it's important. You can take the piss all you like, Marcus, but it matters. It could literally be the difference between life and death. The more of them you have to deal with, the more space you're going to need to do it. You need at least double the space they occupy, and with the best will in the world, you're never going to find that in a city centre.'

David was less than impressed. 'Let's cut the crap. What is it you're actually trying to do here? Are you just playing games? Because I've got to be honest, I'm not best pleased at being caught up like we were last night.'

'No one was trying to catch you out. We were just trying to keep ourselves safe. Not our fault if people keep barging in uninvited.'

'Let's not get caught up in semantics.'

'Look, we've got everything we need here, or we did have until those bloody raiders turned up the other day. I was born and raised here. My family's farmed just outside of Yaxley for the last eighty-odd years, and we intend being here a while longer yet. Well, I do, anyway. What we've done here is make the most of our environment and our experience. We keep the dead moving the way we moved herds of cattle previously, and the way we will again one day. We keep their numbers under control 'cause there's still plenty of them dragging themselves down here from Peterborough way. They're just another type of vermin is all, one that happens to look like us. They won't last forever, that much I'm sure of.'

'You're right about that,' David said, less antagonistic now. 'We've been trying to hold out until the end of winter. If the cold doesn't stop them, decay will. There's only a finite length of time they'll be able to stay mobile.'

'Agreed. Longer-term, things look a lot more positive. It's surviving the here and now we've got a problem with. I'll be completely honest, we were struggling even before those thugs turned up and turfed us out of the warehouse. I'm hoping it's something you might be able to help us with. Quid pro quo. We could all do well out of this if we're smart.'

'Go on.'

Ed paused, a little unsure. 'Truth is, we've been struggling here because there are so few of us. It was hard enough keeping on top of things as it was, but with what's happened now, it's nigh on impossible.'

David connected the dots. 'You want us to provide the manpower?'

'Something like that.'

'Wait, to get rid of Piotr, or to keep your farm running?'

'Both.'

'We've lost a lot of people along the way, but there's still a fair few of us, you know. You'd be looking at the best part of a hundred mouths to feed.'

'I ran a commercial farm, mate. I think I can handle that. I've got plans for expansion once the dead are finished. I've wanted to get a decent number of livestock back on the farm, but it's been too much of a risk until now. I tried with chickens, but the damn things were too noisy.'

David laughed. 'I've heard it all now.'

Ed remained deadly serious. 'You think this is a joke?'

'It's not that, it's just...'

'It's just that you haven't thought about it. Well, I have, mate. It's my job. What we're lacking is the manpower you have.'

'How do you know you can trust us?'

'Because I trust Tony. This is less of a gamble for me than it is for you.'

'And how do we know we can trust you?'

'I could have left you stranded in your trucks.'

'Can't argue with that,' Noah said, perched on a seat nearby, spectating.

'For what it's worth, I think we should do this,' Chapman said. 'The potential gains are huge. This place can give us everything we need for long-term survival, without us having to go traipsing the length of the country to get to Ledsey Cross. Way I see it is we

136

try it, and if things don't work out, we can still move on.'

'Aren't you forgetting something?' Ruth said. She'd been sitting on the edge of the conversation, listening in. 'What about Vicky and the others? We can't just forget about them. If anything, they should be our priority.'

David rubbed his temples and sighed. 'I know how you feel, Ruth, but you know the reality of our situation here. They're not our priority. They can't be. We've always had to put the needs of the majority first.'

'I know, but—'

'But nothing. They'll be okay, you know they will. Sam and Vicky won't take any shit.'

'We've got a chance of setting ourselves up with a future here, Ruth,' Chapman said. 'We can't pass that up.'

'Your friends will find us if they come this way,' Marcus added. 'Same way you did.'

Ruth looked like she was about to protest, but she backed down at the last moment because even though she didn't like it, she knew they were right on every score. The needs of the many outweighed the needs of a handful of people, and both Sam and Vicky did have proven track records at surviving the apparently un-survivable. Besides, what else was she going to do? If they hadn't come this way, they could have gone anywhere. What were the chances of finding a van full of people in an entire country? It was needle in a haystack time. She knew she stood next to no chance.

'Aren't we just glossing over something here?' Sanjay said. 'What about Piotr and his mates? Anything you build here, any successes you have, those fuckers will destroy it all.'

'I know,' David said.

'So, we've got to get rid of them, right?'

'Right.'

'But Piotr's a fucking psychopath. And most of the morons left with him are equally unhinged. Killing corpses is one thing, Dave, but what we're talking about here... I'll be honest, I'm not comfortable with any of this.'

'Neither am I, Sanj. Truth be told, I'm nervous just thinking about it. But right now, I don't see that we have any choice. If we don't take them out once and for all, then we'll just be kicking the can down the road. We can't spend the rest of our lives running from that evil bastard, constantly looking over our shoulders. We're going to have to make a stand at some point.'

'I agree,' Ruth said.

'And me,' Chapman agreed. 'Fuck it. I'm done running. We've got the weapons we picked up from the reservist base, rifles and grenades. Maybe it's time to use them.'

David looked at Ed. 'Can you get our trucks out?'

'Easy. You should be able to move them in an hour or so. The crowds will be gone by then.'

Marcus grinned, a plan forming. 'We don't have any firearms, but there is something else we can bring to the party.'

24

'The human race is on the verge of extinction, of that I have absolutely no doubt,' Piotr said. 'These final days, weeks, months, and possibly even years are the death throes of a dying breed.'

'You're a proper ray of sunshine, you know that?' Kelly said. 'I'm glad you only talk like this after we've had sex. Going on about the end of the world is a proper passion-killer.'

She got up and scooped up her discarded clothing. His trousers were entangled with her underwear. She separated them, kept hold of her knickers, and threw the rest at him.

'Thank you,' he said.

'What, for throwing you your trousers?'

'No.'

'So, you're thanking me for sex then? Great. That doesn't make me feel like a prostitute at all.'

'Not that. Jesus. Thank you for keeping me focused.'

'I don't follow. You don't half talk a lot of crap once you've shot your load.'

'It's not crap. It's important. Don't you get it? The rest of the world is dead, but we're still doing okay. Hell, we're fucking. What greater pleasure is there, what more proof of life than fucking?'

Kelly could think of a few, but now wasn't the time to mention them.

Piotr was still sitting on the bed, ranting. 'Even when there's so much death surrounding us and what's left of the world is on its knees, we can still find such pleasure... don't you think that's incredible?'

'It is,' she said, quickly agreeing. She decided not to tell him that she'd found ten times as much pleasure last night with Damien McAdams, the footballer. She couldn't believe she'd fucked a Premier League footballer. Times past, she'd have been all over her socials telling anyone who'd listen, but both the social networks and all her contacts had been logged off for good now.

And Piotr was *still* droning on.

'The world and almost everyone in it is dead, Kelly, but we're still here doing our thing. I'm not promising you a life like the one you used to have, but stick with me and I'll see you right. You know that, don't you?'

She finished pulling on her clothes then climbed back on the bed. 'I know that. You hungry? I'm starving. I'm going to fetch us some food.'

And she left the room before he could say anything else.

Damien was downstairs with Paul Duggan and several others, all togged up in freshly looted gear like they were about to go on a hike through the wilderness. 'Where you off to?' she asked.

'Fishing,' he said, sounding like an excited kid.

'I thought we could spend some more time together.'

'Later, Kel, I promise.'

'But you said we could—'

He was gone before she could finish her sentence. It was bloody freezing outside. She was glad when the heavy glass door swung shut. It blocked out the cold and it blocked out the wind and it blocked out everything else. Her stomach growled with hunger, and she went to find something to eat.

One of the local lads, Yasir, had told them about the fishing lake in the country park adjacent to the warehouses. Damien wasn't much of an angler by any stretch of the imagination, but Yasir and Paul Duggan seemed to know what they were talking about, and he'd jumped at the chance to go fishing with them. Paul had told him it was a good opportunity to learn an important life skill, but Damien hadn't cared much about that. It was a chance to get outside and spend some time with the lads. He'd missed this kind of freedom and camaraderie. It was a welcome taste of the old world.

'So, what was it like?' Paul asked as they walked down to the lake.

'What was what like?'

'Playing for the Arsenal? Playing in front of all those people?'

Damien spun a well-rehearsed answer he'd given a thousand times before to a thousand different people. Paul lapped it up, and that made him feel good, made him feel important, like he used to. He'd forgotten how much of his life centred around his public image. He'd been worried that his magic would wear off now that everything had changed, and he would become merely ordinary. Paul's reaction was proof positive that his celebrity status should count for something for a while longer yet.

They'd taken everything they needed from the Amazon Aladdin's cave and were now crossing a football-pitch-sized patch of undeveloped scrub to get to the tree line boundary of the country park. Yas took them along a muddy, well-worn path through the trees. 'I used to cut through here and play when I was a kid,' Yas said. 'Been here forever, this place has. They've been building up on all sides, but whenever anyone talked about building on the park, all the locals used to come out in force. Proper little oasis, this is.'

He was right.

The rough path soon merged with another, more substantial walkway, and the park opened up around them. It looked untouched. Unspoilt. A glimpse back into an untainted world that everywhere else had forever disappeared. Paul stopped and looked around. 'Perfect. It's like nothing ever happened out here. I can imagine little Yas playing down here in his shorts.'

'I did!' Yasir laughed.

The country park was cold, wet and miserable today, but at that moment Paul didn't ever want to leave. 'We are gonna find fish here, aren't we?'

'Yeah, loads. Why?'

'Because he doesn't want to go back to Piotr empty handed,' Damien said.

'Don't talk bollocks,' Paul said, embarrassed.

'I'm not. It's true. You're always sucking up to the boss. I don't blame you. I'd probably be the same in your position.'

'It's just down here,' Yas said.

He'd described it as a fishing pool, but when they reached the water Damien thought it looked big enough to be called a lake. They found a convenient spot and began to set up their gear. It was overgrown now, but this part of the bank looked well-worn and had likely been frequently fished from in the past. There was a rough-hewn wooden bench. Damien sat down and watched Paul and Yasir sorting out their rods and tackle.

'Takes me back,' Paul said. 'I haven't done this for years.'

'Did you bring a net?' Yas asked.

'Thought you did.'

'You said you were getting the net.'

'I didn't.'

'Go back and get one.'

'Can't be bothered.'

'We'll have to manage without.'

'Got to catch some fish first...'

Damien had stopped listening to their inane back-and-forth. He was unsettled by the amount of movement he could see on the other side of the water. He hoped it was animals, or other people from the group, but he knew it wasn't either. The clumsy rustling of the undergrowth indicated the presence of the dead.

'Are you sure we're alright out here?'

Paul looked up and squinted into the distance. He shook his head, not about to let his fishing trip be interrupted. 'Don't worry about it. It's just a few creepers.'

'You sure?'

Maybe it was the trees making it look like more of a crowd, the dead disappearing then reappearing in the gaps between trunks.

Paul looked again. He was getting annoyed now. 'It's nothing.

Looks like a group of them that's managed to get through a fence or something. It happens from time to time. Ed's pretty good at keeping them under control, but even he can't keep track of all of them. He says it's like herding cats. Really fucking horrible cats as well.'

'There's quite a lot of them, Paul,' Yas said.

'What's the matter with you two? We've just got to get used to this,' he said as he continued setting up. 'The population of the UK was about seventy million, last I heard. That means there's gonna be bodies wherever we go for a while longer yet. You've just gotta learn how to deal with them.'

'Yeah, I know that, but there's a lot of them round here,' Damien said, sounding nervous.

'Frigging hell, mate, you're not losing your bottle, are you? You played in attack in the Premier League, for fuck's sake. You should be used to a bit of pressure.'

'I am, but this is different, isn't it? I'd fancy my chances against a massive away crowd more than I would a handful of those rotting fuckers.'

Paul sighed with disappointment. It was true what they used to say about never meeting your heroes. Damien was proving to be a real disappointment, gibbering nervously. 'Look, mate, we've come down here to relax and catch some fish. When it comes down to it, staying safe from the dead and catching fish are similar hobbies.'

'Bullshit. How d'you work that out?'

'They're both a lot easier if you keep your bloody mouth shut.'

'Yeah, but look at them. They're coming this way, Paul. Can they hear us?'

Paul was getting annoyed now. 'They can hear *you*, that's for sure. Now shut up and fish. If you don't like it out here, go back.'

He didn't want to admit it, because to do that might give Damien and Yas the impression that he was concerned, but there did seem to be a lot of dead bodies around here, far more than he'd expected to see. There was a sizeable crowd gathered on the other side of the water now. Worryingly, some of them seemed to be edging along one side of the fishing pool now too.

Yasir had also seen them. 'Look, Paul,' he whispered, 'I don't want you thinking I'm bottling it or anything, but there's a heck of a lot of them down there. I don't like it. I've only ever seen them in numbers like that when Ed's been...'

He stopped speaking suddenly.

'What is it?' Damien asked, heart thumping.

'Listen.'

Someone was singing. It was such a surreal thing to hear that, for a moment, neither Paul nor Damien knew how to react. The words were inaudible, but they could just about make out the tune. *The Final Countdown...* a slice of cheesy eighties pop-rock that Paul remembered his dad playing on the car stereo on repeat. Yas recognised it for a very different reason. 'It's bloody Ed, that is,' he said. 'He's always singing that frigging song when he's moving the dead. He sings to make them follow him.'

'So, why's he bringing them this way?'

It took an idiot or a genius to risk making a noise like this out in the open. From what he'd so far seen, Paul wasn't yet sure which of those camps Ed fell into.

'Reckon Piotr's told him to move a load of bodies?' Damien asked.

'Away from the warehouses, maybe, but he's bringing them closer.'

Realisation dawned.

Paul threw his fishing tackle down then sprinted along the edge of the pool to shut Ed up. When he spotted him at the front of the herd, he screamed at him without thinking. 'You fucking maniac. What the hell are you doing?'

Ed stopped singing and stepped off the path. The snaking column of listless figures that had been following him continued to move forward and Paul realised he'd been played. By default, Ed's calculated silence had left him as the sole focus of undead attention. Paul panicked, not knowing what to do or where to go.

He thought he should try and lead the corpses away and back out into the wilderness, but the idea of being followed by them was too terrifying to even consider. Instead he ran for cover, racing back to the warehouse.

He tripped over a pile of fishing tackle abandoned in the middle of the path. Damien and Yasir were already long gone.

25

The alarm had already been sounded at the warehouses. Piotr had been ready for this. He'd expected it. He watched from outside his building as Paul raced across the scrubland like a frightened little kid.

Inside, Harjinder was rallying the troops as boss man had ordered. Though they'd spent much of their time here enjoying the fruits of their labour, Piotr had insisted on some level of preparedness, should the dead attack. Retribution from the disgruntled former occupants of the warehouses had been expected, as had the possibility of other survivors stumbling on their treasure trove by chance. And there had always been the very real possibility that the dead themselves would return in huge numbers, of their own volition.

It didn't matter. Every one of those threats would be dealt with in the exact same way. His lot would wipe the fuckers out.

They'd found an almost endless supply of items on the shelves of the warehouses that could be used to fight. It wasn't like in other countries, where guns and ammo could be bought off the shelf, but that didn't matter. Here, chainsaws, garden tools, power tools, even sporting equipment had been repurposed as weapons with devastating destructive power.

Piotr gave the order to the thirty-odd fighters he had left at his disposal. 'Destroy every single one of them. Living or dead, I don't want anything left standing at the end of this but us.'

And he waited for his people to pull the rip cords and triggers and start their chainsaws and other tools, then followed them down into battle.

Vast columns of the dead emerged from the country park. The

confines of the established paths they'd followed through the greenery had given the illusion of them having formation and intent, but as soon as they were out into the open, they spread out and became more diffuse and erratic. The weapons Piotr's soldiers used today would have been out of the question on all other occasions, but the ugly machine noise proved unexpectedly useful. Just when it looked like the army of the dead was going to fragment and become harder to contain, the abrasive noise of the buzzsaws and nail guns and circular saws gave them a whole new focus, calling them to the slaughter. Piotr wished he'd thought of this earlier. He followed a woman who swept the whirring blade of her chainsaw from side-to-side, slicing up corpse after corpse. It was as if they couldn't wait to be killed. There was an undeniable beauty in the over-powered re-kill. When she cut through them at an angle, the two uneven halves of their blood-slick, dismembered bodies slid apart.

A few metres behind, someone let out a horrific yell of pain. Piotr didn't look around to see who it was – no point, it didn't matter – but he shouted an order they all needed to hear. 'Careful. Watch the people around you.' The adrenalin was flowing. If they weren't careful, the one-sided battle would degenerate into total mayhem. His people needed not to lose control.

A surge from the dead caused him to take a few steps back. Bones crunched under his boots, and he looked down and saw it was one of his men. A recent recruit from Yaxley... he couldn't remember the lad's name. Didn't matter now. He picked up the nail gun he'd had been using and began moving from corpse to corpse, firing nails into what was left of their brains with a pneumatic thump and hiss and a satisfying, rifle-like recoil.

What the fuck?

Now that Piotr had turned around and was facing the opposite direction, he saw that even more of the dead were flooding onto the battlefield, this time from the general vicinity of the fields to the east of Yaxley. A two-pronged attack. No, wait, *three*-pronged – there was yet another wave of them approaching the warehouses from the west.

'It's a fucking set-up,' Piotr said, furious. He backed into Harjinder, and they almost went for each other before both realising just in time.

'It's the locals isn't it, boss?'

'Of course it's them.' He paused to put a nail through the skull of another cadaver. 'We talked about this, Harj. We knew they'd try something eventually.'

The situation had deteriorated with a speed that was completely at odds with the slothful advances of the dead. Paul Duggan felt responsible, like he had something to prove. He wrestled a hedge trimmer from Darren Adams who'd gone down under the weight of a bunch of corpses that had rushed him at once. 'Help me, Paul!' Darren yelled, but Paul wasn't listening. He could see Piotr up ahead now, talking to Harjinder, and he knew he needed to make his presence known.

'Wipe 'em out,' Paul screamed as he ran, and he lowered the whirring blade and hacked through the legs of another four cadavers. Though nowhere near as powerful as the chainsaws others were wielding, the trimmer ripped through the parchment-thin flesh of the undead, felling them like sapling trees.

Harjinder had disappeared. Paul pushed forward again to take his place. Yas blocked his way through.

'You've got to help me, Paul. I'm no fighter.'

'We're all fighters now,' Paul said, plunging the grinding teeth of the trimmer into a dead woman's belly.

'But I can't do this—'

Paul shoved Yas out of the way. The terrified man collided with Piotr, who spun around and fired a nail through his cranium, only realising what he'd done once he looked down at the body by his feet.

'Focus, you fucking morons,' he yelled, and he kicked Yasir's lifeless body in frustration.

Paul edged closer. 'I know what's happening, Piotr,' he shouted, breathless, yelling to make himself heard over the battle noise.

'It's Ed. I saw him. He's led them all here. It's a set-up.'

'Worked that out on your own, did you?'

And then they both froze, because in the few random, vacuum-like seconds between the last attack and the next, they both heard the same thing.

Engines.

David gave the signal, and the convoy moved away at speed. True to their word, Ed and Marcus had left the road ahead completely clear. He remained tense, expecting dead bodies to swarm out across the tarmac at any moment, but none came.

Barbara Moore navigated for David. She was sharp as a pin, and she knew the streets here as well as anyone. After retiring fifteen years ago, she'd lived in Yaxley with her husband until the world's end. Now she was Ed's right hand, helping on the farm. She didn't like physical work these days, but she was keen to get rid of the vile bastards who'd tainted the village with their unwanted presence. 'Left then an immediate left again,' she ordered, and David obliged without hesitation as she navigated them through the maze. 'Next left, then two rights in quick succession.'

He did as she told him and swung the truck back around onto the road they'd originally followed into Yaxley. It too was now artificially clear. He checked the rear-view: Chapman and Sanjay were close behind.

Barbara tapped his arm. 'Keep your eyes on the road, David, and put your bloody foot down.'

Whenever there was any sign of trouble, Kelly looked for Alfonso Morterero and stuck to him like glue. 'What the hell's going on, Alf?' she asked.

He was a man of few words. 'No fucking clue.'

'But he told you to wait here?'

'Yep.'

'In the van?'

'Yep.'

'Why?'

'I'm his driver.'

'I know that much, dimwit. Did he say where he's going?'

'Nope.'

'Are we in trouble here?'

This time Alfonso just shrugged, didn't even bother answering. Kelly was about to speak again when three trucks came out of nowhere and screeched into the warehouse carparks. The first two continued as far as they could, the third stopped abruptly, blocking the exit. Alfonso grabbed Kelly's arm and pulled her down. The two of them sank into their seats, out of sight.

'Fuck,' Alfonso said.

Piotr's ragtag army were fighting for all they were worth. There was barely any fear in the ranks, little nervousness, because they'd been here before, would no doubt be here again, and each time they'd prevailed. The dead were a nuisance, no longer a threat. Their numbers were a challenge, but nothing they hadn't overcome previously. Those dumb fucking yokels thought they'd been so fucking smart leading their undead sheep back to the warehouses, but the fighters had seen worse. Sure, a handful of them had gone down and would be missed, but most were still standing, still slaughtering. When they'd last fought like this in London, they'd been up against an enemy with apparently limitless numbers in its ranks, an endless supply of cannon fodder. Today, though, they were facing just a few hundred of the undead, a thousand, tops. And now they all had shiny new weapons. Easy money.

The fiercest fighting was concentrated around the centre of the scrubland battlefield. This was the point at which the snaking columns of corpses had converged on Piotr's gang, and also the point from which they'd launched their fightback. The epicentre of it all had become a magnet for violence, a hot, swirling mess of blood, sweat, and broken bones. The dead continued to surge forward, and the remaining fighters attacked them with a nervous energy that bordered on glee. The massacre was therapeutic for the men and women who fought, though their strength flagged. The fact there was a clear end in sight now gave them a renewed energy, an incentive to keep attacking. They knew the dead had been brought here as a last-ditch attempt at rebellion. When it failed, as it inevitably would, they'd launch again, a proper planned attack, and get rid of those troublesome natives once and for all.

'They're slowing down,' Paul shouted to Piotr and to anyone else who could hear him. 'Keep going. One last push. We've got this!'

The reduction in the corpse ranks was becoming noticeable now. Though there were still hordes of the undead on the battlefield, the vast numbers that had come here had finally started drying up; now just a trickle of slow-moving stragglers wandered into the kill-space. Paul felt unstoppable. From zero to hero in the space of one quick battle. He'd worried that Piotr might have found out from Damien and Yasir that he'd seen them coming through the country park and had just run for cover instead of trying to stop them but, against the odds, he'd turned things around. Now he was the one coordinating the charge and inflicting maximum damage on the pathetic dead. He was exhausted, but he was going to stay at the centre of it all, cutting down corpse after corpse after corpse with his blood-soaked power tool, determined that the boss would take note.

He looked around for Piotr, because it was pointless trying so hard if he wasn't watching, but Paul couldn't see him anywhere. *Christ, what if he's gone down? Fuck!* For a moment it was hard to contain his excitement. Staying on the right side of the chief was his best option for now, but if something had happened to Piotr out here, he'd be a natural fit to fill the power vacuum left behind.

Hold on.

Is that Steve Armitage up there?

I don't remember him being here with us?

Paul was confused. He could definitely see Steve Armitage – he was a distinctive-looking guy – but what was he doing here? He was hanging back, well away from the centre of the fighting, and Paul could see other people he recognised now too. People he was certain they'd left behind in London: Lisa Kaur, Doctor Liz, Chapman... Fuck. Where the hell had this lot come from?

'Now!' Steve ordered. On his command, they each pulled their pins and hurled their grenades into the heart of the battle between Piotr's army and the Yaxley undead. It was all but impossible to miss. They all hit their mark, and the resulting succession of explosions was devastating. Vast clouds of dirt and body parts were thrown up into the cold December morning air, and when the noise died down, there was absolute silence.

Nothing moved on the scrubland. No living, no undead. No survivors.

Liz Hunter vomited. David went to support her, but she pushed him away. She wiped bile from the corner of her mouth and slowly approached the devastation. 'You okay?' he asked.

'Not exactly.'

'We had to do it.'

'If you say so. I've spent a lifetime trying to prolong life, and now I'm reduced to this. It's fucking disgusting. Completely necessary, I suppose, but fucking disgusting. What have we become, Dave?'

David had no answer.

Behind them, there was a commotion outside the warehouse. Sanjay shoved a group of figures out into the carpark. Dr Ahmad, and several others that David didn't immediately recognise. They were either people who'd taken the easy option and fled from the Tower with Piotr, or those who'd defected when he'd reached Yaxley. Fucking cowards, the lot of them. Total risk avoidance. He looked at them with disdain. 'What shall I do with this lot?' Sanjay shouted.

'Lock them up somewhere. We'll decide what to do with them

later.'

Sanjay did as he was told, as did his prisoners. He didn't anticipate any trouble. All these skiving, treacherous bastards had ever wanted was an easy life. Now they'd got rid of Piotr and his heavies, they'd almost certainly capitulate. David watched him frogmarch them away.

'Result,' Steve said, disturbing him. 'That did the trick.'

'You can say that again.'

Ed wandered over. 'We all good here?'

'I think so. I'd do a roll call to make sure we got rid of Piotr and all his crowd of bastards, but I don't reckon there's enough left of them to be able to do any identifications.'

'Doesn't matter. Fuck the lot of them. They're gone, that's all we need to know. There's about a hundred of us here now. If there's any of them left, they'll think twice about trying anything. We showed them.'

'We showed them we could be as bad as Piotr, that's for sure.'

'Get over yourself, David,' Ed said. 'We did what we had to do. We did it to them before they could do it to us.'

'Yeah, you're right. We just need to—'

David stopped talking abruptly when he heard another engine approaching. Chapman and Lisa grabbed their weapons and sprinted back to the road by the warehouses to head off whoever it was, fearing another strike from the last of Piotr's people.

Chapman relaxed when he recognised the van that had stopped on the other side of the blocked entrance. 'We're good. It's Sam and the others.'

Sam stopped the engine and got out. He walked over to Chapman and shook his hand. 'Thought you might have ended up here. We knew there'd been some activity round these parts, so we'd been loitering, didn't want to stray too far. Then we heard all the commotion. What was all that about?'

'It's a long story.'

'Let me guess. Piotr?'

'Of course.'

'Sounds like we missed a lot.'

'Well, we clearly did,' Chapman said as Dominic and Stan sheepishly got out of the van. 'What the fuck are you doing with those shysters?'

'An equally long story. I'll tell you later. Are we all good here?'

'Really good, actually.'

When Ruth saw Vicky, she broke down in tears. 'Thank Christ you're safe,' she sobbed as she held her.

'You knew I'd come back,' Vicky whispered, not letting go.

Together, Vicky, Sam, Orla, Selena, and all the people they'd picked up along the way walked down into Yaxley. There was much to do, and much to catch up on.

Within a couple of hours – no one was sure exactly when – the van they'd left outside the carpark gates had gone.

26

DAY ONE HUNDRED AND THIRTEEN
CHRISTMAS DAY

In the three weeks since they'd reclaimed Yaxley, much had been accomplished. Georgie was firmly back into the swing of things, recording important information in meticulous detail: who'd survived, who hadn't made it, and who remained unaccounted for. She'd found a kindred spirit in Ed, a man whose penchant for minutia and precise record keeping matched her own. People had tried to persuade her it might be time to stop, that they'd reached their final destination and that the details she'd been keeping were no longer necessary, but Ed had urged her to keep going. Previously, Dominic Grove had wanted the information available to help justify his wild utopian daydreams. Ed argued that the future was less of a concern, that the details she'd been keeping would be invaluable to help sustain them in the present. How many mouths they had to feed, how much manpower they had available, who might prove useful now that they could claim some stability. Then the farming to feed the larger group, what crops they'd need to grow, how many animals they should try and keep, how much food they'd need to produce on an ongoing basis... these were the questions that Georgie's data helped answer.

It was an unexpectedly positive time, though tempered with a pervading sadness that frequently threatened to overtake everything and everyone. This Christmas Day felt like the antithesis of everything Christmas last year had been. 'It's not like it was now,' Selena explained when Ruth questioned her lack of enthusiasm for the holiday season. 'This time last year I was at home with Mum and Dad. My uncle and aunt came up from

Brighton, and Nan came around, and Mum cooked this massive dinner for everyone, and it was amazing. No offence, Ruth, but this ain't a patch on any of it. I'm just sitting here thinking about everyone I've lost, and it hurts. The twenty-fifth of December is just another day now.'

But they tried to celebrate, regardless.

With the contents of the warehouses so accessible, people were tasked with finding a gift for another member of the group, their names picked from a hat. A forced, community-wide, Secret Santa. Selena had written a Christmas list at Vicky's insistence, though gift-giving felt like hollow and perfunctory gesture, as did claiming material items. Last year she'd asked for money, makeup, and clothes. This year she'd only asked for two things:

1 – body armour
2 – a fucking big knife.

They held a communal Christmas meal in the village hall. A predictably meat-free, hotchpotch affair, Phillipa Rochester had done them proud and had cooked enough to feed twice as many people. Much booze had already been knocked back. Songs had been sung, and it had proved to be an unexpectedly emotional get-together. The word 'Christmas' was only occasionally mentioned. It was an opportunity to pause; to look back and to look forward. A chance to take stock.

'Complements of the season,' Taylor said, carrying another crate of beer into the hall that he'd procured from the stores.

'Always the hero, eh, Tony,' David said, half joking.

'Hardly.'

'Must feel good to finally be yourself, though, eh? To have dropped the Superman act?'

'I'm still Superman, mate,' he laughed. 'It's the Clark Kent bit I dropped.'

Chapman, mid-conversation, reached across between them and helped himself to a can. 'The reason we've made it this far,' he said, worse for wear, 'is that we've played it safe and not done anything stupid. If you look back, all the times that Dominic and

Piotr screwed up were because they overreached.'

Dominic was sitting in a corner with Stan, listening intently but keeping his mouth shut for once. He was in no position to argue. He'd finally learnt that the more he said, the more trouble he ended up in. A quiet life here was all he wanted now.

Chapman continued, in full flow. 'What you did here, Ed, wasn't that different from what we were trying, except that you got the scale right. Frigging Dominic was always trying to prove a point, weren't you, Dom?' he called across. 'He didn't realise that none of us cared about tomorrow. We just wanted to survive today. All the people who listened to him are dead now.'

'Ignore him,' Stan whispered. 'He's just trying to get a rise out of you.'

'Dominic wasn't completely wrong, though,' David Shires said. 'Back in London, we were always aiming for something, it just didn't often work out. Might be we didn't fully consider the precarious spot we were truly in at the moment, but I think you have to have something to aim for though, don't you?'

'I guess.'

Liz turned to look at David. 'What about you?'

'What about me?'

'What are you aiming for?'

'I'd like to see everyone here settled and safe. I want Ed to be able to do everything he's trying to do with the farm, and I want the dead to disappear.'

'I'll ask again,' Liz said. 'What about *you*?'

He hesitated, eyes brimming with tears. 'I think I'm just getting all sentimental because it's Christmas, but I still want more than anything to just go home.'

'Home?' Sanjay said. 'What's home these days? It's just where you happen to be, I reckon.'

David shook his head. 'It's more than that. I want to go back to Ireland. And before any of you say anything, I know exactly what I'm likely to find there, but I still want to go. I have to go. I honestly think we're going to be okay here, but I don't know if that's going to be enough for me. No disrespect, but I can't picture myself spending the rest of my days here, in a place I don't know, with people I don't know so well.'

'But all that'll change over time,' Liz said.

'Maybe that's true, but if I don't go back, I don't think I'll ever be completely satisfied. Do you understand where I'm coming from? Until I know for certain what's happened to my family, I can't give up on them.'

'I get that,' Ed said, trying his best to show some sensitivity, 'but the reality is you're never gonna really know, are you? My family is gone, and as far as I know, everyone else here is on their own now too. I think we just have to accept that's the way it is. Play the hand that's dealt us, and all that.'

'I don't know if I can. Even though there might only be a fraction of a fraction of a fraction of a per cent chance that my wife or any of my kids are still alive, I have to take it. Christ, the thought of any of my little ones being on their own over there... I just can't stand it.'

'Merry fucking Christmas,' Dominic muttered under his breath.

27

Vicky, Ruth, and Selena had moved into a small, terraced cottage on a road opposite the village hall. Sam and Joanne had moved in together next-door. Vicky had neither the energy nor inclination to join the party in the hall, and the others took their lead from her. Instead, Sam roasted a couple of rabbits he'd caught over a fire-pit he'd dug in his back garden. He cooked over the open fire regularly. He'd removed several of the fence panels between the two houses and shared dinner with the neighbours most days. Tonight, Vicky had barely touched her food. She loitered by the fire, heat more important than nourishment, and chain-smoked cigarettes. Sam kept her company; the others having gone inside to play board games. He couldn't think of anything more tedious. She watched him watching her.

'Just do it,' she said.

'Do what?'

'Give me your variation on the same hilarious joke everybody's been doing since I got my hands on more cigarettes. Go on, I dare you. Tell me smoking's bad for my health.'

'I wouldn't dream of it.'

She chuckled, and her laughter quickly spiralled out of control, degenerating into an unstoppable, hacking cough. Sam handed her a bottle of Scotch that he'd been keeping in his pocket. She swigged from the bottle of booze, its smooth taste and warming sensation better than any medicine.

'I can't get over you without any hair,' she said.

Sam ran his fingers over his freshly shaved scalp and chin. 'I know. It's cold without that mop. I miss it.'

'Joanne doesn't.'

'She told you?'

'She did. You two getting on okay?'

'It's purely platonic,' he said quickly. 'We're flatmates.'

'Yeah, right.'

'Believe me, the last thing I'm thinking of is a full-blown relationship. I don't think I could handle it. If I let someone in, *really* in, and we broke up, I don't think I'd cope.'

'You serious?'

'Deadly.'

Vicky watched the fire burn and pondered his words. She understood. In a world where so much had been lost and so little positivity remained, trusting anyone else with your happiness felt like a risk too far.

Sam felt obliged to keep the conversation going. 'You never told me how you got on with Dr Liz yesterday.'

Vicky shrugged. 'There's not a lot to say. She can't do anything for me.'

'Then why do you go and see her?'

'Because it makes her feel better. Because it stops Ruth and Selena from nagging at me. I'm serious, there's not a lot of point, otherwise. She says she'll be able to help me with pain relief when things get bad, other than that, there's nothing anyone can do.'

'Yeah, I get that.'

'You know what keeps going around my head?' she asked.

'I can't even begin to imagine. Seriously.'

'It's that frigging Wham song, *Last Christmas*.'

'Ouch. Why?'

'Because this is my last Christmas, why d'you think?'

'You don't know that for certain.'

'Spare me. We do.'

Sam messed with the embers of the fire. 'Have you talked about it with Ruth yet?'

'Nope. I'm trying to keep things normal for as long as I can.'

'Normal, Vic? Since when was anything normal around here?'

She shook her head. 'You know what I mean. Ruth and Selena both know I'm ill, but they don't know exactly how ill.'

'It doesn't take a genius.'

She ignored him. 'Thing is, as soon as I admit it and it's open for discussion, it'll be all we talk about. Ruth will be fussing over me more than she already does, and everyone will start treating me different and... and I just don't want that. You understand, don't you?'

'I do, as it happens.' Sam paused and prodded the dying fire with a stick again. 'So, is that what you've been preoccupied with all day?'

'My own mortality? That's enough, isn't it?'

'I know you better than you'd like to admit, Vic. I think there's something else.'

She plunged her hands in her pockets and paced the overgrown lawn. 'Hand over that Scotch, will you?' She took a slug and grimaced, then took another before handing it back.

'I'm getting itchy feet.'

'Go on.'

Vicky looked around, as if she was sharing a grubby little secret she didn't want anyone but Sam to hear. 'I don't think I want to stay here. The group's done well, and Ed and the Yaxley people have poured their hearts and souls into this place, but I'm not ready to drop anchor. I just don't want this to be the place where I die.'

'You're talking about Ledsey Cross again, aren't you?'

'Kind of. I know it sounds crazy to be talking about leaving somewhere so well-established and with as much potential as this, but it feels even crazier not to try.'

'Do you really think there will be anything at Ledsey Cross that we don't have here?'

'Yes, I do.'

'The people?'

'The people, the infrastructure, the location, the security... If I'm being completely honest, Sam, not going means giving up on the only goal I've ever really set for myself. I can't stand the thought of dying before I've had chance to see it. Does that sound crazy?'

'No crazier than anything else.'

'On the day of the apocalypse, I was supposed to be at a hospital appointment. I was going to find out how long they thought I had left. And that was with all the chemo and other treatments they were going to propose. Now we're three months further on, and I've had no treatments whatsoever. My diet is shit, I'm tired all the time...'

'It's not just about you though, is it?'

She shook her head.

'No. I know how corny this sounds, Sam, but it's about the kids too. Selena, Omar, Isabella and Emily... hopefully they're going to be around long after the rest of us are gone, definitely after I'm gone. I want them to have the best chance possible, and I think Ledsey Cross could be a better option for them.'

'Ruth doesn't agree.'

'I know.'

'I heard her and Selena having a good old moan about it the other day. Her argument was that it's all well and good going to somewhere self-sufficient like Ledsey Cross where there's solar power and what have you, but when all the lightbulbs are gone, all the lightbulbs are gone.'

Vicky laughed. 'She's absolutely right about that! But we've likely got lightbulbs for fifty years! That's a hell of a lot of books read, isn't it? It's philosophy studied, passions realised... it's light in the darkness, for fuck's sake. And who knows what will have happened by then? We're human; we're inventors, creators, and we can't be alone on the bloody planet. They'll find other people. Society might be functioning again by then, on some basic level. It won't be the answer to everything but being at Ledsey Cross with the right people will at least give them the best chance possible. Sorry about the rant.'

Sam smiled at her. 'How long do you think you've got, Vic?'

'Weeks,' she said without hesitation. Both the speed with which she answered and her answer itself took him by surprise. He had no reason to doubt her.

'Does Liz concur?'

'Yep.'

'And there's definitely nothing she can do to—'

'There's nothing,' she said, cutting across him. 'Look, Sam, my mind's made up. I'm leaving here. I'm off to Ledsey Cross and no one's going to stop me.'

DAY ONE HUNDRED AND FOURTEEN

David could smell smoke. He sat bolt upright in bed, stirred with a start from a deep, booze-assisted slumber. The lighting in his bedroom was all wrong, flickering orange, not blue-black. He got up too fast, tripping over the piles of clothes and other things he'd not yet unpacked, pulling on his trousers and shirt as he stumbled across the cluttered room. He felt nauseous. The house was still unfamiliar, and his head was spinning. He crashed downstairs, pulled on his boots and grabbed his jacket, then burst out into the cold of early Boxing Day morning.

One of the cottages at the far end of the road was on fire.

A crowd of people had already gathered outside the house. *Marcus's place*, he thought, and he could see him in the doorway, frantically passing his belongings to the handful of people who were actively assisting.

'How did it happen?' David asked, trying to squeeze into the line and help.

'No idea,' Ed said. 'Marcus is a sensible lad. He doesn't smoke, doesn't take stupid risks... I'm at a loss. He's a lucky bugger, though. If he hadn't woken up, he'd be a goner. It's a good thing Barbara was up and about. She saw the smoke and started hammering on the door until he answered. He was away with the fairies, by all accounts.'

Through the downstairs windows, David could see the fire rapidly taking hold. It was licking against the walls, billowing along low ceilings and jumping from room to room. He could feel the heat from here; the temperature inside must have been intense. He saw wallpaper turning to ash, peeling away from the plaster. Curtains and other furnishings caught light spontaneously, flames jumping through the parched air.

David realised he wasn't helping. He was just getting in the way. There were already more than enough people and a chain had been formed that stretched right the way across the street, passing Marcus's belongings from hand to hand to hand and piling them up a safe distance away.

Lisa had recently settled in another house nearby. On hearing the increasing noise, she got up and came out to help, but now found herself redundant like David. 'Shouldn't we try and put it out?' she asked.

'How? There's no running water. Short of passing buckets from person to person, I don't know how we're supposed to deal with something like this.'

'Makes you realise just how vulnerable we really are, doesn't it?'

'I think most of us realised that already.'

David had sobered up quickly. He walked around the corner, worried that other properties nearby might be at risk. Lisa followed him. Things looked immeasurably worse around the back, but other than to the empty house next-door, there didn't seem much danger of the fire spreading. 'How do you think it started?' she asked.

'No idea. Ed seems to think he's not the kind of lad to leave candles burning or anything like that. I mean, it might well have been an accident, but I reckon if—'

He stopped talking. 'What's wrong?' Lisa asked, concerned.

David didn't immediately answer. Instead, he walked through an open gate at the side of the burning house, into a rectangular garden. The inside of the building was an inferno. The heat kept him pushed back, but he could see sheets of flames in other rooms through the open back door.

'Ed said Marcus came out through the front of the house.'

'So?' Lisa asked, confused.

'So why isn't the gate locked? And why is the back open like this?'

'How am I supposed to know?'

'Think about it... it's the end of December, it's freezing cold, and none of us really have any kind of heating. There's no way he'd have left the back door wide open like that.'

'You think someone broke in? What would he have worth stealing? Bloody hell, you can just take what you want these days, no need to pinch from your neighbour; I'm surprised he bothered locking it at all.'

'You're missing the point.'

'Enlighten me.'

'I'm saying the fire could have been started deliberately. And before you say anything else, I realise exactly how crazy that sounds.'

'But why would anyone set Marcus's house on fire?'

'Beats me. You can't deny what we're seeing here, though.'

People began running past them. The house was still burning, but something else was happening elsewhere in the village that was clearly more of a concern. Sam sprinted past, then Ed, then a whole load of others. David and Lisa followed, though David struggled to match their speed. His mind raced as he ran through the twisting streets. That more of the dead had seen the fire and were advancing towards the village was the only logical explanation he could think of.

But he was wrong.

He was so very, very wrong.

Both the Amazon warehouses were on fire.

The blazes hadn't been burning long, that much was clear, but there was little question that the vast buildings were already lost. If they couldn't put out a relatively small house fire, what hope did they have of putting out these huge industrial units?

A crowd had gathered on the scrubland where Piotr's army had been defeated, the cratered land still heavily scarred from the grenade blasts. But the people here weren't interested in the debris of war, nor were they watching the fierce fires that grew

166

rapidly, lighting up everything. Instead, they were standing around a far more grotesque monument to the unimaginably awful world they now a part of.

Anthony Taylor's naked, lifeless, mutilated body hung skewered on a metal pole sunk deep into the ground at the centre of it all.

No matter how bad things had looked first thing, in the cold light of day they looked immeasurably worse. Apart from the two warehouses and the vast stores of equipment and supplies they'd contained, several streets full of houses had also been lost. Where yesterday there'd stood comfortable homes where people had begun reclaiming their lives, now there were just rows of blackened ruins. Burnt rafters left open to the elements. Charred walls with shattered windows and gaping black holes where their doors used to be. The dark skies over Yaxley were heavy with chugging clouds filled with noxious smoke.

'What he can't have, that fucker just destroys,' Ed said, and he kicked a chair across the floor of the village hall. The detritus from yesterday's Christmas dinner hadn't yet been cleaned up. The place was a pigsty. The party had been so completely engrossing that they'd left it last night and gone to their respective beds in good spirits. Now yesterday's celebrations felt inappropriate and premature. Stupid, even.

'We're completely sure it was Piotr?' Sanjay asked.

'Who else could it have been?'

'But we thought he was dead.'

'And we should have known better,' David said. 'It's been that fucker's modus operandi from day one. He puts everyone else in the firing line and stands back from it all, shouting orders. And like Ed says, if you've got something he wants, he'll destroy it in a heartbeat. If he can't have it, no one can. He's an evil, evil fucker.'

Ed's mind was racing. 'Okay, we need to think about this sensibly. We need to prioritise security. At the very least we should erect some kind of border around the centre of the village and keep it guarded.'

'I agree,' Chapman said.

'Don't over-react,' Sam warned. Chapman turned on him instantly.

'*Over-react*? What planet are you living on, you soft bastard? He could have killed all of us. He could have wiped this place off the map.'

'Yeah, but he didn't.'

'No, Sam, but he's taken out a major asset and left us afraid and vulnerable. We have to take the blame for this. We let our guard down and we let him do this to us. We should have made sure he was dead.'

'How?' Ruth asked. 'After the grenades you couldn't tell how many people had died or if they'd been alive or dead when we hit them. It was a mass of burned-up body parts. It's not like we can do DNA profiling or check dental records or anything like that anymore.'

'Someone moved the van, didn't they? Should have tipped us off, made us wary, but we were busy merrymaking, and he'd have guessed that or even seen it. We let Piotr go; he's still out there. We can't let anything like this happen again.'

'Again, assuming it *was* Piotr.'

'Oh, come on. Do you think there's anyone else who'd be so fucking twisted and spiteful?'

'I agree,' David said. 'Piotr's an awful fucker, alright, but he's not stupid. He planned this carefully. Other than Taylor, no one got hurt, did you realise that? He didn't randomly attack us; instead he attacked our ability to survive. He's done enough to permanently undermine our stability.'

'All's not lost,' Ed said. 'Sure, the warehouses are gone, but we'll still be able to get what we need from Peterborough. It'll just be a lot harder now, a lot less convenient.'

'And that's how we know it was Piotr. Like I said, this was deliberately engineered to cause us problems.'

'Doesn't matter. Chapman's right. We need to up our game and make sure the same thing doesn't happen again. If you're right about him, this could be his first step in a campaign of terror. He'll come back again, and next time, people will get hurt.'

'I'm not so sure...'

'What if it wasn't him? Clearly it was someone. We've been complacent, and I'm not prepared to take any more chances.'

'We'll get lookouts in place by this afternoon,' Chapman said. 'I'm not going to be asking for volunteers – everyone's going to be involved in this. We'll put a rota together. I'll get Georgie to organise it.'

'Agreed. Me and Marcus will go out herding later, start getting a decent number of corpses corralled. It's an idea we talked about early days but never progressed, and I think we need to look at it again.'

'What's that?'

'Surrounding the village with the dead. It should be enough to keep anybody out. I reckon a few thousand should do it, and there's probably still a hundred thousand or so left wandering around Peterborough.'

'Hold on, mate. Is this really the right answer?' Sam asked. 'Seriously? You'll keep the bad guy out, maybe, but you'll also keep us all in.'

'We'll leave some form of access, obviously.'

'I get that, but we're talking about one man and, potentially, a handful of other hangers-on. Don't you think a bloody moat of corpses is a bit of an overreaction?'

'Maybe, but I'm not prepared to take the risk.'

'There must be a better way? One that's less labour intensive? Putting fencing around this whole place and filling it with dead watchdogs? That's not going to be easy.'

'No one said it would be.'

'And once Piotr's gone, what then?'

'We maintain the defences. What else do you suggest? Are we supposed to just wait here like sitting ducks for the next self-proclaimed warlord to come along? Because there will be others, of that I've no doubt.'

Sam struggled to hide his frustration.

They were back to square one.

The positivity of the preceding weeks had been permanently shattered by Piotr's actions. A familiar, gut-churning anxiety had returned. For the briefest of moments, people had begun to think the worst was over, that the fighting was finished and the time for rebuilding had begun, but what had happened in Yaxley had tipped everything on its head again. Several days passed in a whirl: frantic planning sessions followed by hours and hours of graft. They fortified the village as best they could and began making preparations for encircling themselves with a ring of dead flesh as a deterrent. The temperature had dropped. It was markedly harder working in the fields. The fragile optimism that had been felt by the people in the village snuffed out like a spent candle. Even if they had a spark to relight it, they'd no longer be able to sustain the flame.

The living room of the cottage that Vicky, Selena, and Ruth shared was crowded with people tonight. Sam and Joanne were there, and David and Sanjay too. April and the girls from Stanstead. Noah. Ollie, Callum, and Mia from Brentwood. Orla, Liz, Lisa, Marcus... it was standing room only. This meeting hadn't been arranged; it had just happened. One conversation had led to another, then another. One person had spoken to someone else, who in turn had taken others into their confidence... It felt like a betrayal of sorts, but it was never intended as such. It was a group of disparate, frightened people who'd briefly dared to dream, but who'd since been brought crashing back to reality. There was no need for bravado, no need to worry about hurting feelings or causing offence.

'I'm sick,' Vicky said. 'Very sick. And I don't want to die in this place.'

Her comment silenced the already difficult conversation. How were they supposed to respond to that? Her illness was hardly a secret, but it had been something they'd only ever talked around rather than addressed head-on.

Sam cleared his throat. 'I understand that Vic, I really do. We just need to be realistic about what it's going to be like if we move on. I'm just playing devil's advocate here, alright? Despite what's happened, what we've got here in Yaxley is still pretty decent, all things considered. We're relatively comfortable, and even though we've lost the warehouses, there's still plenty of stuff nearby.'

'I know. What Ed and the others achieved here is remarkable, but I don't think it's enough.'

Ruth wasn't convinced. 'Would anywhere else be any better?'

'We can't know either way, can we.'

'It's a hell of a risk. We're talking about leaving all of this behind to go to a place you're not even sure exists.'

'I'm lost,' Mia said, confused. 'What place?'

'You've not heard about the fabled Ledsey Cross?'

'No.'

'Show her, Selena,' Vicky said, and Selena plugged in her phone and connected it to the TV they had set up in the corner. Sam had procured a portable solar-powered generator and various other bits of kit before the warehouse fire. They'd talked about watching movies together, but had quickly abandoned those plans. They'd begun *It's a Wonderful Life* Christmas afternoon, but it had almost ruined the party before it began. All that old films and TV programmes would do was remind them of what they'd lost.

Selena cycled through the photographs of Ledsey Cross that most of them had seen numerous times before. 'I still can't get my head around the fact they're out there,' Orla said. 'No matter how many times you show me these pictures or read me their messages, it still doesn't feel real.'

'I still don't follow,' Mia said.

'These pictures were taken after the apocalypse,' Vicky explained. 'They were sent to friend of mine and Selena's before the networks failed.' She gestured at the screen. 'That lady there is Annalise. Our friend Kath was in contact with her *after* everyone else had died.'

'But that's impossible.'

'Not impossible,' Sam said. 'Unlikely, but not impossible. I reacted the same way you just did when I first found out, but the evidence is there on Selena's phone.'

'It just doesn't seem real.'

'I know,' Vicky said. 'When I was with Kath and we were watching those messages coming through, I thought the same thing. But the proof's right here. While we were fighting just to stay alive in the middle of London, the people in Ledsey Cross who'd survived were living relatively normal lives.'

'For me, that's the draw of Ledsey Cross,' Orla said. 'It might all come to nothing, but the idea of being able to reclaim even a part of what we lost, well, I think that's priceless.'

'I know most of you have heard this before,' Vicky continued, 'but I made a promise to Kath to get Selena there. The village is remote, but not isolated. There's a single route in and out, and it's incredibly self-sufficient. We're talking running water, solar power, wind turbines, the lot.'

'I'm sold,' Noah said. 'When do we leave?'

'Seriously?' Sanjay said.

'Yes, absolutely.'

'It's in Yorkshire, you know; she didn't mention that. Hundreds of miles from here.'

'So much the better. Have you not noticed, Sanj, that the further we get from the southeast, the fewer bodies there are?'

'That's not always going to be the case,' Sam warned. 'I've been thinking about potential routes for as long as I've known about Ledsey Cross. Travelling north will be okay to a point, but sooner or later we'll hit trouble. Liverpool, Manchester, Huddersfield, Bradford, Sheffield, Leeds, Wakefield, York, Doncaster, Hull... if you look at a map of the country, there's a band of towns and cities stretching virtually from one coast to the other. It'll take some planning to find a safe route around them.'

'But it has to be worth the risk, right? If this place is as good as Vicky's saying?'

He nodded. 'I think so, and I'm keen to find out. If I'm being completely honest, I think I'll always regret it if we don't go up there and at least have a look.'

Liz shook her head. 'I'm sorry; I see your perspective, but I feel different. Much as I like the idea, there's no way we can risk uprooting everyone here. There are just too many of us. It's too much of a gamble. And if just a few of us were to go, then I still think I'd stay put. My job is to take care of people. I need to stay with the majority.'

'And I totally understand that, Liz,' Orla said.

'I feel the same,' April said. 'I'd love to go, but I can't justify taking that kind of a risk when I'm responsible for Emily and Isabelle.' She looked at the girls playing at her feet. 'Believe me, I'd love for them to be able to grow up somewhere well away from all this chaos, but that's a long journey and the roads are not safe. Maybe when you find this place, you'll come back and tell us about it?'

There was a lull in the conversation as people considered what they'd heard. 'Tell us what you're thinking, Dave,' Sam said.

He didn't answer immediately. Instead, he swirled the remains of the coffee in his mug, carefully considering his response. 'I think most of you know that I've never intended on settling anywhere other than home. I've made no secret of the fact that I intend to make my way to Ireland, though I'm not delusional. I know what I'll likely find when I get there.'

'So, are you in our out?' Vicky asked. 'Sounds to me like there's a few of us who are keen.'

He thought again. 'I'm in,' he eventually answered. 'Being here in Yaxley is infinitely better than it was in London, but it still feels like we're making do, even more so now that Piotr has fucked us over. I think a contingent of us should travel up to Ledsey Cross, see if it's as good as it looks, or whether it's another dead end. If it's the utopia you think, Vic, then provided the people there are in agreement; the Yaxley contingent should have the opportunity to rethink joining them.'

'And what about you?'

'It's on my way, isn't it. If I can make it there, I'll know I can make it back to Ireland. More to the point, staying here's an equal risk, maybe more so. I don't think we can afford not to go. Say I put my boot through that TV screen, Selena. What do you do?'

'Go and find another one, I guess,' she replied, confused.

'And if I put my boot through that one?'

'Then I'll ask you to stop coming around to our house.'

Light laughter circled the group. 'Good answer! But what if all the TVs are gone, what then? Or what about cars? We get a flat tyre right now and we can find a replacement, but what happens when we can't? Or when all the petrol has been used up or evaporated?'

'Electric cars?' she suggested. 'Scooters?'

'Different issues, same problems. You can see what I'm saying, can't you?'

'You've lost me completely,' Noah admitted.

'I'm saying that right now, we're suspended in a bit of a grace period. We're going to have to get used to living without all this stuff sooner or later, so why not start sooner? Selena, I hope with all my heart that you've got a long life ahead of you, and I think we owe it to you and the rest of you youngsters to give you the best possible start. From where I'm standing, I think that means leaving here and shooting for Ledsey Cross.'

31

DAY ONE HUNDRED AND EIGHTEEN

December thirtieth. There'd been some talk of waiting until the first of January, but what was the point? The dawn of a new year meant nothing anymore, if it ever really had. The arbitrary position of the planet in its journey around the sun today was of no more or less importance than its position this time last week or next. No one yet had any thought of abandoning the calendar altogether or starting again from Year Zero, nothing like that. It was still going to be important to keep track of the days, weeks, and months so they could use the seasons, as people always had, to keep themselves safe, warm, and fed. But as the events of last week had proved beyond doubt, for the most part, anniversaries and other previously significant dates counted for nothing anymore.

Sam had expected a uniformly negative response when they announced their intention to leave, but it wasn't as clear cut as that. Some people were quick to voice their opposition, while a handful of others wanted to come along, and many were as yet undecided. Some of the most vocal critics gave themselves away, the strength of their reactions saying much more about their own desires and insecurities than logical reasoning. Most of the villagers, though, were indifferent: they were already home, no need to search further. Sam was happy with that. Better to leave on good terms. He knew there was every chance they might be back here before long.

Vicky, Selena, Ruth, David, Sanjay, Orla, Joanne, and Lisa were a tight unit, having made it through the journey from the centre of London to Yaxley together. Omar was keen to go wherever Sam went. Other, newer recruits were also keen to come along:

Noah, Ollie, Mia, and Callum from Brentwood, none of whom felt like ready to put down roots and had no special attachment to the village. But the biggest surprise was Marcus. Ed was loath to lose his skills and experience, but he couldn't be persuaded to stay. Piotr had torched his house as a distraction. He'd lost everything the first time on that Tuesday morning in September, and after working so hard to rebuild some semblance of a life, he'd lost it all again in the fire last week. He felt the urge to move on; there was little anything keeping him here.

Thirteen adults, along with Omar and Selena (who felt like neither adults nor kids at times), were ready to set out. They took enough supplies to see them good for a few days and loaded everything into one of the army trucks. A handful would travel in the truck, the rest in a comfortable minibus they'd procured from a local dealership. Simon, a mechanic who'd originally lived in Peterborough, fitted the truck with a makeshift plough to help clear crap from the road.

As the last odds and ends were loaded up and people said their goodbyes, Sam walked over to speak to David. He was standing on his own, staring into the distance. 'Are we being really stupid here, Dave? Are we selfish or naïve or...?'

'No, absolutely not,' David said without hesitation. 'They don't need us here. Chapman and Ed will have this place running like clockwork between them.'

'Likely so.'

'And it's like we've already said, it doesn't have to be as final as it feels. If things don't work out, we come back. And if things do work out, they can come to us. Things are changing, I can feel it. The world's a blank sheet of paper today, Sam.'

'It certainly looks that way, I'll give you that.'

A dusting of snow had fallen during the night. Nothing too heavy, just enough to settle and leave a light covering over everything. It hid the ruination and made the world look deceptively peaceful and unspoilt.

'Should be a good day for travelling,' Ed said. 'Simon's given both vehicles a thorough check over. He's fuelled them up and left you with spares in case you hit any problems.'

David nodded. 'I appreciate it, Ed. And you mean *when* we hit problems.'

Ed laughed. 'Your words, mate. Just take it easy, won't you. The temperature's still dropping. I was out in the fields earlier; it's making quite a difference to the dead already.'

'How do you mean?'

'They're all seized up with the cold. It's like they're on a time delay.'

'That's good,' Sam said. 'It's what we hoped would happen. Their body temperature is ambient. If everything around them freezes, they should too.'

Ed agreed. 'A few degrees lower and they'll freeze solid. I reckon they'll shatter if you hit them.'

'Just when I think this world can't get any more surreal,' David said, smiling to himself. 'A year ago, they were normal folks like us. Now look at them.'

'Take advantage of the conditions, that's all I ask. They're constantly changing, and I wouldn't like to predict what's coming next.'

'Humour me and try,' David said. 'You've interacted with the dead more than anyone else I've come across. What do you think's going to happen?'

Ed hesitated. 'Nah. You'll take the piss if I tell you.'

'Go on then. I'm all ears.'

'It's hard to explain; it's more a feeling I have than anything else. All I know is I started by knocking seven shades of shit out of them in the early days, but I don't do that so much now.'

He stopped again, clearly uncertain.

'What happened to make you change your approach?' Sam asked.

Ed shrugged. 'This is the crazy part. When I showed them a bit of respect, they responded, seemed to, anyway. When I've been close to them recently, I've started to think that they're watching me as closely as I'm watching them. I think, mind you, this is only a guess, but I think they're starting to remember what they were. *Who* they were. It's like the panic's died down, and now they're looking for answers, just the same as we are.'

'I'd like to say that changes everything, but the hard truth is they'll be gone in a few months.'

'No doubt. But a lot can happen between now and then. Right now, they're all still operating individually, but imagine if they start to communicate. Imagine if they start to plan? Don't forget, we're still massively outnumbered.'

32

The desolation once they'd left the village felt never-ending. They'd been driving for hours, but it felt like days. The entire world appeared frozen, theirs the only signs of life. Occasionally they caught glimpses of the dead, but they were only glimpses, never anything more. Largely indistinguishable from their surroundings, the iced-up corpses juddered and shook when the vehicles passed, trying to turn to follow the noise, fighting a losing battle against the frost.

Other than its effect on the undead, the snow was another hindrance. The covering of unspoilt white disguised distances and camouflaged everything. Behind the wheel of the truck, Sanjay found it harder than expected to keep to the roads because they'd all but disappeared. He could no longer see the kerb and instead had to rely on the position of streetlamps and signs to help him make out the route. The plough helped, but to a very limited extent, clearing only directly in front of him. He drove at a far slower speed than he'd have liked. 'Maybe we should have left it a few more days,' he said, and he looked up into the heavy sky. The clouds were so low it was as if he could reach out of the cab and grab them.

'There was no point delaying this,' David said. 'We could have found enough excuses to put it off forever if we'd tried. No time like the present, you know? Leaving was the logical step.'

'I hope you're right,' he said, because he was far from sure that was the case. 'It's hardly been plain sailing so far. We had enough grief getting from London to Yaxley. We've got to go twice that distance again to get to Ledsey Cross.'

'We're not on foot though, are we. And we've made pretty good progress, according to the map. Anyway, we might not have to go that far.'

'Don't you think?'

'I'm not about to get into another argument with Vicky, but as far as I'm concerned, if we find somewhere closer that ticks all our boxes, we won't need to go all the way to Yorkshire. I'm worried how things will be when we get close to Manchester and Leeds. If we can stop before we get that far north, I'd be happy. Maybe head west, towards Wales?'

'You think she'll stand for that?'

'Being perfectly honest with you, Sanj, there's a part of me thinks she's not going to make it whatever. She's in a really bad way. Between us, I don't think she's got long left.'

It was easier to follow than to lead. Sam steered the minibus along the tracks left by the truck, scraped clear of snow and ice. Inside the minibus, it was alternately too quiet then too loud. It played havoc with Sam's concentration. The silence would get too much, too much space for him to think, then Omar would piss someone off in the back or say something he shouldn't, and the resulting noise would have him praying for quiet again.

Joanne sensed his frustration and did what she could to keep him occupied. 'I spy with my little eye, something beginning with S.'

'Snow,' he said without hesitation.

'Nope.'

'Sky.'

'Nope.'

'Sun?'

'You can't actually see the sun for the clouds.'

'No, but you still know it's there.'

'I know the bloody Swedish flag's out there too, don't I. Wrong answer.'

'I give up. I hate this game.'

'Signpost,' she said.

'Where?'

'Back there. And there's bound to be another one up ahead somewhere.'

'That's not how it works either.'

'Oh, so you hate the game but now you're going to argue about the rules? Poor loser, you.'

'I didn't lose. I quit. There's a difference.'

'Not from where I'm sitting.'

Joanne put her feet up on the dash and watched Sam. He felt her eyes on him but kept his gaze fixed firmly forward. 'Problem?'

'No problem,' she said. 'Just trying to work you out.'

'You can't. I'm an enigma.'

'You're an arsehole, I know that much.'

'Thanks. Anyway, we've got more important things to be worrying about than me.'

'Who said I was worrying?'

'What then?'

'Like I said, I'm just trying to work you out.'

'What for?'

'Because I like you, you know that. When we were back in John Kennedy Tower, you didn't say anything about what you'd done. It was only later, when I met Vicky, that she told me about you crashing your bus to give your friends a better chance of staying alive.'

'I don't like to go on about stuff like that,' he said, embarrassed.

'I can tell. And then I was talking to David once we'd got away from the Tower of London, and he was telling me about how you were this great eco-warrior.'

'Hardly.'

'It was something you were passionate about, though.'

'I can't deny that.'

'So now you've gone from *Save the Planet* to *Save the People*?'

'If you say so. Look, what's all this about? How would you feel if I started asking you loads of personal questions?'

'Pretty good, actually. I'd like us to get to know each other better.'

Sam struggled to stay focused. The conversation felt uncomfortable, unnatural. There'd been no time or desire for closeness and relationships since the world had fallen apart. Was it too soon? Should he respond or just try and force a change of subject? He'd always liked Joanne, but since they'd been able to spend those few quiet days together in Yaxley before Christmas, he'd started to wonder whether there might be a chance that the two of them could—

'Jesus Christ,' he said, and he wrenched the wheel hard left. Immediately ahead, Sanjay had swerved off the road. 'What the hell's he doing?'

'Concentrate, Sam,' Lisa shouted from the back. 'He was indicating. You just weren't watching. Too busy chatting up Joanne.'

Guilty as charged, he took the criticism on the chin. He said nothing, just put it down to tiredness and nerves. He needed to stop, and when he pulled up next to the truck and looked around, he realised that was what Sanjay had decided too.

They'd parked up outside a decent-sized pub. It looked like an ideal place to pause for a pitstop. There was a reassuring lack of snow-dusted, human-shaped mounds in the otherwise unspoilt carpark. A fuel station a couple hundred metres further down the road was a potential source of additional food and fuel. Perhaps they'd been serving breakfast at the pub; there were a handful of corpses at the windows, reacting to the engine noise. It was nothing they couldn't handle. Sam's stomach growled at the memory of a full English fry-up.

When the engines were switched off, other than the crunching of the ice under their boots, there was an all-consuming silence that suffocated everything. It felt fragile. No one wanted to be the one who disturbed it.

A semi-frozen cadaver dragged itself across the carpark painfully slowly, pivoting on inflexible legs. Ruth waited patiently then dealt with it with a single swift stab to the temple. Its pathetic resistance was on a time delay, barely able to lift an arm to block her attack.

'The sooner we get inside, the sooner we get warmed up,' David said. Joanne, Callum, and Selena climbed the steps to the entrance. Vicky half-heartedly tried to call Selena back but stopped herself. *You've got to let her do it.* She reminded herself that she wouldn't be around much longer to bail the kid out (not that she needed it, judging by the speed she was moving). Better that she got used to dealing with the dead in relatively one-sided situations like this. She lit a cigarette and leant back against the side of the minibus, watching the others at work.

Selena crashed through the pub door and the dead inside reacted as one to the sudden intrusion, their collective movements as stilted and awkward as the staccato corpse Ruth had just re-killed out in the carpark. Vicky couldn't make out what was happening inside, but it didn't matter because it was only a few seconds before Selena reappeared, dragging a body by its ankle down the steps, the back of its head cracking hard on every downward drop. She dumped it by a wheelie bin. Old habits die hard. Was she expecting a van from the council to come and clear things up?

Inside the freshly de-corpsified pub, people were already making themselves busy. The place looked like it had been recently refurbished. The fixtures and fittings were new but had been designed to look rustic and worn. There was a large fireplace at one end, and, after a quick inspection, they decided it looked safe to use. Marcus, who'd improbably worked as a steeplejack for a couple of weeks during his university gap year, checked the chimney was clear of blockages. There were curtains up at the windows and a reasonable supply of firewood. The potential for comfort made the risk of carbon monoxide poisoning seem inconsequential in the overall scheme of things. The heat and light from the fire and the supply of booze behind the bar would make the long night ahead infinitely more bearable.

The number of people inside the pub was already helping the temperature to climb. 'Okay, let's get some lights up in here,'

David said. 'And make sure all the windows are covered. We don't want any of those nosy undead buggers getting too close in the night now, do we?'

There wasn't much in the kitchen. Other than a few boxes of crisps and other bar snacks, everything else had spoiled or been eaten by vermin. There was plenty to drink but, for now, alcohol was being shunned in favour of tea and coffee. People were outside collecting snow and ice to boil up for water. 'Me and Sam will go and check what's at the fuel station,' Joanne said. 'There might be more food.'

'We've got a load of MREs from the barracks in the truck, remember,' Ruth said. 'They taste like shit but they're warm and filling.'

'Good shout,' David said. 'I'll go and get them in a minute.'

'Let's see what we can find before we resort to eating that muck,' Joanne said, and she followed Sam outside. He stopped at the edge of the carpark and looked back at the pub. 'Trouble?' she asked.

'Nope. Just wanted to see if we could see them from out here.' He watched the building intently for a few more moments. There were some glimpses of movement in the doorway, and a few flickers of light as the final windows were covered. There'd be smoke coming from the chimney soon, but there was nothing they could do about that. All in all, the group's occupation of the pub appeared largely undetectable from the outside. 'We're getting pretty good at this, don't you think?'

'I guess so.'

'If we're struggling to see anything, the dead definitely shouldn't be able to.'

'Maybe it's not the dead we should be so worried about.'

'Sorry?'

'Forget it. It won't matter if it carries on like this. It's bloody freezing out here. The temperature's really starting to drop again.'

Inside, the kiosk was untouched. 'Bingo!' Sam shouted with

excitement as he started clearing a shelf of Pot Noodles and cup-a-soups. 'Give me this kind of junk over that army shite any day.'

'Ace. What flavours you got?'

'Loads. There's bound to be more in the back too.'

They found a trolley in the stores and loaded it up. They struggled to get it through the door without making a noise, then remembered it didn't matter so much. Between the remoteness of their location and the iced-up condition of the dead, for once they could afford to take their chances.

It was almost completely dark now. 'When I was a kid and it snowed, the sky always used to go a weird colour,' Joanne said. 'Kind of a purple-orange, remember?'

'I remember.'

'Must have been the light of the cities reflecting off the snow. And now there's no light, there's no reflection. It's strange.'

'Everything's strange these days,' Sam said, shoving the rattling trolley wheels up a kerb. 'Feels like it's about midnight, but I bet it's not even six o'clock.'

'Doesn't bother me. I could sleep through 'til morning whatever. I'm exhausted but I've done nothing today.'

'You say that, but everything takes effort now, don't you think? We're all constantly on alert, waiting for the next thing to go wrong.'

'Pessimist.'

'Realist.'

'Whatever.'

Sam stopped walking. 'There you go. Listen to that. Someone's having grief.'

He could hear raised voices coming from inside the pub. Christ, a few minutes ago he'd been complimenting them on how well-organised and cooperative everyone seemed, and now it sounded like a full-blown row had kicked off.

'It's probably nothing. Probably just Selena mouthing off at Vicky as usual.'

Between them they lifted the trolley up the steps and wheeled it into the pub. Their entrance was largely ignored. There was a circle of people standing in one corner of the room. Concerned, Sam pushed his way through to the front. Sitting on a chair, surrounded, was Dominic Grove.

'Not again. How the fuck did he get here?' Sam demanded.

'Little fucker snuck himself away with the supplies in the back of the truck, stowed away like a bloody rat,' Ruth said. 'Fucking leech.'

'It's not like that—' Dominic started to say.

'Oh, really?' She turned to face the others. 'What are we doing listening to him? We should just throw him out. Leave him like he left us in London.'

'You don't understand...'

Ruth had had enough. She lunged for Dominic and grabbed him by the throat.

'Hang on! Calm down, Ruth,' David said, tugging gently at her elbow as Dominic grasped both her wrists. 'This isn't helping anyone. We're better than this – you're better than this. He's a lying, cowardly, two-faced, bullshitting little prick, but we're not going to stoop to his level.'

'Ruth!' Vicky called. 'Are you going to kill him here in the pub?'

Reluctantly, she let him go.

Dominic was crying now. He was a bedraggled, scrawny strip of the man he'd once been. 'How the mouthy have fallen,' David said. 'So, are you going to tell us what you're doing here?'

Dominic sniffed and wiped his eyes. 'I just want the same as you all do. I just want to live a better life.'

'Pass me a bucket, I think I'm going to throw up,' Sanjay said, unimpressed.

'I'm serious. I've made a lot of mistakes, I know I have. You know I was a politician, and I carried on, back in London, doing the exact same things I used to do before everyone died. I genuinely thought I could make a difference, but I was wrong. I just didn't want to admit I was wrong.'

'About what?' Orla asked. 'From where I'm standing you've got a list of fuckups as long as my arm. So, tell us, what is it exactly that you think you got wrong? Was it when you abandoned everyone and took the boat from the Tower, or are you finally realising you made mistakes before that too?'

He hesitated before replying, as if the words were stuck in his throat. 'I… I allowed myself to be bullied, you see? I was coerced. I know I should have stood up to Piotr, but you don't know what he was like.'

David laughed. 'Oh, we know all too well, thanks. It's thanks to him that we lost so many people.'

'I know! I know, and I understand that, I really do, but you only saw a fraction of what he was capable of. So much of his anger was directed at me, but I tried to keep it from showing.'

'This is priceless,' Ruth said. 'What do you want, Dom? A fucking medal?'

He shook his head. 'No! No, that's not… Look, I just want a chance. He killed Lynette, you know. Right in front of me. No hesitation. We were talking and… and he just threw her off the roof. I was terrified! What could I—'

'I've had enough of this shit,' Ruth said. She turned to face David. 'We need to get rid of this fucker once and for all. I'll do it. I'll kill him myself.'

'And what will that achieve?' Dominic asked. 'That'll make you just as bad as Piotr.'

'You're in no position to judge,' David said.

'And neither are you,' he immediately answered back, a little confidence returning. 'How many people did you kill to take back Yaxley?'

'We had no choice.'

'And I can tell you now, Piotr would have said exactly the same thing. I bet that's what he did say when he came back and set fire to the warehouses. It's all a matter of perspective, don't you see?'

His tears had quickly dried up.

'He's right,' Vicky said. 'Much as I hate to admit it, he has a point.'

'You can't be serious,' Sanjay said.

'I agree,' David said. 'I'm not proud of what we did, but I stand by it. The rules of the game are different now. We're not living in the same world we used to.'

'We have to do *something*.'

'Yes, but I'm not sure what. He's not coming with us, I know that much.'

'Please, David... don't do anything stupid,' Dominic said, sobbing miserably again. David ignored his pleas.

'Find a room with a lock and shut him in it. Just get him out of my sight. I need time to think about what we're going to do with him.'

33

David needed to stay alert, but having access to a fully stocked bar was a temptation he found impossible to resist. He allowed himself a couple of black spiced rums and Pepsi Max. The first drink went straight to his head. He decided that was a good thing. 'We have to be willing to take these little pleasures when they're offered to us,' he told Sanjay, Ruth, and Noah. 'It's important.'

'I completely agree,' said Noah, who was also comfortably drunk. He'd already indulged of his favourite tipple while no one else was looking.

'You both need to take it easy,' Sanjay warned. 'The last thing we need tonight is a full-scale piss-up.'

'Two drinks hardly constitutes a piss-up,' David said. 'We'll save the celebrations for when we get to Ledsey Cross.'

The mention of Ledsey Cross temporarily silenced the conversation. After a few seconds had passed, Noah cautiously asked a question. 'Are we really going to go all that way?'

'Yes,' Ruth answered without hesitation.

'Perhaps,' David corrected her. 'Hopefully,' he added.

Noah leant forward. 'Look, I apologise if I'm talking out of turn, but how much of this is for Vicky's benefit, and how much of it is a definite plan?'

'It's important to stay positive for Vicky,' David answered, 'but it's even more important to safeguard the future of everyone here and the folks we've left behind in Yaxley. I have every intention of trying to get to Ledsey Cross. It may well be the utopia she makes it out to be, but at the same time, if we find somewhere equally suitable on the way, I'd struggle to find a reason why we'd move on.' He looked at Ruth. 'You understand what I'm saying, don't you?'

She nodded. 'Yeah. I get it. I know how much it means to Vic, but I also know how ill she is. I feel better now we're on the move. Looking at her today, there's part of me thinks she won't make it anyway. She's in a bad, bad way.'

'And she doesn't need to know any different. As far as Vicky's concerned, we're going to Ledsey Cross and that's the end of it. We've got a route mapped out all the way. We stick to the major roads as far as we can go north, then cut east as soon as we've gone past Sheffield and Leeds. We'll pick up the River Wharfe and follow it where we can, because that'll take us into Heddlewick.'

'And that's the village that leads to Ledsey Cross?' Noah asked.

'That's it.'

'Sounds straightforward enough,' Sanjay said. 'So that inevitably means it's going to be anything but.'

Noah swirled his drink around his glass then asked another question. 'So, what happens if we make it up North and the people up there don't want to let us in?'

'They will,' Ruth said without hesitation. 'We've got a connection. Vicky's friend Kath's friend.'

'Okay. We're banking on the goodwill of a friend of a friend of a friend, then?'

'Something like that. What's your point?'

'My point is, if things have changed and they don't want us up there, what do we do? Are we just going to accept it and walk away, or do we take a leaf out of Piotr's book and fight our way inside?'

'Hang on – we're not like that,' Sanjay said, but Noah didn't look convinced.

'I'm not so sure. If it comes down to it, I think most people will do what they have to survive.'

34
DAY ONE HUNDRED AND NINETEEN
NEW YEAR'S EVE

They woke up to several inches of snow. The wintery world had looked strange yesterday, but it looked positively beautiful today. The thicker covering had obscured almost every detail outside, completely erasing, for the moment, every evidence of destruction and decay. A handful of cadavers had, by chance, discovered the group's pub hideout and had made an advance towards it, but the worsening cold had stopped them. Now they stood in the carpark, converging on the building like a gang, all of them frozen mid-step. Snow covered and unable to move, they were like grotesque Christmas decorations, something left for them by Krampus.

Joanne reluctantly sat up, not wanting to get out from under the covers. Sam handed her a mug of coffee and some food. She hadn't cleared away the cutlery and crockery they'd used last night. 'I can't get used to not washing up,' she said. He just looked at her.

'Wait... the world is dead, the streets are filled with walking corpses, and you're freaked out by a bit of dirty crockery?'

'Yeah. Weird, isn't it? It's the fact it doesn't matter anymore. We'll leave this place today and never come back. More to the point, no one will ever come back here. That's the part that freaks me out. It makes me feel insignificant like you wouldn't believe.'

'For what it's worth, I do understand. I went outside for a piss just now, and there was no sign of anyone. Not even any sign of *us*. All our tracks from last night have been covered up and the truck and the van look the same as everything else. It's the strangest feeling. It's like we don't exist anymore.'

They were ready to get on the road again within a couple of hours. The vehicles had been dug out, refuelled from other stationary wrecks, and loaded up. 'We all set?' David asked. His question was met with a few grunted replies and zero enthusiasm. 'Just one thing left to do.'

'Are you sure about this?' Ruth asked.

'I'm sure.'

'It's the most sensible option,' Sam said. 'You get the engines going. I'll go do the deed.'

'Thanks, mate,' David said. He climbed up into the cab of the truck next to Sanjay. Ruth started the engine of the minibus. The combined noise of the two vehicles shattered the tranquillity of the unspoilt winter morning. An immobile, snow-covered corpse did all that it could to react to the ugly noise. It managed to raise its right arm a few centimetres and twist its neck towards the truck slightly, but it otherwise remained frozen to the spot.

'If we got enough speed up and drove straight at it,' Sanjay said, watching with fascination as it struggled against the cold, 'I reckon it would just shatter.'

Alone, Sam returned to the pub. He walked through the detritus of their overnight stay, his footsteps sounding disproportionately heavy on the floorboards. Nights like last night, where they'd been relatively comfortable and had felt unusually safe, gave him a little hope for the future, but there was always a caveat. He could already hear Dominic screaming for someone to come and let him out.

There was still a little residual warmth in the main part of the pub from all their activity, but the office at the end of the short corridor was as bitter as outside. They'd locked the door with a key they'd found in the pocket of a corpse behind the bar, and someone had shoved the back of a chair under the handle, just to be sure he wouldn't get out. Sam paused and took a breath, feeling uneasy.

No point putting it off. Just got to get this done.

He moved the chair, turned the key, and opened up.

'Thank Christ for that,' Dominic said, tears of relief prickling his eyes. He looked like he'd hardly slept. 'I heard the engines. I thought you were going without me.'

'We are.'

Sam was blocking the doorway, no way out. He took his knife from his belt and Dominic recoiled, squirming in his chair. 'Please, Sam, don't... you don't need to do anything you might regret.'

'Jesus Christ, after everything you've done, you have the audacity to tell me what I should or shouldn't do? You're an absolute fucking joke.'

'I know,' he said, sobbing freely now, but unable to wipe his eyes because his hands were bound to the back of the chair. 'I know what I've done, but I don't deserve to die. Killing me will make you no better than Piotr.'

Sam gripped his knife tight. There was something about Dominic's tone that wound Sam up. He could almost see the cogs turning in the odious little fucker's head, could hear the spin-generating machine cranking up, ready to start spewing his usual word-twisting bullshit and help him worm his way out of a situation entirely of his own making. It was the insincerity that stung Sam more than anything – the blatant bluster and the ease with which the excuses just dripped off his tongue. Dominic Grove never showed any remorse or contrition. He'd just pile on layer after layer of off-the-cuff defences, flinging endless fistfuls of shit at the wall until enough stuck. Sam had had enough.

'I am better than Piotr,' he said, 'and I'm better than you, too. I didn't come here to kill you, Dominic, I came here to let you go.'

'Thank you, thank you,' he said with something approaching genuine relief. 'You're doing the right thing.'

'But, like I said, you're not coming with us. You're on your own now, pal.'

Sam leant over Dominic and slashed the plastic cable ties they'd used to bind his wrists behind him. He turned to leave, and

Dominic ran after him and grabbed his shoulder. Sam span around, his knife still drawn.

'I don't want to hurt you,' he warned, 'but I will if I have to.'

Sam's brutal honesty was in direct contrast to Dominic's effusive, empty words. Dominic was in no doubt he meant it. Sam shoved him away, pushing him back into the office.

'Please, Sam...'

'You listen to me, Dominic. The people in those vehicles out there are all I've got left. There were hundreds in London, but thanks to you and Piotr, their numbers have gone down and down again. I can't risk having you around anymore. There's everything you need here. We've left you some food, and there are rooms upstairs we've hardly touched. Make yourself comfortable. Spend the rest of your days here if that works for you. Just make sure you stay out of my life and out of the lives of the people I care about.'

35

The weather was both a blessing and a curse. The effects of the cold on the remaining undead population were welcome, making them easier to spot and therefore avoid (as well as stripping them of their ability to attack), but the snow made driving a challenge, even with the makeshift plough welded to the front of the truck. They'd done well to keep moving at a steady speed for several hours, but it was hard going. The conditions were changing. The clouds had gradually disappeared, and the sun had emerged at the least opportune moment. The glare was unrelenting. Sanjay had one hand on the wheel, the other covering his eyes. 'Forgot to pack my sunglasses,' he mumbled without irony.

David was focussed on the paper maps he'd been carrying since leaving Yaxley. He'd followed their progress carefully all morning because the maps didn't just tell him where they needed to go, they also showed where they'd been. He kept a note of the time it took them to cover each section of road and scribbled calculations on a scrap of paper, keen to work out how long the rest of the journey would take. 'We'll be close to Doncaster before long,' he said. 'That's proper North, that is. You know, we might just do this.'

'Think we'll get to Ledsey Cross today?'

'No way. Tomorrow, though, hopefully.'

'Famous last words,' Sanjay said as he slowed the truck down. David looked up from his map, shielding his eyes from the sun. He could tell from the mountain range of snow-covered, angular humps and bumps that the road ahead was blocked across its entire width. It wasn't the first time they'd had to deal with such problems, and it almost certainly wouldn't be the last. When they

197

stopped, David got out of the truck. Sam and Lisa joined him out in the road. The snow was beginning to thaw, turning to watery grey slush under their boots.

'What do you reckon?' Lisa asked.

'We need to find a way through. We haven't passed a turning in miles, so it's going to be a hell of a long diversion if we have to go back on ourselves and look for another way.'

Long, impenetrable shadows made it hard to work out where one vehicle ended and the next began. The brick-like shape of the colossal, ice-covered relic immediately ahead of them was easy to discern. It was a bus, that much was obvious, but it had stopped diagonally across the road, and it wasn't immediately clear which way it was facing. There was another car pinned between the nearest end of the bus and the barrier that ran along the side of the road.

The bus obscured the view. Sam tried to look over the roof of the car. 'Can't see much from here.'

Lisa crouched down and peered under the chassis, checking for debris. 'We should be able to move it, I think. There's nothing behind. I reckon if we use the truck to push this car back and steer it out of the way, we should be okay to get through.'

'Okay.'

'But there is one problem.'

'What's that?'

'There's a load of bodies on the other side of that bus. Looks like they've drifted here over time and not been able to get away again.'

'Frozen?'

'Some of them. I definitely saw some movement, but it's hard to see how many are free.'

There was little resistance in the ranks. 'We knew what we were signing up for,' Mia said. 'If we'd wanted an easy ride, we'd have stayed in Yaxley.'

Sanjay was ready to push the car out of the way with the truck.

The rest of the group, all but Ruth, Vicky, and Omar, who remained in the minibus, were ready to deal with the repercussions. They'd planned their next move as carefully as they could, but there remained countless unknown variables. Once Sanjay had moved the crashed car, what then? Would the rest of the road ahead be clear? What about the bodies? How many were there, and in what condition?

Sanjay stared into the space but hesitated before re-starting the truck's engine. No matter what condition they'd been reduced to, the prospect of any close encounters with the undead still made him unbearably nervous. The sight of everyone else in the wing-mirrors added to his unease. They were all out in the road, tooled-up. It reminded him of that first morning in Wapping when they'd gone face-to-face against the dead by order of Piotr and Dominic, and though most people had survived that day, in his mind that battle in the streets had marked the beginning of the end for the Monument group. Sam slapped the side of the truck and signalled for him to focus and get on with it.

When he turned the key, the engine immediately roared back into life, and he imagined the dead trapped behind the bus beginning to shake off their frozen bonds. Sanjay edged forward, the plough scraping against the barrier at the side of the road. He immediately course-corrected, but there was barely any margin for error. It unnerved him. *Can I get through that gap? Am I really going to be able to shift that car?*

No time to worry about it now as the plough crunched into the car. For a few stomach-churning seconds it didn't feel like the wreck was going to budge, that it was wedged in too tightly, but with a short, controlled burst of power, Sanjay managed to force it back. He reversed, then accelerated into it again, a little faster, a little more confident. And then he was through.

He'd been warned about the bodies on the other side of the beached bus, but he hadn't been ready for them to look like this. It was as if he'd driven into a forest of branchless, snow-covered tree stumps, all of them planted in random positions across the carriageway. He fought against the urge to steer around them and instead drove straight, cutting a path through to a clearer section of road up ahead. He cursed himself for getting so wound up about nothing. In their petrified state, the dead were no threat at all.

But not all of them were frozen.

From a distance, the corpses had looked like pieces on a chessboard that had been abandoned mid-game. On the edges, where there'd been no protection from the icy winds, they were still locked in position. Towards the centre, though, they'd been shielded from the worst of the weather. Those cadavers had slightly more freedom of movement, and the engine noises had given them the impetus to try to break free and attack.

'I thought this might happen,' David said, holding a heavy wrench he was ready to use as a weapon. 'Just get rid of the fuckers before they start getting frisky.'

He led the one-sided charge and was encouraged when he looked back and saw that everyone was fighting. There were no exceptions, no excuses. Hardened combatants like Sam, Joanne, Orla, Selena, and Lisa were hacking down the semi-frozen monsters with ease. Other, less experienced members of the group were also doing what they could. Mia, Callum, and Ollie had spent more time avoiding trouble than waging war. Noah was even less adept at fighting. He gingerly swung the wooden baton he was carrying in a wide arc as though driving downrange and took out the legs of the two cadavers nearest to him. Another one was desperate to lunge at him, managing, in its silent fury, to lift its feet and break the glue-like layer of frost that had until then been preventing it from attacking. His confidence increasing by the second, Noah destroyed the staggering cadaver with single a brutal swipe to the head that ripped the thing's jaw from its socket.

More of the dead were beginning to move now, the increased activity around them providing them with the impetus to fight back. Orla had an ice-axe she'd acquired while they'd been in

Yaxley. She moved from dead body to dead body, hammering the spike into each skull in turn, clinical and efficient. 'Wish they were like this all the time,' she said between re-kills, panting with effort.

'It's easier than I thought it'd be,' Noah said.

'I know, man,' Ollie agreed. 'Where's the challenge?'

'Yeah, I don't want a challenge. I just want a rest. I'm getting too old for all this.'

For some of the group, this sudden frenzy of one-sided violence was clearly cathartic, and there were still plenty of pickings to be had. Deeper into the largely motionless crowd, it was as if the corpses were being defrosted by the energy of battle. More of them were breaking free from their icy bonds, juddering and shuddering in a way that was eerily reminiscent of their initial unnatural reanimation last September. The increase in undead movement was unsettling. There seemed to be hundreds of them still. It was beginning to feel like a race against time to get through them.

This was a strangely subdued massacre.

Other than the regular grunts of effort and the occasional shouts of warning and encouragement, the fighting was quiet. The living went about their work with a cool efficiency and the dead took their punishment without protest. David watched his people work with pride. Even the least experienced of them moved rhythmically from corpse to corpse now, hacking them down and barely blinking an eye, hardly pausing for breath. They'd done enough, but they kept fighting, making sure that every last cadaver was permanently incapacitated, no matter how small the individual threat it posed. 'That's us finished,' he finally shouted. 'Let's get back on the road.'

36

He'd hardly ventured out of the pub all day, only to empty the bucket he'd been using for a toilet, and even then, only for the absolute minimum amount of time he needed to be outside. Dominic was a social animal, a real 'people person', always had been. He still craved human contact (despite the number of humans having been reduced to little more than zero) and this isolation was unsettling. The thought of having no one but himself to hear the constant stream of words he still spoke aloud was depressing, but he didn't see how things were going to change anytime soon. He thought, and told himself, that he'd better try and get used to it. It was a comfortable enough place, with enough food and drink to see him through several weeks, maybe even longer if he was especially frugal. He'd dragged down a mattress from upstairs and set it up by the hearth, and he'd used the dying embers of last night's blaze to restart the fire. There were plenty of wooden tables and chairs he could smash up and burn, and he was confident he'd find other fuel sources outside, if he looked hard enough.

'All in all,' he said, 'I've got off quite lightly. There are far worse places to be stranded on one's own.'

Except he wasn't completely alone, was he?

There was that crowd in the carpark, for starters.

They remained frozen in position for now, but they wouldn't stay that way for long. He'd been fixated on one of them in particular. The frost had kept its feet fused to the ground, but he swore, as the day had worn on, it had changed position. It had been looking the other way first thing, staring out into the distance at nothing, but now it had swivelled its torso around, though its feet remained planted ahead, and was staring straight into the pub. Its icy eyes were fixed on the window where he'd been standing, watching it watching him. *Horrible bloody thing.* He knew it made sense to go out there and get rid of them before they regained full mobility. He'd got as far as arming himself with a knife from the kitchen, but he hadn't yet plucked up the courage to go and do the deed. Maybe he'd leave it for today. It would surely be cold again tonight, more than likely dropping below zero. Probably best to leave it until the morning.

It was going to be strange having to do everything for himself, though he comforted himself that it would probably only be short-term. Once the dead were properly dead, he'd leave here and see who else he could find. He had the benefit of a public image that would likely serve him well for another couple of years at least.

Okay, so politicians didn't win popularity contests, 'Other than the ones that originally propel one into office, of course,' he laughed. But whomever he came across in this strange new world would likely have heard of him, even if they didn't recognise his face. His pre-apocalypse fame would enable him to get a foot in the door with most any group he came across from hereon in. 'And a foot in the door is all I'll need, isn't it.' Because even now, once he was in front of an audience, they would be putty in his hands. He knew beyond any doubt that he still had the gift of the gab because here he was, doing a number on himself. The thought made him happy. He was on his own, miles from anywhere, at the mercy of both the elements and the dead, and yet he was still managing to convince himself that everything was rosy.

He stoked the fire, poured himself a drink, then picked up a trashy novel he'd found in an upstairs room and started to read. He'd also found some paper and pens. Maybe he'd write his memoirs while he waited here for the dead to reduce to mush? He remembered a conversation he'd had long ago with Stan, of all people, about him cementing his position in the history books. 'Maybe I'll just write those history books myself?' At least that would guarantee he'd be painted in a flattering light. For now, though, all he'd written down was the useful info he could remember from the conversations he'd overheard last night. *Cutting cross-country once they'd passed Leeds, following the River Wharfe, aiming for Heddlewick and the road to Ledsey Cross...*

It was hard to believe the others had still been banging on about the bloody legendary Ledsey Cross. He thought they'd have given up on that futile daydream by now. Then again, truth be told, if he had either the means or the inclination, he'd be tempted to check the place out for himself. 'Locals there would probably welcome someone with the kind of leadership experience I could offer.'

Dominic became unexpectedly misty-eyed over a copy of the last edition of the *Daily Mail* ever printed. He'd been about to tear it into strips to use as firelighters when a wave of nostalgia had washed over him. He read it from cover to cover then folded it carefully and put it in his bag. Even after all he'd been through, he'd still managed to hold onto a few precious mementos of his life before the end of the world. His laminated parliamentary pass. A photo of him and some random royal at the opening of something or other, he couldn't remember what or where. He'd taken them as souvenirs when he'd left his office in Westminster for the final time, not fully realising then the extent to which they'd likely become important historic documents; crucial evidence of the world before this one that had been ended in a single morning without warning or explanation.

It was a clear run between the door of the pub and the petrol station. Much as he wanted to stay indoors, he'd been thinking all day that he should probably go and check the place out. He'd find plenty of useful stuff there, of that he was certain. And the sooner he did it, the sooner he'd be able to properly shut himself away in here, *and doing that*, he reminded himself, *is key to our survival.* He didn't want to fall into the same trap as they had in London and make so much noise trying to stay alive that it attracted the attention of hordes of the undead.

Petrol stations usually sold barbecue stuff, didn't they? They'd have probably had wood and firelighters on display on the forecourt last September, so he might not even have to go inside the building. He'd lose the light in the next couple of hours, so if he was going to do it, he needed to do it sooner rather than later.

'Get a grip, old boy,' he said to himself. *You can do this*!

He wrapped himself up in as many mismatched layers of clothing as he could find and took a single hesitant step outside. The temperature was icy cold – much lower than his new home in the pub – and it chilled him to the bone. But the world out here was reassuringly silent, so he shoved his hands deep into his pockets and half-walked, half-ran across the carpark.

Someone came at him from out of nowhere. His first instinct was that it was one of the dead, but when he realised he'd been rugby tackled by a big fucker who weighed many times what even the heaviest corpse did these days, he knew he was really in trouble.

Winded, he lay on his back in the slushy snow and looked up into the darkening sky. A familiar face leered over him and grinned. 'Well fuck me,' said Piotr. 'Dominic fucking Grove as I live and breathe. What's a snivelling little prick like you doing out on his own in a place like this?'

205

37

There were another three of them along for the ride with Piotr. They were his driver from London, Alfonso Morterero, Harjinder, and a woman from Yaxley called Kelly whom Dominic hadn't seen before. He recognised the van they'd turned up in – it was the same one he'd arrived at Yaxley in with Sam, Vicky and the others. When they'd first found him, Piotr had threatened to kill him, but Dominic had so far managed to persuade them he was more useful alive, though he sensed it wouldn't take much to make Piotr go back on his decision.

They were inside the pub now, soaking up the heat from his fire and plundering his supplies. They'd already hit the booze. Dominic resolved to stick to soft drinks. He needed to stay in control.

'So, where did you disappear to, you slippery little bugger?'

'I lost you in the madness at Stansted. I tried to find you, but you remember what it was like there. Me and Stan got separated from the rest of you, so we just laid low. The others came through a few days later and we managed to get ourselves picked up. We didn't get to Yaxley until after all the trouble had blown over. Didn't find out what they'd done until way after the event, otherwise I'd have done what I could to help.'

'Sure you would've,' Harjinder said, watching from a distance.

Piotr remained unimpressed. 'None of that explains why you're out here. Did you think you'd just strike out on your own? You've never struck me as a lone survivor type of guy.'

Dominic's throat was dry as a desert. He took a sip of his lemonade. It was only when he lifted the glass to his lips that he realised just how badly his hands were shaking. *How do I spin my way out of this one?* 'I saw what you did there at Christmas. I saw what you did to Taylor.'

'And?'

'And I'll be completely honest, I didn't think it was going to stop there.'

'So you decided you'd get out before it got nasty?'

'It was already nasty enough, Piotr, but yes. I could see things getting a lot worse, and if I'm honest, I didn't want to hang around for the afterparty.'

'But it still don't add up. You always take the easy option, Dominic. You wouldn't have left on your own, would you?'

Dominic hesitated again, thinking through his options, trying to find the least worst way of describing what had happened over the last twenty-four hours. 'A group of them left Yaxley. They're off hunting for the mystical Ledsey Cross, wouldn't you know. I stowed away in their truck, and they were none too pleased when they found me.'

Piotr laughed. 'Yeah, I can imagine. Who was it? Shires and his usual playmates.'

'That's right.'

'And they left you out here on your own to freeze? Poor little Dominic.'

'I'm doing alright for myself, thanks very much.'

'Yeah, whatever.'

Dominic was beginning to feel a little more confident. 'So why are you here, Piotr? They're fortifying their village because they think you'll be back.'

'Why would I go back there? There's nothing left. I set fire to it all,' he said, unemotional.

'But they killed so many of your people. I thought you'd want revenge.'

Piotr shrugged. 'You've got me down all wrong, Dom.'

'So, why are you *here*?'

'We found their tracks and followed them till the snow got too heavy last night. Figured they wouldn't have left unless they thought there was something worth leaving for. If money counted for anything these days, I'd stake everything I had on them going to Ledsey Cross.'

'Doesn't take a rocket scientist to the work that out. But they're long gone. They left hours ago. How did you find me? Was it luck, or are you just very good at finding needles in haystacks?'

Harjinder waved a brick-like gadget at him. 'Thermal imaging camera. Picks up body heat. Grabbed it from the warehouse before we torched it. You'd be surprised how much you can see when the rest of the world is ice cold.'

'And I'm supposed to believe you just happened to be driving past and you spotted me with that?'

'Credit me with a little intelligence,' Piotr said. 'I was sure they'd head north. We got back on the road first thing and just kept following the same route. I'll be honest, though, I didn't expect to find you. I wondered where you'd disappeared to, you slippery little fuck.'

'Why go to so much trouble to track them down?'

Piotr shrugged. 'I thought it would be a good opportunity to catch up with my old friends, say hello, maybe knock back a couple.'

'So, basically, you feel you owe them a beating.'

'You're surprised?'

'Is this what your life has become? Settling scores?'

'You disapprove?'

Dominic back-pedalled furiously. 'I didn't say that, it's just...'

'Just what then?'

'Just that the whole world is yours for the taking. Why are you so interested in what that pissant group do now? They're just a bunch of nobodies. There's only a handful of them left out here anyway.'

'But you took a chance on them.'

'That was different.'

'Was it? How? We both have to admit, no matter what we think of Shires and his pals, they're good at staying alive. Even if they don't get all the way to Ledsey Cross, I expect whoever's left will have a plan and they'll get themselves set up somewhere decent. Wherever it is, whatever they make of it, I will take it from them.'

'And what about me?'

'What about you? I could just leave you here to rot.'

'But we've always got on alright, haven't we? We achieved great things together, you and me, remember?'

'Oh, I remember. I just can't recall what it was that you brought to the party.'

'Don't be like that,' Dominic said. 'All of the work we did to build the base around the Monument and reclaim the land, build up security, those ideas came from me.'

'The bullshit came from you, yes, but it was me and my people that made it happen. And as it turned out, your ideas were pretty shitty, don't you think? All you did was design us a massive prison cell.'

Dominic didn't argue. He knew that wouldn't have helped. For all his bluster, he also knew that, on some level, his intelligence and ability to communicate intimidated Piotr. But he could talk his way out of this mess, he knew he could.

'I think you need me.'

Piotr laughed. 'I don't think anybody ever needed you.'

A pause. Dominic waited, letting the tension and expectation build. 'I can help you.'

'Yeah, right. Because you've been so helpful so far. Fucking idiot.'

'No, I'm serious. I was stuck in here with them all last night. They, er, locked me in the office.'

'Looks like they'd had enough of him too, boss,' Harjinder said. Piotr ignored him.

'So what?'

'I heard all kinds of stuff,' Dominic said. 'Where they're going.'

'We've already established that.'

'I know the routes they're taking.'

'So, tell me.'

Dominic's heart was pounding, but he'd been in tighter spots

209

than this. Having this thug threaten him was nothing compared to the pressure of a live TV interview straight after another government U-turn; having to parrot the correct lie whilst knowing there were hundreds of thousands of people listening to your every word. 'No,' he said.

Piotr smacked him in the face. It stung like a bitch, but Dominic didn't budge.

'Tell me.'

'No.'

Another smack. While he was unsighted, Piotr nodded to Harjinder who grabbed Dominic's hand and flattened it against a table, then raised a hammer above it, ready to break every bone.

'How long do you think you'll last out here with one hand?' Piotr snarled.

'About as long as you'll last going around in circles trying to find them,' Dominic said, spitting blood. 'Go on, Harj, do it. I'm not talking.'

He prayed that Piotr would see sense, well aware that he was counting on the goodwill of someone who'd literally crucified the last person who'd crossed him. But his fingers remained intact, and the hammer hadn't fallen. Yet.

'We're wasting our time,' Harjinder said.

Dominic swallowed hard and shook his head. 'Here's the deal – you take me with you, and I'll help you find them. Then, when you've sorted them out, I'll get you to Ledsey Cross.'

'Ledsey fucking Cross...'

'I know what we've both said about that place in the past, but they wouldn't be going if they didn't think it exists and is worth the effort. Just stop and think about it. It could all be yours.'

'And what's in it for you?'

'I'm a changed man. I just want an easy life. I'll get you there, then I'll disappear. I'll stay well out of the way and keep my mouth shut.'

'That'll be a first.'

Kelly tapped Piotr's arm. 'It's not a bad idea. It's freezing out here. If we don't use him, it'll take us an age to get anywhere.'

'He might be lying.'

'I'm not,' Dominic said, nervously watching the hammer poised over his hand. 'I could tell you anything, send you off in whatever direction I choose then run the other way. But if you take me with you, I've got to get you to the right place, haven't I? I'd be an idiot to risk double-crossing you.'

The room was still and silent as Piotr considered his options. Harjinder waited for his cue, keen to exert a little violence and break the deadlock.

It was rare for Alfonso to offer an opinion, but he cleared his throat and risked speaking. 'I know you, Piotr; as long as Shires and Vicky and the others are out there, it'll be like an itch you'll never be able to scratch. We can get rid of them for good, and at the same time guarantee a decent outcome for us.'

Piotr thought for a moment longer. 'You're right. Grab anything useful you can find here. We're leaving.'

'What, now?' Dominic said, surprised. *Relieved*. 'But it's getting dark out there.'

Piotr laughed at him. 'You really are a useless little prick. Are you scared? The temperature's dropping again so the dead won't be an issue, and we saw tracks leading away from here. We'll follow them as far as we can, then you can make sure we keep heading in the right direction.'

'Okay.'

'But listen to me, Dominic. You mess with me, and I'll find the biggest crowd of dead bodies you've ever seen, I'll fire them up, then I'll have Harj here break all your fingers and your knees and leave you on your own right in the middle of them. Understand?'

'Completely.'

38

In the short days and long nights of late December in the UK, daylight was at a premium. The uncertainty about what they'd come across in the miles ahead compounded their reluctance to take unnecessary risks. Though they'd likely have at least another hour of light ahead of them, the road they were following would soon pass between Pontefract and Knottingley, two reasonably large centres of population. There'd been unanimous agreement within the group that stopping and making camp sooner rather than later was preferable to pushing on and risking getting stuck near the two towns. Better to wait until morning, then make the final push to Ledsey Cross.

But Christ, even after so many weeks and months had passed, even out here in the middle of nowhere, the awful sights they uncovered were still occasionally so horrible that they were almost impossible to take in. They'd found a building that had appeared perfect for the night: isolated and protected by a tall border fence all round. The remaining frost and snow had masked its original purpose, and it was only when Sam and Joanne broke in to take a look around that they realised where they were. It had been a boarding kennel, and the two of them walked in silence along row after row of the furry, frozen husks of never collected family pets. Joanne had seen so much death over the months that she thought she'd become immune to such pain, but there was something about seeing all those helpless animals, imagining each of them dying terrified and alone, that cut her to the core. She could hardly speak. Between them, she and Sam said just enough to stop anyone else going inside to check.

A mile further down the road was a garden centre. The entrance to the building at the hub of the site was at the end of a long, sloping driveway, and they left the vehicles up on the flat. They already had enough to do tomorrow without having to dig out the truck and minibus, if it snowed again. The temperature had dropped with the disappearance of the sun, and even a heavy frost would leave them struggling to get back up the incline. They could already hear the part-thawed slush cracking and popping as it began to freeze.

This place was a much better find. It was disorientating to see ice-covered summer displays outside: rows of dead summer plants buried under snow, garden sheds and outdoor furniture hidden under mounds of white. 'I keep forgetting,' Sanjay said to no one in particular. 'Our clock's still ticking, but everyone else's stopped last September.'

They huddled together in the heart of the spacious, brick-built store at the centre of the site. They took supplies from a small café, then collected snow for drinking water and boiled it up on gas stoves they found in an outdoor living section. Though it took an age for all eighteen of them to be fed and watered, they all had hot drinks and decent, not-entirely unpalatable, dehydrated food. Chocolate and other snacks kept the energy levels up.

'We're whispering,' Noah said. 'Why are we always whispering these days?'

'We sound loud because everything else is so quiet,' Orla suggested. 'You're right though. There's no need while it's so cold.'

'It's been months, but it still feels strange to have to be so quiet,' Lisa said.

'It's not natural,' Vicky agreed.

'We'll get used to it,' David said.

Lisa wasn't so sure. 'Is that what we want?'

'I could put some music on,' Selena said, already fishing in her rucksack.

Sanjay looked worried. 'Bit risky, don't you think?'

'Not so much while the dead are still frozen,' David said, and

Selena took his comment as tacit approval. She whipped out a phone from the selection she carried, then rummaged deeper for a portable speaker and a power block.

'This is solar,' she said, briefly waving it at him as she worked. 'Got it from the warehouse.'

David watched her sorting the various connections with the kind of impressive digital dexterity that he'd never possessed. He wondered how long those skills would remain intact? For how long would there be technology like this left to use? It was odd to think that the human race had reached the peak of its technical abilities and was now on the most rapid of declines. The song Selena started to play – not as loud as he'd expected, and not as awful either – was enough of a distraction to take his mind off everything for a moment.

Vicky looked exhausted, her cheeks sunken and hollow. She looked around the room, soaking up the music and the moment, and her thoughts turned to all the many people they'd lost along the way. She stopped herself and instead forced her mind to focus on those who were still here. This group of people, formed and reformed from other groups and sub-groups, had all demonstrated an incredible aptitude for survival. She watched Joanne and Orla, who'd only recently got to know each other, working with quiet cooperation to make sure everyone had eaten enough. Some folks had worked hard to make the building safe, while others had done a stock-take of their new surroundings, noting everything that might be of use. 'I feel good about what we achieved today,' she announced. 'I was worried we weren't going to make it, but watching the way we've all come together, I'm starting to think we might just be able to do this.'

Ruth pulled her closer. 'I've got to admit, I didn't ever think we'd get this far. For what it's worth, I think you might just be right.'

'I think you *are* right,' David said. 'Look at us now and look at what we got through to get here. I know the temptation's been to always look on the dark side over the last weeks and months, and

Christ alone knows that's been justified at times, but we also need to acknowledge when things go well. We're fed and watered and reasonably warm; we've all seen much worse. We ought to get some sleep tonight so we can be ready to hit the road early. With a good wind at our backs, tomorrow could finally be the day we get to Ledsey Cross.'

It was three in the morning. The world was unexpectedly bright. The sky had been clear for much of the preceding day and there'd been no noticeable increase in cloud cover through the night so far. The temperature under the starry sky had dropped to sub-zero again, ensuring that every corpse in the vicinity – maybe even the entire country – had again frozen solid, their immediate threat neutralised. The moon was three-quarters full, and in the darkness of everything else, it appeared lit up. In turn, the light it cast was reflected equally brilliantly off the remaining snow and fresh ice. It was almost as if dawn had broken several hours too soon.

The van raced across the beautiful, alien-looking landscape at the kind of speeds people hadn't dared drive at for months. Until tonight there'd always been the danger of herds of wandering cadavers getting in the way, or the endless congestion of the pileups that frequently blocked the roads. None of that mattered now: the dead were held safely at bay by their icy binds, and the other vehicles that had travelled this way in only the last twenty-four hours had left clear tracks to follow.

'There,' Dominic said. 'Stop here.'

Alfonso slowed down and switched off the lights. There were two vehicles at the side of the road a couple hundred metres ahead of them.

'You sure those are their vehicles?' Harjinder asked.

'I think so.'

'You think so? You need to do better than that.'

'I hid in the back of the truck; didn't get a proper look at it.'

'It has to be them,' Kelly said. 'There's no snow on them.'

'It's them. One hundred per cent,' Dominic said.

'You'd better be right,' Harj threatened.

Piotr's groan silenced them. 'We've been following their tracks, you idiots, which lead right to those there. Anyway, children, there's no one else left alive, is there.'

He scanned the area with a pair of binoculars. Harjinder got out and looked through his thermal imaging camera. He was back inside in seconds. 'Well?'

'That's it, boss. Big heat mass in that building down there.'

'Okay. Right. Alf, stay behind the wheel and wait for my signal. Harj, you're with me.'

Noah was fumbling around in the dark, trying to find somewhere to pee. One of the major downsides of the endless quiet, he'd discovered, was the absolute lack of privacy. You literally couldn't fart without everyone hearing it. He should have gone last night, but the ghosts of this building had freaked him out, then sleep had got the better of him. Now he was having to feel his way through the inky black, trying to get far enough from everyone else so he could do what he needed to do without waking the rest of them up. It had been a while since he'd used a toilet for the purpose it was intended. The physics of them still worked – you only need flush them with a bucket of water afterwards. But these days the conveniences weren't always that convenient. Typically, the shape of the dried-up bowl amplified the noise when you peed standing up. He'd taken a piss in Lakeside when he'd been on his own in the very early days, and by the time he'd been ready to shake himself dry, there'd been a crowd of corpses waiting for him outside the cubicle. Noah laughed to himself. There truly was no aspect of life that hadn't been turned on its head by the apocalypse. *You never saw that one in the movies*, he thought.

It was cold inside the building, but it looked a hundred times colder out there. He was running out of options, his bladder aching. When he saw a large, bowl-shaped, gravel-filled plant pot on the other side of the dust-covered tills, he jumped the barrier and unzipped his flies. Christ, the relief was blissful. To hell with the noise.

There were lights outside. Someone up by their vehicles.

He thought David or one of the others might have gone to fetch something from the truck, but that couldn't have been the case because there were so few of them here now, and he'd stepped over all the regular drivers on his way over to pee. Could it be the dead? Was it the first shards of sunlight reflecting off the metal and glass? Or, *alright*, was it what he thought it was? *Is someone really trying to steal our bloody van?*

'Trouble!' Noah yelled, and his voice echoed throughout the building, waking everyone else immediately. He shoved the glass door open and ran out into the icy morning, the drop in temperature hitting him like a punch to the gut. It felt like the cold was squeezing the air from his lungs and he struggled to keep running. Sanjay, Sam, Callum, and Joanne, all overtook him and raced up the slope. They struggled with the fresh ice, though, legs having to work twice as hard to cover half the distance. Sanjay veered off the tarmac and onto the verge at the side, the unevenness of the frozen grass and mud giving him more grip and more speed. Their truck was already moving away, but he reached the side of the van and slammed against it. In the passenger seat, Harjinder looked at him, grinned, flipped him the bird, then accelerated away. Another van followed the two stolen vehicles. With his hands on his knees, struggling to breathe, Sanjay watched it disappear. Alfonso Morterero saluted. Next to him, Dominic gave a little wave as they disappeared.

Back inside the Garden Centre, the angry barbs and retorts were already being hurled back and forth. 'What the fuck did you leave the keys in the ignition for?' Marcus demanded.

'We always do that,' David said, equally furious.

'You just handed our future over to a band of thieves.'

'Until just now we didn't think there were any thieves left out there.'

The arguments were pointless, everyone knew it, but with no obvious solution to their predicament, they were all they had.

'Well?' Ruth demanded when the others returned.

'Piotr,' Sam said, struggling to catch his breath.

'What? You're certain about that?'

'I didn't see him, but I definitely saw that bastard Dominic Grove and Alf too. They don't have the brains or the balls between them to have done this without Piotr. Christ, he used to have to remind Alf to breathe.'

'What the fuck is wrong with these people?' Mia asked. 'I know you lot never got on, but why can't they just fuck off and leave us alone?'

'Because Piotr's brain doesn't work like the rest of ours do,' Ruth said. 'He just wants us to know who's boss.'

'But he didn't have the balls to come and face us, did he?' Ollie said. 'Cowardly fucker.'

'I hate that piece of shit,' Omar said.

'Did he even know for sure that it was us?' Callum asked.

'Yes,' Sam replied without any hesitation.

'How?'

'How do you think? Dominic bloody Grove's got the old gang back together again. The two-faced little wanker. This is on me. I should have finished him off yesterday.'

'I don't understand,' Callum said. 'If this guy hates you lot so much, why leave us here? Why not try and get rid of us?'

Vicky shook her head. 'He's not as stupid as you think. He knows exactly what he's doing. He knew he was outnumbered, same as he did in Yaxley. And the thing you need to remember about Piotr is that he might well be a malicious bastard, but self-preservation is always at the top of his list. He didn't need to risk attacking us. All he needed to do was reduce our chances of staying alive.'

'And that's exactly what he's done,' David agreed. 'We're stranded now.'

'It's worse than that. Where do you think Piotr's going now? I guarantee he's on his way to Ledsey Cross.'

'God help them,' Orla said. 'Does he know the route?'

'He can read a map, can't he?' Noah said.

Vicky shook her head. 'It's not that straightforward. It's a small place, hard to get to. Unless he knows about Heddlewick, he might struggle to find it. That's the one advantage we still have. We know exactly where we're going. He doesn't.'

'Then we better get a bloody move on,' David said.

'How?' Mia asked. 'We've just lost all our kit, or did you not notice? They've taken our vehicles and Vicky's sick and—'

'And what's the alternative? Have you got a better solution? Because from where I'm standing, we either stop here, try and get back to Yaxley, or keep going. Ledsey Cross is closer, and with Piotr on the warpath, it seems to me the people there are going to need us as much we need them. We need to get there before he does.'

'We should have a vote. We need to know what everybody thinks.'

'Fuck that,' he said. 'People keep telling me I'm supposed to be in charge, so I'm calling it. Get your shit together. I want us out of here in less than an hour. Got it?'

They'd stripped the clothing section of the store to protect themselves against the cold; there were shelves and bins of Wellies and garden boots and they'd bagged up anything else of worth. It was noticeably warmer this morning and there'd been no fresh snowfall. Though there were clouds on the horizon, for now the sky overhead remained a clear electric blue.

They'd walked north for an hour already, the remaining snow increasingly turning to slush beneath their boots. They followed the tracks cleared by their truck, though they knew they'd disappear before long. But there was no way they could go any faster. Much to her chagrin, Ruth had been pushing Vicky in a wheelbarrow. But she was still slowing them down. Selena walked alongside, stopping the barrow from tipping over. It was impractical and uncomfortable. It was all they could do just to keep going.

At the front, Sam leant across to David. 'This is never going to work. First civilised place we find along this road, we should stop.'

'I was thinking the same thing myself. If we can find some replacement vehicles, we can keep moving.'

'And if we can't, then we need to forget about going any further.'

'You can be the one to break it to Vicky.'

They'd pulled ahead of the others. Sam stopped and took a folded-up map from the inside pocket of his jacket. He covered his eyes to shield them from the sun and scanned the horizon. David unzipped his jacket and took off his hat.

'I'm too hot. This weather's so bloody unpredictable. You don't realise how much you used to rely on the weather forecast and a mixed wardrobe until you don't have access to either.'

Sam looked up from the map and pointed ahead and to their right. 'I reckon that's Knottingley.'

'What's there?'

'No idea. Somewhere to rest and reset, I hope. I say we stick on this road as far as we can. Looks like it'll take us right into the centre.'

'And you think we can risk that?'

He shrugged. 'I think we have to. The night will slow the dead down again. Being nearer to the middle of town should give us maximum options for finding transport and anything else we need. We're not going to make it much further on foot. We're going to start losing people if we're not careful.'

David laughed to himself. 'When we left London there was over two hundred of us. Now there's sixteen.'

Sam looked at Ruth and Selena struggling with Vicky. He'd been stationary for a couple of minutes, and they still didn't seem to be any closer. 'I know. Let's do what we can not to lose anyone else, eh?'

For a long time, the town didn't appear to be getting any nearer. The disappearing snow still lay heavy in the fields and the white covering made everything look the same, obscuring their progress. The only visible landmarks were the towering stacks of a distant power station, many miles ahead. One of the towers was blackened, dirty smoke still billowing from its truncated stump.

And then, almost without warning, they were there. They followed the curve of the road around onto the Pontefract Road, the main route into Knottingley. Now their surroundings began to change more rapidly. The ice had sloughed off the south-facing roofs of a housing estate in large sheets. The sun glinted off windows.

It broke Sam's heart to see that Ruth had abandoned the impractical wheelbarrow and resorted to carrying Vicky on her back. It seemed to him more of an encumbrance, *but*, he thought, *she was probably lighter than the rucksack that Sanjay now carried on Ruth's behalf.* They waited and regrouped beside the wreck of a vehicle transporter that had veered off the carriageway, carved a deep furrow across a sliver of open land, then come to an undignified halt smashed into the corner of a house, reducing it to a lop-sided ruin. The road they had been following looped the long way around, but there was a shortcut to be had here if they were able to pick a safe path through the rubble and ice.

They paused a couple of streets later. 'Tell me this is where we're thinking of stopping,' Ruth said to David.

'Somewhere around here, yes,' he said. They were both watching Vicky but trying to make it look like they weren't. Her body may have been failing, but her hearing was still pin sharp.

'We should keep going,' Vicky said. We can't afford to let Piotr build up any more of a lead than he's already got.'

'Not an option,' Sam told her. 'David's right. We're in no state to keep going, you especially, and we're definitely in no condition to take on Piotr like this. Anyway, you're assuming the folks at Ledsey Cross won't be able to take care of themselves. From what you've said, I reckon they'll be okay without us.'

'Maybe so, if they were warned,' Selena said, getting agitated. 'I can't stand the thought of Piotr doing anything to Annalise and the others. I know there's enough of them there, but they don't know what he's like.'

'You can argue all you want, but we're stopping here tonight,' David said, cutting across the chatter. 'We'll be stronger tomorrow, rested, and we'll have replaced a lot of the kit we've lost.'

'I know that,' Vicky protested, 'but—'

'But nothing. I've made my decision. The town centre isn't far. A couple of us will go and check things out so we don't walk straight into anything disastrous. The rest of us will wait here.'

Vicky fished in her pockets for a cigarette and her lighter, figuring she should shove something in her mouth to stop herself answering back. It was pointless arguing. Didn't matter how much she protested, in her current condition she was pretty much helpless.

42

Knottingley was compact enough for Callum and Sam to be able to scout relatively easily. There was a high street with traditional shops on one side, more modern-looking buildings on the other. It looked like they'd be able to find enough food and other supplies here to get them through tonight and tomorrow. 'You know what gets me?' Callum said, his voice low as a whisper.

'What?'

'All these shops... look at how many of them we're never gonna need again. There are restaurants and takeaways, a pawn brokers, a bookies, couple of charity shops and thrift stores... me and the others used to talk about it when we were back in Brentwood. We'd have a few beers, then one of us would always be wanting to order a pizza or a curry.'

They kept going, and found that further to the north, the industrial part of the town was bordered by the River Aire. They'd nothing to compare it with, but the water looked fierce. The noise it made was deafening. A freshly defrosted corpse bumped past Sam, more interested in the sound of the current than in him. He watched as it toppled into the river and was carried away by the ferocious, churning flow. He hoped the waters didn't let up. With everything else so quiet, the river would be a magnet for the dead.

They found an old-fashioned guesthouse on the way back to the others. Thankfully, there had been plenty of vacancies at the critical moment last September. The bedrooms were clear, and there were enough beds, sofas, and other spaces for them all to be able to rest tonight. 'This'll do us, Callum,' Sam said. 'Let's get back.'

They'd not been gone long, but when they retraced their steps, there were bodies waiting for them in the roads they'd run along. The remaining undead population was thawing out and becoming more mobile. Even though the temperature was only a couple of degrees above freezing, the fact it was above freezing at all had altered the equation in favour of the dead. Sam cursed himself. In their haste to find shelter, they'd been less careful than they normally would have been. The trek through the winter landscape this morning, coupled with their experiences over the last couple of snowy days, had lulled them into a false sense of security.

'Godawful time for these fuckers to wake up,' he grumbled as he drew his knife and approached the nearest corpse. The creature hesitated, still struggling to move, but its fury and intent were clearly undiminished. He caught one of its flailing wrists, but the damn thing continued to fight. Increasingly agitated, it began to thrash about with such force that its arm tore away at the shoulder, the already feeble flesh further weakened by the combined effects of the freeze then the thaw. Surprised, Sam hit it across the face with its own dismembered limb, whacking it with such force that it tripped over its feet and collapsed in front of him.

'It's only a flesh wound, pal.'

'That would be funny if it wasn't so disgusting,' Callum said, watching nervously as more of the dead closed in. They took slow, dragging steps through the slush, and were easy to outrun.

The rest of the group had attracted a similar amount of attention. David, Joanne, and the others fought quietly and efficiently, but even with all their experience, it was impossible to massacre in silence. The noise of every individual kill dragged more of them out of the shadows.

'Tell me you found somewhere decent,' David asked Sam in a glimmer of space between attacks.

'There's a guesthouse. Bit grim and old-fashioned, but it'll do.'

'Will it keep us safe from these nasty fuckers?'

'As much as anywhere.'

'Then I guess we follow you.'

'This way,' Callum said. He gestured for them to follow him, then raced off. Sam held back, happy to bring up the rear. They couldn't afford to get split up and lost here. With the light ebbing away and the dead locals becoming more active, he had neither the time nor inclination to be hunting down lost sheep in the suburbs.

Just Ruth, Vicky, Selena, and Omar remaining now. He tried to help Ruth with Vicky, but she batted his arms away. 'I'm alright,' Vicky snapped, angry. 'Let me go, both of you. I can walk by myself. You just focus on clearing the way.'

There were more of the dead still coming, but they were slower than ever, shuffling as much as staggering. It was impossible to know if it was down to the level of their decay, the aftereffects of the freeze-then-thaw, or a combination of both. It didn't stop them getting in the way, but it made them easier to bypass. Even now, Sam was awash with relief that they were continuing to exhibit the same kinds of behaviours he'd witnessed in the apocalyptic ruins of central London, still playing that bizarre game of follow-my-leader, ignoring everything except the actions of the corpse in front of them. As they went, he was mindful of those that had shown glimpses of consciousness returning. Back in Yaxley, Ed had confirmed that he'd seen it too. There was upwards of thirty of them in the street ahead now; he didn't fancy any of them making direct eye contact with him or asking directions.

The closest corpses broke away from the crowd. Ruth, Selena, Sam, and even Omar each moved quickly to head off the cadavers nearest to them. Sam hadn't seen Omar fight much before, and he was impressed by the kid's tenacity. The body he was dealing with loomed over him, almost double his size. Omar repeatedly swung a metal pole into its pelvis, the bones audibly cracking, until it dropped down to his level, then he battered it into submission with admirable dedication.

They were so focused on the advancing horde that they'd taken their eyes off Vicky. When Sam looked around, he saw that she'd continued walking. Her exhaustion was such that she could barely lift her feet, and she dragged herself along in a way that was uncomfortably comparable to that of the dead. The similarity was such that the corpses themselves appeared to be fooled; several of them parted, allowing her to move between them; the rest ignored her completely. Sam couldn't understand what he was seeing, but he knew that right now, it didn't matter. He signalled to the others, and they followed in Vicky's inexplicable wake.

The rest of the group was already at the guesthouse. That they'd reached the shelter was obvious because there was another glut of death already loitering in the slushy street outside, even more moving towards the building. It was a small-scale recreation of their London nightmares – death attracting death attracting death. Sam put on a burst of speed and shoulder charged through the bulk of them, sending them toppling in all directions and leaving the way to the building's ornate porch clear. The front door flew open, and Selena and Omar rushed for cover. Sam waited, holding back the dripping crowds until Ruth had half-dragged, half-carried Vicky the remaining distance to safety. He followed them inside. Lisa slammed the door shut behind him then helped Marcus drag a table across it.

The building was damp and stank of mould. When Sam looked up, he saw faces peering back at him from every angle. Worried expressions from doorways further down the hall. Expectant faces peering down from between banister posts like naughty kids who'd been sent up to their rooms, and the portraits on the walls, smugly judging how he dealt with the end of the world. Through the frosted glass in the doorway, he could see the mass of decay swarming outside. 'Jesus, was it worth it?' he asked, thinking out loud.

David was confused. 'Was it worth what?'

'We should have stayed in Yaxley.'

'We couldn't. You know that. It's just hindsight.'

'Yes, but what have we achieved? We're no further forward now than when we were stuck in that hotel on Fleet Street. Same shit, different location.'

'That's not true.'

'It *is*. All that effort and for what? If anything, we're in a worse position.'

'No, mate, we're not. Okay, so things look a bit shitty tonight, yeah? We're knackered. But look at the bigger picture. We're nearly through this. You've seen how fragile the dead have become; we're close to the end of them. That's one clusterfuck off our plates, right? And we're closer to Ledsey Cross than we thought we'd ever get.'

Sam wasn't listening. His brain was racing. On autopilot.

'I've got to get back out there. We need food and drink. We can't afford to get stuck in here without—'

David gently put his hand over Sam's mouth until he'd stopped talking. He frowned at him. 'You don't need to do anything else for a bit, Sammy. Have a sit down. Get your shit together. Joanne and Sanjay have already gone out to get what we need. They went out the back way so yes, they're reasonably safe and yes, they both know what they're doing. Stop always trying to be the hero, you infuriating sod. Sit down and let someone else take the heat for once.'

It was against his nature, but Sam did as he was told.

There was a small dining room just off the hallway, the tables laid ready for a final breakfast that was never served. There were two dead diners sitting at a table in the corner where they'd spent the last four motionless months slumped against each other, decaying together. Sam pulled up a seat next to them.

A small crowd had gathered around another table.

Vicky was struggling. Selena passed her a bottle of water that she sipped, despite clearly needing to gulp. Whenever she tried to swallow, she was racked with violent coughs and splutters. It was impossible to drink when she could barely breathe. Ruth had her arm around her shoulder. She looked like a giant in comparison. Vicky kept trying to talk, Ruth kept trying to stop her. 'It's okay…

get your breath back.'

'But. Did you-did you see them?' Vicky managed to say.

'Who?'

'The dead outside?'

'What about them? Come on, Vic, save your energy. We can talk about this later.'

But she clearly had no intention of waiting. She spoke again, her words interrupted by more coughing. 'Did you see how they... reacted?'

Blank expressions.

'They didn't,' she closed her eyes, 'they didn't attack me.'

'It was the way you were moving, love, it had to be,' Ruth said, sounding more hopeful than anything. 'You've slowed right down. It's no surprise after the last few days.'

Vicky shook her head. She managed to swallow a little water at last, then continued. 'It's more than that. They can smell death on me, and they know it's getting closer.'

43

The conditions over the last four months had worn the guesthouse down to a ruin. The limitations of the building were increasingly noticeable because it was raining again. Doors and windows had been left open and there was a hole in the roof that they'd not seen from the front. As a result, part of the ceiling in one of the second-floor bedrooms had collapsed. Water was now soaking through the carpet and had started dripping into the room below. 'Thought you said this place was alright,' Noah grumbled to Sam as they looked through an increasingly crowded lounge window for Sanjay and Joanne. Sam wasn't in the mood for any bullshit. He was nervous. It felt like they'd been gone for hours.

'Feel free to fuck off and find yourself somewhere else to stay. There's plenty of room. We'll be out of here first thing.'

'Tetchy,' Noah said, and he wandered away.

At the end of the entrance hall was a reception hatch. On the other side, a small square office then a kitchen beyond. Noah checked in all the stainless-steel cupboards and drawers for any food they'd overlooked, but he wasn't the first person to have been in here, and held out little chance of finding anything. Behind the guesthouse was a large gravel carpark, surrounded on all sides by high walls. The snow had all but completely disappeared now, leaving vast, reservoir-sized puddles behind. He froze when he saw someone out there, then relaxed when he realised it was one of the Brentwood lads. It must have been Callum, because he could see Ollie out there now too, and Lisa. They were running towards the gate at the side of the guesthouse. Either the dead were attacking in large numbers, or Joanne and Sanjay were back.

Driving a small, snub-nosed coach, Sanjay accelerated and ploughed into the substantial throng that had gathered outside the guesthouse. He slammed his foot on the brake and skidded to a halt, bringing the van to a juddering stop in front of the building, then reversing down towards the gate and taking out a handful more corpses. He blasted the horn for someone to open up, but Ollie and Callum were already on it. They hadn't needed any prompting; the chaos out in the street was audible across the whole of Knottingley. As soon as they were safe and the gate was closed, Sanjay rolled the coach forward to block it.

They were already drenched so barely noticed the standing water as they emptied the coach. 'Busy out there?' David asked once they got everything inside.

'Like you wouldn't believe,' Joanne said, shaking herself dry. 'Safe to say the locals are all defrosted and on the move again. Until we turned up, I don't think there'd been much activity at all around here.'

Sanjay leant against the door, panting. 'We found the coach then paid a visit to the nearest shops, just like we'd agreed. We just grabbed whatever we could get our hands on, so I don't know what we got. We were only inside a few minutes, but it was long enough. I thought we were going to be stuck there.'

'And now they're all on their way over here?'

'Looks that way. It was unavoidable, Dave.'

'I'm not blaming you two. We knew this would happen. Who knows, they might freeze again tonight.'

'I don't think so. It's much warmer than it has been. Even if there is a frost, it's only going to be enough to slow them down; won't stop them completely.'

With most people now helping themselves to the spoils of Joanne and Sanjay's supermarket haul, David took the opportunity to go upstairs to get a better view of what exactly what was going on outside. Alone, he climbed the steps to the second floor. The lonely ascent, coupled with a gnawing nauseous feeling in the pit of his stomach, reminded him of when Taylor had taken him to a high vantage point in London so he could fully appreciate the scale of the dire situation they'd found themselves in at the Monument. Okay, so there'd been hundreds of thousands of corpses in central London and there were only a fraction of that here in Knottingley, but only the scale was different, the balance was just as unsettling.

Lisa had followed him upstairs. She handed him food and drink. 'No thanks,' he said. 'I don't think I could keep anything down.'

'Take it. We all need to try and keep our strength up.'

He opened the out-of-date energy bar she'd given him, sniffed it, chewed a corner, then put it back in its wrapper. 'That's fucking horrible.'

Lisa watched the bodies in the street below. 'This is nothing we haven't had to deal with before, you know.'

'It feels different.'

'I don't see it. In London we had—'

'For one, this isn't London,' he snapped, the tone of his voice immediately silencing her. He sounded angry or... afraid? He shook his head. 'I'm sorry, Lisa. I have a bad feeling about this. This is very different to London. *They're different*. Look at them.'

She rested her forehead against the glass and looked down. 'We just got screwed over by the weather again. If it had stayed cold, they wouldn't be here.'

'No, but they *are* here. And the longer we wait, the more there will be.'

He wasn't wrong. Lisa looked along the road outside in either direction. More corpses were coming this way. 'I get that you're worried, but it's nothing we can't handle. Sam was talking about going out later and trying to draw them away. It'll work. Even if we have to go out there hand-to-hand and fight, we can do it. They're in such an awful state now, Dave. They're virtually falling apart.'

'You're really not seeing it, are you?'

Lisa was confused. 'See what?'

He gestured down into the road again. 'Look again.'

She sighed. 'You're going to have to give me something more to go on.'

'Look again!'

She did as he told her.

And then she saw it.

Down in the street around the front of the guesthouse, the dead weren't swarming, weren't pushing or shoving, they were *waiting*. Now that she'd seen it, she couldn't unsee it. Like everyone else who'd come from London, she'd become used to seeing vast hordes of these vile, horrific creatures scrambling ever closer to wherever the last of the living were hiding out. They'd shown no concern for themselves, and only a limited awareness of their surroundings, but *Christ*, she thought, the monsters outside this building seemed to be holding back, even biding their time. Lisa recalled the horrific scenes she'd witnessed in the capital: the toxic glut of compacted remains, where putty-like flesh had been squeezed into every available gap, shaped by the force of countless more of the dead endlessly pushing from behind. There were far fewer of them here than in London, but what she was witnessing now was infinitely more terrifying.

'Doesn't matter how hard we try, how quiet we are, they'll find us,' David whispered. There was a note of panic in his voice that Lisa had never heard before. One thing they'd all been able to rely on was his optimism and control, but those qualities seemed to be in short supply now. 'It's almost dark now,' he continued. 'If this rain keeps up and the clouds stay low, it'll be pitch black tonight. Impenetrable. We won't know the full extent of what's happening out there until morning.'

'But we can't risk leaving, can we? So, what are our options?'

'Honestly, Lisa, at this moment in time I'm not sure we have any.'

44

The rain was hammering on the roof, clattering against the windows. In parts of the guesthouse, it was as if the inside was outside, such was the amount of water running down the walls and dripping from the ceilings. Noah continued to make his displeasure known. 'We're barely any better off in here than we would be camping in the carpark.'

'Be my guest,' Sanjay said.

'I'm not trying to be difficult, I just don't understand how anyone thought this was a good place to stop.'

'Put a fucking lid on it,' David snapped. 'We've got enough to deal with already without you lot being at each other's throats.'

'I'm just trying to say—' Noah began.

'Yeah, well don't. If you've not got anything positive to say, do us all a favour and don't say anything at all. In fact, just do that.'

The atmosphere in the second-floor bedroom at the back of the hotel was unbearable, the tension hard to stomach. They'd all crowded into the same room because it was the furthest, driest point from the bodies in the street out front. It was sparsely furnished with just a badly assembled flat pack dressing table and wooden chair alongside a three-quarter bed. Vicky lay on the grimy mattress. She tried to sit up, but Selena pushed her back down. 'Take it easy, Vic.'

'We need to go.'

'We've already been through this,' Ruth said. 'We're not going anywhere tonight.'

'We have to. We've got to get to Ledsey Cross before Piotr does.'

'We're not going anywhere until the morning,' David told her.

'This is bullshit. We can't just sit here waiting.'

'We're going nowhere. With the greatest respect, you can barely make it across the room without help right now. You need rest. We all do.'

'We can rest when we get to Ledsey Cross.'

'And unless you rest, you won't bloody get there! Christ, woman, you're infuriating at times.'

She almost smiled at that. Almost.

'Look, one thing you need to keep in mind is that whatever trouble we're coming up against, anybody else who's left alive will be too. The odds are stacked against *everyone*, Piotr included.'

'Piotr especially,' Orla said.

'We just need to be ready to get out of here at the crack of dawn,' Sanjay said. 'And we can do that easy. Jo's got us a decent bus, and Sam says...' His voice trailed off. He looked around. 'Where is Sam?'

It was second nature to him now. Strange how used he'd become to being in such close proximity to the dead, as if it was the most normal thing in the world. Back in the early days, September and October, every step had been a nightmare, surreal and horrific. He'd studied the undead masses with a mix of fascination and disgust, keen to understand what drove them to move. But now things were very different. Now they were nothing more than rotting meat that kept getting in his way. The fact they'd once been people with personalities and histories and connections counted for nothing now. Now he couldn't stand the fucking sight of them.

He slipped out of the back of the guesthouse with Callum, his partner of choice. The kid had proved that he knew what he was doing on more than one occasion recently. Sam preferred to do this kind of thing on his own, but in unfamiliar territory like this, it was too much of a risk. They climbed over fences and dividing walls to get a decent distance away from the crowd of corpses in the street. With the rest of the town so quiet, they figured that one of Callum's trademark disturbances would be sufficient to distract enough of the creatures to relieve the pressure on the front of their hideout. There was only an hour's daylight remaining at most. They needed to take advantage of it.

'We've got to get far enough away to get them to shift from outside the guesthouse but stay close enough to make sure they all hear it. Too far out and we could just split them. We could end up with two crowds to deal with.'

'This should do it,' Callum said, and he opened his jacket and showed Sam his tools of the trade, donated by Selena: a fully charged phone and the battery-powered speaker she'd used in the garden centre shop last night. 'It had better work. We're all out of tech after this.'

'Has this trick ever not worked?'

'No.'

'Then have a little faith, ye.'

They were a couple hundred metres away from the guesthouse, but the density of the crowd in the street didn't appear to have reduced. 'This ain't normal,' Callum said.

'There's no such thing as normal anymore, mate.'

He shook his head. 'It's like David was saying earlier... they're not acting like they used to.'

'We're assuming that's a bad thing. They might be losing control, not regaining it. Have you thought of that? It would explain why they're just standing there.'

'Doesn't explain why they came here in the first place, though. Look, can we just get this done. I want to get back.'

The rain was relentless. They'd reached a crossroads. Sam gestured north and they walked away slowly, their movements largely camouflaged by the atrocious conditions. Occasional cadavers pivoted towards them on unsteady feet, but by the time they'd realised there was something different about Sam and Callum, they'd already gone. Callum pointed at a Georgian townhouse. They broke in with minimal effort and dealt with the building's sole remaining occupant with a similar lack of fuss. On the top floor, Sam prised open all the windows and leant outside.

'Fuck.'

'What is it?'

'There's frigging hundreds of them.'

The brooding clouds were low and heavy, but there remained just enough light to allow them to see the full scale of the crowd they were trying to wrangle. The arrival of the last of the living into Knottingley had triggered another relentless procession of the dead. It looked like every single corpse that had defrosted and remained mobile in the desolate town was now dragging itself closer to the guesthouse.

'Fucking hell,' Callum agreed. 'They're everywhere.'

'We've brought them all out of the woodwork, haven't we? I bet nothing at all has happened in this place until today.'

'Now we're the fucking circus come to town. Are we ever going to get a break?'

'I doubt it. We're the minority now. It's not our world any longer. Never was, to be honest. We just assumed it was.'

'Yeah, heard you was a tree-hugger,' Callum said. 'Load of good you lot did, saving the whales and all that.' Sam ignored him.

'Just get that music playing, will you.'

Callum obliged and the pair of them went back downstairs to escape the blaring noise. They stood with their backs against the wall of a living room preserved in aspic, watching the herd outside. They'd expected them to turn and crowd towards the house *en masse*, but they didn't. Some of the nearest corpses reacted, but the vast majority continued about their unnatural business undisturbed.

'What's going on?' Callum asked.

'There's obviously something that's a bigger draw here than your shitty taste in music.'

'Like what? Bloody Green Day? The only other thing is our lot hiding in the hotel.'

'I know. And that has to be it.'

'But I don't get it. It was only a few days ago we tried this trick in Brentwood, and it worked perfect, same as always.'

'Because there was nothing else nearby to distract them.'

'Hang on, are you saying those things outside are fixating on the rest of our people *instead* of the music?'

'That's exactly what I'm saying, and I know exactly how that sounds and what that means. Whether or not they know we're deliberately trying to trick them into coming this way doesn't matter. Fact is, they've made a conscious decision to stay focused on the guesthouse instead.'

'Fuck me.'

'My sentiments exactly. This changes *everything*.'

'We have to get back,' Callum said, but Sam was already on his way. He slid a patio door open and stepped out into a water-logged, jungle-like garden. The rain was still coming down hard, so cold it took his breath away. At the end of the lawn, he paused again under the sparse overhanging branches of a fruit tree.

'There's one thing I still don't understand. We expected there to be a lot of activity around here, but what we're seeing is off the scale.'

'What about the river?'

'I was wondering the same thing. I'm going to take another look.'

'I'll come with you. Makes sense to stick together.'

'One to report back when the other gets washed away?'

'Yeah, something like that.'

The gate opened out onto an alleyway that ran between two rows of back-to-back houses. They jogged to the end of the alley then slowed their pace dramatically when they stepped out onto the street and merged back into dead. They matched the creatures' slothful gait step for dragging step and were all but completely ignored. They took a sloping route through the crowds, avoiding any sudden movements, then disappeared down a driveway between a gym and a tyre replacement depot.

Something was off.

Something was very wrong here.

'Can you hear that?' Callum asked.

A deep rumbling noise could be heard over (*under*?) the sound of the rain. It was like an endless roll of thunder. It didn't fade or move, it was just... there. No wonder the dead had been drawn to this place. The sound in this part of Knottingley was all consuming, everywhere and nowhere. And the ambient noise was natural, not mechanical.

When they reached the carpark at the end of the long, warehouse-like gym building, the source of the noise was revealed. The cars that had been left on the far side of the carpark were up to their wheel arches in water; much of the tarmac resembled a lake.

Sam followed Callum who used a low wall to climb up onto the roof of one of the stranded cars. 'Christ, would you look at that.'

The river they'd seen when they'd first explored Knottingley had swollen to several times its original size. Sam stared in disbelief at the vast, raging, mud-brown torrent. 'I think we might have seriously fucked up stopping here.'

'But how could it have got so bad so fast? I mean, I know the rain's been heavy but still...'

Sam gestured around them. 'The rain's been heavy for weeks, so the ground was already saturated. And the drains and sewers are fucked. We saw that in London, and it's only going to have got worse since then. And on top of everything, we've had heavy snow with a fast thaw.'

'The snow's all gone now, though. It should start easing off, shouldn't it?'

Sam shook his head. 'I wish. I think it's going to get a lot worse before it gets any better.'

'How come?'

'It's to be coming down off the hills. There's going to be an absolute load more water coming this way.'

45

It was dark by the time they made it back. 'Where the hell have you two been?' David demanded when Sam and Callum finally returned to the guesthouse. They'd looped around the back of the building and climbed over the carpark wall. Sam dragged him into the kitchen, out of earshot of everyone else.

'We're in trouble.'

'We're always in trouble.'

'No, Dave, this is different.'

Sam paused, and in that moment of hesitation, David felt his legs weaken with nerves. In all the time he'd known Sam, he'd almost always been nothing but unfailingly positive. He'd found solutions when others had only seen problems. He'd conjured up escape routes out of thin air. He'd risked his life, been left for dead, and still come up smelling of roses. David knew things had to be bloody awful for him to be talking like this. He looked terrified, lost. 'Tell me.'

Sam took another breath and steadied himself. 'I don't think we're getting out of here, Dave.'

'What do you mean? Of course we are.'

He shook his head. 'It's worse than we thought. We've led everyone into a dead end.'

'I don't understand. The dead are here because we're here, yes, but we always knew that would be the case. We were unlucky. The thaw came and they were able to get mobile again, that's all. We can get through this, mate. We always do.'

'I'm not so sure. We tried to distract them with noise again. It's always worked before, but not this time. They can see through it.'

David almost laughed at the ridiculousness of what he was hearing. 'What? For Christ's sake, Sam, get a grip.'

'I'm serious. We started more music playing, and they just kept going. They walked straight past, following the queues to this place.'

'Bullshit.'

'Go out there and have a look for yourself if you don't believe me.'

'Then we'll just have to take a leaf out of Piotr's book and get rid of them, won't we?'

He shook his head. 'Not that easy. There are too many. And there are bigger things happening here.'

'Like what?'

'Like the river that runs through this place. Callum and I didn't think anything of it when we saw it earlier, but with this bloody rain and all the melting snow... there's a serious risk of flooding. It's too dangerous for us to try getting away now.'

'But surely the noise of the river should be drawing the dead away from us if it's that bad?'

'Same as the music. They're choosing to ignore it and focusing on us.'

'This is absurd.'

'Tell me about it!'

'So, what do you propose we do?'

'We need to be honest with everyone about the mess we're in and get them all onside. Then we secure the building, batten down the hatches, and hope we're still in one piece in the morning. If we are and the water level hasn't increased, then we make a fucking run for it.'

They worked without pause to get the place ready. Out back, Callum, Ollie, Orla, and Noah had blocked the gap under the bottom of the carpark gate with whatever they could find. It was imperative that they kept the coach dry and operable. They'd need it to get them out of Knottingley – if there was anything left of Knottingley to get out of in the morning, and any way of getting out.

Inside, the rest of the group had confined themselves to three adjacent rooms on the second floor of the guesthouse. Before tonight there'd always been a glimmer of hope, even on the darkest days. Here today, though, there was nothing. Trapped in a rundown B&B, stranded miles from anywhere by the rising water and hounded by the dead, today it felt like they'd reached the end of the road.

Ruth refused to take the news lying down. Sam had explained their position, but she didn't want to listen. Sanjay was similarly incensed, as was Joanne and Marcus. They supplemented the makeshift weapons they already carried with tools taken from the garden sheds and garages of neighbouring properties, then she led them out onto the street in front of the guesthouse in the incessant rain. Several of them wore head-torches. They'd fight their way out of Knottingley if it came to it.

Sam had warned them about the noise outside, but it was still remarkable. The river roar was even louder now, an ever-present, all-consuming roar. It was everywhere at once, disorientating some of the dead and sending some of the corpses staggering off in random directions, hunting for the source of the drifting din and colliding with others that remained focused on the guesthouse and its occupants. The group were used to an enemy that, for the most part, all herded in the same general direction, but this was wholly different, absolute chaos. Would it make them easier to deal with, or just add another unwanted layer of complication to the carnage? Ruth knew there was only one way of finding out.

She had a long-handled axe that she'd found in a shed next-door, and she swung it in wide, indiscriminate arcs around her, wiping out sizeable swathes of foetid corpses. She advanced into each blood-stained space she cleared until she'd reached the middle of the street. The other volunteers followed her lead, fanning out and forming a semi-circle around the front of the guesthouse, hacking and reaping their way through, cutting down whatever undead that shambled into range.

The fighting felt different this time.

Until tonight, the enemy had all but queued up to be cut down, their blunted instincts driving them forward irrespective of the physical danger they faced. Tonight, though, their confused, independent movements presented a new challenge. Joanne illuminated one of them with her head-torch and lunged at it, only for it to step back out of range. Sanjay swung at another nearby but missed and nearly wrenched his shoulder from its socket, his fist making contact with thin air. He'd dismissed a couple of earlier incidents, explaining them away to himself as a result of the awful conditions and the increasing piles of slippery limbs and entrails littering the ground, but he was becoming increasingly concerned. 'Fucking thing just backed away from me. Did you see that? That fucking thing just backed away!'

Ruth ignored him, focusing on a trio that had lurched into range, but Joanne was not so dismissive. 'This isn't right,' she shouted, fighting to make herself heard over the rain and wind and the river roar. '*What are they doing?*'

They both lowered their weapons momentarily because the behaviour they'd seen was now being repeated all around them. Some of the corpses – overall a small minority, but enough for them to be noteworthy – were unquestionably trying to retreat. They were moving away from the direction of attack, colliding with others who continued to numbly stumble into range of Ruth's axe swinging. This level of conscious control had been all but invisible when they'd looked out at the crowds as a whole, but down here among the masses, such subtle shifts in behaviour were increasingly noticeable. And now he was actively looking for it, it was all Sanjay could see. For every six or seven cadavers still clamouring to get at him, one or two more were trying to get away.

Ruth and Marcus were doing enough to hold back the dead tide, because although the size of the crowd out here was huge, they were nowhere near as tightly packed as they had been in London. Joanne took a step back to try and make sense of the madness. A corpse collided with her, and she instinctively shot out a hand and caught it by the wrist. She let it go and the damn thing just stood there, looking directly at her. Its cloudy, unfocused eyes were staring into the light from her torch, its mouth opening and closing like a landed fish. But there was no aggression. The creature wasn't fighting. 'What the fuck is going on here?' she demanded, knowing full well it wouldn't answer. The damn thing just continued to stare straight back at her, vacant and unblinking, neither retreating nor attacking. Another surge came from the crowds behind it, and it was swallowed up.

Joanne was distracted when Ruth, Sanjay, and Marcus raced back past her towards the guesthouse. She was about to turn and follow them when she realised her feet were wet. When she looked down, she saw that the street was awash with murky water. It was only a few centimetres deep, but it was everywhere, and it was getting deeper. She could feel the force of it increasing too, flowing down the road. She looked around, and though the range of her head-torch was limited, she saw enough.

Many of the dead that had gathered outside the guesthouse were being knocked off their feet as the speed and depth of the water flow increased. When she looked down again, Joanne saw that it was up to her ankles. She retreated to the guesthouse, having to push through a brace of corpses that had followed the others inside. She tore at their flaccid flesh, feeling her way through the decay and stumbling over the waterlogged remains of others that had already gone down.

Sam was waiting in the porch for her. He grabbed her outstretched hand and pulled her inside.

The hallway was wet. They'd done what they could to stop it, but water was already getting in.

'You okay?' he asked her.

'Not sure.'

'Looks like the river burst its banks.'

'No shit,' she said, numb, not knowing how else to respond.

46

The guesthouse reeked of dirty water. There was water throughout the ground floor now, and there was absolute panic on the floors above. They'd done what they could to try and stem the flow, but no matter how much furniture they'd piled up, it didn't seem to have made a scrap of difference. Still, most of the group remained downstairs, trying.

'Out of the way!' Marcus yelled as he crashed down the staircase, his arms loaded with pillows and bedding stripped from bedrooms. He splashed along the sodden carpet and stretched over to wedge the bedding into gaps in the mound of furniture they'd piled up at the door. It was hopeless, but he kept trying. He'd stop one trickle, only to see water start running from somewhere else.

In the adjacent lounge, Sam and Noah were blocking the windows. The miserable light made it even more difficult to look for gaps. There were large numbers of sickly cadavers pressed up against the outside walls of the guesthouse. 'How are they even standing their ground?' Sam asked.

'They're not,' Noah said. 'See?' He gestured for Sam to look through a small crack between the piled-up furniture.

The corpses were being carried along like driftwood, catching on the corners of the building and bunching up. Here, where the porch of the guesthouse protruded, large numbers of them were already wedged in, forming a dam of the dead. He moved an upturned chair and pressed his face against the glass to get a better look. Jesus, the water was at waist level with the grotesque monsters now.

David went from room to room, collecting stragglers. 'We've done as much as we can,' he said to Sam and Noah. 'Time to move to higher ground.'

When he left the lounge again, he collided with Joanne coming the other way. 'It's not so bad out back,' she said. 'There's some water coming under the gate, but we've done enough to stem the tide.'

'Think it'll hold?'

'I think it has to.'

The kitchen and dining room were clear. David ran back towards the staircase then stopped when he realised Sam was still in the lounge, trying to drag a sideboard out into the hall. 'Did you not hear me? We're done, Sam.'

'Not yet. Just give me a minute. I want to get this in front of the door if I can. Give me a hand.'

'Fuck it,' David yelled at him.

'It'll only take a sec.'

'No, Sam, look!' He shone his torch at the front door so that Sam could understand his panic. Water was spurting through the gaps around the doorframe under huge pressure. 'I'm not asking, I'm telling. Whatever you're doing, it won't make any difference now.'

Sam scrambled over the lump of furniture left wedged in the doorway, leapt the banister and followed David, but they'd only made it halfway up the long staircase when the door gave way. It flew open with astonishing force as though the door had been blown by explosives, and the surge of stormwater and dead bodies that flooded into the guesthouse was such that the blockade they'd built was instantly destroyed as if it had been made from paper and matchsticks. For a moment, frozen with horror, all Sam could do was stare as the torrent tore through the ground floor of the building.

And then he saw the dead.

He'd expected them to have been blasted to oblivion by the deluge, and many of them were, but their numbers were such that many others were carried along by the water. A few of the spidery corpses were, by chance, swept towards the stairs. One stuck an arm between the balustrades and was able to catch hold. Its limb was painfully thin, barely any meat left on its bones, yet its grip was impossibly tenacious. And again, as had been the case outside, where one became wedged, others became stuck also, the bones of one becoming a platform for others, clogging each passageway. Another was flung against the wall by the force of the water. Finding itself several steps up, it began to climb, the rising flood aiding its buoyancy. David booted it under the chin, sending it backflipping into the swirling, broth-like mire that now filled the entire ground floor of the guesthouse.

No way out, David thought as he and Sam climbed the stairs like rats. *Christ, there's absolutely no way out.*

For now, the coach remained relatively secure in the carpark out back, but how long that would be the case was anyone's guess. But even if they managed to get out of this building, there was no way they'd get out of Knottingley now. The roads all around would be impassable, and if the floodwaters didn't get them, the dead inevitably would. Irrespective of how the behaviours of some of the cadavers appeared to have changed, there remained many, many more that still bayed for the blood of the living.

The water level appeared to have stopped rising, but it was academic now. The flood had given the dead an unexpected advantage, lifting them up and allowing them increased access to the staircase and the floors above. Had they left doors and windows less secure, most of the tide would have swept through, but they'd done a bang-up job of it, and made a fairly stable tidal pool. Several of the floaters had already reached the first floor. 'They won't get up here, will they?' Selena asked from the second-floor landing, panic in her voice.

David wanted to tell her that they wouldn't, wanted to reassure her they were safe, but he wasn't going to lie.

'There's a loft hatch,' Lisa said, and she shone her torch at the ceiling. Ruth, almost double her size, crouched down and let her climb up on her shoulders. She opened the hatch and looked around. They'd already seen that a small section of the roof had collapsed near the eaves, but it hadn't got any worse, and the attic space appeared otherwise secure. It had been properly boarded and there was a pull-down access ladder. She grabbed the cord and asked Ruth to lower her down.

'Get up,' she shouted as people herded out from the bedrooms towards the steps. 'Carry as much as you can and get up there.'

No one objected: going higher was a natural human reaction. The fear of what they were climbing towards was nothing compared to the nightmare below that they were trying to escape. Though the dead remained individually lethargic and weak, and only a handful of them had so far made it up to the first floor, in the chaos of the moment it was easy to believe that either the guesthouse would completely fill with foul-smelling water, or that scores of the dead would be able to get up the stairs and attack.

The entire group climbed up into the freezing, damp attic space. The last one, David pulled the ladder up behind him then leant down to close the hatch. He paused for a moment and listened. The driving rain hitting the roof and windows. The roar of the river running down the street outside. The churning of the water inside the building and the bangs and crashes as furniture and corpses were thrown around by the force of the flood.

He pulled the hatch shut and sealed them in.

47

DAY ONE HUNDRED AND TWENTY-ONE

The first day of the new year had been an unprecedented ordeal, a new low. It had begun with Piotr's raid on them at the garden centre and had gone downhill from there. They'd expected to be at Ledsey Cross by now, but their destination felt further away than ever. And was there even any point in trying? If Piotr had already found the place, there'd likely be nothing left of it. He'd have destroyed anything of value by now.

Some of the group had slept intermittently through sheer exhaustion, others lay awake for hours, too scared to close their eyes for even a second, listening to the world outside being battered by nature and to the guesthouse being swamped by both the floodwaters and the dead, all of it being mixed into a toxic soup.

It was still raining when the first orange-purple hints of morning began to appear in the otherwise inky-black sky. There'd been little change through the long hours of darkness now ending, but the conditions did seem to have eased slightly. Sam tried to see what was happening outside, but it was impossible. He stuck his head out of the hole in the roof, but the angle was all wrong. David had tried opening the loft hatch a couple of times before dawn, but it had been equally difficult to make out any details, except that below them remained a swirling chaos.

It felt like everyone was waiting for someone else to take the lead and ask the questions that were inevitably going to have to be asked. How were they going to get out? If they managed to escape from the building, would they be able to get out of Knottingley? Was there any point trying?

'So, this is it, is it?' Noah asked, finally breaking the wordless deadlock. 'Are we just going to sit here until our last few scraps of food run out?'

'We've only been waiting for your brilliant suggestion, Noah.' Sam asked, unimpressed. 'Why don't you go down and have a look around?'

'I'm asking, not volunteering,' he replied quickly. 'Christ's sake, you'd have to be crazy to go back out into all that shite. I saw enough last night to last me a lifetime.'

Marcus laughed. 'A lifetime, seriously? I'm starting to think a lifetime for us might just be the rest of today and maybe tomorrow.'

'Can't we have a bit of positivity here?' David asked. 'Are we just going to throw in the towel?'

'I wish I'd stayed in Yaxley,' Noah said.

'Yeah, I wish you had too,' Sam agreed.

'Fuck you.'

'No one made you come with us,' David reminded him.

'I know that. But with the benefit of hindsight, leaving what we had there was a really fucking stupid move. Since then, all we've had are problems. Big ones. We should have learnt our lessons earlier and just put up with what we had. The grass is always greener, and all that crap. I'm getting homesick for Lakeside, for crying out loud.'

'It's not as bad as you're making it sound,' Vicky said, struggling for volume. 'You've just spent a shitty night in a wet attic. At least the dead aren't a threat.'

Her comment was met with a moment of silence. Had she lost it? Had the sickness got to her brain? 'Bullshit,' Noah said.

'It isn't. You can't see it because you're not looking for it.'

'Looking for what?' David asked.

'You just assume they want to kill us. I don't think they do.'

'Why else would they be hounding us constantly? Why else would they attack us whenever we get anywhere near them?'

'They don't. Maybe they once did, but now? You're misreading the signals.'

Noah laughed. 'This is fucking priceless.'

Vicky ignored him. 'That's why they were outside and wouldn't go. They know we're in here; I think they think we can help them.'

'I've heard it all now.'

'Just watch them. Put yourself in their shoes. Their behaviour has been changing, it's been changing all along. I think they're starting to understand what's happened to them. I think they're gravitating towards us because they want us to help.'

'Don't tire yourself out, love,' Ruth said.

'Stop assuming the worst. Have a little faith. Look how far we've come.'

Noah remained unconvinced. 'And look how far we've got left to go! Since I fell in with you lot, it's been the same pattern repeating itself over and over. Someone has a good idea, we all support it, it goes wrong, we're all fucked. Wash, rinse, repeat.'

'It's not like that.'

'It *is* like that. That's exactly what it's like.'

'There's always a way out,' Sam said. 'Things are shitty now, sure, but they'll improve. They have to.'

'Oh, change the bloody record will you.'

But Sam wouldn't. 'We might end up stuck here for a few more days until the floodwaters recede, so what? If Vicky's right about the dead, that changes everything.'

'The dead aren't our only problem.'

'Right, I know that. Piotr might get to Ledsey Cross before us. So what? He's one man, and Vicky says there are loads of people there, a strong, well-organised community. Hey, Selena, how many did you say there were?'

Nothing.

No reply.

Ruth switched her torch on and shone it around frantically. 'Jesus and Mary! Where's Selena?'

Their bickering always annoyed her. It was wasted energy, that was what Kath had told her once when she'd been arguing hell for leather with Vicky about something unimportant, and she'd never forgotten it. None of them had even noticed her prise open the loft hatch a while earlier and drop down. She hadn't used the ladder, hadn't wanted them to realise what she was doing and start another argument about how it was too dangerous and how someone older and more responsible should go down instead, or worse, that one would go with her. Sometimes she thought they didn't understand about life in their new world; hadn't thought as much about it as she had. None of the old rules applied, did they. It didn't matter that most of them were older than she was, some of them double her age. Fact was, they'd all been living through this hell for an equal length of time. When it came to dealing with the apocalypse, they were all equally experienced.

The soles of her shoes squelched on the sodden landing carpet. Even up here, it seemed, the water had found a way of getting in. She saw that a window had blown open during the night, letting in the elements. The smell inside the guesthouse was rank. She'd gotten used to the stench of decay, but this was on another level. She covered her mouth and nose with her scarf, though it barely made any difference.

The building was by no means silent, but it was reassuringly quiet. Last night's maelstrom had passed. Above her head, Selena could hear the pointless conversation droning on in the attic. Elsewhere, a constant soundtrack of drips, dribbles, trickles, and splashes kept silence at bay. *Definitely much quieter outside this morning*, that was for sure. The rain and wind had dropped. The roar of the water had receded.

A couple of corpses had made it as far as the first floor, but she dealt with them quickly and efficiently, barely missing a beat. The motionless body of a long-dead woman lay halfway along the next set of stairs, sprawled face-down and face-first as if she'd simply washed up on the tide, hair splayed like seaweed. Selena stepped across and sank her knife into the woman's exposed right temple, just to be sure. She then crouched down and peered through the banister to try and get an idea of both the damage to the building and the level of the undead threat that remained. From where she was looking, she couldn't see any corpses that were still mobile. There were plenty that had been dashed on the rocks, some relatively whole, but most appeared to have been torn apart in the chaos overnight. There were a couple stuck behind a sideboard that was wedged in the doorway of the lounge, but despite the fact they struggled incessantly when they saw her, she was confident they weren't getting out. The front door was blocked by junk, inside and out. Selena thought it was safe to keep going.

The drip, drip, dripping kept her on her toes. It was hard to tell whether what she could hear were the dribbles of water escaping from nooks and crannies in adjacent rooms, or the slippery flesh and liquefied remains of corpses creeping up on her. The small dining room was a chaotic mess of body parts, so random that it was impossible to work out which limbs belonged together. Some still twitched. It reminded her of a programme she'd watched on TV once about fishing out at sea, when a net had been emptied on the deck and most of the fish were still flapping.

She checked each remaining downstairs room but found only one more corpse that was capable of movement. It had, somehow, become impaled on a strip of hooks in the kitchen, out of reach. It looked like it had been hung there purposefully, a grotesque and rapidly deteriorating hunting trophy.

Suddenly, coming down alone seemed like a really bad idea, and she didn't like being here on her own at all. A drawer in the kitchen had been pulled out and emptied all over the floor. Selena helped herself to a couple of knives and looked out of the back of the building. The carpark was mostly dry, and the coach appeared okay. The work they'd done to block the gap at the bottom of the gates seemed to have done the trick.

She was going the wrong way. It was the front windows she needed to look out of, but she was delaying the inevitable. As long as she stayed in the kitchen, staring out through this grubby window at the square, wall-enclosed scrap of wasteland out back, she could avoid the fact they were stuck here. That much she was beginning to accept. There'd be no Ledsey Cross today, no happy ending. Why not close the book now? Avoid the end until it came to find her? So she delayed acknowledgement and clung on to a few more precious seconds of inactivity and relative calm.

That the front door was open and neither water nor corpses were getting in was a good sign, she supposed. She slipped in mud as she approached the front of the building. Every ground floor surface was coated with a layer of the stuff, everything greasy to the touch. Here, the place felt more like a section of a cave system than a residential building. She took a deep breath and began to disassemble the heap of junk that separated her from the outside world. She took hold of a tree branch as thick as her wrist and yanked it towards her, but it wouldn't budge. She tried again – same result. Once more, and the branch came away, bringing with it much of the rest of the blockage. She was on her backside before she realised what had happened, and she scrambled for one of the knives she'd just picked up, ready for attack.

Nothing came.

Cautious, Selena inched back towards the doorway.

She stopped. Then grinned. Then laughed out loud.

The road outside the guesthouse was still a river, though the water was nowhere near as deep and ferocious as it had been last night. But what really took her by surprise, what delighted her more than anything that had happened in the long days since their exodus from London had begun, was the fact that the street was otherwise completely clear. The water last night, when the rain had been relentless and the level of the swollen river had been at its highest, had coursed with such force through Knottingley that it had washed away the dead from the streets.

As long as they could get the coach started and get out of the carpark out back, she thought they might actually have a chance of getting the hell out of here and reaching Ledsey Cross.

48

Though the first few streets were precarious, the water still wheel-deep, they were clear again once they had got back onto the A1. After that, they made progress with newfound speed that would have seemed incomprehensible just a short while earlier. Though the cleansing effect of the floodwaters hadn't reached far beyond the very centre of Knottingley, it didn't matter. The dead had been badly affected by the extreme weather conditions of the last week. The cold, the snow, the permafrost, the sudden thaw, the torrential rains... they'd all combined to wreak havoc on the undead monsters. Their decaying flesh, already barely enough to keep holding their sagging, corrupted bodies together, was now weaker still. For the first time, the dead appeared vulnerable. Some had been reduced to little more than puddles of flesh. The flesh of others, those that had been subjected to the full force of the floods, had been swept away, pared from their bones. Some were almost completely devoid of meat now; their gleaming, jet-washed skeletons appeared impossibly clean.

Sanjay drove, Vicky and Selena with him up front. Selena had her phone in her hands, plugged in to keep it alive. She was glued to the brightness of the screen. Though satellite-based navigation systems had been down since just after the beginning of the end, she'd had the foresight to download off-line copies of certain maps before the networks had died. She was a smart kid. Having copies of maps of the centre of London had saved their skin on more than one occasion in the early days of the catastrophe, but she'd also thought ahead and taken copies of maps of the area around Ledsey Cross. That they were now following those maps was such a long delayed, much doubted dream that it didn't seem real. 'We're well past being level with Leeds now,' Sanjay said. 'I can hardly believe it. I never would have thought we'd have made it this far.'

'Less than twenty miles left I reckon,' Selena said. 'We could walk it if we have to.'

'Speak for yourself,' Vicky said. She had her eyes closed and was resting her head against the window. Even thinking was exhausting now; she had barely enough energy to breathe. Sanjay looked over at her. He'd spoken with David about her before they'd set out. They'd always known that delivering Selena safely to the people at Ledsey Cross was all that mattered to Vicky. David had wondered if she was doggedly holding on just to make sure it happened.

He nudged Selena. 'Look, at that! A sign for Heddlewick.'

She'd been looking old beyond her years recently, the pressure of their situation weighing as heavy on her as everyone else, but now she grinned at him, excited. 'I know. Can't believe it! Crazy name, though, don't you think?'

'It's very Northern-sounding, I'll give you that much.'

'Annalise won't believe it when we get there. Kath told her that me and Vicky were gonna come. We said it was gonna take a while to get here, but I didn't think it would be four months.'

'I'm sure she'll still be expecting us. Vicky told me that Annalise was close to your friend Kath. She said Kath was stubborn, that she wouldn't have given up.' He looked across and saw that Vicky had fallen asleep. 'Between you and me, Selena, she said you reminded her of Kath, not that I ever met her, of course. She said you could be just as cantankerous.'

'Not sure what that means, but I'll take it!'

They were deep into open countryside again, the last vestiges of the chaos-filled urban and suburban areas left far behind. Out here, the world felt vast and endless. At times up on the hills there was no sign that things were any different to how they'd always been. If there'd been any human remains up here, they'd likely have decayed away to nothing or simply been swept away by the rains. Sanjay stared out of his window, transfixed by the normality of this perfect, unscarred part of the world. At moments like this, he felt optimistic. He hoped this was what the view from Ledsey Cross would be like. Clean. Fresh. Unspoilt. Natural.

After climbing for a while, the road descended before plateauing again. Here, the route became harder for Sanjay to follow, the coach cumbersome and the roads littered with debris. The floods, the driving rains, and the frosts and thaws of the last few days had clearly had a substantial impact on this part of the world. Up ahead, a minor landslide had all but obscured the entire way. He was forced to slow to a crawl and drive in the gutter to keep them moving forward. 'And to think,' he said to himself, 'we used to believe we were the ones in charge.'

'What are you on about?' asked Selena.

'Nothing,' he said. He could have told her about how he'd seen more potholes in the road in the last couple of miles than he expected, or how weeds and tree roots had already made inroads and would eventually chew their way through the tarmac, breaking it into useless, tar-coated pebbles. He didn't bother mentioning how roads blocked now would stay blocked forever. What was the point? The kid had enough to contend with. *She's never even driven a car*, he thought sadly. By the time she got to his age, driving would likely be a thing of the past.

The power station they'd seen from a distance on their long and lonely walk into Knottingley loomed into view. They were much closer now, but it was still many miles away. The damage wrought on the towering structure was sobering even from way out. At some point there'd been a huge explosion at the station, that much was blindingly apparent. One of the colossal cooling stacks had collapsed to half-height. 'Are we safe being this close?' David asked Sam.

'As safe as anywhere. It wasn't a nuclear plant, if that's what you mean.' Sam could tell from David's reaction that was exactly what had concerned him. 'There was Derwent to the south, and

Heynsham further north, but nothing more local than that.'

'How do you know?'

'Spent enough time protesting about them, didn't I?' He lowered his voice so as not to scare the others. 'Don't breathe too easy, though. We've talked about this before. I've no doubt there have been meltdowns all around the world since everyone died. Whether lethal amounts of radiation reach us or not depends largely on the wind direction. Just put it from your mind, Dave, because there's fuck all we can do about that noise.'

Noah overheard Sam. 'I'm less concerned about the radiation and more worried about the dead. An explosion like that will have been felt for miles around. Leeds, Manchester, Sheffield... who knows how many corpses might have come this way to investigate.'

Sam shrugged. 'Again, my advice is the same. Put it from your mind because there's fuck all we can do. We'll deal with whatever we find, same as always.'

'Yes, but—'

'But nothing, Noah. Seriously, forget about it. We're not going to get a lot closer to that power station, anyway. We'll be turning off towards Heddlewick before we get anywhere near.'

After twisting and turning on the descent from the hills, the road now stretched out ahead of them again, wider and more direct. There was a single vehicle stalled up ahead. Sanjay slowed down. David leant forward from the back, concerned. 'Trouble?'

'Possibly. Is that our minibus?'

He stopped a short distance away. 'It is, you know, it's definitely ours. I remember the registration ending EXC. It's the van we took from Yaxley. Doesn't look like there's anyone in it, though.'

'I'll go and see what's going on,' Marcus said, and before anyone could protest, he let himself out of the back and crept towards the abandoned vehicle. He became more confident as he got closer. The others watched in silence as he opened the driver's door and leant inside. He turned the key in the ignition. The lights came on, but nothing happened.

'No fuel,' he said when he returned. 'Tank's empty. They've just left it.'

'That's good, isn't it?' Selena asked. 'The less equipment they've got, the better.'

'Logically, yes, but this is Piotr we're talking about,' David said. 'I don't trust anything that fucker does. It could be a trap.'

Vicky wasn't convinced. 'Seriously? He's already taken everything we had, and I'm sure he wouldn't imagine us coming up on him so soon anyway. He'll be long gone by now. Get going, Sanj. The only thing this is telling us for certain is that Piotr's closer to Ledsey Cross than we are.'

Sanjay drove on. A river ran through the fields over to their left. In places its route was hard to make out, its banks having burst, drowning the land around it. There were bodies here also. More than they'd seen herding together since they'd left Knottingley. 'Where have this lot come from?' he asked.

'Market day, apparently.' Sanjay smirked at him. 'Doesn't matter where they came from,' Sam said, 'it's where they're going that we need to worry about.'

The dead here looked like they were migrating, all of them moving in the same direction, wearily walking the same well-trod path, all heads bowed. They no longer had the physical strength to keep looking up, but it looked for all the world like they were miserable sods, plodding towards homes destroyed by war. None of them reacted when the coach approached. Perhaps the sound of the engine was drowned out by the noise of the river, but it seemed, as they passed even the nearest ones, that they simply couldn't be bothered.

'It could be other survivors,' David said.

'Attracting them? The people from Ledsey Cross?' Selena said hopefully.

'Maybe. My money's on our friend Piotr drawing them deliberately. Just take it easy, Sanj. And keep your eyes open.'

Several miles further down the road, a once-impressive looking manor house came into view. It was a huge, ornate building, no doubt originally the home of some long-forgotten lord and lady, subsequently passed down to generation after generation, each less deserving than the one before, each pounds and acres poorer. Sam had always hated all aspects of the gentry, despised the privilege. He couldn't deny feeling a certain degree of smug satisfaction today because here he was, on his way to what could prove be one of the best places left in the country to survive and live a reasonably fulfilled life, while the owners of the estate were likely shoeless now, dragging their feet along with the rest of the faceless undead masses. When all was said and done, all the wealth in the world had counted for nothing. He'd had barely a couple of pennies to rub together for years, yet he'd outlived and outlasted them all.

Sam was so consumed with his pointless self-congratulations that he almost missed the significance of what he was looking at. The vast grounds of the country estate were enclosed within a high stone wall which should have been impenetrable, and yet scores of the dead were traipsing aimlessly across the once well-tended gardens like sheep. 'Slow up, Sanj,' he said as they approached the estate's open gates.

'That would have made a cracking hideout,' Joanne said.

'Yeah. I think it did.'

From here they could see all the way along the curving, unfeasibly long and sweeping driveway to the house's grand main entrance. Sam started hunting in his backpack for his binoculars. It reminded him of some of the exclusive gated developments he'd seen in London, not the grandeur, but they too were places that the undead had wandered into in large numbers and had then been unable to reach the exits or even comprehend that they needed to.

'We're wasting time here,' David said, conscious that there were bodies beginning to gravitate towards the road. 'Keep going, Sanjay.'

'No, wait,' Sam said as he focused the binoculars, trying to get a clear view of the area around the front of the building where a number of vehicles had been parked. They were out of keeping with their surroundings: dirty and battered; functional, not flash. 'There was definitely a group living here.'

David was losing his patience. 'So, what? Look at the number of bodies in the grounds, Sam. Whoever was here fucked up. They didn't make it. End of story.'

Sam shook his head. 'No, there's more to it than that. A lot of them have been massacred. There are bits of them all over the place.'

'So?'

Sam sighed and put the glasses down. 'So, I think the bears are still here, alright, Goldilocks? There are too many of the dead loitering around the house. Why would there be so many of them out here in the middle of nowhere?' He lifted the binoculars again.

'Maybe it's because we're right between the power station that exploded and Leeds and Bradford, they came for tea, nobody home, now they're stuck. It makes complete sense.'

'David's right,' Joanne said. 'The dead marched this way because of the explosion, and this poor bunch of bastards happened to have set-up camp mid-route.'

'What a shitty way to go,' Ruth agreed. 'This could have been us.'

'We're wasting time. Let's go,' David said.

Sam went to put down his glasses but stopped. 'Jesus. David, that's our truck. The one Piotr stole.'

'Are you sure?'

'One hundred per cent. The plough's a dead giveaway.'

'What kind of state is it in? Can you see anyone?'

'Doesn't matter,' Sanjay said. 'If Piotr's here we need to get moving.'

The door of the manor house flew open. A man came racing out, pushing into the swollen group of corpses still jostling for position near the entrance to the building. He burst through, then sprinted along the drive towards them.

'Son of a bitch. We've got a live one coming.'

'Who?'

Sam didn't recognise him. 'No idea. It's not Piotr.'

He handed the binoculars to David, who took a few seconds to locate the man then bring his face into focus. 'It's Alf Morterero.'

'Alf who now?'

'Scum that worked for Piotr.'

Before anyone could say anything else, Sanjay hit the gas. The wheels of the coach skidded, but the weight of the vehicle, embarrassingly, stopped them moving away with any speed. Behind, Alfonso came bursting out of the gates. He thudded into the side of the coach. Sanjay kept going, leaving him grasping at the air where the coach had just been. 'Fuck him,' Sanjay said. 'Fuck him and Piotr and all the rest of them.'

Alfonso kept running for as long as he was able, then pulled up, hands on his knees.

At the back of the coach, Marcus pressed his face against the glass, watching until the desperate lone figure disappeared with the curve of the road. 'I hope him and the rest of those cunts rot in hell.'

49

Sanjay drove as fast as he could, desperate to get them to Ledsey Cross. 'Slow down or we might not make it at all,' Selena said. 'We'll make it.'

They almost missed the turning to Heddlewick. Since passing the manor house the road had climbed again along one side of a steep, wooded valley. Sanjay braked hard and stopped the coach, then reversed back. Selena shook Vicky's shoulder. 'Look, Vic. This is it.'

Tantalising glimpses of tightly packed slate roofs appeared below them, visible through the trees. 'I can't believe it. We've done it,' Ruth said.

'Not yet we haven't,' Vicky reminded her.

'I know, I know. I'm trying not to get ahead of myself, but it's hard.'

'You sound nervous, Ruth,' David said.

'You don't say. I'm more nervous than I've felt in a long, long time. There's a lot at stake here.'

He nodded.

'It's only now that I'm starting to allow myself to believe we might actually do it. The distance seemed impossible when we first left London. All along the way we've had setbacks; I didn't know if we'd get here.'

'I always knew we would,' Selena said (even though she didn't). 'I think when I meet Annalise I'll just start crying. She'll be gutted that Kath's not with us. We didn't get to tell her what happened before the networks went down. She knew we were coming though, didn't she, Vic? She said she'd be waiting for us, no matter how long it took. Hard to believe she's so close.'

'Just on the other side of the valley,' Ruth said.

David nonchalantly wiped a tear from the corner of his eye, hoping no one had noticed. 'Take us home, Sanj,' he managed. He was overcome with emotion, daring at last to believe they'd almost reached their journey's end, that they were on the verge of joining that wonderful, welcoming community of people he'd heard so much about. They still had a way to go, of course, but since they'd worked out the route, he'd subconsciously envisaged the river Wharfe to be the finishing line. He'd tried to visualise this part of the route so many times, had tried to imagine how it would feel when they were finally driving over the bridge that would take them to the promised land... His heart raced as Sanjay followed the slope of the gently descending route through the trees, carefully coaxing the boxy coach around each twist and tight turn.

He braked hard.

'What the fuck?'

Immediately ahead of them, the road had disappeared. Part of the hillside had collapsed, taking with it almost all of the tarmac. The coach's front wheels skirted the edge, half of the driver's side tyre gripping thin air. He'd reacted in barely enough time to stop them dropping over into the abyss. Sanjay reversed up until they were completely on solid ground again. 'Looks like we'll be walking the rest of the way,' he announced. 'I'm not going off-road in this thing.'

'How far do you suppose?' David asked.

'About four miles I think,' Selena replied. 'We can walk it.'

'Looks like we're going to have to.'

'Wait and see what's in Heddlewick first,' Sam said. 'We might be able to get a couple of vehicles going.'

'Let's just keep moving,' David said. 'Sooner we get this done, the better.'

They unloaded everything out of the coach, spreading the weight of their meagre belongings fairly between them.

'We'll go and scout ahead,' Sam said, and with David's agreement, he and Joanne clambered down the forested bank then worked their way around to the point at which the road was accessible again.

'Was this definitely the only route into the village?' Joanne asked as they walked down. 'Piotr couldn't have come through another way?'

'I don't think so.'

The road was becoming progressively steeper. 'Christ, imagine if we'd been here a few days earlier, trying to get up and down here in the snow.'

'We never would have made it. The floods were bad enough in Knottingley, but the river runs right through the heart of this place. As long as we can get to the bridge, I reckon we'll be okay.'

They were level with the first few buildings now. They were traditional grey stone cottages, rugged and weathered. Joanne couldn't resist peeking in through a ground floor window. Everything inside was as it had been left on the day everyone had died, a snapshot of a life frozen in time.

'You okay?' Sam asked.

She shrugged. 'Guess so.'

'Tell me what you're thinking?'

'It's just, I've always felt sad looking at places like this, you know? Like longing for something you'd think anyone could have, whilst knowing I never would. But for the first time, I'm thinking that maybe there's something like this waiting for us over that hill.'

'We could come back here if it comes to it,' Sam said. 'I'd be quite happy living in a nice little pad like that. Would you?'

'What, be happy with a place like that or be happy living with you?'

'Either,' he said quickly. 'Both.'

'Yeah, I could live with that. As long as you keep your hair cut. It looks so much better short.'

Sam shook his head and carried on walking. A short distance further, he stopped again. This time he was silent, staring ahead. He didn't know what to say.

Apart from the few outlying buildings they'd already passed, much of the rest of the village had all but completely disappeared. Where they'd expected to see a river winding gently through the heart of the place, there was now a thunderous, fast-moving torrent of mud-brown water more than fifty metres wide. Along the way, vast amounts of debris had been collected and had now built up against one side of the bridge like a colossal dam. It was only when Sam looked closer at the rubbish that had been accumulated that the scale of it truly came into focus. There were cars that had been thrown around like toys. The water was almost level with the road across the bridge. Wedged under one of its outer arches was a double-decker bus, just its top windows and roof now visible above the raging torrent, looking like it was fighting for air. An incalculable number of corpses filled the gaps like a logjam. The scene looked like a flooded scrapyard built atop a burial ground. Some of the buildings down by where the banks of the river had originally been had collapsed. Parts of their ruins stood resolute against the flood; others had all but completely submerged, just partial walls and odd corners remaining.

'We can still get over there, right?' Joanne said. 'I mean, I can just about still see the road.'

'That's the way our path lies. No going around, that's for sure.'

'Aren't there other crossing points?'

'Inevitably, but chances are they'll all look like this.'

'We need to get closer, then. Get a proper idea of what we're dealing with. See if we can work out a safe route over.' She took another couple of steps then stopped again. Further down the road there was a very visible muddy tidemark. 'Jesus, look how high the water got! What must it have been like here last night? The scale of this is just unthinkable.'

A noise like boulders crashing together silenced their conversation. Down below, the bridge was taking a continual battering. Frequent plumes of fast-moving, dirty water jetted up like waves crashing against a seawall.

'I'm really not sure about this,' Sam said. 'Apart from the fact we'll almost certainly be killed if we end up in the water, we don't have a clue what's going on under the surface. The bridge could be about to collapse, there could be sinkholes, unstable pillars... anything.'

'But like you said, we have to get over.'

The others were slowly coming down the road towards them. Sam was conscious that he hadn't yet achieved what he'd set out to do. From up here on the side of the valley, the view of what was happening on the other bank of the river was limited to the part of the village nearest the water and this end of the bridge, everything else obscured by trees. He shouted back to David. 'It doesn't look completely impassable. See the cars in the road down there? The water's below the windows. It's waist height, tops.'

Sam carried on walking, emerging from the trees, and the other side of the grossly swollen river gradually came into view. On the far side the land remained relatively level for a while before it climbed up into the hills. There had been sports pitches over there and more homes, along with fields, parkland, and other open spaces. But little of that was visible because, beyond the sunken village, between the water and the hills, for as far as they could see along the opposite bank in either direction, the land was packed solid with thousands upon thousands of swarming corpses.

'Fuck me,' Ruth said, catching up. 'I know we saw stuff like this in London, but I didn't expect it out here. Jesus Christ, there are so many of them. Where the hell did they all come from?'

'The power station,' Sam said. 'Has to be.'

'But you said yourself, that's still miles from here.'

'I know, but think about it... Leeds, Bradford, Halifax, Huddersfield... this might sound extreme, but with nothing else happening up here and nothing but open countryside between those places and the power station, it was kind of inevitable. It explains what we saw on the way here. A mass migration along the river, triggered by the explosion at the power station. They follow each other like lemmings. When there's nothing else to distract them, they just keep coming.'

'Yes, but that doesn't explain why they're *here*, does it?'

'Well, that's just down to shit luck. The power station is upriver, so if thousands of them had already reached it, the flood would have swept loads of them up and dumped them back this way. Also, we saw something similar in London, remember? It's the topography. Because of the slope, loads of the dead ended up lining the banks of the Thames. For the record, I doubt this has just happened here. I bet there are crowds like this all along the river, filling every dell. Problem is just that this is the point where we need to get across.'

The group had bunched up together, all of them looking for routes through the utter chaos up ahead. 'You can see the road to Ledsey Cross,' Sanjay said, pointing across the valley. It snaked over the landscape, tormentingly free from obstructions. 'We'll be fine once we get onto it.'

'Just the small matter of a raging torrent, a flood, and a massive population of dead bodies to get through first,' Noah reminded him. 'You really couldn't make this shit up.'

'Maybe we should wait,' Callum said. 'Unless it pisses down again, the river level should keep going down, yeah? There's nothing stopping us holing-up in one of these tidy little cottages, is there? Then we try again later.'

Noah was quick to respond. 'Yeah, right, dumbass. Nothing stopping us apart from Piotr and however many more of his mates are holed-up in that bloody great house with him.'

'What if just a few of us went across first?' Sanjay suggested. 'If a few of us can get to Ledsey Cross, we might be able to bring back people to help. They might have equipment we can use. Transport.'

'We have to keep going and we have to stick together,' Ruth said, before anyone else had chance to speak. 'For Vicky's sake if nothing else. I need her to know we've made it.'

David looked around for Vicky. She was at the back of the pack, Selena keeping her upright. 'Okay, let's do it,' he said. No more questions. No more discussions. It was late morning, and even if they managed to get across and get through the dead, they still had several hours' trek ahead of them. The sooner they started, the sooner they'd be done. He led the way down to the water.

On closer inspection, both ends of the bridge were relatively dry, despite the water frequently lapping over the surface. The bridge had a slight arc that only became noticeable as they drew level with it. The road, despite being strewn with debris, was elevated on either side of the river, visible above the flood. 'I reckon the water level is still a few metres higher than normal,' Sam said. 'I don't know anything about this place, but judging from the steepness of the banks, I think the bridge was high over the water originally. I reckon the road came out in the middle of the village on that side. Look over there.'

He pointed across to where a section of the opposite bank had fallen away, exposing a jagged stone face. Half-houses teetered precariously, ready to collapse at any moment.

'Well, this should be fun,' Vicky said, her voice a fragile rasp. 'And what's the plan once we get to the other side? Swim for it?'

On the far side of the bridge, he first hundred metres or so of land remained underwater. Sam gestured towards a carpark and a couple of large stores, a small retail park right on the edge of the undead hordes. 'It looks a bit less crowded over there. I think there might be barriers keeping them out of the carparks. Let's aim to get over there, then regroup.'

'And then?' Noah asked.

'And then we fight our way through, I guess. And we just keep fighting until we make it through to the other side of them.'

'But there's got to be ten thousand or more,' Marcus said.

'I'm all ears, mate. What's your alternative?'

'If there was more space on the other side, I could have tried some of Ed's tricks from Yaxley. He was bloody good at herding corpses, though even he'd struggle with a crowd like that. Trouble is, there's nowhere to move them to. They're occupying virtually all the space over there.'

'Don't think of it as a crowd of ten thousand,' David said, 'think of it as a crowd of about a thousand each.'

'Impressive maths skills. How is that supposed to help get more space?' Noah grumbled.

'I'm just trying – badly – to put things in perspective. Sam's right, there doesn't seem to be any alternative to fighting our way through. This is it, I guess. Everything we've done to get here and all the battles we've fought, it's all been leading up to this. We get over that bridge, through that crowd, and into Ledsey Cross, or we capitulate. That's what it boils down to. Pack it in and go back to Yaxley, maybe.'

'As if I didn't feel under enough pressure already.'

Sam followed the road down towards the bridge. He stood on the road, a narrow and precarious strip of dry land. Down here beside the engorged river, the noise was deafening. He glanced back over his shoulder and saw that, although the others had followed, they were holding back, waiting for him to take the lead. 'Oh, fuck it.'

It was impossible to know for sure whether the foundations of the bridge remained solid, but Sam reassured himself with the thought that, individually and collectively, the weight of their small group was of very little consequence. It might have been a different story, had they been able to get their minibus down here – not that they'd have got very far. The crossing was impassable by vehicle. Many of the decorative stone balustrades had been destroyed and the resultant rubble strewn across the tarmac. There was no way they'd have been able to drive over.

The first few metres were easy, but an unexpected surge sent a flood of brown water spilling across the road around Sam and cascading out through the gaps between the balustrades on the other side. He held onto the stonework for support, the force of the ice-cold water almost taking his feet out from under him. He tried to shout a warning back to the others, but they couldn't hear him over the noise.

He clung onto the wall and edged slowly forward. He didn't know how the others were going to make it – Vicky was too weak, Omar too small, Ruth preoccupied with Vicky, David busy trying to keep everyone else safe, Noah complaining... He couldn't risk checking on them because to lose focus on his footing for even a second might prove disastrous. On the other side of the bridge, the river had an almost lake-like calm to it, but he knew it was a deception. Below the surface it was fast-moving, with devastating currents ready to snatch away anyone lucky enough to fall in. He saw the loitering dead on the fringes of the crowd on the other bank being swept away with ease, dragged under and whisked away with sobering speed, thrown around like dolls. And all that separated him from the same fate was this battered ruin of a bridge and perhaps a metre of air. The raw power of the water was petrifying. He doubted even the strongest remaining member of their group would stand any more of a chance than the helpless corpses he'd just been watching.

Focus on the bridge. One foot in front of the other. Just keep moving.

He didn't risk looking back again until he was more than a quarter of the way across. Sanjay and Joanne were right behind him, then David, Ruth, Vicky, and Selena. He cursed his selfishness. Should he have helped them? Perhaps Sanjay should have gone first, and he behind. Vicky was dragging herself along, sandwiched between Ruth and Selena. If the water took her, she wouldn't stand a chance, and neither would her aides. There were dead bodies he'd seen that had more meat on their bones than Vicky now.

The rest of the group were more spread out. Marcus brought up the rear. For a moment Sam struggled to see Omar but then spotted him wedged between Mia and Ollie, his bobbing head just level with their waists.

Focus!

Sam rested his hand on the next balustrade and immediately felt it wobble. He'd been about to put all his weight on it but snatched his hand away at the last second as a huge chunk of masonry fell away and dropped into the water, showering him with spray. He was terrified, his feet frozen to the spot with fear. When he took his next step, would the whole of the bridge disintegrate into the river? He looked down at his boots, and when the water washed away, he saw that he was straddling a vicious crack that was several centimetres wide in places. He shouted a warning to Sanjay and pointed at the ground. There was nothing they could do. If the bridge was going to collapse, no amount of screaming and shouting would stop it.

He prodded the ground with the toe of one of his boots, then took another couple of tentative steps forward. The constant spray from the water continually battering the left side of the bridge and the mass of rubbish that had accumulated against it was freezing, and the wind here was unexpectedly fierce. They'd been shielded from the worst of it on their descent into the village but here, midway across the river, there was absolutely no protection. In desperation, Sam dropped to his knees and started to crawl, trusting that the others would follow his uncertain lead. He glanced back again and was relieved to see that they had.

Almost halfway.

The noise was a thousand times louder down here, but there was at least some shelter, and Sam felt a little less exposed. If the road began to crumble, he could at least lie flat and try spreading his centre of gravity the way you were taught to save yourself on thin ice, but who the hell was he trying to fool?

KEEP FUCKING MOVING!

Sam crawled onwards then paused, braced against a brutal gust of wind, then continued, and now he realised that he'd started to descend the gentle slope of the bridge. He wanted to get up and run, figuring he was over the worst of it now, but that wasn't going to happen. There was a car lying on its roof up ahead, blocking the way. He'd glimpsed it from further back, but it was only now that he could see how it had fallen. Carried by the raging water, it had crashed nose-first into the side of the bridge then been forced up and over, flipped onto its back. It was now wedged in position like a stranded turtle with its bonnet scraping the road and its rear-end propped up against what was left of the opposite wall.

Under or over?

Sanjay caught up and squeezed past. 'I'm smaller than you,' he yelled into Sam's ear, struggling to make himself heard. 'I'll go first.'

Before Sam could either protest or agree, Sanjay was flat on his belly, crawling through the limited triangle of space between the road, the wall, and the precariously balanced car straddling both. Aware of the others bunching up behind him, Sam held his breath, waiting for Sanjay to get through.

Another section of the right-side wall gave way, and the roof of the car slapped down onto the road, blocking it fully. There was immediate panic, then momentary relief as Sanjay picked himself up on the other side of the wreck. 'Fuck me, that was close,' he said.

'I'll go over,' Sam said to Joanne, and he was about to climb over the upturned chassis when she shot out an arm and stopped him.

'Are you fucking crazy? Don't!'

The front of the car was now facing upriver, and water was hammering against it relentlessly. The movements were slight, but noticeable. With every second, the vehicle was inching further and further back, closer and closer to oblivion.

'We could push it over?' David suggested.

'We can't risk that. Without the car there, the water will just come flooding over the top.'

David could see it. The slope of the road and the force of the water here was such that the car was now acting as a temporary plug. They had to take advantage of it and fast. There'd be no way they could compete with the thunderous river flow.

Omar slipped past. 'Fuck this,' he said, and he yanked the back door of the car open, then crawled on his hands and knees across the headliner of the roof and out the other side.

'Move, move, move!' Sam shouted, because it was clear their best, perhaps only option was to follow his lead.

Joanne was next. She reached back for Vicky's outstretched arm and she and Selena manhandled her through, followed rapidly by David, then Ruth, then the others.

From first place to last.

Once everyone else was through, Sam dived into the wreck and pulled himself out the other side. He moved with a frantic speed. He'd seen enough disaster movies to know that the last one through almost always bought it in the end. He'd either get his foot stuck, or his clothes would snag, or the flood would wash the car clean off the bridge with him still in it...

He was still imagining nightmare scenarios when Noah and Callum grabbed his shoulders and pulled him out the other side. Sam picked himself up and saw that the others were running now, racing down the slope and heading for shelter in the ruins of the flooded village before they faced the dead.

'Go,' Callum said, and he turned back.

Sam was confused. 'What?'

'We need to make sure he can't follow us.'

'Who?'

'Who else, brainless? Piotr. I'm gonna shift that car.'

'He's right,' Noah said, and before Sam could stop them, they were behind the wreck they'd just crawled through, pushing for all they were worth.

'Don't! Just leave it,' Sam yelled, because from where he was standing, the dangers were obvious. Callum and Noah either couldn't hear him or were ignoring him. Callum took a couple of steps run-up, then slammed into the side of the car with force. It was balanced precariously now, remaining wedged in position by only the faintest of margins, perhaps only by the thickness of a layer of paint.

'Let me have a go,' Noah shouted over the roar. 'It's about time this old dog showed you pups how it's done.'

Callum stepped out of the way. A combination of a mighty shove from Noah and a shunt from the water sent the upturned car, and then Noah himself, flying over the side of the bridge. The wash caught Callum waist high. He fell and scrambled away on his backside, terrified that he too would be swept away by the force of the unstoppable flood. More of the stone balustrades began to crumble, the ground disappearing around him. Sam yanked him up by the scruff of his neck and the two of them ran for drier ground as a huge chunk of the bridge collapsed into the river behind them.

The bridge was made impassable. There was no way for Piotr (or anyone else) to follow them. And there was no way for them to go back. Sam finally released Callum, many steps past the need to hold him. They looked back briefly; another living soul, sacrificed in an instant. Callum couldn't speak.

'Stupid shit,' Sam said, shaking his head. 'No more heroics, Cal.'

'Yes sir,' he mumbled.

50

The adrenalin had staved off the cold, but its effects were fading fast. They'd need to get out of their wet clothes, but there was nothing dry left anywhere in Heddlewick. They waded away from the end of the bridge in a tight group, holding on to each other in a chain for support, terrified that one or more of them would be washed away. Out here, though, they'd escaped the worst of the river's flow. The foul-smelling water in this part of the village was relatively calm.

There was a hardware store on the edge of the flood with a large outdoor storage area enclosed by a wire-mesh fence that, from here, seemed to have held. The goods stored inside the yard had been scattered as if a hurricane had passed through, but the penned-in space looked relatively dry and free of dead flesh. Marcus was the first to reach the fence. He worked his way around to the entrance then ushered everyone through.

Space to breathe at last.

'I can't take much more of this,' Marcus said, hands on his knees, panting hard.

'Hopefully you won't have to,' David told him.

Callum walked over to Ollie and Mia, exhausted. Mia put her arm around him, hugging him briefly. 'You did us a favour,' she said. 'We can forget about Piotr and the others now.'

There was no time to grieve for Noah; no sense considering any loss, as they were nowhere near safe. Maybe they'd have chance later. Sam climbed up onto a mound of bags of gravel and sand and tried to work out what their next move should be. 'How's it looking?' Joanne shouted.

He didn't immediately answer.

There was no point even thinking about trying to salvage

278

anything from what was left of Heddlewick. Almost every building had been lost to the flood, and though some on the fringes appeared accessible now, everything inside would have no doubt been ruined. A little food to give them strength for the fight ahead and some warm clothes to take the edge off the cold was all they'd probably need, but almost the entire village was waterlogged. The stench was horrific. Bloated bodies floated in the streets.

Between the hardware store and the vast hordes was a modest modern retail park, completely out of keeping with its surroundings. From here he could see a frozen food store, a clothing store, a KFC drive-thru, and a fuel station. It looked like an ideal staging point. A place where they could regroup and rearm before they faced the dead.

Sam climbed back down. 'To be honest, it could have been a lot worse.' He explained what he'd seen. 'For the sake of another hour, it's worth stopping. My guts are churning and I'm sure you're all the same, but we need to be ready to deal with those crowds.'

Lisa looked at the huge expanse of death that was waiting for them. In the madness of the river crossing, she'd trivialised the undead problem, had almost dismissed it. But now they were close, the scale of the remaining challenge was overwhelming. 'It's not fair. The harder we try, the harder it gets.'

'Bollocks. Don't talk like that,' Sanjay said. 'Focus on the positives. Look how far we've come to get here, not how far we've got left to go.'

'Spare me the inspirational bullshit, Sanj. I've had enough.'

'It's not bullshit. It's bad luck is all. We're trying to get to a place that was intentionally remote. We were always going to hit problems. We've almost done it now, though.'

'Yeah, but it's problem after problem after problem.'

Sanjay grinned. 'You only just worked that out? It's the end of the frigging world, Lisa. Did you think we'd skip along a yellow brick road? Just a shit-ton of rotting bodies to deal with, a few more miles walking, then we're literally home and dry. No more complications.'

'Sanjay's right, we can do this,' David said. He turned to Sam. 'Lead the way, mate.'

There were a handful of corpses trapped inside the clothing store, but it was nothing they couldn't handle. The group stripped and changed at speed; all modesty forgotten. There was nothing to hide or keep precious; they couldn't afford it. Any embarrassment they might once have felt had gone the way of brushed teeth and matching socks: consigned to history. Except for Vicky. She remained much more modest. She didn't want any of them to see how badly her body had been ravaged by disease. Whenever she caught a glimpse of herself in the mirror, she was reminded of the corpses outside. She thought her body looked like that of an emaciated child.

They moved from one store to the other quickly and quietly, the river muffling the little noise they made. The stench in the frozen food store was as bad as expected, but they knew there should be a decent stash of dry food they could snack on. Ollie and Mia led the way, zigzagging around rows of chest freezers filled with mush and mould.

The display of snacks and crisps had already been pilfered. 'Oh, that's just fucking typical,' Mia said, disappointed. She kicked through the wrappers on the floor.

'Looks like the rats beat us to it,' Ollie said. Sam crouched down and studied the debris. He picked up a handful of crisp packets and an empty Coke.

'Rats that can open bottles? I don't think so. Somebody was here.'

'Somebody is still here,' an instantly recognisable voice said. In that moment, everything else became background noise.

Piotr.

He was standing in the doorway to a storeroom that had been ransacked, its contents chewed up and vomited onto the floor. He was brandishing a pistol. David recognised it as being from the stash of weapons they'd taken from the base in Brentwood.

'I have to give you credit, old man, I didn't think you'd make it this far,' Piotr said. 'The conditions haven't exactly been kind to any of us. I'll admit, I'm almost impressed.'

'Why don't you just fuck off and leave us alone?' Sanjay said, unable to contain his anger. 'Could you not have found yourself a rock to crawl under somewhere else?'

Piotr just laughed. 'Nope. Sorry. It pains me to say it, but I'm glad you're here, I could do with your help.'

'And what makes you think any of us are going to help you?'

Piotr shot Sanjay in the head.

'That's why.'

Though the bloated river still roared in the distance, and despite the gun shot having whipped the nearest of the dead into a frenzy outside, it was as if the rest of the world had stopped, frozen in time. David looked down at Sanjay's lifeless body in absolute disbelief, unable to even begin to comprehend what had just happened, let alone speak. Omar dropped to his knees next to Sanjay, tears streaming down his face. He glared at Piotr.

'I know, kid, you hate me. You wish I was dead. You think I'm a despicable cunt. To be fair, you're probably right.'

David still couldn't look away from the body of his friend. He was paralyzed, unable to move, barely able to think. Sanjay, who'd quietly fought so hard and who'd given so much for the good of everyone else, who'd never complained, who'd always been among the first to volunteer no matter how hard the task... to have had his life snuffed out with such brutal speed and inconsequence was impossible to process. Piotr had killed him on a whim, with as little thought as if he'd just switched off a light.

Piotr emerged fully from the storeroom, his pistol still pointing into the crowd, and they saw that he was injured. He was dragging a badly busted leg behind him, his trousers soaked with recent blood. He hid it as best he could, but he was clearly in a huge amount of pain. 'We had a bit of an accident, if anyone's concerned.'

'We're not,' Sam said.

'We stopped to check out a fancy big house in the country, just down the road from here. You might have passed it? Anyway, turned out it was full of corpses. Turns out this whole area was until the floods came.'

'We saw it. Saw your friend Alf, too.'

'Yeah. He and Kelly got themselves into a bit of trouble there. We got split up.'

'And you didn't bother going back to pick them up?'

'No.'

'You just abandoned them?'

'Yep. You didn't pick anyone up either, I notice. Anyway, I thought they were dead. There were lots of bodies around there and we had to take our chances. Harjinder got us this far before the floods hit.'

'So where is he?'

'Gone. Lost. Drowned. He was such a loyal little doggie. He bravely went out in the storms last night to make sure we were safe here and got himself swept away. Idiot.'

'You really brought your A-team with you, didn't you?'

'They got me this far. That was all I needed them to do.'

'How did you know about this place?'

'Ah, yes! I had help from the last remaining member of my team.'

He moved to one side. Very reluctantly, Dominic Grove emerged from the inconspicuousness of the shadows.

'Now isn't that just perfect,' Sam said. 'Shame you two didn't go swimming with your mate.'

Piotr laughed. Dominic didn't. 'Yeah, sorry to disappoint you. After all this time, though, Dom has *finally* proved his worth. See, you people are too careless, too trusting... You locked him up out of the way, but he heard you talking. He heard you planning your route to Ledsey Cross, and he heard you talk about this village. He remembered the details and shared them with me, and now here we all are. So, it looks like you're stuck with us now.'

'Fuck you both.'

'No, I'm serious. I wouldn't be having this conversation if I didn't have to. Like I said, I need your help. And I don't want to sound overdramatic, but I've got more than enough bullets left to kill as many of you as it takes until you decide to play ball. To be honest, though, I don't think I'll need that many.'

'You two really are peas in a pod,' Ruth said, advancing towards him. 'We should have got rid of both of you a long time ago.'

With predatory speed, Piotr reached out and grabbed Omar by the shoulder. He dragged him closer and rested the pistol against the back of the boy's head. 'Try it. You know I'll do it, so it's just a question of how many more of you you're prepared to lose before you realise I'm serious.'

Dominic edged forward and cleared his throat. 'Look, I know what you all think of me, and I realise how hard this must be, but we're going to have to work together if we want to get to Ledsey Cross.'

David looked up from Sanjay's body and faced Piotr, ignoring Dominic completely. 'I don't get it. You've come this far. Why do you think you need us?'

'Have you not seen the size of the crowds out there?' He gestured in the general direction of the corpses outside. Many of them had begun to drift over towards the store, peeling away from the main mass in dribs and drabs in response to the raised voices and gunshot noise. 'I'm not going to be able to get through that lot on my own.'

Sam shook his head. 'I've got news for you. We were going to struggle as it is. If we're lumbered with a cripple, I don't reckon we'll make it either.'

'The irony is I only need you because my leg is fucked. I can't drive.'

'So you've got a vehicle?'

He nodded. 'One of yours, actually. Your van is in the carpark. Did you not notice?' He paused, giving them chance to look outside. It wasn't immediately obvious, tucked away neatly between two other abandoned vehicles, but Sam recognised it as the van they'd taken from the barracks in Brentwood. The same van that had disappeared from outside the warehouse after the Yaxley people had ambushed Piotr's group.

David looked at Dominic. 'What about you? Can't you do it?'

'I don't drive,' he said, sheepish.

'Fucking useless.'

'This is good news for you,' Piotr said. 'It's a win-win situation. Let's be honest, you were never going to make it out of here on foot.'

Ruth was still fuming. 'He's a cold-blooded killer. I don't know why we're wasting our time with him.'

'Because he'll do it again,' Dominic said quickly. 'And again and again. At least this way some of you have half a chance.'

'Bit more of a chance than Sanjay, eh? More of a chance than Lynette?'

At the mention of Lynette's name, Dominic shifted his weight uncomfortably. Piotr picked up on his obvious unease and grinned. 'What did Dominic tell you about Lynette?'

'That you pushed her off a roof by the Tower,' Ruth answered, barely able to contain her anger now.

Unfazed, Piotr looked across at Dominic. 'Seriously? Is that right, Dom? You told them *I* killed Lynette?'

'I-I didn't, I didn't say that,' he stammered. 'What I meant was, it was one of those situations when no one can be exactly sure what happened and—'

Selena, who'd been trying to melt into the shadows and shield Vicky from the violence, shouted up. 'I know you were both up on the roof with her when she died.'

Dominic shook his head furiously. 'No. It wasn't like that. What happened to Lynette was a tragic accident. She'd had enough and she, she...'

His voice trailed away. Behind him, Piotr was laughing. 'Seriously? You just can't help yourself, can you. Once a politician, always a politician. You could just shut up, ignore the bitch, but no. You have to keep digging and digging and digging. Always making things worse.'

'It's not like that,' he said again.

'Let's sort this out once and for all. Dominic, did you tell these people that I killed Lynette?'

Dominic's eyes were wild now, constantly flitting around but never settling on anything or anyone long enough to focus. His mouth opened and closed, his mind racing as he tried to spin his way out of trouble. But all he came up with was dead end after dead end. 'Yes,' he eventually admitted, barely audible. 'I'm sorry. I was wrong and was afraid and I should never have—'

'And did I kill her?'

Another pause, followed by another admission. 'No.'

'There,' Piotr smiled. 'Was that so hard? Now then. Did she jump to her death because the poor cunt couldn't face going on any longer?'

'No.'

'No. Right. Now, why don't you clear things up once and for all? Tell everyone what really happened.'

'I pushed her.'

Other than the sound of corpses slamming up against the windows, there was a numb stillness throughout the store.

David broke the silence. 'You were both up there. Why should we trust either of you?'

Piotr blew the top of Dominic's head off. What was left of his body slid heavily to the floor.

'Looks like you'll have to take my word for it,' Piotr said. 'Right, now bloody Lynette's no longer a worry, let's get to work. We can finish this fascinating conversation when we get to Ledsey Cross.'

'And how exactly do you think we're going to get through that crowd out there?'

Piotr adjusted his position and grunted with pain as he momentarily took his full weight on his busted leg. He tightened

his grip on Omar. 'I'm glad you asked. I've been sitting here all
night working it out. Got it all planned.'

51

To his credit, Piotr's plan seemed sensible. To a point. 'This will split the crowd in two. We'll drive straight up through the middle of them,' he told the rest of the group huddled in the back of the van. He was on the front seat with David behind the wheel. Between them sat Omar, trembling. He'd not spoken a word since he'd been collared, Piotr's pistol resting against his chest.

'You do realise how hard it's going to be to distract so many of them at once?' David said. 'The noise of the river is too much. You fired that frigging gun and only a few of them reacted, or did you not notice?'

'You think I hadn't thought of that? That's why it's not noise we're using, mate, it's light. Two explosions at the same time, in different parts of the village. Remember how much trouble a bit of fire caused back in London?'

'We remember,' Ruth said from the back. 'We also remember whose fault it was and who it was who fucked off and left us to deal with the consequences.'

He shook his head. 'Give me a break. Look, I get it, we're never going to be friends; I'm all broke up about it. Just do me a favour and put a fucking lid on your whining until this is done. Do this right and there will be plenty of time later to squabble about who did what.'

'Leave it,' Vicky told her softly. 'Don't react. Fighting is all he's got left. The more ammunition you give him, the stronger he'll be.'

Piotr sat up in his seat, grimacing with the excruciating pain of his mangled leg. 'You look in a bad way,' David said.

'I am.'

'Is it broken?'

'Maybe. Probably. Doesn't matter. Again, plenty of time to worry about it later. Right now, you just need to focus. Things are going to get a bit hectic around here.'

David shook his head. This grim new world of theirs was a bizarre place. He was staring into a milling crowd of thousands of bedraggled creatures, with not a single heartbeat among them, on the banks of a flooded village in the middle of nowhere, being held at gunpoint by a psychopathic ex-construction worker... never mind things getting hectic, they were already absolutely fucking insane.

The van had been abandoned facing the enormous undead gathering. Harjinder had left it there by chance, but its position was just about perfect. They were midway between the hardware store where they'd sheltered after crossing the bridge, and the fuel station they'd seen. From here they had a relatively clear run onto the road to Ledsey Cross. Piotr's orders were simple: when the time came and the dead crowds parted, drawn in two directions at once by the mad-made distractions, David was to drive the van through the gap in the middle before it closed up again around them.

A classic Moses in the Red Sea scenario.

It sounded straightforward. It was anything but.

'What is taking them so long?' Piotr asked. 'Those kids you sent down there, do they know what they're doing?'

He turned his head to look over his left shoulder and, for a fraction of a second, David considered snatching the pistol from him. Clearly sensing his urge, Piotr tightened his grip on both Omar and his weapon. He pressed the muzzle of the gun so hard against the side of Omar's head that the kid whimpered in pain. Piotr chuckled then grimaced, slightly relaxing back the gun and giving Omar a shake like a scruffed pup.

'Chill out, Piotr,' David said. 'Mia and Ollie know what they're doing. They're experienced. They won't let us down.'

'They'd better not.'

David just looked at him. '*Or else?* Fuck me, Piotr, you're beginning to sound like a fucking pantomime villain.'

He glared back and, for just a second, David thought he might truly have overstepped the mark. But then Piotr's face cracked into a broad grin, and he laughed out loud. 'Pantomime villain! That's me alright! I'll take that as a complement!'

'It wasn't meant to be. I was just making an observation because—'

Part of the hardware store exploded. How Mia and Ollie had managed it was unclear, but there was no doubt that they'd fulfilled their brief: find everything flammable in the store – gas cylinders, fuel, whatever else – then set it alight and get the hell out. David twisted around and craned his neck to see what was happening. 'I see them,' Marcus shouted from the very back of the van. 'They're on their way.'

The two kids were racing towards the carpark as a tsunami of rot began to slip and slide back the other way. They pushed back against the corpse tide, safe in the knowledge that the huge explosion they'd caused behind them was enough of a distraction to render the two of them almost completely invisible. With an enormous burst of yellow-orange flame belching up into the grey behind them, to the weakened eyes of the dead everything else had become background noise.

And then another massive detonation.

Cued up by the first blast, Sam and Callum executed their part of the plan with relative ease. Despite months of inactivity, enough flammable liquid remained in the petrol station pumps and tanks, and in the vehicles abandoned mid-fill on its forecourt, to fuel a second explosion which dwarfed the first. The two men had to take the long way around, splashing through the outermost streets of the flooded village, then climbing back up towards the van.

David moved his hand towards the ignition in readiness. 'Hold steady,' Piotr warned. 'Give our dead friends a bit longer to really get moving.'

'It's not our dead friends I'm worried about. My people are out there.'

'Hold,' Piotr said again.

Ahead of them, David could see movement stirring deep within the undead hordes. Hundreds of them were already drifting away from the fringes, but the expected chain reaction hadn't yet worked its way to the centre. Piotr's stated intent had been to divide them, to send one half one way and the rest the other, but there was confusion at the heart of the crowd. Some of the lethargic figures that had started to drift towards the burning ruin of the hardware store had now been distracted by the fuel station blast and were moving the other way. And at the centre of it all, the dumb bastards were colliding with each other as they tried to go in opposite directions, blocking the way through. Much activity, little movement. The road to Ledsey Cross remained congested with rotting flesh.

'This isn't going to work, Piotr,' David said.

'It is.'

'It *isn't*. Look, will you? Can't you see what's happening? The fuel station is closer, and the blast was bigger. There are more of them moving that way. We were never going to equally split the crowd. I think we need to—'

'You think! *You think*! Bloody stop talking and get ready to drive when I give you the fucking word.'

Behind them, Mia and Ollie reached the van and were let inside by Orla. Sam and Callum were also closing in fast, but David was struggling to keep track of them in the constantly shifting crowds.

'Go,' Piotr said.

David shook his head. 'Sam and Callum aren't in yet.'

'I said go!' Piotr yelled, and he cocked back the pistol and jabbed the barrel so hard against Omar's chest that the kid yelped in fear.

David started the van, revved the engine hard, then swung out onto the congested road.

*

'Now there's a fucking surprise,' Callum cursed as he and Sam raced back towards the van. He pulled up slightly. Sam shoved him in the back to keep him moving.

'Don't slow up,' he said, manhandling bodies out of the way. 'The fires are dying down. It's only going to get worse.'

Through a momentary gap in the confusion of criss-crossing figures now swarming all around them, Sam saw the van ploughing into the crowd. Though the glimpses of movement were intermittent and irregular, the vehicle seemed to be making progress. David was maintaining enough speed to keep pushing through the undead.

'Ignore everything else. Just focus on the van.'

'Yeah, hadn't thought of that,' Callum said under his breath. Truth was, he was too scared to focus on anything else, certainly too scared to focus on the vastness of the crowd that they'd now become a part of. There were dead bodies coming at them from every conceivable direction, all angles at once. Even those that had been maimed by the van and lay damaged on the ground still wouldn't give up. Flailing arms reached out for them as they sprinted through the mire, broken stumps swiping at their feet. One caught Callum's ankle and he went down hard. Before he'd fully realised what had happened, Sam had dragged him back up again.

The gap between their position and the back of the van suddenly seemed to be reducing. A moment ago, they'd been chasing distant taillights. Now Sam could see the panicked faces of the passengers in the back.

David accelerated then changed down and crunched through the gears. 'What the hell are you doing?' Piotr yelled at him. 'I thought you knew how to drive.'

'There are too bloody many of them,' David said through clenched teeth. The treads of the van's tyres were slick with dead flesh, unable to get any grip on the equally slippery surface of the road. 'We've got no traction. If the road was clearer, we'd have half a chance.'

'How the fuck did you lot manage without me?' He turned around in his seat and gave his orders. 'All of you, get out in front and start shifting bodies.'

They'd prepped for this. It wasn't a surprise. Lisa, Orla, Marcus, Ollie, Ruth, Joanne, and Mia were tooled up and ready to work. They opened the back and jumped out, the vehicle barely moving forward at all now. Selena and Vicky remained in their seats.

'You too princess,' Piotr yelled at Selena. He knew Vicky was utterly useless, not even worth the leverage of threatening her life. Selena was ready to fight back, but Vicky knew it wasn't worth the risk.

'Just do it,' she whispered, her voice barely a rasp.

'I'm not going to just—'

'Do it,' Vicky said again, and Selena did as she was told.

Lisa, Orla, Joanne, and Ruth carried makeshift shields they'd brough with them from the frozen food store; the Perspex lids of chiller units that had been prised off and cannibalised. They were remarkably effective – rounded in shape, relatively lightweight, and see-through. The four women formed a line and moved in unison from the rear of the van around to the front, pushing back a decent number of bodies that the others who followed them bludgeoned into submission with hammers and axes and whatever else they'd managed to lay their hands on.

Sam and Callum were close now. Sam could see what was happening and it came as no surprise. To have expected them to carve a path through such an expansive of riled, undead creatures had been the kind of delusional, bullshit idea Piotr seemed to excel in.

Initially, the forward attack was working. Whether it was due to their collective strength or the fact that large numbers of the dead remained uncoordinated, distracted and confused by the sudden abundance of stimuli, it didn't matter – the group out front had so far managed to punch a hole through the seething masses that allowed David to keep the van moving forward. But no one was under any illusions. From his seat behind the wheel, David had the clearest view of the carnage. They'd covered less than a third of the distance they needed to.

'We're not going to make it,' he said.

'Bollocks,' was the only answer Piotr had for him.

'You're not listening to me. I'm not trying to be difficult, Piotr, I'm just pointing out a fact. We're not going to make it. We've slowed down to a crawl.'

'If they can keep the road clear, we can keep crawling.'

'But what if they can't? We've lost the advantage of the explosions, in case you hadn't noticed.'

'There's still some fire.'

'Yes, but it's too far away and it's going to burn out in minutes. Jesus, you still don't fully understand how the dead react to us, do you? They're not going to be interested in a couple of distant fires now. All they're going to be focused on is this van and the people in and around it.'

'Just keep driving,' Piotr told him again, and all David could do was comply.

Sam pushed and shoved his way through the rancid, writhing crowds around the back of the juddering vehicle. It would jump forward a metre or so, then get stuck again, wheels skidding in gore. Its progress had become so unpredictable, so erratic, that Ruth, Lisa, and Orla had begun to pull away.

From the rear, much of the fighting up ahead remained unseen. Sam felt like he was drowning in rot. What was left of these corpses was unimaginably horrific; most had bloated from the amount of rain and flood they'd suffered, and their corrupted stink was made infinitely worse by the river water stench itself. They virtually disintegrated when he hit them. He glanced back to look for Callum, but all he could see was death. He was about to put on a burst of speed to try to get around the front of the van, but there was no sign of him. Regardless, he dropped his shoulder

293

and raced forward. He overtook the vehicle with ease, then jumped back out of the way when Marcus swung an axe just in front of him. Wrong-footed, he lost his balance and almost fell back into the disintegrating crowd. A hand roughly grabbed a fistful of his jacket and pulled him to safety. It was Joanne. She yanked him back into the circle of protected space she and the others were struggling to defend. 'Where the hell have you been? You took your time. We could do with some help.'

Sam didn't have enough breath left in his lungs to respond. It was all he could do to fall into line and keep pushing more corpses away. But every cadaver he grabbed hold of now seemed to be fighting back with equal voracity. But were they fighting? Christ, it was as if they weren't interested in him at all now, as if all they wanted was to get past him and get closer to the van... like they were trying to stop themselves from being dragged back into the free-for-all.

He felt himself slowing down. Either that, or the ferocity of the desperate dead was increasing. His foot became snagged in a pile of limbs, and as he fought to free himself, the van lurched to the side and nudged into him. It was just a glancing blow, but it hurt like hell. Behind the wheel, David didn't even notice. Unbalanced, Sam looked down when one of the hideous creatures caught hold of his leg and wouldn't let go.

It was Callum.

He'd taken a long route around and was on his hands and knees now, crawling between swaying, spidery undead legs, struggling to get into the precious bubble of space around the vehicle and stand up. Sam dragged him to his feet and the two of them backed into Selena. She recoiled, unsighted, and in doing so a gap appeared in the fighting line: the three of them on one side, Marcus and Joanne on the other. The dead poured through between them. Selena did what she could to retake her place in their rough formation, and both Callum and Sam fought alongside her. Individually the undead were insignificant, but in numbers such as this they were unstoppable.

Ruth, Orla, and Lisa were fighting with such conviction up ahead that they hadn't noticed they'd become separated from the others. Joanne yelled for them to slow down, but the disorientation was such that no one could tell who was shouting or where they were shouting from. Ruth turned around to look for Vicky, but all she could see was more rancorous cadavers spilling into the undefended space behind. It reminded her of a vast festival crowd, but it was as if every attendee was on the same bad trip, hallucinating and panic-stricken. This mess was as far removed as she could imagine from those joyous collective celebrations of light and noise she remembered and missed.

'Keep going,' Lisa pleaded. 'We're almost there.'

Ruth shook her off. Her desperation to find Vicky was such that she heaved her freezer-lid shield around and started moving back the other way.

Despite his elevated position behind the wheel, David was unaware of the fragmentation of the group. He'd lost sight of all of them, focusing instead on keeping the van moving forward. But that was becoming impossible. There simply was no way of driving over the uneven bloody chaos of the battlefield. The tarmac had disappeared, indistinguishable from the muddy, bloody mush of everything else. 'We're slowing down,' Piotr said. 'Why are we slowing down.'

'There's nothing I can do. I can't get any grip.'

'Get the others to push.'

'*What others*? Can you see them? Fuck knows where everyone's gone.'

He stopped the van then tried again, shifting into a higher gear and trying to pull away, the way he'd been taught to drive in ice and snow. It didn't have any effect. Every time he accelerated, the wheels spun faster, and the engine noise increased, but the van didn't move. The effect on the nearest of the dead, though, was dramatic. They surged closer, slamming up against all sides of the vehicle at once, drenching it in their gore.

David tried reversing, but even that didn't make any difference. Back into first, then into reverse, then first gear again... their only movement was a useless back-and-forth rocking, barely noticeable amongst the constant bangs and crashes as corpses threw themselves against the van's windows and metal walls. He hit the horn to try and alert those still fighting out front.

'What the hell are you doing?' Piotr screamed.

'The only thing left that I *can* do. Look, Piotr, we're going nowhere. We need to get out and walk. I know your leg's bad, but we don't have any other option. This van's not going any further.'

'Keep. Bloody. Trying!'

'There's no point.'

David let the engine die. For the first time, Piotr lifted his pistol from Omar's chest and pointed it at David.

'I'll fucking kill you.'

'Go on, then. How will that help you, exactly? Don't you get it, you fucking moron? This is all you've got left. The worse you make things for us, the more of us you kill, the bigger your struggle's going to be. It's really not that difficult to understand, is it. People are irreplaceable now. You killed the fittest member of our group. And finished off your sick entourage, didn't you? No one's got your back, Piotr. We're only waiting for you to fail again. This is why you've fucked everything up so badly, time and time again.'

Piotr had an expression on his face that David hadn't seen before. Equal parts fear, indecision, helplessness.

'Listen to me, we can get through this,' David told him. 'We've got through worse. We just need to—'

He stopped talking. Vicky was trying to get his attention. She reached for his shoulder with bony fingers. He took her hand in his.

'Don't waste your breath,' she said. 'If he doesn't get it by now, he never will.'

The back door of the van flew open. It was Ruth. Struggling to move at all now, Vicky slid back along the floor towards her. Ruth kept the undead at bay with her shield so Vicky had space to get out. Around her, the dead watched but didn't surge towards her. She looked into the multitude of decaying faces staring back at her, knowing that all they saw now was just another corpse, someone else like them who'd been ravaged by disease, barely able to keep moving... hardly even existing, straddling the border between life and death.

Piotr was panicking. 'What the hell are they doing? Are they crazy?'

In the unexpected madness of the moment, he didn't react when David seized his chance and threw Omar to safety, shoving him out of the driver's door. He figured the dead were less of a risk to the boy than Piotr.

Piotr hadn't even noticed. He was distracted by the first of the undead now trying to crawl into the back of the van, reacting to the engine noise and to the volume of his voice. Fucker was panicking.

'Not a fan of being this close to them, are you?' David said. He laughed at him. Couldn't help himself. 'Jesus, Piotr, you're pathetic. I've seen you ordering people about, screaming and shouting at folks to get them to fight for you, but I've never seen you deal with a single one of them yourself.'

Piotr wasn't listening. He was petrified by the corpses that had made it into the back of the van, forced forward by an abundance of others surging from behind. He fired the pistol into the multitude. The first shot burst the head of a rancid-looking creature like a brain-filled balloon. The next, fired frantically, shattered a window but somehow missed everything else.

Many corpses reacted predictably, hurling themselves forward again, increasing the pressure inside the van. Outside, some of the others appeared initially to back away from the noise. Piotr couldn't take his eyes off the ghastly creatures. He was frozen with fear. Too much to take in at once. All out of lackeys. All out of options.

David sensed his disorientation and grabbed the pistol. Piotr fired instinctively, but only succeeded in putting a bullet through the padded roof of the van. He was caught off-guard by the angle of the recoil, and David easily ripped the weapon from his grip. Piotr looked at him, helpless. 'Please—' he started to say, but David had had enough.

'Did you seriously think I was going to let you inflict yourself on the people at Ledsey Cross?'

'But I... It wasn't—'

'Oh, fuck off, Piotr,' David said.

He'd never fired a pistol before, and he hoped he'd never have to do so again, but he screwed up his face, anticipated the recoil, then shot Piotr through the kneecap of his otherwise uninjured leg.

His screams were worse than the gunshot noise.

David scrambled out of the van and forced his way upstream, through the flood of corpses all moving the other way, reacting to the chaos. There was movement everywhere he looked, so much that he couldn't make sense of any of it. Which way was he supposed to go? Where were the others? He caught glimpses of some of his friends fighting in different spaces, well away from each other, looking as lost as he felt. And he looked back at the van and could still see Piotr thrashing around furiously inside, his desperate noise drawing more and more of the undead closer. David still had the pistol. Did he try and shoot the fuel tank, like they did in the movies, and cause another explosion that would temporarily distract the dead? Did he shoot as many corpses as he had bullets left for? Or did he shoot Piotr again and put him out of his misery?

Did he fuck.

He left the bastard to scream and shout and bleed out alone, and it felt good. Maybe too good.

David turned around again and walked straight into Vicky. 'I was looking for you...' he started to say. She was shaking her head.

'No time. Just walk. Don't fight.'

'What?'

She smiled at him, and even that seemed to take more effort than it ought to. 'You heard. Just walk. Don't fight them. Follow me.'

She began dragging herself deeper into the mob and David did as she said. Up ahead he could see some of the others battling hard to stay afloat, in clear danger of being swallowed up and overcome by the tidal dead. Some of the creatures were shuffling towards the van, but many more continued being drawn to the areas where his friends were desperately trying to stay alive. They'd truly split up now – the intended single survivor group having divided and subdivided. Some people were on their own, others in twos and threes, but they all fought with a uniform ferocity, a desire to stay alive. It didn't seem to matter. They were outnumbered whatever: several thousand cadavers for each individual one of them.

The harder they fought, the stronger the undead resistance seemed to become. David pushed more of the wretched creatures away as they crowded closer to him. Vicky turned back and shook her head again. 'Don't.'

'Don't what?'

'Don't fight. I told you. They're as frightened as we are.'

With Ruth alongside her, she kept walking forward. She didn't react when the dead clattered into her, didn't try and re-kill any of them; to her they became lost, disoriented brethren, and she just walked through them.

Between them.

Alongside them.

With them.

All David could do was follow her lead. He matched her almost step for step, struggling as much with her lethargic pace as he did with the constant urge to lash out at the unpredictable, foul-smelling monsters that crowded into him from every direction.

And then, up ahead, were Selena, Omar, and Ollie. Vicky changed direction slightly so that she didn't miss them. She was in such a poor physical condition now, grey-skinned and bedraggled, that none of them recognised her at first. Omar realised when he saw David behind, and he was about to say something when David subtly gestured for him not to. With a faint, barely perceptible change of expression, he signalled for Omar to do as he did and keep walking. Selena, realising that the brittle creature that had just brushed up against her was Vicky, did the same.

Sam and Marcus, next, fighting in a muddy pocket of space.

Then Mia and Callum. Then Lisa, Joanne, and Orla.

Those with shields naturally fell into formation around the others, maximising the available protection, or at least giving them space to breath. When anyone spoke or reacted, the dead around them reacted too. But when they remained quiet and followed Vicky's example, they were able to pass through the hordes almost completely unchallenged. Way behind them, Piotr's angry wailing continued for a while longer, but soon it stopped, and the world became unnaturally quiet. The river roar faded away, muted by the distance. Soon the only noises were the dragging of weary feet along the road.

They'd reached the outermost edge of the crowd, the point where the gradient of the road had increased such that the dead could no longer climb. Vicky kept walking for as long as she could, then collapsed. The others crowded around her. Ruth and Selena kneeling at her side. Had she died? Someone had half a bottle of water. Ruth lifted her head and poured it into her mouth. She reacted, swallowing a little, but coughing up more. 'I'm okay,' she said, her words barely there.

'Like hell you are.'

Sam edged closer. 'What happened just now, Vic?'

'She's done in,' Ruth said. 'Let her rest.'

Vicky shook her head and, with Ruth's help, sat upright. 'We're kindred spirits, them and us, just the same. I don't have long left, Sam. I think I understand them now.'

'I don't understand any of this.'

'And I don't expect you to. I was right. The dead didn't want to kill us. They're just adrift, like we are. They just want their suffering to end.'

'I see it,' David said, 'and it makes sense now. In massive numbers, anything they did would always be misinterpreted as aggression, as an attack. But with the rest of the world dead, who else could possibly help them but us? They came to us because they had nowhere else to go.'

52

They cut down two sapling trees and strung jackets between them and made a stretcher to carry Vicky, threading the wood through the sleeves. David had been thinking again about all those they'd lost along the way. 'Did you know Gary used to be a marathon runner?'

'What, our Gary with the dodgy knees and ankles?' Sam said. 'I don't believe it.'

'It's true. When things were getting really shitty, he'd tell me all these running anecdotes to make things seem better.'

'And did it work?'

'Sometimes, I guess. Passed the time.'

'Have you got a nugget of Gary's wisdom to share with us now then, Dave?'

He shrugged. 'Maybe. He used to say that no matter how knackered you were, how hard you'd run, when the finish line comes into view, you'll always somehow find your second wind. All I'm saying is, let's hope Gary was right because I feel like I've just run all the marathons.'

Ruth and Joanne were at the front of the stretcher, David and Sam carrying the back. Selena walked alongside, holding Vicky's hand. She smiled at Vicky and kept talking to her, but she knew she didn't have long left. She hoped they'd reach Ledsey Cross in time; it seemed beyond cruel for her not to get to meet Annalise and all the others now. Selena's stomach was churning with an impossible combination of emotions. Nervous excitement combined with sorrow and dread. They were like oil and water, refusing to mix.

There was only this road, so they knew there'd be no wrong turnings at this late stage. They'd seen a signpost outside

Heddlewick that had confirmed it was five miles to Ledsey Cross. The group was largely silent, numb with exhaustion and apprehension. David, keenly able to compartmentalise, was imagining a hot bath and a comfortable bed, though he knew he was shooting high; such things were the absolute height of luxury these days. It was hard to believe they were so close. He could almost hear the water running and the kettle boiling, could almost smell real food cooking. And his stomach began to growl with hunger as he remembered the taste of bacon sandwiches, and optimism surged. He might just... if everything Vicky had told him was true, then the people here could make bread, and he'd seen pigs in the background of the photographs she'd shown them of the farm. *Christ*. He'd give everything he had for a bacon sandwich. *Trouble is, I've got nothing left to give.*

Sam was wondering how many people would be at Ledsey Cross? In the pictures it looked like there were more than a hundred. Had their numbers increased in the four months since the networks had died, and they'd last been in contact? He hoped they'd have room for a handful more and, in time, that the others from Yaxley might make the journey north too. He looked side-eyed at Joanne and smiled shyly.

Selena was thinking about Kath's friend Annalise, and how she was going to break it to her that Kath hadn't made it. She thought Annalise would be upset, but perhaps not surprised. The journey had been an ordeal for even the strongest of them, and though Kath had been tenacious and stubborn as hell, she'd also been old and physically unwell. This world was no place for those who weren't strong enough to survive. That thought brought her back around to Vicky, and she gave her brittle hand another gentle squeeze. 'Almost there, Vic,' she said, and though she couldn't be completely certain, she thought she felt Vicky squeeze her hand back in response.

The long road was undulating with countless twists and turns, never straight for any decent length. There were climbs and there were more climbs. It was tree-lined in places, and though the group still expected corpses to come at them from out of the shadows, they didn't. It was a relief. It was a good sign.

They'd lost all track of time. This had been another endless day. Sam wondered if they should have found somewhere to shelter for the night, but they were so close now it seemed more sensible to keep going and, anyway, there wasn't anywhere suitable. For the sake of a little more effort, they'd be able to spend the night in relative comfort and with other people. It would be good, he thought, to see houses with lights on inside, maybe a streetlamp or two. There was a concern (that he only shared with David, not wanting to cause another round table discussion) that the villagers might have set traps to keep out the dead. David agreed that they needed to watch out. He'd been caught out around Yaxley, after all.

No traps, yet, but there were no lights yet either. The day was drawing to a close and night was setting in. With everything else so dark, they'd expected the village to shine like a beacon. And what about the noise? They were sure they'd have heard the sounds of life in Ledsey Cross from a distance.

Wait.

They were surrounded by buildings now. *Were they here?*

Dark, empty buildings.

In one house, a corpse clattered against a window in response to their movement outside.

Sam felt nerves twisting his gut. Surely this wasn't it? They must have taken a wrong turn or just followed the wrong road altogether.

No, we didn't.

He stopped at the side of the road and lit up a sign with his torch.

WELCOME TO LEDSEY CROSS – PLEASE DRIVE CAREFULLY.

After coming so far, he could now barely bring himself to take another step. They'd reached the village at last, but it was as cold and as lifeless as everywhere else.

53

There was a community centre. They bundled themselves inside to escape the cold of the night and the crushing, almost unbearable disappointment. The building – along with all the other buildings nearby from what they could tell – appeared to be in good repair. All of it was untouched. There were corpses trapped indoors here and there, as there were everywhere. The bulk of the mobile dead, though, had long since drifted away.

'I don't understand,' Selena said, sobbing. She was heartbroken. Disconsolate. 'But what happened?'

Vicky, who they'd laid on a bed made from cushions and blankets, gestured for her to a come closer. Her voice was an exhausted whisper, but the acoustics of this empty, almost church-like place, amplified her words so that everyone could hear. 'The same thing happened here as happened everywhere else.'

'But Annalise... Kath spoke to her... She was texting her non-stop.'

Vicky shook her head. 'I had one phone and Kath had the other. She did have a friend called Annalise who lived here, but all those messages were from me. She put my number in her phone as Annalise, and we talked and talked for as long as we could.'

'But the photos?'

'I edited them on her phone. Made copies and changed the dates so it looked like they were taken after they actually were, after everyone had died.'

Selena could hardly speak. Tears were streaming down her face. 'You lied to me.'

'I know. I'm sorry. It was the only way.'

'Bullshit.'

'It's true. Without Ledsey Cross, you'd have given up a long time ago. We all would. We all needed something to aim for.'

'So many of us died getting here, and it was all just bullshit!'

Vicky tried to sit up, every movement now an effort. 'Not all of it. This place is just as good as Kath said, that wasn't a lie. It is self-sufficient. It is isolated. There's farmland and plenty of natural resources. It's perfect for all of you. You can make new lives here. There's everything and everyone you need.'

Other than Vicky's rasping voice, there was absolute silence now. Everyone was gathered around her in the shelter and warmth of what did appear to be a strong and comfortable building. She looked from face to face to face and smiled.

'The fact you got here shows you've all got what it takes to survive. Hundreds didn't make it. You'll do well here. When you're ready, go back and get the others.'

Ruth rested a hand on Vicky's shoulder, sensing her getting tired. 'Take it easy, love. We can talk again in the morning.'

Vicky shook her head. 'I don't think so,' she said, and she lay back down. 'Don't be upset. We did it. I was never trying to get to Ledsey Cross for the people, I just wanted to get the people to Ledsey Cross.'

By the morning, Vicky had slipped away, lost in her sleep. As the sun rose, David and Sam stood in the centre of Ledsey Cross and looked around the silent village. 'For what it's worth,' Sam said, 'I think she was right. With a bit of work, this place could be as good as we imagined. We'll have a look at the solar panels later, see if we can get some lights working. I reckon the water supply is salvageable too. I'm no plumber, but between us we should be able to reverse engineer it or something.'

'Doesn't matter,' David said. 'We can carry buckets from a stream if it comes to it. From memory, Vicky said something about there being a lake not far. Fancy a spot of fishing?'

'Never thought I'd hear myself say this, Dave, but yeah, I do.'

'Marcus says he'll have a look around the farmland. He's no expert, but he's got more experience than the rest of us combined. He was talking about hunting for livestock. There's got to be some cattle, sheep, or pigs that have survived somewhere.'

'I was thinking along the same lines, actually.'

'Great minds, and all that,' David said.

Sam paused. He watched his friend as he studied their surroundings. He sensed his mind racing at the same speed as his own, considering all the possibilities, probabilities, and potential complications they were likely to encounter. 'So, how long are you staying for?' he asked.

David looked confused. 'What?'

'It's just that as long as I've known you, you've always said you'll keep going until you get back home to Ireland and find out what happened to your family.'

He shook his head. 'I don't think so. I know what happened to them – same as what happened to everybody else. No, Sam, the only family I've got left is here. This is my home now.'

ABOUT THE AUTHOR

David Moody first released Hater in 2006 and, without an agent, sold the film rights for the novel to Mark Johnson (producer, Breaking Bad) and Guillermo Del Toro (director, The Shape of Water, Pan's Labyrinth). Moody's seminal zombie novel Autumn was made into an (admittedly terrible) movie starring Dexter Fletcher and David Carradine. He has an unhealthy fascination with the end of the world and likes to write books about ordinary folks going through absolute hell. With the publication of new Autumn and Hater stories, Moody has furthered his reputation as a writer of suspense-laced SF/horror, and "farther out" genre books of all description.

Find out more about his work at:

www.davidmoody.net
facebook.com/davidmoodyauthor
instagram.com/davidmoodyauthor
twitter.com/davidjmoody

"Moody is as imaginative as Barker, as compulsory as King, and as addictive as Palahniuk." —*Scream the Horror Magazine*

"Moody has the power to make the most mundane and ordinary characters interesting and believable, and is reminiscent of Stephen King at his finest." —*Shadowlocked*

"British horror at its absolute best." —*Starburst*

"As demonstrated throughout his previous novels, readers should crown Moody king of the zombie horror novel" —*Booklist*

If you are the original purchaser of this book, or if you received this book as a gift, you can download a complementary eBook version by visiting:

www.infectedbooks.co.uk/ebooks

and completing the necessary information
(terms and conditions apply)

CPSIA information can be obtained
at www.ICGtesting.com
Printed in the USA
BVHW040942100123
656000BV00012B/300

9 781739 753535